BERLIN CALLING

ALSO BY KELLY DURHAM

The War Widow

Wade's War

The Reluctant Copilot

The Movie Star and Me

BERLIN CALLING

A Novel

KELLY DURHAM

LAKE UNION
PUBLISHING

Published by Lake Union Publishing, Seattle

www.apub.com

Amazon, the Amazon logo, and Lake Union Publishing are trademarks of Amazon.com, Inc., or its affiliates.

ISBN-13: 9781503942967
ISBN-10: 1503942961

Cover design by Rachel Adam Rogers

Printed in the United States of America

For Ina and Harry

PROLOGUE

Berlin, Germany
December 1944

Maggie was tired of peeing into a bucket. She was tired of the stink, the filth, the indignity. It seemed that whenever she needed to relieve herself, the guard picked that moment to peer into her tiny cell. Most of all, Maggie was tired of the fear that constantly gnawed at her mind.

The sleepless nights in the basement cells of the Gestapo's Prinz-Albrecht-Straße headquarters were interminable, the darkness punctuated with the constant sound of dripping, the scurrying of rats, the moans of sniffling and weeping men.

Maggie knew the sands in her hourglass were running out, that soon the footsteps in the corridor would stop at her door, that the stomach-churning sound of the jailer's key would click in her lock, and that she would be dragged upstairs to interrogation.

She expected her interrogation to begin at any time, and she knew that she was in grave danger just by being here. What she didn't know was how much the Gestapo already knew—and how far they would go to find out.

A dark thought popped into Maggie's mind: *Well, maybe I'll find Clive after all.*

CHAPTER 1

Heidelberg, Germany
July 1938

Maggie O'Dea was finishing her second beer with her classmates when she noticed the German boy.

It was a sunny Saturday afternoon, and Maggie and her friends were enjoying a break from their summer classes at the University of Heidelberg. The boy was lean and handsome, with an athletic build and blond hair. He was a little taller than the other boy who'd entered the Biergarten with him. When the two looked toward Maggie's table, she looked away—back toward Constance, sitting across from her, who was in the middle of telling a funny story.

The two boys—Maggie guessed they were about her age—kept glancing over at her table, but she pretended to ignore them. Instead, she continued to hold court with her classmates, entertaining them with jokes about the food in the cafeteria (always potatoes), opinions about their professors, and a spot-on imitation of Frau Hess, their dormitory housemother.

After a beer, and several furtive glances, the blond boy stood and approached them. "Excuse me. You are English?" he asked, smiling from the end of their picnic-style table, the sun over his shoulder.

"English?" Maggie slammed her stein on the table and shaded her eyes with one hand. "Certainly not! I'm Irish American. Damn the English!" Her retort had the desired effect, catching the boy off guard. Maggie's green eyes flashed in the afternoon sunlight. "Within my body, sir, reside the soul of a poet, the compassion of a saint, and the fortitude of the downtrodden. *English?* Ha! Don't they wish!" Then she belched. Addie and Constance erupted into giggles, but Doris, clearly mortified, looked as though she'd like to crawl under the table.

The boy threw his head back and laughed. He gracefully stepped over the bench of the table and sat down next to Maggie as Addie scooted to her left. "My most sincere apology, Fräulein! You must allow me to make amends by treating you and your friends to another round." Before the girls could object, he caught the attention of the waiter hovering in the shade next to the counter and placed his order with a whirl of one upraised finger.

"Permit me to introduce myself," he said. "My name is Kurt Engel. And this"—he motioned to his friend to join the party—"is my comrade Arne Becker." Arne smiled and slipped onto the opposite bench next to Constance and Doris, who was still decidedly uncomfortable.

Kurt took control of the conversation and soon learned that Maggie and her friends were students. He revealed that both he and Arne were native Heidelbergers who had grown up together and who were home on leave from the military.

"Tell me," Kurt asked Addie, "what do you think of our hometown?"

"Oh, it's beautiful," she replied, obviously pleased with the attention from the handsome young men.

"You are quite right," Kurt agreed. "Heidelberg is the most beautiful German city. In fact, Arne and I are going up to Philosophenweg this evening to watch the illumination of the castle. You must all come with us!"

After finishing their beers, the group—minus Doris, who pleaded that she must attend to her studies—crossed the Neckar River and hiked up the ridge to the heights above the city. Kurt and Arne had brought a small backpack stuffed with bottles of beer, cheese, and bread, a small blanket rolled and strapped to its outside. In the shade of an oak tree, just off the trail, the blanket was spread and the conversation rejoined.

"So, American girl," Kurt said, opening a bottle of beer and handing it to Maggie, "why such anger toward the English? I thought you Americans liked all things British."

"As I told you earlier, German boy, I am not simply American, I am Irish American, combining the most desirable qualities of the Old World and the New. I loathe the English! They are wholly arrogant imperialists, never content until they can conquer and control native peoples!"

"Like the Irish, I suppose?"

"Yes! Like the Irish! The Indians, Egyptians, Palestinians—the list goes on. Even where they have permitted self-government, they maintain a royal governor." The warm beer and warmer sun had further loosened Maggie's rarely timid tongue. "They are parasites. Imperialist parasites. Here is a tiny nation of, what, fifty million? Yet they rule the world!"

"Not for long," Kurt said, drawing a chuckle from Arne. He leaned closer to Maggie on the blanket. "You are very wise to come to Germany and to study our language and culture. Germany is now the dominant power in Europe. Our Führer is a genius."

"Perhaps, but he has such a funny mustache!" teased Maggie, eliciting snickers from Addie and Constance. Kurt and Arne traded glances. "He reminds me of Charlie Chaplin."

"Chaplin is English, is he not?" Kurt teased back with a smile.

"Damn him, too!" Maggie said, tipping her bottle back and taking a gulp.

"Herr Hitler has worked a miracle in Germany over the last five years. He put our people back to work, he strengthened our economy, and he is rebuilding our military power as well."

"And according to the newspapers," Maggie replied, "he now hopes to annex part of Czechoslovakia, right?"

Kurt cocked his head as though surprised. "Only the ethnic Germans living east of the arbitrary border created after the war. Uniting all true Germans makes the future for Germany very attractive"—Kurt paused, catching Arne's eye—"just like our lovely guests!"

"A toast, then, to the ladies," Arne said, raising his bottle and clinking it against Addie's. Arne's toast changed the tenor of the conversation, away from world politics and on to more immediate concerns. "How long is your course of study?" Arne asked Addie.

"Four weeks," she replied. "Then we plan to travel about Germany and see more of your beautiful country."

"Excellent! You must visit Munich and go south into Bavaria. Garmisch-Partenkirchen was the site of the last winter Olympic Games. Dresden is a beautiful city of music and art, Florence on the Elbe. And Rothenberg, a medieval village on the Tauber River . . ."

He went on, but Maggie's attention strayed to Kurt. He was sitting very close to her, so close she could smell his scent. She took in his short, blond hair and muscular build; his lively eyes; his full lips and even, white smile. *My God*, she thought, *he looks like an Aryan movie star!*

Later, as the summer evening grudgingly gave up its light, she leaned against him. He put his arm behind her, their shoulders touching in the dark. The illumination of the castle began shortly after ten o'clock. It was a summer tradition in Heidelberg, dating back to the early part of the century. It was history as a tourist event, drawing visitors from all over Europe. The illumination reenacted two events.

"The first illumination, in 1613," Kurt explained to Maggie, "was staged by Prince Elector Frederick the Fifth to honor his new bride."

"How romantic," Maggie cooed as the red flares surrounding the castle grew in brightness, bathing its stone ramparts in crimson light.

"She was English," he whispered in her ear.

"Slut." Maggie smiled in the darkness.

Kurt resumed his narrative. "The second event was more tragic. The French destroyed the castle during the Nine Years' War, blowing it apart with explosives and then burning it. That was in 1689. Fortunately, the French have been more reasonable lately."

As the red flares faded, Kurt encircled Maggie's waist with his strong arm and stole a kiss. Maggie liked it.

"I'm glad you're not English," she said.

"So am I!" He laughed.

◆ ◆ ◆

Maggie and Kurt spent more and more time with each other as the summer days passed. After classes, Kurt would call to take her to dinner, sometimes with her friends, though he made it clear he preferred to enjoy her company without distractions.

"My leave is up next week," he said in between bites of veal at a small sidewalk café on Dreikönigstraße. "I've been reassigned to Berlin."

"Oh, Kurt," she groaned. "Do you have to leave so soon? I feel we're just—well, we're just getting started." She reached out and took his hand. "It's just that I want to get to know you better!" She smiled.

"Why don't you come to Berlin with me?" he ventured. Without waiting for a reply, he added, "It is the greatest of cities! Fine restaurants, the best music and theater, so much to do all the time. And the most beautiful women! Of course, when you come, they shall all go jealous! You must come!"

"I would love to, darling, but first I have to finish my studies here. I promised Father that I would always finish what I start."

"You are close to your father?"

"Yes, very," Maggie answered, pushing the peas around on her plate. "Father worked very hard to take care of me and Maureen after our mother died. He said I should always be proud of who I am, and that the best way to do that is to finish what I start."

"I am sure, dear Maggie, that I shall be no less in love with you in the two weeks it takes you to finish your coursework. Then you can follow me to Berlin! Yes?"

Maggie tilted her head to the side and smiled. "I think that would be marvelous, darling," she said. "But what would I do in Berlin all day while waiting on you to wine me and dine me? Surely you don't expect me to become a kept woman? I would need to work at something, and I'm here as a student. I can't legally take a job."

"Nonsense!" Kurt scoffed. "Even National Socialist rules can be circumvented!"

◆　◆　◆

The following Sunday morning, Maggie met Kurt on the platform of Heidelberg's Hauptbahnhof, its main train station. He was shortly to board a Frankfurt-bound train, where he would transfer to the Berlin express.

"There you are!" Kurt beamed as Maggie approached in a yellow dress, white sweater, and sun hat. "I thought you had already forgotten me!"

"It will take more than a long-winded priest to make me forget you, Kurt Engel." She smiled, catching his hands and leaning forward to kiss him on the lips. "You're not in uniform?"

"No, I'll change on the train before we arrive in Berlin."

"Where's Arne?"

"His train to Karlsruhe left earlier," Kurt replied. "Now, you are coming in two weeks?"

"No." She watched Kurt's smile disappear, then beamed at him. "I am coming in twelve days!"

Kurt's face lit up and he laughed. "I hope I can wait."

"I hope you can't," Maggie said with a sideways glance and sly smile. "Remember your first assignment upon reporting for duty, Kurt:

you must arrange a job for me. Father is very generous with my allowance, but he also believes in work. He expects me to earn what I get. If I am to stay in Germany, that means a job."

"Yes, ma'am!" Kurt replied with a mock salute. He reached out and took Maggie gently by the shoulders, staring into her green eyes. "Ah, Maggie, I do wish you were coming with me now. I don't know how I shall cope the next two weeks—I mean, twelve days!" He leaned down and kissed her, his hands finding her waist and pulling her close. She felt his warm breath on her neck and his lightly stubbled cheek against hers. "I must go," he said as the conductor blew his whistle.

"Good-bye, darling," Maggie said, squeezing his hand. "I'll see you in Berlin on the twenty-ninth."

The engine belched steam, and the cars shifted as the train began to pull away. Kurt released Maggie's hand, grabbed his suitcase, and swung himself up onto the coach. *"Auf Wiedersehen, Liebchen!"* he called over the gathering noise of the train.

Maggie blew him a kiss.

CHAPTER 2

Berlin, Germany
July 1938

It was nearly six o'clock in the evening twelve interminable days later when Maggie stepped off the train and onto the platform of Berlin's massive main station. The sun was still high in the summer sky, its yellow light filtering through the glass skylights above the platforms. The station was crowded with people moving in every direction. There were men in business suits, women in dresses and hats, and everywhere soldiers in uniforms.

Maggie's eyes were adjusting to the alternating patches of bright light and dim shadows when she spotted Kurt not a dozen feet from her. He was wearing his stone-gray uniform, his officer's cap tilted at a rakish angle. Kurt was facing away from her, standing in the shade and looking toward the rear of the train, which extended out into the bright sunshine.

"Oh, excuse me, sir, can you please help me?" she said in a voice tinged with mock distress. Kurt whirled, his face alight, and drank her in with his startlingly blue eyes as she played out her scene. "I was looking for my friend. He's quite handsome, a sweet, strapping German boy.

I've been saving myself for him, but I've gotten so, so—well, should I say eager? I just can't contain myself any longer!" she said, rushing into his arms.

Kurt threw back his head and laughed, attracting the curious, then envious glances of businessmen and others heading toward their trains and their weekends. "Maggie! You are even more beautiful than I remembered," he said, "as if that was possible!" He wrapped his arms around her and kissed her, pulling her tightly against his chest. "I could not wait for you to get here! Now, my dear," he said, looking around, "let's get your bags."

In a borrowed car, Kurt drove Maggie north, out of the city center, and eventually onto a tree-lined street. He turned right into the gravel lot of a two-story block of apartments arranged around a central parking area.

After carrying the fifth heavy suitcase up to his second floor flat, Kurt sat for a minute, a light sheen of perspiration glistening on his forehead. "Maggie," he said, "I am glad you have so many bags so full of so many things."

"Why is that, darling?" Maggie said, opening two beers.

"It means you are planning to stay!"

"Of course that's my plan." Maggie smiled, handing him a beer. "But do remember that discussion we had about a job."

Kurt pulled her down onto his lap. "All taken care of, *Liebchen!*" he said, nuzzling her neck. "I used all my initiative and skills, strength and cunning to procure a work permit for you," he said, handing her a brown paper booklet the size of a passport. "Not only permission to work, but I have also scheduled you for a job interview with a friend of mine on Monday!"

"You are wonderful!" Maggie said with sincere delight, twisting around in his lap to face him. "You did all of this in just two weeks?"

"Twelve days," Kurt corrected, with exaggerated modesty.

"Why, Kurt!" Maggie kissed him. "Whatever shall we do until Monday?"

"Let me think," he said, running his hands over her hips.

Maggie grinned. "I hope you didn't use *all* of your strength finding me a job!"

◆ ◆ ◆

"You understand, of course, Fräulein, that my acquaintance with your friend, regardless of how cordial, does not guarantee you a position here?" asked Herr Direktor Johann Bauer in an official tone.

Bauer leaned forward with his elbows on his desk, chubby fingers clasped together on top of a buff-colored folder. Not all applicants were as pleasant to interview as the pretty young woman seated across from him. A pudgy man, Bauer combed his dark brown hair over the top of his head in a futile attempt to mimic Hitler. Like the Führer, Bauer also kept a neatly trimmed mustache that extended only the width of his nostrils. His khaki summer suit was stretched tightly across his round shoulders, his National Socialist Party pin prominently displayed on his left lapel. The top of his shirt collar was invisible beneath the roll of his neck.

"From your file," he continued, "I see you scored high marks in your summer coursework in Heidelberg and that you have worked summers in a newspaper office in America."

"Yes, Herr Direktor," Maggie replied. "I worked for two summers as a cub reporter for the High Glenn *Bugle*."

"High Glenn?"

"My hometown. Of course it's just a small place in New York, not a city like Heidelberg." She was anxious to impress Bauer, the head of the foreign service in the Ministry of Public Enlightenment and Propaganda's Broadcasting Division. Bauer's department transmitted official German communiqués to all corners of the earth, on multiple frequencies and in a variety of languages.

"Beautiful city, Heidelberg," Bauer mused, a far-off look in his eyes. He shifted his gaze back to Maggie and let it linger there a moment, as though he were finding the city's beauty reflected in her. "You speak German very well, and there is, of course, no question of your abilities in English." He smiled. "Have you fluency in any additional languages?"

"No, Herr Direktor. Though I do have a good ear for languages, and I am willing to learn."

"That won't be necessary, Fräulein. Much of the department's activity is directed to our listeners in Great Britain," Bauer continued. "I should think you would be able to contribute in translations and transcriptions. You do type, do you not?"

"Yes, Herr Direktor. I can type forty words a minute, and I can also take dictation," she said, exaggerating only a little.

"And, although you are American, you are somewhat familiar with the English, I take it?"

"Oh yes, Herr Direktor. I am quite familiar with the English," Maggie answered, color rising in her cheeks, her eyes taking on a renewed intensity. "My father immigrated to America from Ireland when he was a young man, mostly due to the English."

"I see," said Bauer, who liked what he saw, both in Maggie's file and in her attractive presence. Too often, he thought to himself, the Broadcasting Division got the hand-me-downs from the ministry's main office on the Wilhelmstraße. Well, here was one young beauty he would hire before Joseph Goebbels could intercept her. "Very well, my dear," Bauer continued, adopting a more paternal tone. "I believe we can make good use of your talents!"

"Wunderbar!" Maggie exclaimed, causing Bauer to laugh.

Bauer pushed back from his desk and stood, struggling to button his coat across his broad belly. "Please follow me, and I will introduce you to Herr Schmidt, the head of our English language service."

Bauer waddled around his desk and led Maggie down the main corridor of Broadcasting House, the sprawling, modern headquarters of the Broadcasting Division. The structure on Masurenallee, a twenty-minute subway ride from Berlin's center, was built to house Germany's burgeoning radio propaganda effort. The huge building—shaped like half a wagon wheel, spokes and all—covered most of a city block. Maggie followed a step behind and to Bauer's left as he led her to a glass door labeled *Englische Abteilung* and pushed it open.

"*Guten Tag*, Herr Schmidt," the Direktor said, sending a pale, serious-looking young man in a dark suit jumping to his feet, a startled look on his face. On Schmidt's desk lay the morning's *Völkischer Beobachter*, the official Nazi Party newspaper, next to an ashtray in which burned an unfinished cigarette.

"*Guten Tag*, Herr Direktor," stammered Schmidt. "This is an unexpected surprise!"

"Yes, I suppose most surprises are," Bauer said. "Everything is in order, I trust?" the Direktor asked, looking around the office at the five empty desks.

"Yes, Herr Direktor. Most of the staff start their day after lunch."

"Why after lunch?" Maggie asked.

"Oh, you must excuse me," Bauer said, turning from Schmidt to Maggie and then back. "Allow me to present Fräulein Margaret O'Dea. Fräulein O'Dea"—Bauer gestured toward the younger man—"Herr Schmidt, the section leader of our English language service."

Schmidt bowed slightly to Maggie. He seemed uncertain, Maggie thought, perhaps a little in awe of Bauer. "A pleasure to meet you, Fräulein," he said, dropping eye contact and looking back to Bauer as if awaiting an explanation.

"Fräulein O'Dea is the new translator and transcriber you requested, Schmidt."

"Of course," the younger man said. "Thank you, Herr Direktor."

"Well." Bauer turned back toward Maggie. "I will leave it to you young people to carry on from here. Welcome to Broadcasting Division, my dear. I am sure you will find the work fascinating and fulfilling. Herr Schmidt will acquaint you with your duties. Good day to you both!"

Bauer pushed his way back through the doorway and disappeared into the corridor. Schmidt exhaled and stared after him.

Maggie cleared her throat. "So, Herr Schmidt, where do we start?" she asked cheerfully.

Schmidt turned his gaze toward her as if noticing her for the first time. He was slightly taller than Maggie, with a lean build and a handsome face. His dark hair was oiled and combed straight back, and his wire-rimmed glasses sat crookedly on his long, thin nose. "Ah, well," he mumbled, clearly trying to figure out what to do with his new employee. "Can you write?"

"Yes, Herr Schmidt." Maggie laughed, bringing a tinge of color to Schmidt's white face. "I can read, too!"

"Forgive me," he said sheepishly. "I meant can you write radio copy, the script a broadcaster reads on air?" Schmidt was beginning to recover his composure, and his posture relaxed.

"I suppose I can. I've done some writing for my hometown newspaper, and I've listened to enough radio broadcasts. It certainly doesn't sound that difficult. Why don't you give me an assignment, and let's see how you like it?"

"An excellent idea, Fräulein O'Dea," Schmidt said.

"Just call me Maggie," she said, smiling.

Schmidt grinned as though thinking that Maggie's assignment to his section might be a fair trade for suffering through a visit from the Direktor.

◆ ◆ ◆

Schmidt leaned over Maggie's shoulder as she typed, a hand on the back of her chair. Maggie pounded away on the keys and, reaching the end of the page, ripped the sheet from the carriage, leaned back, and cocked her head upward to look Schmidt in the eye. "OK," she said, "how's this?"

Schmidt held the page between his long, white fingers. His eyes scanned it rapidly. To Maggie, he appeared deep in thought, carefully considering what she'd just written. She waited, eager that this first impression of her work would be a positive one. He looked up at the ceiling of the silent office, pursing his lips, then back at the page. "Mmm," he mumbled. Maggie leaned slightly forward, searching for a hint of his reaction.

"Maggie," Schmidt began slowly, "I think this is excellent. I think we might use this tonight."

Maggie squealed with delight and jumped up. She grabbed the startled Schmidt and hugged him, giggling with satisfaction. When she released him, she saw that his face was flushed, a shy grin spreading across it. "I must remember to compliment your work often." He laughed.

◆ ◆ ◆

Schmidt had assigned Maggie a short piece on the problem in the Sudetenland, that portion of western Czechoslovakia inhabited by more than three million ethnic Germans. Maggie had condensed the lead article in the *Völkischer Beobachter*, lifting out the main points. Since the spring, Hitler had been issuing bellicose statements insisting that the Sudeten Germans should be reunited with the German *Reich*. His bloodless *Anschluss* with Austria had emboldened the Führer in his quest for territory and German reunification.

Now, in the early afternoon, with most of his English-speaking on-air talent at their desks or lounging in chairs, Schmidt stood at his desk in the middle of the office and read aloud Maggie's script.

"Lord Runciman, a member of Great Britain's House of Lords, continues his diplomatic mission to Prague. Runciman spent much of the last two days shuttling between representatives of the ethnic German population and officials of the Czech government in an attempt to defuse tensions in the Sudetenland. Officials in the region report widespread looting and rioting around the city of Karlovy Vary. Reports indicate that native Germans have been made the target of random violence by roving bands of Czech thugs. Members of the Henlein Party, representing many Sudeten Germans, have appealed for the Czech government to immediately restore order or permit assistance from German law enforcement officers who are monitoring the situation from observation posts near Zwickau. The German foreign ministry issued a warning to Czechoslovakia's President Beneš that crimes against Sudeten Germans and their property must not go unpunished. No response has been forthcoming from the Beneš government."

Schmidt paused and looked up from the paper. "Well, what do you think?" he asked.

"I think we should change it to say the Henlein Party represents *most* Sudeten Germans, not *many*," said Robert Hipps in a slow drawl. Hipps, from Mississippi, had been listening intently, his eyes not on Schmidt but on the pretty girl to his right. "Other'n that, I think it's fine."

"How about that part about the foreign office issuing a warning to Beneš?" interjected Julie Clay, another American, with a more cultured accent. "Is that part true?"

"Of course it is, Julie," Schmidt said. "We always vet our message with the foreign office."

"Well, then," Julie replied, "I agree with Robert. I think it's good, damn good. Who's taking it on air?" she asked, clearly hoping it would be her.

"I was thinking that since our target audience is primarily the British, Clive should read it," Schmidt said.

"If he's sober," Robert stage-whispered to Julie, bringing a knowing chuckle from several desks.

Maggie sat in the corner, her eyes moving from person to person as they spoke. The on-air talent was a fascinating mix of Americans, English, and the occasional German. Typically, they broadcast from early evening until late into the night, depending on whether their target audience was in London, just one hour behind Berlin, or in New York, six hours earlier.

"All right then," Schmidt continued, "let me introduce the author of this segment, our newest section member, Maggie O'Dea."

Maggie stood as if lifted by the sprinkling of light applause that rose from the others.

"Maggie joined us just this morning. She came to Germany earlier this summer as a student and has decided to stay for a while. Welcome, Maggie!" The brief introduction concluded, Schmidt turned to the others. "Now, the rest of you take this as guidance for your talks tonight. Embellish as you see fit, but don't stray too far from the main points as written. Draft your talking points and review them with me before 1700."

As Robert, Julie, and the others turned their attention back to their own work, Schmidt motioned Maggie back to the center desk. "Off to a good start, Maggie," he said. "They usually love to rip one another's work to pieces. They accepted yours substantially intact." Surrounded by his staff, Schmidt was no longer nervous or tense. He was in his element, writing, directing, counseling. He was assertive and in control—far different than he had first appeared with Bauer and, thought Maggie, far more appealing. She stood by as he scribbled a note across the top of

Maggie's paper, intrigued by the change a couple of hours and the right colleagues had made in the man.

"Come, Maggie, and I'll introduce you to the star of our little operation, Clive Barnes," Schmidt said, gathering up some papers and making his way to the door of the office. Once in the hallway, he resumed his introduction of Barnes. "Clive is our most popular broadcaster, at least among our English listeners. He uses the on-air name of Lord Lyon. Perhaps you have heard him?"

"I've heard of him, Herr Schmidt," Maggie replied. "But the things that usually appeal to English listeners don't usually appeal to me."

"Oh?" Schmidt glanced at her as they walked down the corridor. "How so?"

"I don't like the English. They feel they're entitled to rule over others, to dominate the world."

"Yes, this may be true," he agreed, "and this is why it worries me." It was Maggie's turn to glance at him. "What worries you?"

"I fear our countries may be on a conflicting course. This business with Czechoslovakia seems to me very dangerous. If the British, or the French for that matter, choose to support the Czech government, Germany will have a difficult time," Schmidt explained, staring down as they continued walking, then looking up when they reached a wooden door with no label on it. "Here we are." He knocked and, without waiting for a reply, pushed the handle and walked in, Maggie right behind him.

"Hello, Dieter!" said a fat, smiling, bald man sitting on an upholstered love seat. Barnes made Direktor Bauer look tiny. He had a massive head fringed with gray hair, three long, lonely strands of which ventured across the top of his otherwise hairless pate. His left foot was propped up on a pillow, and his red smoking jacket hung open, unable to corral his girth. A cigarette in a long ivory holder was clenched between his teeth, a tumbler of clear liquid in his hand. "And who is this enchanting young lady?" Barnes asked in a rich, deep voice.

"Good afternoon, Clive," Schmidt said. "Allow me to introduce the newest member of English Section, Maggie O'Dea."

Without attempting to stand, Clive extended a meaty hand. "Delighted, simply delighted to make your acquaintance, my dear. Please forgive me for not standing. A touch of the old gout, you see," he said, motioning with his cigarette holder toward his elevated foot. "May I offer you a libation?"

Schmidt intervened. "Sorry, Clive. Too much to be done just now. Perhaps later. Maggie here has drafted a report that will form the basis of tonight's commentary."

"Has she, now?" Clive sat up a little straighter and reached for a pair of half lenses. "Let's see what we have with which to work," he said, turning his attention to the page Schmidt proffered. "Mmm," he hummed, scanning the sheet. "Yes, yes. Quite right. Just the right tone, I'd say. Puts our friends in their preferred role as mediators and controllers. Yes, they like that. Well done, my dear!" Clive said with an admiring look at Maggie. "This will do quite nicely. Thank you, Dieter. I will see you before five o'clock with my outline."

Schmidt and Maggie nodded good-bye and retreated to the hallway.

"So, your name is Dieter," Maggie said as they headed back toward the English Section office. "I thought for a while there that you were just plain Schmidt."

"Forgive me," he said with the shy grin. "Bauer does put me off my game a bit, I'm afraid."

"What's wrong with Bauer? He seems like a pleasant, if swinelike, bureaucrat," Maggie added playfully.

Dieter turned toward her, the smile gone from his face. "Not here, Maggie," he whispered.

Nonplussed, Maggie fell back into step as Dieter continued down the corridor.

◆ ◆ ◆

"You must never ridicule Bauer, or any of the party members, in public," Dieter explained later as they sat under the awning of a sidewalk café near Broadcasting House. "They don't take criticism well." The summer sun was still high in the sky, the temperature hot for Berlin. Dieter had loosened his tie, but he kept his coat on, his cuffs extending from his sleeves as he reached for his beer.

"I'm sorry," Maggie said, and she was. "I have something of a playful streak. I like to have fun," she continued, a wisp of a smile struggling to stay in place.

They had finished their afternoon work, reviewing each broadcaster's talking points. Few of them read from a true script. Most simply wrote an outline based on the day's guidance from Bauer's office. The outlines were approved first by Dieter, then by a military censor, and then by an official from the propaganda ministry. The evening's broadcasts, which usually began at seven o'clock Berlin time, started with a news summary, during which Maggie's report would be read along with the other news of the day. Following the news, Dieter's English Section talent would spend the next several hours elaborating, explaining, and analyzing the world events that had been reported. English Section's day wouldn't be completed until the wee hours of the morning, when the final North American transmissions concluded.

"You're new here, Maggie. Berlin is like any capital, filled with powerful men. Powerful men don't like to be made fun of. The National Socialists in particular haven't much of a sense of humor. Playful or not, you must guard yourself. You can never tell who's listening. Bauer is a powerful man and a party member. It wouldn't do for you to be overheard making jokes at his expense. He's an ardent National Socialist and a member of Minister Goebbels's inner circle."

"Is that why he makes you uncomfortable?"

Dieter hesitated. "Yes, in part, at least," he said. "Radio is the most powerful medium of communications in existence. Our government, Minister Goebbels in particular, recognized this at an early stage. That's why we have the best facilities and equipment in the world. And that's why the expectations for our work are so high. You must understand that we are the voice of Germany to millions of listeners. I don't mean just in Britain and the United States. There are other sections broadcasting to South America, Africa, Eastern Europe, and even the Soviet Union—not that they have many radio sets there," he added, as though trying to lighten the conversation. "I don't tell you these things to frighten you. I just want you to understand the limits we must observe." Dieter leaned forward, glanced theatrically around, and said, "But, off the record, I agree: Bauer is a fat oaf!"

Maggie giggled. "Thank you, Dieter." She took a swig from her beer. She was pleased with her new job. She liked the work so far. The people seemed a fascinating collection of adventurers and charlatans. And she appreciated Dieter's concern.

◆ ◆ ◆

Kurt's hand kneaded Maggie's breast as he kissed her. As he started to roll onto her, Maggie abruptly shifted her weight, catching him by surprise and rolling him on to his back. His eyes widened. Maggie smiled and climbed on top of him, causing him to gasp.

Their evening had been a pleasant one, each relaying the events of the day to the other as they enjoyed a meal at a small restaurant near Kurt's apartment. Maggie had shared her successes, first in landing the job and then in meeting her colorful colleagues and earning their praise for her maiden efforts. Kurt, after swearing Maggie to secrecy, told of preparing his platoon for deployment. To where, he could not say, but they both guessed it would be toward Czechoslovakia, and they both guessed it would happen soon.

As they had strolled along the oak-lined street back toward the apartment, Kurt had said, "As much as I enjoy your company, I think we should find you an apartment of your own. I have no control over my comings and goings. If our regiment is deployed, it will happen very quickly and most likely without warning. Perhaps a place closer to where you work would be more suitable."

"Oh," Maggie had said, "you're probably right. You always are." She'd put her arm through his and leaned against his shoulder. "I'd probably appear more respectable, too, with a place of my own." She'd laughed.

Now, as she began to move atop him, Kurt's hands slid down to her hips. "My God, Irish American girl!" was all he could say.

Maggie leaned forward until her breasts met Kurt's chest, her hair covering his face, and kissed him on each cheek as he continued to breathe heavily. Then, slowly stretching her arms around his shoulders, she held tight, reluctant to let the moment pass.

CHAPTER 3

Berlin, Germany
August 1938

Within a week, Maggie was installed in a one-bedroom flat on Soorstraße near Broadcasting House, and Kurt and his regiment—the Leibstandarte SS Adolf Hitler, the Führer's personal bodyguard—had deployed somewhere to the south. He did not know precisely where they were headed, and Maggie knew better than to ask.

With no Kurt to distract her and a short walk to work, Maggie spent most of her waking hours in English Section. She continued to write the daily news report and occasionally assisted the on-air talent with their talking points, either typing notes for them or making suggestions about content. The talent soon learned that Maggie was the best informed of the team, starting each day with a thorough study of the morning papers. Maggie also listened to the BBC at night, something Dieter and her other German colleagues were not legally permitted to do. This gave her insight into current British opinion, the workings of the British propaganda apparatus, and how her team might be able to turn these to their advantage.

August gave way to September, and the summer days grew both shorter and cooler. Maggie began to break out her sweaters. She enjoyed the crispness of the morning air on her walks to Broadcasting House. She missed Kurt, but never Mass, where she would always light a candle and pray for his safety. As far back as she could remember, Mass had been a regular part of her routine, first with her mother and father, then with her little sister.

On Monday, September 19, the headlines in the morning papers were large and bold. England and France had deserted their erstwhile ally Czechoslovakia and were urging the Beneš government to cede the Sudetenland to the Reich. Germans on the street gathered around newsstands and the loudspeakers from which the propaganda ministry's official news bulletins flowed. It seemed that war had been averted. The people were more relieved than excited. Except for the party members.

As she entered the building with a throng of morning workers, Maggie saw Direktor Bauer and several other high-ranking Broadcasting Division officials standing on the second-floor balcony, smiling and laughing. Although she did not see him at first glance, she quickly noticed the object of their attention was the propaganda minister himself, Joseph Goebbels. A small man, barely five feet tall and weighing just one hundred pounds, Goebbels nonetheless commanded the attention of the larger men around him. He had dark hair with matching, intense eyes. Though slightly built, the propaganda minister possessed an impeccable wardrobe: his suits, ties, and shirts were expensive and stylish. Maggie found herself staring as she ascended the stairs. As she turned down the corridor toward English Section, she heard a loud explosion of laughter from the group around Goebbels. *No doubt enjoying Mr. Chamberlain's unwitting capitulation,* Maggie thought. Maggie felt Hitler had clearly bested his English counterpart. She smiled to herself. *Too bad.*

"Good morning, Maggie," Dieter said as she entered the office. No matter what hour she arrived, Dieter was always there, as fresh as though he had just emerged from a barber's chair. "Look lively this morning, won't you? We have a distinguished visitor in the building."

"Yes, I saw him on the way up"—Maggie dropped her newspapers on her desk—"holding forth with the big shots."

Dieter shot her a warning look. "Careful, now," he said. "Bauer says he's here to give us some new direction concerning the Sudeten issue."

Bauer was proven correct. Goebbels, in a meeting with the Broadcasting Division's directors, laid out changes in their coverage of the crisis over Czechoslovakia. With England and France already pulling away from their Czech ally, Goebbels ordered an intensification of the attacks against the Beneš government in particular and the Czechs in general. The strategy was already evident in the morning's newspaper headlines, which Maggie spread before Dieter. WOMEN, MEN, CHILDREN MOWED DOWN BY CZECH GUNMEN! one headline screamed. CZECHS TERRORIZE SUDETEN GERMAN LAND another banner hailed.

No longer would the region be referred to as the Sudetenland; henceforth, in the German press at least, it would be *Sudeten German Land*. With the British and French in a diplomatic retreat, Goebbels had directed that world opinion be informed by tales of Czech perfidy and atrocity.

◆ ◆ ◆

On Thursday, September 22, British Prime Minister Chamberlain returned to Germany, this time to meet with Hitler at Bad Godesberg on the banks of the Rhine River. Dieter relayed to his team the guidance from the Wilhelmstraße.

"We must continue to portray the prime minister as a statesman ready to surmount any obstacle to procure a peaceful resolution to this crisis," Dieter told his staff, looking up from a sheaf of papers on his desk. It was early afternoon and the daily briefing was underway. Dieter, as always, was neatly dressed in his dark suit and white shirt. Maggie sat nearby, wearing a new red sweater and taking notes. "We must convince our listeners that Chamberlain is acting in the best interests not only of Europe but also of the British Empire." Maggie snorted, drawing a chuckle from Julie Clay seated beside her. "Maggie will share some key points," Dieter said and sat down.

Maggie stood and moved to the middle of the room. She had continued to work hard, and her good efforts were respected by her colleagues. When she spoke, they listened carefully, knowing that she had Dieter's ear and that he would study the content of their outlines to ensure Maggie's main ideas were included.

"As Dieter said," Maggie began, "we want Mr. Chamberlain to come off looking like a statesman. That means respectful references to him, using his proper title as prime minister or mister. We also want to convey that he is aligned with the Führer on this issue; that the two are in concert on the ultimate outcome—that is, the return of Sudeten German Land to the Reich. Of course, the holdup at this point is over procedural difficulties only, not substantive differences. Chamberlain favors an international commission to supervise the return of Sudeten German Land, while the Führer favors immediate occupation. In the scheme of things, that should be represented as a minor disagreement, if you discuss it at all. And remember, both sides are simply working to reunite ethnic Germans with their Fatherland."

"Maggie," Robert Hipps asked, lighting a cigarette, "what should we say about the French?"

"Nothing. We'll leave that to French Section. We should focus on the fact that Great Britain and Germany desire the same outcome— the same *peaceful* outcome. We might also inject some of the reports we continue to receive from the region about mistreatment of ethnic Germans by the Czechs, but again, our main point tonight is to bolster Chamberlain, to make him appear to be a heroic figure, as farfetched as that may seem, working tirelessly for peace right alongside the Führer."

Dieter stood. "Any more questions then? All right, let's get to it. Outlines by 1700." As the English Section staff turned to their writing tablets or typewriters, Dieter tapped Maggie on the elbow and motioned her into the hallway.

"Well done as usual," he said, patting her gently on the shoulder. "You've established an excellent rapport with the rest of the team. They respect your work ethic and your judgment." Maggie beamed, pleased at both Dieter's recognition and his touch. "Now, let's go brief His Majesty," Dieter said as they turned and headed toward Clive Barnes's private office.

Lord Lyon was easily the most charismatic of English Section's broadcasters. He had a deep voice, well suited to radio. He had oratorical ability, too. He knew how to tell a story, building detail upon detail, before bringing his listeners to the climax. He modulated his voice in accordance with his location in the story or outline or script. And, although he occasionally read a script on air, his listeners would never know it. He seemed to just talk, as one might to a neighbor or a friend. The only serious concern with Clive was his romance with the bottle.

Maggie waited just behind Dieter as he knocked on the wooden door and pushed it open. Dieter turned quickly, shielding Maggie's view. "Perhaps you'd better wait in the hallway, Maggie," he snapped in annoyance. "It looks like I'll have to have another frank conversation with Clive."

"Oh, nonsense, Dieter," Maggie replied, pushing past him to find their corpulent commentator slouched on his love seat in nothing but his underwear, snoring heavily. "I can handle this fat English bastard!" Maggie strode over to Clive's desk. There she found a glass, which she filled from a pitcher of water. As Dieter watched, she calmly walked over to the slumbering Clive and hurled the water in his face. His massive head snorted and spat, and his arms came up off his belly as if trying to regain lost balance. "Wake up, dear!" Maggie called out sweetly.

Clive's eyes cracked open just far enough for him to see a red blob standing in front of him. "What in God's good name are you doing, Maggie?" he croaked.

"Why, I've come to get you up, sleepyhead," she cooed as if talking to a two-year-old awaking from a nap.

"My dear," Clive grumbled, shifting his oversize frame on the seat, "I am not quite sure I am ready to get up! And I seem to be all wet!"

"Of course you are, darling!" Maggie replied, her voice like honey.

"Of course I am what?" Clive snapped, his fat fingers rubbing at his bleary eyes.

"Ready to get up. And wet," Maggie allowed. "It's time to get to work now. And if you start right now, I might just stay and help you."

This began to rouse the big man, who looked with favor on Dieter's daily visit to his inner sanctum primarily, Maggie suspected, because he brought her with him. "Oh, all right," Clive growled, struggling to pull himself up. "There, hand me my robe. No, the gold one!" he commanded, pointing to a coatrack behind the door. "It won't do for both of us to wear red in such a small office. We might put someone's eye out!"

This brought a giggle from Maggie and an audible sigh of relief from Dieter.

◆　◆　◆

At four thirty, the door to the English Section office burst open, and Clive struggled in, holding some papers in one hand while leaning on Maggie for support. His right hand was around her waist, resting just above her hip, and Dieter could tell his posture was less the product of his gout than his delight in Maggie's company.

"Hello, Dieter!" his voice boomed. "With help from my young colleague here"—he cocked his head toward Maggie—"we have achieved a milestone in broadcast journalism!" By now the others in the office had completely stopped their work to listen to the great man's boasts. "These pages," Clive continued, waving the sheets in the air, "will fire the hearts of our British friends and rally them around their great and selfless leader, Mr. Chamberlain. Why, by this time tomorrow, Chamberlain and his cabinet will be revered throughout their island kingdom and indeed to the far corners of their empire!"

A smattering of applause rose from Robert, Julie, and the others in the room, and Clive bowed slightly, acknowledging the greatness of his oratory and the discernment of his audience. Dieter looked over Clive's notes and penned his initials to the bottom corner before sending him off to the censors' offices.

"Maggie," Dieter said as Clive disappeared down the corridor, "thank you for working with Clive today. When we first walked in, I thought there was no way he would be ready to broadcast. You were wonderful!" He was looking into her green eyes, unable to suppress the small, dumb grin on his face, shaking his head in wonder. "I don't know how you did it."

"It comes from having a younger sister," Maggie said with a smile. "When our mother died, I took care of her. I learned that people are less likely to be difficult if you are sweet and cheerful—at least outwardly." She laughed. Maggie grabbed her sweater under both arms and twisted. "I'm afraid Clive has international hands." She laughed again.

"What?"

"Roman and Russian!" Maggie giggled, adjusting her skirt.

"Heavens, Maggie!" Dieter was startled. "I will speak to him immediately!" He turned to follow after Clive.

"No, Dieter," Maggie said, placing her hand on his forearm. "It's nothing. He's just a horny old bastard, that's all. He appreciates it when a woman pays attention to him. That's another reason I was able to get him going."

Dieter stopped. He looked Maggie squarely in the eyes and said, "All right. This one time. But if it happens again, you will report to me at once. Agreed?"

"Why, Dieter," Maggie replied, seeming genuinely touched, "I believe you're jealous." She patted his arm and smiled.

Dieter blushed. Indeed, he was.

◆ ◆ ◆

Instead of heading home, Maggie stayed at Broadcasting House that evening to listen firsthand to Clive's broadcast. The studios were across the inner courtyard of the complex, through a guarded door and down a series of steps. Dieter accompanied Maggie on this, her first visit to the studio. "I think you will be impressed," he told her as they crossed the well-manicured garden inside the courtyard. "Our facilities are truly state of the art."

Dieter led Maggie past the sentry, who matched their names to an access roster, and then down the stairs. At the bottom, they entered a brightly lit corridor that led to a large control room equipped with all manner of consoles and switches. A team of electrical engineers sat monitoring gauges and dials.

"This way, Maggie," Dieter said, passing through the control center and into a dimmer room. Here, on an elevated platform behind a console, sat Herr Direktor Bauer in a comfortable-looking swivel chair. In his hand Maggie noticed a pair of earphones connected by a black cord to the console. Below Bauer, at a series of floor-level consoles, sat several of Dieter's counterparts. Here, too, there were sets of earphones, a microphone on a small stand, switches, dials, and buttons. Just in front of these consoles was a glass wall, at the top of which was mounted a bank of clocks displaying times in the various capitals of the world. Behind the glass sat a series of separate rooms: one room for each of the broadcast sections. Within each of these, where the on-air talent would actually face their listeners, was a small table covered with green felt, upon which sat a large broadcast microphone, earphones, and a vertically mounted red light bulb. This, Maggie assumed, was the on-air light she had seen in so many Hollywood movies.

In the glass room before Dieter's console, Clive Barnes carefully balanced his bulk on a wooden chair, his elbows resting on the table, his script spread out before him. Maggie thought it ironic that Clive was now fully dressed, wearing a natty, gray, pin-striped suit with a blue-and-white-striped bowtie. A matching handkerchief protruded from his breast pocket. Except for his girth, Maggie thought, he might just have stepped out of a Savile Row shop. And no one would see him, save Bauer, Dieter, herself, and the others in the observation room.

Dieter pulled up an extra chair and plugged a spare set of earphones into a jack on the console. "Sit here," he said, gesturing to Maggie. Dieter had gotten tense again. He was looking down at his notes and at the controls on the panel, occasionally glancing at Clive behind the glass window. This, Maggie figured, was where Dieter's work was evaluated, his abilities put to the true test and his worth considered. Bauer, sitting above his section chiefs, kept an eye on the clocks and inconspicuously switched back and forth between the broadcasts of the German, French, and English sections.

As eight o'clock approached—seven o'clock in London—Dieter tapped softly on the glass. Clive looked up and nodded, then, noticing Maggie, gave her a wink and a smile. Dieter checked his dials, then the clock. He held up his left hand, his fingers extended. Again, Clive nodded. Dieter nodded back and began lowering a finger every second until the second hand on the London clock hit twelve. The red light went on. Dieter pointed to Clive.

Through her earphones, Maggie heard the deep-throated rumble of Clive as he said, "Berlin calling . . . Berlin calling . . . Berlin calling . . . Good evening to my countrymen on the far side of the Channel. This is your friend in Berlin, Lord Lyon, with observations on today's news." For the next fifteen minutes, Lord Lyon held forth on the indomitable determination of Prime Minister Chamberlain and Chancellor Hitler to work together to craft a peaceful resolution to the Sudeten crisis. He described with florid prose the high character of the two leaders, their deepening respect for each other, and the personal relationship they were building—a relationship, Lord Lyon said, which would stand their two great nations in good stead in the perilous days ahead. "It is uncommon in the annals of history that two powerful and sovereign nations should subjugate their own national interests to the common good of the greater continental community," Lyon preached, "yet this is the great drama being played out before us. And if it should come as a surprise to us, if it should catch the casual observer off guard, it is only because our character does not ascend to the high standards of Mr. Chamberlain's and Herr Hitler's. This"—he paused for effect—"is Lord Lyon in Berlin. Good night. God save the King!" The red light flickered off.

Dieter keyed the intercom microphone. "Well done, Clive! Outstanding performance!"

"Thank you, my boy!" Clive boomed, his voice still audible only through the earphones. Clive was standing now, gathering his papers and stuffing them into a folder.

"Excellent work, Schmidt," came the voice of Direktor Bauer, who had descended from his throne and come up behind him. "Lord Lyon was in peak form tonight."

Dieter stood and turned to face his boss. "Thank you, Herr Direktor. Much of the credit is due to Fräulein O'Dea." Dieter motioned toward her. "She spent much of the afternoon with Lord Lyon helping him sober up and prepare his script."

Bauer, looking surprised, turned toward Maggie. "Well, Fräulein, I must repeat myself: excellent work. Whatever it takes, yes? Keep this up and the English will be only too eager to follow the Führer's lead." He bowed curtly and strode back up the two steps to his elevated seat.

Maggie noticed a light sheen of perspiration on Dieter's forehead. He quickly stowed the microphone and earphones and turned off the switches on his console. "Come, Maggie," he said, "let's call it a day. Mikhail can take over for now." Mikhail was one of Dieter's production assistants.

Maggie waited until they were back up the stairs, past the guard, and into the courtyard before she grabbed Dieter by the arm, spinning him toward her. "That was fantastic!" she exclaimed, pecking him on the cheek. Dieter blushed again, his face attempting to match the shade of Maggie's sweater.

"You, Maggie," he said, his fingers brushing his kissed cheek, "you are the fantastic one!"

◆ ◆ ◆

English Section's work intensified over the next week as Chamberlain and Hitler, though in agreement on the final resolution of the Sudeten crisis, failed to come to terms on how to bring it about. On Friday, September 23, as Chamberlain and Hitler met, the Czech army mobilized, calling up reserves and preparing to deploy from its garrisons. War seemed imminent; the German people seemed anxious. Each night, English Section's broadcasters added their spin to the news reports coming from Prague, London, and Berlin. They continued to laud and honor Chamberlain and his progressive statesmanship. They condemned the brutality and smallness of Beneš and the Czechs. On Monday, September 26, Hitler spoke to a partisan crowd of party loyalists in Berlin's Sportspalast. He demanded the Sudetenland—and he wanted it by Saturday, October 1. Europe hung in precarious balance between war and peace.

On her way home from work on Tuesday evening, Maggie had to wait for thirty minutes while a motorized army division rolled by. Truck after soldier-filled truck passed, stirring up swirls of dust in their wakes, all headed southeast. Maggie thought of Kurt and wondered where he was and what he was doing. She hoped Chamberlain and his French allies would be able to prevail upon the Czechs to do the right thing: reunite the German people and avoid war! On Wednesday, news broke of a meeting between Chamberlain, French premier Daladier, and Hitler and his ally, the Italian dictator Mussolini. The four were to meet in Munich the following day. English Section continued to present Hitler's position as the pathway to peace, which rational leaders would be obliged to follow.

Finally, at twelve thirty in the morning of Friday, September 30, the leaders of Europe's four great powers signed an agreement ceding the Sudetenland to Germany as of the following morning. No international commission was convened, nor was any representative of the Czech government invited to participate in the negotiations.

The mood on the streets that Friday morning was jubilant. Workers who had feared war just days earlier were now laughing and slapping one another on the back, boasting at what their Führer had accomplished. Dieter was animated by a mixture of excitement and relief, the tensions of the previous week leaking from his body like the air from a balloon that had been about to pop.

"I can't believe he actually did it!" Dieter said between bites of lunch at a café near Broadcasting House. It was cooler. Fall had arrived almost unnoticed in all the excitement. Both Dieter and Maggie wore coats as they sipped beer and munched on wursts. "I'm amazed at Hitler's willingness to gamble—and astounded that he won everything without giving up anything!" Dieter shook his head and stared down at his plate.

"Ha! The English got what they deserved," Maggie gloated, then cocked her head. "You don't seem to like Herr Hitler as much as everyone else does," she observed. "Isn't returning three million Germans to the Fatherland a good thing?"

"Sure, but Hitler scares me. One of these days he'll go too far."

"Come on, Dieter! He just took from England and France exactly what he wanted, and Chamberlain doesn't even realize he's been humiliated." Maggie took another sip. "It's high time someone put jolly old England in its place. Chin up, friend! Hitler has broken England's stranglehold on power. A little competition will be good for everyone."

Dieter looked at her with his gentle smile and again shook his head. "I hope you're right, for everybody's sake."

◆ ◆ ◆

Hitler wasn't able to keep to his original timetable for occupying the Sudetenland that Saturday. It was only on the following Monday, October 3, that the Leibstandarte SS Adolf Hitler led the occupation forces across the border. In its ranks was *Obersturmführer* Kurt Engel. English Section cast the German troops as liberators, helping the ethnic Germans in the Sudetenland throw off their evil Czech oppressors. The stories presented were upbeat: tales of soldiers hailed as liberators and great acts of kindness by the Führer's forces toward those whom they had come to rescue.

"Another good day," Dieter observed as he walked with Maggie toward her apartment. With darkness falling earlier as autumn deepened, Dieter was concerned about her walking home alone. "I've been thinking of making some reassignments, Maggie," he said casually as a cool breeze swept the leaves from the sidewalk in front of them. Dieter glanced at Maggie. Her red cheeks reflected the crispness of the evening air, her green eyes shifting to meet his. "I'm thinking of naming an additional producer to work mainly with Clive. He requires a great deal of supervision, as you have noticed, yet he is far and away our most popular and influential commentator. What do you think of this idea?" The two had stopped strolling and stood on the sidewalk facing each other in the dim light of the street lamps.

"Well," Maggie began thoughtfully, "it makes sense. Heaven knows the old fart needs some continuity that is missing now. He's on some days and off some days. A dedicated producer would help, I guess. Upon whom would you confer this high honor and pain in the ass?" she asked, tilting her head to the side and smiling.

"Oh, it would have to be someone with mature judgment; someone Clive respects; someone who knows how to get the job done regardless of the circumstances," Dieter mused out loud. "Yes, it would have to be the most capable person on the staff. It would have to be you, Maggie."

"You say the sweetest things!" Maggie batted her eyelids theatrically and laughed. Then, more seriously, she added, "Thank you, Dieter. Thank you for your confidence in me, from the very first day." They began walking again, heading toward Maggie's building at the end of the block.

"Of course, you would have to be willing to accept a pay increase and a new title. And of course greater autonomy in creating Clive's broadcasts." Dieter teased, "Did you ever expect such excitement on your first day back in August?"

"Oh, I didn't know what to expect that first day." Maggie smiled, her hands thrust down into the pockets of her coat. "I didn't know if I would be working for an ogre or if I would even be working at all! And, I have to confess, I was a little nervous with you at first," she said, darting a look at Dieter. "I was afraid you might let Bauer push you around." Dieter said nothing. "But," she continued with a light note in her voice, "instead I've learned that you are indeed a master of your craft, a true artist, painting pictures with words and telling a story that moves hearts and informs minds."

Dieter shook his head and grinned. "You sound just like a propagandist!"

They were still laughing as they came to the steps leading up to Maggie's building. "Well, here you are," Dieter said as Maggie fished in her purse for her key. "Thank you for an excellent week, Fräulein O'Dea," he said formally, with a short bow. "And good evening."

"Thank you, Dieter," Maggie said with a smile.

Dieter turned back toward the Kaiserdamm and the U-bahn station. Then he stopped and turned around to face Maggie. He took a deep breath, grabbed her by her shoulders, and kissed her. Maggie kissed back.

◆ ◆ ◆

With the Sudeten crisis past, Europe's attention turned from east to west, where, in Spain, German forces were augmenting the Nationalist army of General Francisco Franco. During October, English Section reported on a major battle along Spain's Ebro River—a battle that sounded the beginning of the end for the Spanish Republic.

CHAPTER 4

Gandesa, Spain
October 1938

Erich Greinke shifted gingerly onto his left side. His ribs still hurt like hell, and the stitches that ran from just under his right arm to just above his navel itched. He would have scratched, but that would put too much pressure on his wound and cause even more pain. Still, the worst of the discomfort was behind him. According to Dr. Sandoval, Erich's ribs were already healing, and his torn flesh had avoided infection.

Sunlight filtered through the dirty window of the old schoolhouse, bathing the cot across from Erich's in a warm glow. It was too late to comfort the former occupant, who had expired during the night and been quietly removed while most of the other patients had slumbered on, unaware. Now there were five men left in the makeshift ward, their wounds ranging from a shattered arm to severe head trauma. Erich reached carefully over to the small wooden stand beside his cot and glanced at his wristwatch. The dial showed a quarter past eleven, still half an hour or more until he could expect lunch. He picked a cigarette out of the nearly empty pack on the stand, rolled gently onto his back, and stared at the wooden slats that formed the former classroom's ceiling. Erich had gotten used to the pain, which was only a problem now if he moved suddenly. He had gotten used to the bedpan—after all, it wasn't much worse than field sanitation. It was the boredom that he resented. There were no magazines, no radio, no news from the outside world. Day after day, hour after mind-numbing hour, Erich lay on his cot with no distractions other than a daily visit from Dr. Sandoval, three skimpy meals, and the ministrations of the one nurse who attended the small ward. Erich had no idea how many other patients were in the hospital or how many other staff members worked there.

When he had attempted to talk to Sandoval about more than his injury, the doctor had quickly but courteously steered the conversation back to medical matters. The doctor was tight-lipped about what was happening outside and whether the Nationalists still held the upper hand in the fighting. Sandoval's visits generally came in the evening. The doctor wore some kind of uniform, but so far as Erich could tell, it included no badge of rank. His boots were always muddy and his eyes red from fatigue. Erich figured the doctor spent most of his days near the battle lines, caring for the wounded there, then retreated to his hospital with the seriously injured after darkness halted the day's fighting. Fortunately, Sandoval spoke some English. The nurse, a wrinkled, deeply tanned old crone with hands as rough as a blacksmith's, spoke only Spanish. If she could make Erich understand with gestures, so be it. If not, she used her thick, powerful arms to manhandle him into the desired position, with mostly painful results.

Erich lit his cigarette and took a deep, long pull. He thought again about what he would do when he got out of the hospital and out of Spain. He had considered trying his hand as a correspondent, putting his journalism school training to a test reporting on the tumultuous state of affairs in Europe. He had been raised by first-generation German parents in Milwaukee and spoke German almost as well as a native. Although he had never been able to master Spanish, he was confident he could make his way in the German-speaking countries.

Erich exhaled a cloud of blue smoke, grateful for the relaxing sensation. He plucked a small piece of tobacco off his tongue and adjusted his left arm beneath the back of his head.

A door slammed in the hallway outside, and Erich heard the tramp of boots and the murmur of voices. He turned his head toward the classroom door in time to see Dr. Sandoval enter, three other men trailing behind him. Two of the men were wearing the gray uniform of the German Condor Legion, which had been fighting alongside the Spanish Loyalists for more than two years. The third man was older, Erich guessed in his fifties, with silver hair and prominent blue eyes. He was dressed in a muddy, but expensive, shooting jacket, olive-colored pants, a khaki shirt, and leather riding boots. As the four men moved from cot to cot, Erich could hear Dr. Sandoval offering comments on each patient. The older man seemed to be an attentive listener, occasionally asking questions and nodding with understanding.

"And here we have Señor Greinke," announced Dr. Sandoval with a smile as the small group stopped at the foot of his cot. "A countryman of yours, Colonel Donovan."

The silver-haired man smiled and stepped forward with his hand extended. "How do you do? I'm Bill Donovan."

Erich struggled to push himself up into a sitting position and grasped Donovan's well-muscled hand.

"Mind if I visit with you for a few minutes?"

"No sir," stammered Erich. "I'd appreciate the company." Erich, along with most American boys of his generation, was well acquainted with "Wild" Bill Donovan, the most decorated American soldier of the Great War. Donovan had been awarded the Congressional Medal of Honor for his courage and performance under fire while leading a battalion of the Sixty-Ninth Regiment of the New York National Guard. After the war, he had become a crime-fighting prosecutor in Buffalo, had run unsuccessfully for governor, and had been portrayed in a Hollywood film, *The Fighting 69th*, by actor George Brent. Here was an authentic hero, sitting beside Erich's cot as Sandoval and the Germans moved on to the next patient.

"Well, Mr. Greinke," Donovan began, his clear, blue eyes locked onto Erich's. "Just how did you come to be here? I haven't seen many of our countrymen on this side of the lines."

Erich chuckled, then grimaced. "It only hurts when I laugh," he said with a smile. Donovan smiled knowingly. Donovan had been seriously wounded in France in 1918. Despite his wounds, he had rallied his troops to hold off a German counterattack. "I'm here for a couple of reasons, I guess. I was looking for an adventure, a glorious one, in the service of a noble cause." He smiled again, self-consciously. "My father sort of steered me toward Spain. He said the Republicans and the Communists were trying to eliminate the Church from Spanish life and that good Catholics should come to its aid."

"And what do you think now?"

"I don't think God chooses sides. Our methods of resolving conflict are so inhumane that I can't believe God's proud of us, even if we think we're doing the right thing."

Donovan listened, nodding.

"The other reason I'm here is that a little over a week ago I found myself on the business end of a Republican mortar shell. It broke two of my ribs, sliced me open from here"—Erich pointed to his armpit—"to here"—he drew an imaginary line to the middle of his stomach. "It hurt like he . . . the dickens, but my squad leader bandaged me up and got me out of the line to an aid station, and then Dr. Sandoval brought me here."

"Your squad leader sounds like a pretty resourceful fellow," Donovan prompted.

"I figure he saved my life." Erich shifted his gaze from Donovan's face to the opposite wall. "He's a German fellow, a good Catholic, too, from Oberursel, near Frankfurt." Donovan listened silently. "He was tough, though. He'd boot us in the ass if we weren't taking care of business, but he also made sure we had food and some kind of shelter at night. You know, in all the misery of combat, he was almost chivalrous. And he was always smiling. We were never in a situation he couldn't handle." Erich looked back at Donovan.

"He sounds like a good comrade."

"Yes sir," Erich agreed. "What about you? What brings you to Gandesa?"

"I'm just here as an observer." Donovan smiled, leaning forward, elbows on his knees. "We've heard a lot about the German rearmament, and I thought I would call on a few old friends and take advantage of the opportunity to see firsthand how they fight. They're testing some new weapons here in Spain. I thought I might have a look. Did you have any experience with their Mark III tank or their dive bomber?"

"No sir. I wound up in an antiaircraft section somehow. At first, I was working with a Nationalist unit, but I kept having language problems. I was making all my comrades nervous. For some reason they didn't want to take the time to explain things to me once bullets started snapping past our ears." Both men smiled again. "When they found out I could speak German, they put me in with Sergeant Müller's team."

"Were you equipped with their new 88 mm gun?" Donovan probed.

"Yes sir." Erich nodded. "Very versatile. We used it at first against aircraft, but the airplanes the Republicans were flying weren't all that capable, so I'm not really sure how effective the 88 is against modern aircraft. I can tell you it was deadly against their tanks. We used it as a direct-fire antitank gun and as a conventional artillery piece. I saw it knock out tanks at a range of two kilometers."

"What's its rate of fire?"

"With a good crew, a German crew, fifteen rounds per minute." Erich was enjoying Donovan's attention and decided to take a chance. "Can you tell me what's going on outside? I don't get any news in here. Nobody tells me anything."

"Well," Donovan lowered his voice, "it appears that the Republicans have shot their bolt, so to speak. Premier Negrin launched a major attack along the river as a strategic move. He had hoped it would entice the British and the French to ally themselves with his government. Of course, they've been occupied with other matters."

"Yes, of course," Greinke agreed, without knowing what the other matters might be.

"At any rate," Donovan continued, "it looks like the Nationalists have broken the Republicans' strength. Unless Negrin can pull out some secret reserves from somewhere, it seems to me that the worst of the fighting is over."

Donovan leaned back, straightening up. "What are your plans for when you leave here? Dr. Sandoval says you're nearly well enough to be released and that your discharge won't be long delayed. Will you go back to your unit?"

"Oh no, no sir. I've had enough of this noble cause." Erich shook his head as he stubbed out his cigarette. "I've decided war is never glorious in the present tense. No, I think maybe I'll get a job as a reporter for one of the news services back home. I earned a journalism degree from Wisconsin and I've racked up a little real-world experience, which ought to help me land a job. Europe is a pretty interesting place right now."

"It certainly is. Likely to become more so," Donovan said as he reached into the breast pocket of his khaki shirt. "Here, Mr. Greinke," he said, extending his hand. "This is my business card. I'd be happy to assist you in finding future employment. If you come back to the States, to New York, please look me up."

Erich fingered the card.

William J. Donovan,

DONOVAN AND RAICHLE,

2 Wall Street, New York City

"Thank you, sir. I may just do that."

"I enjoyed visiting with you, Mr. Greinke. I hope your speedy recovery continues." Donovan stood to leave and tilted his head toward Sandoval and the two Germans who were standing by the door talking and occasionally glancing in his direction. "I see my hosts are ready to depart. I hope to see you again." He smiled and again extended his hand. Erich shook it and lay back as the four men left the ward.

Erich looked again at the card Donovan had left. He turned it over in his hand while his mind turned over his future prospects. William Donovan was somebody! He traveled in the highest circles of politics and society. Even though he was an ardent Republican, he was a friend of President Roosevelt's. He was big money; he was Establishment; he was, well, interesting. Erich wondered whether Donovan's offer was an empty promise. From what he knew about the man—war hero, successful attorney, prosecutor—Erich doubted it.

The door to the ward creaked open as a stooped, white-haired man struggled to push a wooden cart into the room. Erich eased himself into a sitting position as the old man handed out the patients' lunches. Soup again.

CHAPTER 5

Berlin, Germany
November 11, 1938

"Attention, please!" Dieter Schmidt shouted above the hum in the English Section office. The commentators and the rest of the staff, including Maggie, turned from their desks to face the center of the room, where Dieter stood. "We have quite a challenge in front of us. In tonight's broadcasts, we have been directed to address the rioting from last night and to correct some of the misimpressions it has created."

"What misimpressions?" Robert Hipps snapped. "The Jews got just what they deserved! That little kike bastard is lucky he's in Paris and not here in Berlin." Robert was referring to one Herschel Grynszpan, who, four days earlier, had walked into the German Embassy in the French capital and shot embassy official Ernst vom Rath three times in the abdomen. Rath's death two days later had infuriated Hitler and inspired Goebbels to unleash a maelstrom of anti-Jewish rioting throughout the country.

"It may come as a surprise to you, Robert," Dieter resumed with a trace of irony, "but not all of our listeners feel that one man's murder is properly balanced by the murders of nearly one hundred others, even if they were Jews. Unfortunately, in the United States and Great Britain the backlash has been rather severe. Some of our affiliated political movements have been dealt a rather serious blow by the reactions to the riots. For example, the *Daily Telegraph* in London called it 'racial hatred and hysteria by otherwise decent people.' We have to deal with this in a way that helps our listeners get a fuller picture than they have gotten from their own domestic press. Maggie," Dieter said, looking down at his notes, "would you please list the main points of tonight's coverage?"

Dieter had been nothing but proper since the recent Friday-night kiss. He had maintained a professional relationship with Maggie based on respect and trust. The Monday following his indiscretion, he had called Maggie aside and apologized. "I am really quite ashamed of my behavior," he had begun. "I allowed my baser emotions to take control of my actions, and for this I sincerely apologize," he had said, unable to make eye contact with her.

In truth, Maggie had quite enjoyed the kiss, even though she felt a prick of guilt when Kurt's handsome face flashed into her mind. She enjoyed the attention Dieter paid her. She appreciated the fact that he found her physically attractive as well as intellectually provocative. "Dieter," Maggie had replied, gently lifting his chin with her hand until his eyes met hers, "you have nothing to be ashamed or embarrassed about. I am flattered by your affection and I consider you already, in the short time we've worked together, to be a dear friend. Nothing you did Friday night changes that."

Dieter had smiled weakly, but outside of the office, he had consciously kept his distance from Maggie for several weeks. The private lunches and the evening escorts had stopped.

Now Maggie cleared her throat and, consulting a tablet in front of her, said, "We have a real uphill public relations challenge on our hands. Somebody has even given Wednesday night an unfortunately memorable label: *Kristallnacht*, Night of Broken Glass. Our job is to make sure it doesn't stick. Here are some ideas to help us do just that."

◆ ◆ ◆

Following the briefing, Maggie departed the office and made her way down the corridor to the private chambers of Clive Barnes. Clive had been delighted when Dieter had named Maggie as his producer. He liked the girl—liked to look at her, especially when she leaned over to help him at his desk or to pick up something from a low shelf. And, in truth, he knew Maggie was competent and reliable, qualities he held in high regard since he so often lacked them himself.

"Come in!" his familiar voice boomed when Maggie knocked on the door. "Hello, my dear!" Clive said as she pushed through the door. "I hope you have some marvelous ideas today, because from what I saw it's going to be hell putting a happy face on Wednesday night."

"All I saw was an orange glow in the sky and smoke. And I heard lots of noise: fire engines, police, singing, marching. There aren't any Jews left in my neighborhood," Maggie said. "What did you see?"

Unlike Maggie, who rented a small apartment near Broadcasting House, Clive kept a suite of rooms in the heart of the city at the Adlon Hotel. "Ah, Maggie," the big man frowned, swinging his oversize head back and forth, "it was anarchy, pure anarchy. Police were standing on the corners watching and doing nothing as these mobs tramped through the streets, smashing windows and lighting fires. My correspondent friends tell me that all of Berlin's synagogues were set afire and that many were completely destroyed. They also tell me hundreds of Jewish businesses were vandalized and looted. And that's in addition to several score of Jews who were apparently beaten to death. I tell you, my dear, it is a sad, sad day for Germany. You know, it's almost as if the Germans can't handle success."

"That's way beyond the scope of violence that the newspapers described."

"I saw much of it with my own bloodshot eyes, my dear." Clive shook his massive head again. "Hooliganism like this gives Hitler, Goebbels, and their crowd a terrible black eye."

"Well, it's our job to make sure the black eye starts healing right away!" Maggie said, beginning to wonder how much of the truth she really knew.

◆ ◆ ◆

As the clock ticked upward to eight o'clock, Maggie sat at English Section's control console, fingers held high where Clive, on the other side of the glass, could see them. Earphones in place and Dieter sitting beside her, Maggie dropped her last finger, pointed to Clive and switched on the red on-air light.

"Berlin calling . . . Berlin calling . . . Berlin calling . . . Good evening to my countrymen on the far side of the Channel. This is your friend in Berlin, Lord Lyon, with observations on today's news. And what a news day it has been! The rightful outrage of the German people has been twisted into tales of monstrous behavior. The originators of these calumnies, which would otherwise have been dismissed out of hand, are usually reliable observers of German culture and affairs. How is it that trusted correspondents have completely bungled the scope and scale of these events?

"To be sure, the events of Wednesday night were regrettable and disappointing. Yes, there was, tragically, loss of life in Berlin. But, my friends, there was loss of life Wednesday night in London as well, and even in New York. I can tell you the reports from Berlin have been greatly exaggerated. Publishers must, of course, sell newspapers, and bad news sells best. But let's not let the lawless rampage of a handful of youthful ruffians sour the ripening friendship between the peoples of

Great Britain and Germany—a friendship forged in recent days by the fires of common sacrifice and mutual admiration."

Lord Lyon continued to hold forth for several more minutes, building toward his conclusion. "A murder—the cold-blooded shooting of an innocent diplomat, an embassy official peacefully working in his office on a typical day, tending to his routine duties. A tragedy? To be sure. A criminal act? Of course. Provocative? Without question. But vengeance is not the character of the great German people. We may—indeed, we must—condemn violence, but we must also recognize Germany's role in maintaining peace on this continent despite the actions of a lunatic assassin bent on destroying the bonds of trust so painstakingly established between Germany and her neighbors. Let us not throw in with the cynics who attempt to sow distrust, suspicion, and hatred by knowingly promoting untruthful, embellished accounts of tragic events. Instead, let us work together to overcome this lawlessness. Let us work together to overcome fear and hatred. Let us work together for the triumph of peace and goodwill. This . . . is Lord Lyon in Berlin. Good night. God save the King!"

The broadcast over, Maggie closed down her console and made her way back through the control room to the access hallway that led to the on-air studios. She met Clive as he emerged from his broadcast booth. "Good job, Clive," she said, reaching up to pat his massive shoulder. "You did a good job with what you had to work with."

"Pabulum!" he muttered. "Pure nonsense! Come, Maggie," he ordered. "I need a drink!"

Maggie needed one, too.

◆ ◆ ◆

Kristallnacht, despite the efforts of Dr. Goebbels's propaganda ministry, dealt a serious blow to German prestige. World reaction was aggravated by the official German response to the riots. Hermann Göring, the Reich plenipotentiary of the Four Year Plan, imposed a 1 billion Reichsmark fine—not on the perpetrators of the carnage and destruction, but on their victims, the Jews themselves. In response, President Roosevelt recalled his ambassador for consultation. In Great Britain and the United States, *Kristallnacht* caused many who had been pro-German to reconsider their loyalties, making English Section's work more difficult.

◆ ◆ ◆

"Maggie," Dieter said, tapping her on the shoulder following the completion of Lord Lyon's broadcast one evening in early December. "May I speak with you for a few minutes?"

"Of course, Dieter," Maggie replied, smiling. She was enjoying working with Clive. Although Clive could be infantile at times, especially when he had been drinking, he was usually quite charming. And there was no disputing his talent. Where Robert and Julie were often strident and off the mark in their commentaries, Clive, as Lord Lyon, seemed instinctively to strike the right note with his listeners. As a result, he was by far the most popular of the Broadcasting Division's personalities. The English daily newspapers had even begun to publish his broadcasting schedule and run a synopsis of his previous evening's talk. Maggie's days lasted longer, as she routinely sat at the control console through Clive's eight o'clock broadcast, but she liked the work, and she knew Dieter was to thank.

"Let's go up to the canteen," Dieter said as Maggie gathered her papers and stuffed them into a folder.

The canteen on the main floor of Broadcasting House served food around the clock. Full meals could be purchased during the daytime and through early evening. Lighter fare was available after hours for the broadcasters and staff transmitting to the Americas and East Asia.

Dieter followed Maggie through the short serving line, ordering an egg salad sandwich and a bottled beer to wash it down. They wandered among the mostly empty metal tables until they found a spot near the only potted plant in the dining room, the sole source of color among the black and white institutional furnishings of the cafeteria.

"Does this mean we're friends again?" asked Maggie with a sly smile as Dieter set his tray down opposite her on the table.

"I'm sorry, Maggie," Dieter said wistfully. "It's just that you captivate me so. I don't know how to act around you anymore. I don't know how to treat you."

"Oh, Dieter, just treat me as a friend," Maggie replied warmly, reaching out to lay her hand on his forearm. "I treasure your affection. Let's not let it get in the way of our friendship." She winked, drawing a smile from him. "Now, Section Leader," Maggie said officially, taking a bite of her sandwich, "as much as I enjoy visiting with you, I suspect that you have an ulterior motive in asking me to dine with you in such posh surroundings!"

Dieter smiled, Maggie's playfulness relaxing him. "I wanted to talk to you about Clive. He seems to be on something of a roller coaster: up one day, down the next. I certainly have no complaints with his commentaries. His ability to take our direction and turn it into a reasonable address is one of the reasons he is our most popular speaker."

"And of course he has the most capable producer in the whole division."

"Of course." Dieter smiled again. "But I'm concerned more and more by his drinking. It makes him unstable."

"Yes, he was a bit wobbly on his way to the studio this evening," Maggie joked.

"I don't mean physically, Maggie," Dieter replied with a serious note in his voice. "I'm worried that he may go off half-cocked once he gets on the air."

"I understand your concern. He hasn't been quite the same since that *Kristallnacht* business," she said, "but I can handle the big man. You can count on me."

Dieter chewed on a mouthful of his sandwich before responding. "I know you can, Maggie, and I'm honestly a little in awe of your ability to manage the man. He has an ego as large as his belly, yet you seem to be able to get him to do whatever he needs to do. How is that?"

Maggie smiled at the compliment. She stopped eating and locked her green eyes onto Dieter's. "Have I ever told you about my sister?" she asked, wiping the corner of her mouth with her napkin.

"You mentioned her once."

Maggie looked momentarily away, as if she was trying to reach a decision. When she looked back to the waiting Dieter, her eyes were calm and focused. "I was ten when Maureen was born. My mother was forty-five, and she had a difficult pregnancy. She was sick a lot, tired, and she never really felt good. I remember her telling me that I had been easier, an easier pregnancy. Anyway, Mother died in the delivery room. She was bleeding and the doctors couldn't stop it." Tears were forming in Maggie's eyes as she remembered. Dieter was silent and still.

"My father was heartbroken," Maggie continued, her voice thickened with emotion. "They adored each other. Even though Father worked long hours, when he came home he would stay up late with Mother in their sitting room telling her all about his work: what loans had been made, who was having trouble making his payments, who was in trouble with the law—just all the stuff a small-town banker comes to learn about what's going on with the people we'd see at church or at the store. Anyway"—Maggie blinked away tears—"there we are: Father and a ten-year-old daughter and a newborn. He hired a nanny and a wet nurse, and after Mother's funeral, we brought Maureen home. She was fat and pink and she cried and slept and ate and filled her diaper." Maggie smiled, prompting Dieter to smile back. "But Maureen wasn't as normal as we thought. At her two-week checkup, Dr. Dukes took

Father into his office and told him that Maureen had Down syndrome. Do you know what that is?" Maggie stared into Dieter's brown eyes.

"No."

"It's a form of mental retardation. It varies in its severity. Of course, you can't tell how severe it is in an infant."

"I'm sorry, Maggie, about your mother and your sister," Dieter ventured, unsure what to say or how to respond.

"It's OK, Dieter. It's part of our family; it's part of my story. So, here's my father: hardworking family man, active member of the church and the community, and he's just crushed." Maggie took a handkerchief from her pocket and dabbed at her eyes and nose. "And you know what he does?" She looked at Dieter, who shook his head. "He says to me, 'Maggie girl, little Maureen is the last gift your mother's given us. We've to love her up just as fine as your mum would.' And that's what we did. We continued to have help from Sue, the nanny. She was a wonder. But every chance he got, Father was holding Maureen and singing her his sad, silly old Irish songs. And I was right there with him. Instead of sitting with Mother, like he used to when he'd come home, we'd eat supper and then play with Maureen or read to her or sing. She loved singing. Father was a saint to her. I'd take care of Maureen on Sue's day off. It may seem like quite the daunting task for a ten-year-old, but I didn't know any better. Mother and I had talked and laughed about what a big girl I'd become and how big a help I'd be when the baby arrived, so it just seemed natural to carry on when she was gone.

"I learned that Maureen wouldn't do things just because her big sister wanted her to. She did things because she wanted to. The trick was to get her to want to do the same things I wanted her to do. I guess that's how I learned how to work with people. My baby sister taught me."

Dieter sat silently for a minute, his body tense with the emotion of Maggie's story. "Does Maureen still live with your father?" he asked finally, forcing himself to meet her eye.

"No," Maggie replied. "People with Down syndrome often suffer physical defects as well. Maureen had a weak heart. She died two years ago." Maggie stared at the rest of her sandwich. When she looked up, Dieter's eyes were filled with tears.

"You amaze me, Maggie O'Dea. Really you do," he said softly. He reached across the table and held her hand.

◆ ◆ ◆

Maggie finished addressing the envelope and hurriedly grabbed her overcoat, scarf, and gloves. She stuffed the letter in her pocket and stepped out onto Soorstraße. The crispness of autumn had surrendered to the harshness of winter, and the wind licked at her face like an icy tongue. She would drop the letter into the yellow Reichspost box on her way to Mass. As she walked briskly along Soorstraße heading toward the Kaiserdamm, a light snow began to fall.

The letter was addressed to her father—a Christmas greeting that she realized would be more likely to reach him around New Year's. In his Thanksgiving letter to Maggie, Niall O'Dea had written of their hometown of High Glen and how it was growing, bringing new people to town and new business for the building and loan. He had shared some of the local gossip, including the story of how the mayor's dog had ended up at the pound without collar or license. Maggie had laughed at that one. He had written about Mary, Maggie's stepmother, who was redoing the colors throughout the house and whose close supervision of the painters had brought forth appeals for intervention, appeals he had no intention of heeding. Niall had closed his letter with words of love and encouragement:

> You never cease to make me proud, Maggie. And Mary,
> too. We're proud of your independence and your adven-
> turous spirit, your strong will to stay and make your

way there in Berlin, and the capable, intelligent woman you are. Know that we miss having you here with us, but that you're never more than a thought away.

Love, your dear ol' Father

Maggie had sniffled at that closing sentiment.

If her letter was late reaching her father, it was only because Maggie had immersed herself in her work. Partly from her need to excel and partly from her desire to please Dieter, Maggie had arrived early and stayed late throughout the fall. The uproar over *Kristallnacht* had calmed somewhat, chased from the headlines by the coming of Christmas and a more relaxed international scene. Without an immediate crisis at hand, Maggie had noticed the return of the "old" Dieter, the one from her earliest summer days at Broadcasting House. He had been warmer, more casual toward her ever since their conversation about Maureen. As she turned onto Witzlebenstraße and picked out the cross on top of Saint Canisius Church, her thoughts lingered for a moment on the warmth of his hand on hers. Maggie preferred the confident, cordial Dieter, even if he did subdue his affection for her.

The narthex of Saint Canisius was dark and cold, the stone floor slightly damp from parishioners whose wet feet had tracked across it on this Saturday evening. Dozens of votive candles flickered as the cold wind pushed through the door with Maggie. As her eyes adjusted to the dimness, Maggie loosened her scarf and unbuttoned her coat. She moved quietly down the center aisle and slipped into a pew on the right. At the altar, a young priest was chanting something that Maggie couldn't make out as she knelt to pray. Maggie was halfway through the Our Father when she sensed a presence to her right. *Someone's come to pray,* she told herself. As she finished, she crossed herself and sat back against the pew. She stole a glance to her side and noticed a soldier in a gray greatcoat and black boots. She looked up to find the dancing blue eyes of Kurt Engel. His face was weathered and red, his short hair tousled. He smiled at her and gently reached down to take her hand. They sat quietly for a couple of minutes before Kurt gave a gentle tug and, sliding to the right, stepped into the side aisle. Maggie followed him, grabbing her scarf but leaving her coat unbuttoned.

Kurt was waiting just outside the door. "Hello, Maggie." He smiled, and Maggie remembered the first time she had seen him on that summer afternoon in Heidelberg. Maggie flew to his arms and wrapped her own around his bulky coat.

"I thought you'd never come back!" she said quietly, fighting her desire to squeal with delight.

"I thought of you the whole time I was gone."

"Oh," Maggie said with a smile, tilting her head, "you're just saying that because it's true!"

◆ ◆ ◆

Kurt's return was fortuitous. Activity at Broadcasting House wound down Christmas week as a program of classical music by Germany's great composers replaced the usual news commentaries by English Section broadcasters. Maggie was pleased that she had both free time and Kurt, who after his months in the field had been granted generous Christmas leave. They were inseparable. They took long walks, with Kurt telling Maggie of his adventures in the Sudetenland, how the German residents there had been maltreated by the Czechs and how they had rejoiced when the gray-clad soldiers had rolled into their cities and villages. Kurt's stories reinforced Maggie's belief that the reunification of the Sudetenland had in fact been a proper objective.

Maggie took her turn telling Kurt about her work, her promotion to producer, and her mostly skillful handling of Lord Lyon. "After *Kristallnacht*," Maggie explained, "Clive started drinking more and more. Dieter told me to keep him under control, which of course

I did." She smiled, pleased that Kurt wasn't the only one making a contribution.

"This *Kristallnacht*," Kurt said as they strolled under gray skies toward a small Gasthaus on the corner of the Kaiserdamm. "We didn't hear much about it, only that the Jews were celebrating the murder of one of our diplomats and they started to tear things up."

Maggie raised an eyebrow. "That's what you heard? It was more like a bunch of hooligans declaring open season on Jews! Clive told me that some of the foreign correspondents at the Adlon Bar told him one hundred Jews were killed on that one night! There were fires all over the city, and shop windows were broken. It was a real mess."

"Well," Kurt said, "I wouldn't put too much stock in what the British journalists write. They always exaggerate things."

"But dear, Clive saw this himself. He didn't read it in the papers."

Kurt stopped, his hand on the Gasthaus door. "He's a fat Englishman. He's like all the rest of them: scared of Germany's rising power." He shrugged. "And besides, it was only Jews."

Maggie searched his expression for a moment. Kurt's cold blue eyes and unsmiling face chilled her. She wanted to challenge his slanted knowledge of *Kristallnacht*, but her resolve failed her. *This isn't the time or place,* she convinced herself.

◆ ◆ ◆

On New Year's Eve, the day before Kurt was to report back to his unit, he and Maggie curled up in her apartment listening to the radio. The main program of the evening was the annual New Year's Eve address by Joseph Goebbels.

"What an amazing year 1938 was!" the minister of propaganda began. "It is hard to conceive the progress National Socialism has made since the last New Year! During this momentous year, our beloved Führer has, through his visionary leadership and skillful organization, reunited more than ten million Germans to the Reich! The dream of all true Germans, the Greater German Reich, has been fulfilled!"

Maggie sat with her head on Kurt's shoulder, listening. "Did I tell you that I saw Goebbels?" she asked Kurt, looking up. "He is a wee little man." She giggled.

Kurt turned his face toward hers. "I'm not," he said, staring directly into her green eyes.

"I know," Maggie cooed as Kurt began kissing her on the neck.

Goebbels continued to drone on as the lovers fumbled with each other's clothing. "Nineteen thirty-eight has been the most blessed year in German history!" Goebbels boasted. "Nineteen thirty-nine brings a new year of unlimited opportunity; a year that will be filled with new successes and new victories; and a year in which the world will again acknowledge the greatness of the German people and their Führer!"

CHAPTER 6

New York City
January 1939

Erich Greinke followed the pretty receptionist down the expensively paneled hallway of 2 Wall Street. He thought she was beautiful, and he imagined that if he closed his eyes he would still be able to follow the trail left by the pleasant scent of her perfume. In fact, everything at the law offices of Donovan and Raichle had, so far, been appealing, from the comfort of the armchairs in the waiting area to the thickness of the carpet and the quality of the reading material.

Erich had been scanning the front page of the *Wall Street Journal* while he waited, but had found it impossible to concentrate. Every time a phone rang, a door opened, or someone walked through the reception area, he was distracted again. He was a little nervous, he admitted to himself. He was dressed in his best—if only—suit, which, after the weight he'd lost in Spain, didn't fit well. He was sitting in the office of a legendary figure in the most important city in the world. He wasn't sure what kind of help he might expect from Donovan, or even if the offer Donovan had extended during his visit to Gandesa had been sincere. He was eager to find out. He was relieved when Carol, the receptionist, had finally smiled and said, "Mr. Greinke, if you will follow me, I'll show you to Mr. Donovan's office."

Carol ushered Erich through an open doorway and into a large office with windows facing both Wall Street and Broadway. Donovan stood behind a massive, dark wooden desk, holding a black telephone to his ear with one hand and waving Erich to a chair with the other. Suddenly conscious again of his own attire, Erich took note of the war hero's finely tailored gray suit, the coat of which was draped over the back of his desk chair. His white shirt featured French cuffs and complemented his maroon-and-silver-striped necktie. Carol pulled the double oak doors closed behind her as she backed out of the office, leaving the two men alone.

"How good to see you, Mr. Greinke!" Donovan smiled as he returned the phone to its cradle. He stepped around the large desk and reached out to shake hands. Erich stood to meet his host. "I'm glad you took me up on my offer," Donovan said with what seemed to be genuine satisfaction. "Please, have a seat." Erich sat back down and Donovan sat in the matching chair beside him.

"Thank you for seeing me, Mr. Donovan," Erich began. "I'm sure you have many more important things to do."

"Nonsense!" Donovan smiled. "To tell the truth, I'm grateful for the company of a man who has actually been on the front lines of life. So many of my colleagues view the world as if it exists only in laws, codes, and regulations. They often miss the humanity of humanity. I see you're all healed up."

"Yes sir," replied Erich, who had indeed recovered fully from his wounds. Still uncomfortable in the setting, he plunged ahead, looking straight into Donovan's pale-blue eyes. "When we talked in the hospital, you mentioned that you might be able to help me find a job. If your offer is still open, I would very much like to request your help," he said, just as he had practiced.

"I would truly be delighted to help." Donovan smiled again. He leaned back in his chair. "In fact, I was hoping you would visit. I have a contact that is looking for someone with a background like yours. First, though, do you have any reservations about returning overseas?"

"No sir, that would be fine. As long as it's not back to Spain," Erich added. "What do you have in mind, if you don't mind me asking?"

Donovan chuckled. "Not at all and no, it's not back to Spain. Our firm does a good bit of international work, mostly business-related—acquisitions, patent rights, things like that. So, I maintain contacts throughout Europe. I think I may have shared a bit of this with you during our brief visit in Gandesa." Donovan paused, looking for confirmation.

"Yes sir, you mentioned that."

"I, and many of my friends, see ominous clouds on the horizon, Mr. Greinke. Europe is a frightening place right now. Herr Hitler has pushed the British and French around very publicly, and I fear he may attempt to do so again"—he paused—"and with dire consequences. You've seen firsthand what the German war machine can do. I'm working with some contacts within the government to build a network of intelligent, worldly young men to act as observers in the capitals of Europe and to report what they see, hear, and learn." Donovan stopped for a moment and leaned forward. His friendly smile yielded to a more serious expression. "I've done some, shall we say, checking up on you, Mr. Greinke, and I wonder if that type of position might interest you."

"Aren't there already military attachés at our embassies? Don't they already do the kind of thing you're talking about?"

"Yes and no," Donovan said, leaning back again. "There's a lawyer's answer for you," he chuckled, the smile returning. "The military men are pretty good at reporting on troop movements, new weapons, and things of that sort, although I have to tell you that the information you shared with me about the Germans' 88 mm gun certainly scooped them. Where they fall short is in reporting about political matters. Let's face it: decisions to annex Austria or Czechoslovakia are not military in nature, they're political. Hitler makes a political decision, and then his generals are told to implement that decision. We need smart guys on the front lines who can comprehend the political climate and understand who is influencing the decisions. Sound like something you'd be interested in?"

"Yes sir. It does," Erich answered. "Have you already thought where you'd like to send me?"

"Berlin," Donovan answered succinctly. "You have the language skill, you already have knowledge of the German military, and you understand the human cost of war, Mr. Greinke. That's not to be underestimated. My gut tells me that you also have a healthy respect for the Germans. It's important to respect your adversary."

"I respect the Germans all right. I saw how efficient they can be in combat."

Donovan paused, then looked Erich directly in his eyes. "I believe war is likely, Mr. Greinke, but, if men like you and me do our jobs well, we may be able to delay it until the United States can get its military ready." Donovan reached over to his desk and grabbed a dark-green file folder. "I'd like to send you down to Washington to speak with Henry Cotton at the State Department. He'll fill you in on the details of how things are organized, the resources you'll have—which won't be much— and how to make your reports. When can you leave?"

"Today, I guess. Will I be working for the State Department or for you?"

"Oh, you'll be assigned to the State Department," Donovan said, rising and moving to the corner of his desk. "But make no mistake, Mr. Greinke, you'll be working for your country." Donovan picked up the telephone. "Carol, please ask Clark to bring the car up. Mr. Greinke needs a lift to Grand Central." Donovan glanced at his watch. "Please call ahead to the ticket office and book a seat for him on the Orange Blossom Special leaving at 1:20 p.m. Then call the Mayflower in Washington and reserve a room for him." Donovan put the phone down and came back to the front of the desk. "I'm grateful for our meeting, Erich," he said, using Greinke's given name for the first time. "We have important work to do, and I'm looking forward to your contributions."

Erich stood and extended his hand. "Thank you for your confidence, sir."

◆ ◆ ◆

As he rode in the back of Donovan's limousine, Erich couldn't help but marvel at how things had changed in just two months. He sat back, smiled, and enjoyed the ride as the buildings of lower Manhattan slipped by.

CHAPTER 7

Berlin, Germany
March 1939

"That was wonderful!" Maggie exclaimed, linking her arm through Kurt's as they exited the cinema. "I love the movies! Adventure, romance. Did you like it, Thomas?" she said, glancing over her shoulder. Thomas Müller, an officer in Kurt's battalion, had joined Maggie and Kurt for a matinee showing of *The Adventures of Robin Hood*, an American film that had just been released in Berlin.

"I liked it," Thomas replied as the trio strolled along the Kurfürstendamm. Traffic was very light on the wide boulevard on this Sunday afternoon. "I like the action pictures and the westerns." Kurt had invited Thomas to come along rather than leave his friend in the barracks on this sunny, if cold, afternoon.

"Oh sure," Kurt snorted. "It was fine if you like fancy English fags running around in tights."

"Errol Flynn isn't English, dear," Maggie corrected.

"No matter. I think the Leibstandarte would have routed Robin Hood's merry band *and* the Sheriff of Nottingham in short order," Kurt said, laughing. "Come to think of it, Thomas and I alone could defeat that band of green fairies. After all, we were not meant for occupation duty. We are meant to spearhead the attack! Thomas"—Kurt looked back at his friend, who trailed them by a couple of steps—"you would look dashing in green tights, don't you think?"

Thomas smiled. He was half a head shorter than Kurt and thickly built. He had a plain, broad face highlighted by deep-blue eyes. Maggie thought he was cute, with his dimpled smile, but not handsome like Kurt. "Do you think so?" he asked, holding out his arms and theatrically examining his gray uniform. "Actually, I was thinking they would look very sweet on *Sturmbannführer* Thyssen."

Kurt howled with laughter at the thought of their battalion commander in Robin Hood's tights. Thomas smiled, clearly pleased to have made his friend laugh. Thomas was new to Kurt's unit, having been assigned to the battalion staff only after it had been withdrawn from its duties in the Sudetenland and returned to the garrison for refitting and training.

"Let's get a bite to eat," Kurt said, pulling Maggie toward the door of a restaurant on the corner of the Kurfürstendamm. "All of that swashbuckling made me hungry."

"All you did was sit and watch, my friend." Thomas laughed again. "I should let you two go ahead. I think I'll turn back."

"Please stay, Thomas," Maggie pleaded. "I need to get to know you better so I can be sure Kurt is in good hands when he goes to the field. Besides, I may be able to find just the right girl for you!"

"Just like a woman!" Kurt laughed, drawing a playful punch in the arm from Maggie.

"Thank you, Maggie, but I have a girl. She lives in Frankfurt. We are not all so fortunate as Kurt to have our ladies so near."

As Maggie protested Thomas's early departure, a motorcycle bearing a uniformed rider braked to a halt at the curb. The soldier stepped off the bike and saluted Kurt and Thomas. "By order of Field Marshal Brauchitsch, all officers are directed to report immediately to their units!" Brauchitsch was the chief of the general staff. His message delivered, the courier jumped back on the motorcycle and sped away, searching for other stray officers at leisure.

"Oh, must you go?" Maggie cried. "To think, I go from having two handsome escorts to being all alone at the whim of a messenger!"

Kurt smiled and wrapped his arms around her. "Never fear! Adventure calls, and Robin Kurt and Friar Thomas must don our green fairy garb and disappear into the forest to rob from the rich and give to the beautiful, auburn-haired girl!"

"I, too, must take flight, fair maiden," Thomas said with an exaggerated bow. "But first, m'lady, a ribbon from your hair."

"Move on, you hairy dog," Kurt snarled. "She wears no ribbon in her hair, and if she did, it would be my prize, not yours!"

"Bested by a better man! I take my leave, fair damsel." Thomas smiled and waved as he turned to head back toward the Leibstandarte's barracks.

Maggie looked up into Kurt's blue eyes. "I like your friend," she said. "He's sweet."

"He's a good soldier," Kurt said. "You be a good soldier, too. As soon as I find out what's going on, I'll send word." With that, Kurt leaned down and kissed her. He held her tight for another moment, then released her and, smiling, ran to catch up with Thomas.

◆ ◆ ◆

Maggie didn't have to wait for a message from Kurt to find out what had prompted his early return to duty. On Monday morning, Dieter greeted her as she opened the door to English Section's office balancing a cup of coffee and several morning papers.

"Good morning, Maggie," he said wearily, looking up from his own newspaper. He was, as ever, neatly dressed, but stubble covered his chin, and his eyes were red and puffy.

"You look like you spent the night here!" Maggie said, draping her coat over the back of her chair.

"Not here," he answered, stretching his arms wide and yawning. "I was at the propaganda ministry with Bauer. We were called in about midnight for some briefings. Something is up in Czechoslovakia—again."

Maggie nodded. "That explains it."

"Explains what?"

"We went to the cinema yesterday, and when we came out a motorcycle messenger nearly ran us down to tell Kurt and Thomas they had to report back to duty right away. You haven't met Thomas."

"I haven't met Kurt, either," Dieter reminded her. "The circumstances never seem quite right, do they?" He decided to steer the conversation in a more comfortable direction. "At any rate, it seems Slovakia has declared independence."

"Slovakia?"

"It's one of the regions of Czechoslovakia. At least it was," Dieter explained. "OK, here's a quick history lesson: After the Great War, Slovakia, which had belonged to Hungary, and Bohemia, the home of the Czechs, which was occupied by Austria, were joined together to create Czechoslovakia. I guess with the partition of the Sudetenland, the Slovaks feel now is a good time to separate."

"So, what's the story from the Wilhelmstraße?"

"Broadcasting Division has been told to support the direction of the foreign ministry, but of course Ribbentrop and his minions haven't figured out what that direction might be."

"Ah, ah!" Maggie wagged her finger at Dieter, smiling. "No criticisms of the foreign minister. It would be unseemly."

Dieter chuckled. "We're not sure what angles to play on this Czech thing because they haven't decided what official policy is. For now, we wait and go ahead with our routine stuff: spring just ahead, Germany's economic miracle, the Führer's magnanimity."

Maggie giggled. "Well, hopefully, this situation won't last long."

Dieter returned to his newspaper, hoping in fact that it would last quite a while and that it would keep Kurt Engel tied up for a long time.

◆ ◆ ◆

"That's Fred Oechsner of United Press, Wallace Deuel of the *Chicago Daily News,* and Otto Tolischus of the *New York Times.*" Paul Rand was pointing out people sitting around the bar at the Adlon Hotel. "By the bar there, that's Chesney Nutt from the Atlanta paper." Rand, a junior undersecretary at the embassy, had drawn the short straw and been delegated to show Erich Greinke around Berlin. For Rand, who seemed to Erich to possess all the initiative of a paperweight, that was a handy excuse to visit one of the watering holes favored by members of the American press corps.

Erich had arrived earlier in the week and had taken half a day to move into a small apartment on Calvinstraße, though in truth, carrying two suitcases up three flights of stairs had been the sum of the experience. He'd been spending most of his time getting acclimated to his job as passport control officer. He had not shared his real responsibilities with Rand or with anyone else at the embassy save for the first secretary, Mr. Kennan. Since the recall of Ambassador Wilson following *Kristallnacht,* Kennan was the ranking diplomat, pending the arrival of a new chargé d'affaires.

Now, he and Rand sat at a booth, watching people at the bar of the city's most famous hotel. Erich had let slip that he was interested in journalism, that he had studied the subject in school. Rand was only too pleased to show off his knowledge of who was who among American correspondents in Berlin. "A lot of times you come in here and see Shirer. You ever hear him on the radio back home?"

"Yeah," Erich replied, "I've heard him and Murrow on their news roundup. Pretty neat how they do that."

"Yeah," Rand continued. "I know him pretty well. I would introduce you to him. He must be out of town."

"Sure, maybe next time." Erich scanned the smoky, dimly lit room. "Who's the big man in the booth at the end of the bar?"

Rand twisted in his seat to look over his right shoulder. "Him? Oh, that's Clive Barnes, English fellow. Ever heard of Lord Lyon? He broadcasts to England on the German shortwave service. Supposedly lots of people listen to him in England to hear what the BBC won't tell them."

"What's an English guy doing working for German radio?" Erich asked, taking a sip from his drink and continuing to stare at Barnes.

"Same thing the Americans do," Rand replied. "They mostly comment on the news, you know, like the analysts you hear back home on NBC or Mutual. Same thing with these guys, only they analyze from the German perspective."

"And there are Americans doing that, too?"

"Oh yeah." Rand nodded. "One of them is a real Jew-hater from Mississippi. One's a society dame from Philly or somewhere."

Erich made a mental note to find out more about the American broadcasters. Following his Wall Street meeting with Donovan, Erich had headed to Washington. During an intensive six-week training course with Mr. Cotton at the State Department, Erich's instructors had repeatedly emphasized that correspondents were excellent sources of information. They could travel with relative freedom, and their jobs, after all, were to report on what was happening, from Bremerhaven to Bavaria. Since the Adlon Hotel was just across Pariser Platz from the American embassy, cultivating friendships with them seemed as though it would be simple enough. Erich figured his cover duties in the passport office would be routine enough to allow time for developing his own network of knowledgeable contacts.

"How about another? My treat," Erich said, tapping his glass with his index finger.

"Sure, sure," replied Rand, clearly beginning to like the new guy. "If you're buying, I'm drinking!"

◆　◆　◆

Two days later, in response to the unrest created by the Slovaks' pronouncement of independence, the Germans invaded Czechoslovakia. Hitler proclaimed the annexation of Bohemia and Moravia into the Third Reich.

"So, we focus once more on Czechoslovakia, do we?" Clive asked his producer that Wednesday afternoon.

"I would say yes, Clive, except that there isn't much left of it," Maggie replied. "I brought you a map, though, darling. I've marked the different areas in different colors for you." She pointed to western Czechoslovakia. "This is the Sudetenland. Of course, we've already been over all of that. Now, this part," she said, pointing to a yellow-shaded section that covered most of the rest of the western half of the country, "is what Herr Hitler is calling the Protectorate of Bohemia and Moravia. The pink part to the east there is Slovakia. That forms the southern border of Poland and extends between Hungary to the south and Romania to the east."

"Wonderful, my dear," Clive said grumpily, pulling another cigarette out of a pack on his desk and stuffing it into his holder. "Be a dear and give me a light." Maggie glanced around and found the lighter on Clive's footstool. She scooped it up and flicked the wheel, holding it in place for the light. "Maggie, I love you," Clive said, taking a drag through the holder. "You are the perfect woman: smart, beautiful, and here."

"Thank you, dear." This had become part of the daily routine with Clive. He enjoyed flirting with his beautiful young assistant, and Maggie enjoyed playing along. "I'm afraid you're just too much man for me."

"Yes. Well," Clive continued with a twinkle in his eye, "just remember that my marriage proposal remains open. Now"—he cleared his throat—"just how the devil do you expect me to use a map on the radio?"

◆ ◆ ◆

"And so, my friends," Lord Lyon continued, "we see that Czechoslovakia, as we have come to know it, was not really a unified country at all. It was cobbled together from the rubble of the Great War, joining distinctively different peoples with varied cultures and languages. The events of the last few days should not be viewed with alarm. Rather, these should be seen as the natural course of events when free people are free to determine their own destinies. The Slovaks, who threw off the heavy hand of their Hungarian masters after the war, now peacefully dissolve their still young union with their Czech neighbors. And our Czech friends are the beneficiaries of the good offices of their German neighbors, who have guaranteed order and public safety in the Protectorate of Bohemia and Moravia."

Lord Lyon had in fact made effective use of the map, even though it was invisible to his listeners. He had described the regions that had composed Czechoslovakia and given a brief history of each. He had portrayed the Germans as the good guys, the concerned neighbor who had come to help.

"Why, the humanitarian nature of this action by Herr Hitler is obvious to all serious observers. Mr. Chamberlain and Monsieur Daladier have explained quite clearly, and I might add quite correctly, that the agreements reached in Munich last year are not in any way compromised by today's events. Quite the contrary. We see in the establishment of the protectorate a clear pronouncement by the German Führer that he will guarantee peace in the region—guarantee it with the strength and goodwill of the German people. This . . . is Lord Lyon in Berlin. Good night. God save the King!"

CHAPTER 8

Berlin, Germany
April 1939

"Next, please!" Erich Greinke called out from behind the caged window of the embassy's passport control desk. A long line stretched from the window back down the hall toward the lobby. It seemed to Erich as if all kinds of people were represented in the queue, from Germans to Americans; from those seeking to emigrate to those ready to return home; from those on holiday to those under duress.

A short, older man wearing a simple, brown suit approached. "Gut day, sir," he said smiling. "Mine vife und I go to Amereeka!" he proudly exclaimed, handing over his passport. Erich looked it over carefully and decided it was likely forged. He eyed the little man, whose forehead was beaded with sweat. His plain, plump wife stood looking over her husband's shoulder. Erich reached out to take her passport as well and carefully compared the photos to the two would-be emigrants before him. He quickly stamped the US entry visa into both passports and handed them back.

"*Gute Fahrt,*" he said. Have a good trip.

The little man smiled even more broadly, took the passports back, and took his wife by the hand. *"Vielen Dank!"* he replied, relief visible in the brown eyes behind his wire-rimmed glasses.

Despite his official instructions, Erich sometimes approved questionable documents. From his contacts among the foreign correspondents, he was well acquainted with the persecutions already being visited against the Jews. What he could safely do to assist their exodus, he would.

"Next, please," Erich called to no one in particular, looking down at his watch. He was eager to break for lunch, his stomach growling loudly. When he looked back up, he nearly lost his breath. Before him stood the most beautiful woman he had ever seen. He stared for a brief moment, but wanted to stare longer.

"How may I help you, Mrs. . . . ?"

"It's Miss," the woman said. "Maggie O'Dea."

"I'm sorry," Erich said, but he wasn't. "How may I help you, Miss O'Dea?"

"Call me Maggie," she said, flashing a beautiful smile that seemed to underline her vivid green eyes. "It seems my passport has gone for a swim. I'm afraid it's quite ruined." She held up her passport, which had indeed been mostly destroyed by some prolonged immersion.

"Well, it certainly looks clean!"

Maggie laughed. "Oh yes. Some friends and I were sailing on the Tegeler See last weekend, and I'm afraid they were not much better sailors than me. They—well, actually, we—managed to flip our boat over. My passport wasn't the only thing that got soaked."

"I can imagine," Erich responded, a picture of an auburn-haired mermaid forming in his mind. "Wasn't it a little cold for sailing?"

"Not until we went into the water!" Maggie laughed. "Up until then it was a warm, sunny day."

For the next few minutes, Erich explained the passport replacement process to Maggie, adding as many details as he could in order to prolong the encounter. "I notice on your form here that you haven't listed a telephone number, Maggie."

"Oh, I don't have a phone. But I listed my address on Soorstraße," she said, pointing with her delicate hand to the appropriate line on the form.

"I see. Yes, that will be fine. And you have two replacement photographs of yourself?" Maggie handed them over. "If you will check back with us in about a week, we'll get you all fixed up." Erich smiled. Although he would have liked to ask her to lunch right then and there, he didn't want to appear too forward. Knowing that she would have to come back to pick up her new passport left him confident that he would have another chance to see her. Plus, he had her picture and her address. *Not a bad start,* he thought.

◆ ◆ ◆

When she returned to pick up her new passport the following Friday, Erich Greinke put a move on Maggie O'Dea. "Say, Maggie," he began as she signed for her new documents, "you've been in Berlin for a while. How about you show the new guy around town tonight?"

Maggie smiled her beautiful smile and replied, "How about you join some of my friends and me for dinner? We're meeting at Alois's Tearoom at seven o'clock.

"That's a date!" Erich exclaimed.

◆ ◆ ◆

Erich walked the short distance from the embassy and caught the southbound S train at Unter den Linden station. He transferred to the westbound A Line at Potsdamer Platz. Exiting the Wittenberg Station, he found his destination midway down the next block. Alois's Tearoom, at 2 Wittenbergplatz, was a step up from the Gasthauses that dotted the neighborhoods of Berlin. Here there were white tablecloths and tuxedoed waiters, as well as oversize portraits of the Führer. This was only fitting, since the proprietor was one Alois Hitler, the great leader's half brother. Alois was a portly, gregarious man who seemed to share nothing in common with his famous brother save their last name. Although Alois didn't mind the notoriety his family relations brought his restaurant, he warned his patrons through a mural painted in German script across one wall of the dining room: *Sup di full un fret di dick un holl dien Mul vun Politik!* Drink a lot and eat a lot, but don't talk politics.

Politics weren't at the top of his mind as Erich stood in the foyer of the restaurant, letting his eyes adjust to the dimmer inside light. He scanned the tables looking for Maggie's auburn hair. When he described Maggie to the tuxedoed maître d', the man's face split into a broad smile. "Of course, *mein* Herr, please follow me."

Erich followed through the crowded main dining room. It was filled with diners, many of them wearing military uniforms. A steady hum of conversation mixed with the bustle of the servers, the rattle of cutlery and dishes. In a smaller room were several tables, including one where Maggie sat with—to Erich's chagrin—two men wearing the gray uniforms of the Schutzstaffel, the SS. Their attention was focused on their lovely companion, and they didn't notice when the maître d' paused a few feet from the table, bowed slightly to Erich, and swept his right arm toward Maggie's party.

"*Danke.*" Erich nodded to the man, but he wasn't feeling particularly thankful at the moment. He took another step toward the table, and Maggie glanced up. Maggie stood, causing her companions to look around.

"There you are!" Maggie greeted him, catching his arm with her hand and guiding him toward the table. "Let me introduce you to my friends." By now, the two men were standing facing Erich, one of them wearing a sly grin. "Erich Greinke," Maggie continued, "allow me to present Obersturmführer Kurt Engel and Obersturmführer Thomas Müller." Turning toward Kurt and Thomas, Maggie explained, "This is the gentleman I was telling you about from the embassy."

"How are your ribs, Erich?" Thomas Müller was smiling broadly, his dimpled face betraying his delight, as Maggie and Kurt exchanged bewildered glances.

"All better," Erich laughed, slapping his former squad leader on the shoulder and thinking the evening wouldn't be a total loss, after all.

◆ ◆ ◆

"So we're walking through this farmer's yard, and we come to a pasture gate"—Thomas was telling Maggie and Kurt about the war in Spain—"and there's this little brown peasant boy standing there. He looks up at me and says, '*Señor*, for just one peso, I guide you and your men through the minefield.' So, we scrape up half a peso and hand it over to this kid. 'You get the rest when we're safely across,' I say. He says, 'You must be sure to step exactly where I step.' Well, he's maybe seven years old and he has little, narrow, seven-year-old feet, I mean really tiny." Thomas held his hands a few inches apart to illustrate his point.

Maggie was leaning forward with her elbows on the table, intently following the story. Kurt had leaned back in his chair, his arm draped over the back of Maggie's. Erich was nursing a coffee and smiling, looking from Thomas to Maggie and back. He was working hard not to stare at Maggie.

"So, here we are," Thomas continued, "big German soldiers wearing big black boots, except for Erich, who had on some old hunting boots or something, and we're trying to step in this boy's footsteps and tiptoeing and trying not to lose our balance." Maggie's smile spread to her eyes as she pictured the scene. "Finally, we get to the other side of this pasture! We pay the kid the other half peso and give him some rations because he looks half-starved. And we're standing there catching our breath and here comes this goatherd with, I don't know, maybe thirty or forty goats."

"Right through the middle of the pasture," Erich interjected, as Thomas laughingly shook his head.

"What happened?" Maggie asked, wide-eyed.

"Nothing!" Thomas laughed. "There were no mines in that field. That little rascal made monkeys out of us!" Erich nodded his head, chuckling.

"Probably a Republican bastard," Kurt said, drawing a sideways glance from Maggie.

"And it was only a day or two later that Erich was wounded and had to be evacuated," said Thomas.

Erich looked up from his coffee and nodded, then placed his hand on his friend's shoulder. "Thomas here saved my life. I'll spare you the details," he said, looking at his watch, "as it is already getting late."

Thomas leaned back in his seat and asked Erich, "And after all that, you'd had enough of Germans, no?"

"Oh no, absolutely not," Erich protested, "just enough of war. I don't like it much. In fact, I don't like it at all."

"But it is man's highest calling." Kurt had jumped back into the conversation, a challenge in his voice. "There is no contest like combat, no task to compete with leading men into battle in the service of a cause greater than oneself!"

"Spoken like someone who's never been there," Erich replied coldly, locking eyes with Kurt. The German tensed, leaning forward like a snake preparing to strike.

"OK, boys," Maggie interjected, laying her hand on Kurt's forearm.

"Yes," Thomas said, darting a quick look her way, "enough of this seriousness! In not a few more minutes, I will turn into a pumpkin! And I'm not pretty orange!" He laughed, stood, and stretched, looking around the nearly empty room. Two waiters stood nearby, waiting for their chance to clear the table. The others stood, too. "I'm glad Maggie invited you to join us, my friend," he said, playfully jabbing Erich in the ribs.

"Me, too," Erich replied. "Maggie, Kurt"—he nodded—"thank you for including me in a most enjoyable evening."

Kurt nodded his head but didn't speak. Maggie stepped forward and took Erich by the arm. "It was our pleasure!" she said, and Erich felt she meant it. The combination of her perfume and her touch was intoxicating. As Maggie steered him toward the front of the restaurant, Kurt and Thomas trailed behind. Stepping out into the cool evening air, Erich turned to face Maggie. "I'm sorry I popped off at Kurt," he said so only she could hear.

"Oh, don't worry." She smiled, looking up with her green eyes. "He'll get over it!" She hoped she was right.

CHAPTER 9

Berlin, Germany
August 1939

"Maggie," Dieter asked, "can you get Clive home? I'm afraid he's a bit sloshed, and I don't trust him to get there by himself." It was ten o'clock, and Lord Lyon had completed his evening broadcast. "I would take him myself," Dieter continued, "but we've been called to a meeting at the ministry."

"Of course, Dieter." Maggie was tidying up her desk, putting things away as she prepared to leave.

"You know the Adlon Hotel on Pariser Platz? He has a suite of rooms there." Dieter pulled on his suit jacket and grabbed a small black portfolio in which he always kept a notepad and spare pencils. "Thanks, Maggie," he said, giving her a gentle squeeze on the shoulder. "I'll see you in the morning." With that, he was out the door and down the corridor.

Clive had, in fact, been nipping at the bottle for quite a while by the time Maggie coaxed him into his coat and hat. "Come along, dear," she cooed. "I'll take you home."

"At last!" Clive exulted. "Finally, you've seen the Romeo in me burst forth! You know my undying love and devotion for you, Maggie, only you!" He slurred his words as he struggled to put one foot before the other.

◆　◆　◆

The A Line train was not crowded at that hour. Maggie had a bit of trouble maneuvering Clive during the change of trains to the C Line at the Stadtmitte Station, but otherwise their journey was uneventful. Shortly after ten thirty, Clive, leaning on Maggie's arm, was strolling through the Adlon's lobby. "Come, my dear," he said, shifting his consequential bulk toward the open door of the Adlon Bar.

"Don't you think you've had enough for one night, Clive?" Maggie was weary, having started her day early, as was her custom, with a review of the morning papers. The morning editions had blasted angry headlines warning the Polish government against further aggression toward Danzig, the formerly German and now Polish port city on the Baltic Sea. Lord Lyon's broadcast, which Maggie had helped author, had described Danzig as the German city it had once been and had castigated the Poles for threatening peace by attempting to hang on to something that was not rightfully theirs.

"Just one drink, my love, just one. Come along!" Suddenly the big man seemed fully in control of both his physical and intellectual faculties again. "Here we are!" he sighed, settling his oversize figure into a booth at the end of the bar. "Georg!"—he waved to the barman—"my usual, if you please!"

Georg nodded, and within a couple of minutes he set a Beefeater and tonic in front of Clive. "*Bitte sehr*, Herr Barnes!" He bowed, then turned his attention to Maggie. "And for the Fräulein?"

"Whiskey, neat," Maggie replied, drawing raised eyebrows from Georg. "I'm Irish."

"I'm terribly worried, Maggie," Clive began as Georg bustled away. "I'm afraid our friends may go too far this time."

"You mean Danzig?"

"I mean Poland. Chamberlain and Daladier were badly outmaneuvered at Munich. As weak as they are, I don't think they will be outfoxed the same way again. It would bring down Chamberlain's government."

"But Danzig should be returned to Germany, don't you think? I mean, it was a German city until after the war, wasn't it?"

"I'll tell you what I think." Clive paused. "I think there is a young man over there who has been ogling you ever since we arrived. And I further think he is coming this way."

Maggie turned to see Erich Greinke making his way past the patrons at the bar.

"Well, hello, Maggie!" he said.

"Hello, Erich." Maggie smiled, shaking his hand. "May I introduce Clive Barnes, one of my colleagues from Broadcasting House? Clive, this is Erich Greinke. He works at the US Embassy."

"How do you do, Mr. Barnes?" Erich nodded as Clive's huge hand swallowed his.

"Quite well, quite well. Any friend of Maggie's is a friend of mine! Won't you join us?" As Erich sat on the bench next to Maggie, Clive waved to Georg behind the bar. "What are you drinking this evening, Mr. Greinke?" the big man asked.

"What you're having looks just fine."

"Georg, two more of these," Clive said, tapping the rim of his glass with his thick index finger. "And one more for Maggie!"

"Clive, you said just one!" Maggie protested, but her grin gave her away.

"What do you do at Broadcasting House, Clive?" Erich asked.

"I'm a commentator. English Section, of course."

"Oh, of course!" Erich exclaimed, pounding his fist once on the table. "Lord Lyon!"

"Quite so, my boy." Clive grinned, clearly pleased to have been recognized.

"I heard you when I was in London, on the way over from the States. Yes sir, you're very popular across the Channel."

"Thank you, my boy, thank you."

"So, Maggie works for you?"

"Maggie is of great help to me, this is true, but I think it is not quite accurate to say that she works for me. I rather prefer to think that we work together. Isn't that right, my dear?" He cocked his head lovingly in her direction.

"Thank you, Clive." Maggie smiled. "And what are you doing out so late on a school night?" she asked Erich.

"I was meeting Thomas for a drink. He's off to the field tomorrow. I figured Kurt had probably told you already," Erich said, watching her face for a reaction.

"Yes, he did mention something about that. Some exercise or something," Maggie said, bluffing, wondering why she was hearing this news from Erich instead of from Kurt.

"Anyway, Thomas had just left when the two of you walked in and I said to myself, 'Here is a perfect end to the evening: drinks with a famous broadcaster and a beautiful girl!'"

"You flatter me more so than Maggie, young squire. She is, as you say, quite beautiful. I, on the other hand, am simply quite drunk, rather sleepy, and in need of a toilet." Clive pulled a ten-Reichsmark note from his pocket and laid it on the table. "Drink up until it's all gone, and be sure to leave a handsome tip for Georg. Lady, gentleman"—Clive struggled to his feet—"I bid you good night!"

When the Englishman had lumbered into the lobby, Erich said, "I didn't expect to find you here tonight."

"Nor I you," Maggie replied with a smile, reaching for her drink.

"I've been meaning to ask you, Maggie"—Erich looked over to the bar, making sure Georg was out of earshot—"why are you working for these guys?"

"I enjoy working with Clive—even if he is English. He wants people, especially other men, to think he's gruff, but he's usually pretty much the teddy bear you saw tonight."

"I don't mean Clive. He's likeable enough. I mean the Germans. Why are you working for them?"

Maggie was taken aback by Erich's direct question. She looked directly into his blue eyes. "I love the Germans," she said indignantly. "They're industrious and disciplined, good Christians, most of them. They're neat. They're a lot like Americans!"

"I love the Germans, too. Both of my parents are German. They came to America as children. It's the Nazis I'm talking about, Maggie. Why are you working for them?"

"I like my work. We're helping to bring ethnic Germans back into Germany through peaceful means. Plus, I like Berlin. It's the most exciting city in the world right now, and I'm part of it!" Maggie was uncomfortable with Erich's inappropriate questions. How dare he challenge her! She would have left the bar, but he was still sitting beside her. She couldn't get out of the booth unless he moved. "Besides"—Maggie took the offensive—"you worked for them, too! You fought for them in Spain when most other Americans fought for the Republicans. Thomas told us all about you!"

"I was young and naive. What's your excuse?" Erich asked, then took a swig from his glass.

"Well, for one thing, the Nazis aren't the English!" she blurted.

"What?" Erich sat his glass down and stared at Maggie. "Are you kidding me? Surely you can come up with a better answer than that."

"All right, mister," Maggie snapped, no longer caring to remain polite, "tell me how the Nazis are any worse than the English. After all, you're far more worldly than poor little me."

"Well, let's see." Erich looked toward the ceiling for a moment, pretending to think over Maggie's question. "The Nazis invaded their neighbor and took them over—no wait, make that two neighbors. I almost forgot about Austria. You know, everybody there already speaks German, so maybe that doesn't count." He grinned sarcastically. "And then there's the little issue of the Jews. Theft, vandalism, imprisonment, murder—all sanctioned by the state. How's that, Maggie? Am I getting through to you?" Erich's grin had faded away. He was deadly earnest.

"Gee," Maggie said, smiling, "I'm sure glad you enlightened me, Erich. For a minute there I thought you were getting confused. I thought you were going to tell me how the English subjugated the peaceful kingdom of Ireland and stripped it of basic freedoms, declared war on its inhabitants, and destroyed its economy!" All of this she said sweetly, but her Irish temper was near its boiling point, her checks flushing.

"Oh please, Maggie! Next you'll be blaming the English for the potato famine!"

"Listen, friend." Maggie had lowered her voice now, adopting what she hoped was a menacing tone and leaning toward Erich. "It's not just the Irish. Ask the South Africans. Or the Afghanis. Oh, I know," she said, taking on a brighter tone, "let's talk about India! You're so eager to condemn the Germans—"

"The Nazis," Erich corrected.

"Whatever," Maggie resumed. "You're so eager to condemn the Germans, but look at what the English did in India: they massacred two thousand unarmed men, women, and children just for assembling in a garden. Sanctioned by the state, as you like to say—the officer in charge exonerated by a board of review. Oh, you may think the English are high and mighty, Mr. Greinke, but I see them for what they are: arrogant, bloody, violent imperialists."

"I think you're missing the point, Maggie," Erich began again. But it was too late.

"Mr. Greinke," Maggie said formally, holding up her hand, "I've had enough of your questions and quite enough of your company." She lifted her chin up and said, "If you will please excuse me?"

Erich slid off the edge of the bench and stood to the side. "Think about what you're doing, Maggie—and who you're doing it for."

Maggie did not pause, but walked straight past the bar and into the lobby. Erich stood, smiling, enjoying the view as Maggie walked away. He clearly had a great deal of work still to do on Maggie O'Dea.

◆ ◆ ◆

The following morning, Maggie excused herself from the English Section office and made her way to Clive's private office. At this hour, it was unoccupied, the great man no doubt still sleeping off his hangover. In addition to privacy, Clive's office boasted another luxury: a telephone. Maggie picked up the receiver and asked to be connected to the headquarters of the Leibstandarte SS Adolf Hitler in northern Berlin.

"Heil Hitler," a voice answered.

"May I speak with Obersturmführer Engel?" Maggie asked.

"Maggie? Is that you?" a surprised voice asked.

"Yes, yes it is. Thomas?"

"Yes," Thomas laughed. "I'm the duty officer today."

"Oh, Thomas, I'm trying to reach Kurt. Can you find him for me?"

"You're out of luck, Maggie. He's out on a training exercise."

"Damn!" Maggie spat. "When will he be back, Thomas? He didn't say anything about going away."

"Maggie, this really isn't a good conversation to have over the telephone," he said uneasily.

"Can you meet me somewhere later and tell me what's going on?" she pleaded.

"Sorry, old girl, I'm set to leave later today as well. But I will let Kurt know you called. Got to go, Maggie! See you soon!" The line went dead.

Maggie jammed the handset down onto its cradle. "Damn it!"

◆ ◆ ◆

Maggie sat at Clive's desk reading the morning papers by the light from the lamp. In reality, she was only staring at the papers. She was still fuming that Kurt had gone off without so much as a by-your-leave. She was annoyed at Thomas as well for not telling her what she wanted to know. The jangle of Clive's phone startled her, causing her to curse again as she snatched up the receiver.

"Call for Fräulein O'Dea," said the operator.

"Yes, put it through, please," Maggie replied.

"Hello, Maggie?" came a familiar voice.

"Yes, this is Maggie."

"Maggie, this is Erich Greinke. I just called to apologize for last night. I, well, I guess I had a little too much refreshment, and I'm afraid I wasn't very gentlemanly."

"You certainly weren't!" Maggie snapped, her recollection of the previous evening adding to her annoyance.

"Anyway, I'm sorry, and I was hoping you would let me express my regret in a more tangible manner."

"What'd you have in mind?" Maggie was curious.

"Well, how about you let me take you to dinner?"

Maggie hesitated. "OK, Erich, on one condition: I can bring along two friends."

"It's a deal! How about Friday evening after Mr. Barnes's broadcast? Meet me at a little place called the Kleist Eck. It's only a few blocks down the Kaiserdamm from Broadcasting House."

"See you then," Maggie said curtly and hung up.

Erich smiled as he put down the phone. He wasn't sure who Maggie would bring, but he knew it wouldn't be Kurt or Thomas.

◆ ◆ ◆

"Dieter, would you do me a favor?" Maggie asked with a sweet smile later that afternoon.

"Probably," he replied with a grin, "as long as it isn't expensive or dangerous."

"It should be neither. I simply need an escort to dinner Friday night."

"Why, Maggie," Dieter bowed, "I'd be honored. What's the occasion?" Maggie filled him in on Erich's invitation, without giving any details of their conversation in the Adlon Bar. "Sounds like fun," Dieter said, "and the price sounds about right, too."

◆ ◆ ◆

Erich thought the evening would be fun, too. His plan to befriend Maggie had gone off track at the Adlon. Tonight, he intended to set things right again. He didn't know who Maggie would bring with her, but he was still surprised when she showed up clinging to the arm of a lean young man in a conservative gray suit. With them was an attractive, slender blonde with the lightest blue eyes Erich had ever seen.

Maggie introduced Erich to Dieter Schmidt and Elise Karlsen, a member of Broadcasting Division's Scandinavian Section. Maggie, too, had a plan for the evening.

"I appreciate all of you coming tonight," Erich said after they had been seated at a small table toward the rear of the Kleist Eck's dining room. "I don't know if Maggie told you, but I was rather abrupt with her over drinks the other evening, and this is my attempt to make amends."

"Nothing to make amends for, Erich. All is forgiven," Maggie said, smiling and taking the high road, even as she took Dieter's hand in hers. Dieter tried not to look shocked. Erich tried not to look disappointed.

"So," Erich resumed, "tell me about your work. I find broadcasting to be fascinating. Of course, I haven't heard everything you work on, but I did hear Lord Lyon a couple of times when I was in England on the way over. Did Maggie tell you that she introduced me to him?" He directed his question to Dieter.

Maggie replied, "It was Tuesday, Dieter, when you asked me to escort Clive home."

"Yes, I remember," Dieter said. Then to Erich he asked, "And what do you make of our esteemed colleague?"

"Oh, he was very interesting! Seemed like a pleasant gentleman as well," Erich replied, causing Dieter to raise his eyebrows and glance at Maggie.

"He is talking about Clive, isn't he?" Dieter asked Maggie, causing her to giggle.

"Elise," Erich resumed, "what do you do at Broadcasting House?"

Elise smiled. "I am a production assistant. We broadcast in Norwegian, Swedish, and Finnish, and I assist our commentators with scripts, research, coffee, snacks . . ." She laughed; then Elise turned the tables on Erich. "What, exactly, do you do at your embassy?"

"I'm the deputy assistant second undersecretary for identity documentation and personal international travel control," Erich said rapidly, causing the others to laugh. "No, in all seriousness, I'm the passport control officer. That's how I met Maggie. She came in one day with a ruined passport, and I helped her get a replacement."

"I'll bet that's exciting!" Elise said with a roll of her eyes, earning another round of laughter.

"Only when it leads to new friends," Erich said charmingly. He was a completely different person from the one who had alienated Maggie three nights earlier, she thought. She was beginning to think maybe she had been too hard on him.

"How long have you been in Berlin, Elise?" Erich asked.

"Six months now. It's quite an exciting place to be." Maggie observed the exchange, pleased that Erich was paying attention to her attractive colleague. "How about you, Erich? How long have you been here?"

"Oh, I'm the new kid on the block. I've just been here a few weeks. I was in Spain for a while and then spent some time back in the States before I started my job here."

"Erich fought with a German unit in the Spanish war," Maggie explained. "He was the comrade of an officer in Kurt's battalion."

A heavyset waiter interrupted the conversation to take their orders. Once he waddled away, Erich resumed the conversation. "Radio seems like a pretty exciting business—all those movie stars and singers and everything. Do you work with a lot of entertainers?"

Dieter glanced at Maggie and chuckled. "That's not really the kind of broadcasting we do."

"Oh," Erich said, feigning disappointment. "I guess you all work more in news than in entertainment."

"Exactly," Dieter replied. "The English, of course, have the BBC to provide the official news from London. Because BBC is run by the government, its perspective is by nature one-sided. Our job is simple: we provide the other side of the story so our listeners can make informed judgments based on multiple points of view. The English don't have a system like yours in America, with several commercial networks providing differing perspectives. Here in Europe, we provide a counterbalance to the English point of view."

Erich was diplomatic enough not to point out the issue of government control existed with both the BBC and the propaganda ministry. "Do you have correspondents all over the world, like CBS?" Erich asked.

"Some, of course, but we also rely on local contacts to keep us informed. For example, Maggie here combs through the newspapers every morning. We also listen to what other broadcasters are saying, your CBS, for example. So, we're taking information in from a variety of sources, some government-operated, some commercial."

"Well, you certainly seem to have a lot of responsibility," Erich observed, pleased that Dieter was treating him as a student to be enlightened. As the waiter returned, balancing four plates of steaming food, he asked, "Do you go on air yourself, Dieter?"

"No, my job is more supervisory," Dieter answered. "Fortunately, I have talented colleagues like Maggie"—he nodded at her—"who help us adapt our broadcast scripts from the propaganda ministry's daily guidance."

"The ministry is just around the corner from you, actually, Erich," Maggie interjected, "on the Wilhelmstraße."

"With guidance in hand," Dieter resumed, "we—people like Elise, Maggie, and I—shape it into more refined talking points for our commentators. Of course, they apply their individual styles to it, and that's what our listeners hear over the airwaves."

"And you have others like Lord Lyon who do the actual broadcasting?"

"Yes—well, none exactly like Clive." Dieter chuckled. "He is by far the best known of our English language commentators. I'm told his schedule is even printed in the London papers, he has become so popular."

"Yes, that's right! I've seen it." Erich continued to play the star-struck fan.

"Same with our section," Elise added, continuing to focus her attention on Erich, who turned to face her.

"And your studios are there, too?"

Elise described the broadcasting control room and the underground on-air studios, complete with the monitoring consoles, red on-air lights, and large wall clocks. Erich seemed enthralled with it all.

Maggie noticed that Elise seemed enthralled with Erich. Just as she had planned.

The dinner conversation avoided the thorny political issues being played out in Europe and stuck mostly to work, occasionally straying to some of the more interesting characters both at the US Embassy and at Broadcasting House. The dinner party broke up shortly before midnight. Erich settled the bill, and each of the four diners headed in a different direction—but not before Erich obtained Elise's phone number.

Yes, Maggie thought, *this is going to work just fine.* Erich had the very same thought.

◆ ◆ ◆

A letter from her father had arrived in Friday's mail. Tired from a long day's work and a pleasant evening with friends, Maggie didn't open it until Saturday morning. In his letter, Maggie's father asked her to consider coming home. He cited alarming reports from the newspapers in the city that another European war was imminent. His letter concluded:

> Pray consider my request. It's your own safety that
> is my greatest concern. If another war comes, I fear
> Berlin will become a dangerous place, and I'd feel so

much more comfortable with you on this side of the Atlantic. Your mum and I raised you to make your own decisions, and I have confidence in your ability to do so, as does Mary. Whichever you decide, to stay or to come home, you're always in my heart.

Love, your dear ol' Father

Maggie was touched by his concern, and she longed to hold his hand and hear him sing. But she was not about to leave Berlin.

Maggie got out a sheet of paper and put the date at the top: August 19, 1939.

Dearest Father,

Just received your loving letter of August 1. The war clouds don't look nearly as dark to those of us closest to them. Instead, they appear more like the ones that floated overhead and then dispersed last fall. We are all confident that things will be worked out now as they were then.

Berlin is a great and wonderful city. There is something going on all the time, with the government here, the cinema, opera, theater, etc. We have beautiful parks and lakes and rivers, and we have spent a great deal of our free time out of doors during these warm summer months. I have made many new friends, most of them German, of course, but also American, and even—can you believe it—an Englishman!

As many jobs as you've made me work (just kidding!), I've never had one so fascinating as my work at Broadcasting House. We are on the inside of what's going on here. The work is exciting, and I directly assist the most famous (at least in England!) of our broadcasters. His radio name is Lord Lyon. He's obese and often inebriated, but mostly delightful, and I truly believe he relies on me.

As to coming home, dear, I think I will not. Berlin is very safe. Göring, the chubby head of the air force, has said that if war does come, we can all call him "Meier" if even one enemy bomber gets through to the city! In fact, should war come, as I think it will not, I fear it would be far more dangerous to attempt to journey across the Atlantic than to simply hole up here and ride it out. With what I know of the German military (remember I told you about Kurt?), I should think the game would be up rather quickly.

The only thing, in fact, that argues in my mind to come home is the chance to see you and listen to your silly songs and your warm laughter. You are my Dear One. Give my regards to Mary.

Love, your girl, Maggie

Chesney Nutt was laughing so hard that no sound was coming forth. Tears leaked from the corners of his eyes, his gnarled hand grasping a half-finished bourbon and water. Erich, sitting across from him in one of the booths in the Adlon Hotel's smoky bar, smiled, enjoying his friend's delight.

"Jus' think about it now, buddy boy," Ches resumed. "Here you got Dr. Goebbels, who just hates the Bolsheviks. I mean, he's been poundin' on 'em for years, and not without cause, mind you—godless, murdering, incompetent bastards. And all of a sudden, bingo! He's got to spin a tale as to how they've been Germany's best buddies all along.

I tell you, Erich"—Ches paused to hiccup—"I'd give your left nut to be a fly on the wall down at the propaganda ministry right now!" Ches giggled, flushed from his drink and his laughter.

Erich had met Ches, chief European correspondent for the *Atlanta Journal*, at an embassy press briefing. The embassy had advised Americans to consider leaving Germany in light of the increasing tensions over the Polish situation and the possibility of war. Erich had supplied Ches with the names and addresses of several Americans living in Berlin to interview for a story. The two had hit it off. Now, on this August Wednesday evening, Ches was returning the favor by sharing drinks and his analysis of the rapidly developing political situation.

"What do you think Hitler's up to with this Russian deal?" Erich asked, flicking ash off the end of his cigarette.

"I think it's pretty simple: he's just closing the back door," Ches said. "I was in Paris a lot during the Great War, and the hope then was always that we could squeeze the Germans from the west and the east at the same time. Once the Russians dropped out of the war, it looked like the Germans had it won, at least until the United States came to the rescue. Hitler doesn't want to risk having to fight on two fronts this time. Hell, he even wrote about the dangers of two fronts in *Mein Kampf*. You ever read that, Erich?"

Erich shook his head. "No."

"Scary stuff when you think of the military machine Hitler has built. That boy's got an overdose of hatred in his system." The bar was quieter than usual. Many of the correspondents were staking out the foreign ministry or the propaganda ministry, waiting for the next official statement concerning the newly signed nonaggression pact with the Russians.

"What about Poland, Ches?"

"Well, buddy boy, I sort of wonder if that's not part of the deal Hitler cut with the Russians." Ches took a long pull from his glass. For a little fellow, Erich thought, he sure could drink. "The way I see it, Herr Hitler and Mr. Stalin have already carved up Poland like a prize hog. My guess is that one way or another, Hitler's going into Poland, and he's going to take back what used to belong to Germany: Danzig and the Corridor, at least. Stalin, on the other hand, probably gets eastern Poland to add to his happy empire."

"So you don't think Hitler's going to back down?"

"No way is he gonna back down," Ches replied, enjoying his role as sage. "Think about it, Erich. He's gotten too much, too fast, too cheaply. Why should he back down now? He's like a card player on a hot streak where every hand's a winner."

"What about the British and the French? Will they step up this time, or is this Czechoslovakia all over again?"

"Now that, my friend, is the question!" Ches stated decisively, tipping his nearly empty glass toward Erich. "The fate of Europe hangs on the answer! Time for another round, Georg!" Ches called out, motioning the barman over. Ches was short and slightly built. His thinning hair was mostly gray, his face deeply lined. Ches was only fifty-two, but Erich thought he looked much older.

Chesney Nutt told people who were curious enough to ask that he'd been a newspaperman his whole life. That wasn't far from the truth. His first job, at age ten, had been hawking the morning edition on Peachtree Street. His dependability and street sense had led to a job as a stringer for the paper at the turn of the century. Within two years, he was on the payroll, covering the police beat and becoming well acquainted with the law enforcement officers as well as the white and colored riff-raff of the South's most vibrant city. When the paper's news editor was arrested during the bust-up of a prostitution ring on the city's east side, Ches used his friendship with the cops to get the terrified husband and father released with no charges filed. As a reward, the editor had promoted the youthful reporter to the paper's newly created position of European correspondent. Ches had been in Europe on and off ever since. He'd covered elections, riots, the Great War, floods, earthquakes, famines, and plagues. His contacts were legendary among his peers. He liked to boast that he knew many of the continent's major newsmakers, from England and France to Poland and Germany. And most of the bartenders.

"Another round, Herr Nutt?" Georg asked when he reached the table.

"Yes, Georg. But first, let me ask you a question. You're a well-informed person. You keep up with what's going on around here. Is there going to be peace or war?"

"Oh, peace, surely, Herr Nutt." Georg smiled. "The Führer knows what he's doing. He's just reclaiming German territory, after all. He'll work everything out. You will see. I will bring you your drinks." Georg bowed slightly and turned back toward his bar.

"Do you think he's right?" Erich asked, his eyes following Georg.

"I hope so," Ches said, looking down into his empty glass. "I do hope so."

◆ ◆ ◆

Elise Karlsen initiated the Saturday-afternoon picnic. She invited Dieter and Maggie, mistakenly assuming they were a couple, based on the Friday-night dinner with Erich, whom she also invited. The late August weather was hot and muggy for Berlin, and the city's inhabitants responded by taking to the parks and lakes.

In the sprawling Tiergarten, Berlin's large, forested park, Elise picked a shady patch near a small pond. Erich spread out an old quilt and helped the lithe young lady arrange the food and drink from several small bags they had carried to the spot. Elise wore a white blouse and light blue slacks that showed off her athletic build. Erich enjoyed her graceful movements and the warmth of the sunlight filtering through the overhanging branches.

"You look lovely," Erich said to her as she finished arranging the food and settled in by his side. This prompted a pretty smile in response.

"I'm glad you could come," she said, flashing her blue eyes and popping a grape into her mouth. "I hope I don't wilt in this heat! It never gets this warm at home!"

Erich had been surprised, but pleased, by Elise's invitation. He had been delighted to learn that she had also invited Maggie and even Dieter. He always enjoyed spending time with people in general, pretty girls in particular—and especially two as attractive, and independent, as Elise and Maggie. Plus, the outing offered him a renewed opportunity to learn more about the operations of the Broadcasting Division even as the propaganda battle was reaching a fever pitch. The morning's newspapers had been filled with heavy, black headlines proclaiming chaos in eastern Poland and all manner of vandalism and villainy directed against its German-speaking population. The most ominous article reported that Polish troops were poised along the border. Nothing good could come from that, Erich thought, true or not.

"I picked up a couple of papers this morning," Erich said, enjoying his view of Elise. "It seems that your work must be very interesting right now."

"Yes, very," Elise said, leaning forward. Without another word, she kissed Erich, a gesture he was only too happy to return. "That was nice," she said, her eyes locked on his.

"Do you think so?" Erich grinned. "Perhaps we should try it again," he said with mock seriousness, his heart beginning to race, "just to make sure." But, as he leaned in again, the stillness of the moment was interrupted.

"All right, you two! Knock it off!" Maggie O'Dea called from fifteen yards away. Elise and Erich sat back and caught their breath. Maggie and Dieter were carrying a picnic basket between them, each holding one end of the handle. "We just can't leave you two alone for a minute now, can we?" She laughed.

"Impeccable timing, Maggie," Erich laughed, trying to keep the disappointment from his voice. He stood to shake hands with the new arrivals as Elise moved food and drink to the center of the quilt to make room for them to sit.

"Been here long?" Dieter asked with one eyebrow raised.

"Not long enough," Erich replied, causing Elise to blush. He reached into one of the bags and brought out bottles of beer, passing them around one by one. "Elise and I were just talking about this morning's headlines."

"Oh," Maggie teased, "is that what you call it? We call it something else where I come from!"

Erich decided he'd rather give than take. "So, Maggie, what have you heard from Kurt?" He stole a furtive glance at Dieter, trying to gauge his reaction, then shifted his focus back to Maggie.

"Not a damn thing!" Maggie bit off her words. "You'd think he would have the courtesy to let me know when he's going away, but I get nothing. Thomas wouldn't even tell me!" She frowned as she tipped her bottle back and took a swig.

"Well, we can probably all guess where they are, anyway," Erich said. "Don't you think so, Dieter?"

Dieter nodded, pushing his glasses back up on his nose. "I think it's safe to assume they are somewhere east of us."

Erich continued to guide the conversation. "What do you think is going to happen, Dieter?"

"I think there will be a great deal of saber rattling like there was over Czechoslovakia," he said, "and in the end, I think the outcome will be much the same. Nobody wants to go to war, particularly not over Poland."

"So, you definitely think Hitler is going into Poland?"

Dieter paused for a moment. "My personal opinion? I think everything will be worked out and that there will be no war."

"What about you, Maggie?" Elise jumped in. "What do you think is going to happen?"

"I'd say Dieter is right, as usual." She winked at her colleague. Dieter smiled at her compliment. "It's all very similar to the Czech situation last year."

"It seems that way to me, also," Elise responded. "The Poles are the ones acting aggressively. I expect the French and British to rein in their ally."

"I certainly hope they do," Maggie said intensely, her lips pressed into a thin line. "As much as I'd like to see the Brits get their asses kicked!"

"Maggie, such language!" Erich said, causing the others to chuckle. A soccer ball came bouncing toward their blanket, the escaping plaything of two small, blond boys. Dieter scooped it up and booted it back toward them.

"OK, Maggie," Erich resumed, slicing a piece of cheese. "I know you don't like the English—you were clear on that the other night." Without looking up, Erich began cutting slices off a sausage. "I grew up in a German household in Wisconsin; I don't really know much about Ireland."

"Do you know any Irish history?" Maggie asked after a moment.

"Not much. Elise? Dieter?" Erich handed a small plate of cheese and sausage around.

"Well, in the first place," Maggie began, "you need to understand that England ruled Ireland by force, a lot like it had tried to govern its colonies in America. Of course, it didn't work in America because the colonists rightfully saw themselves as English subjects wrongfully deprived of their rights as Englishmen. You might think that the English would've learned from King George's folly, but, alas, they did not. In Ireland, they suppressed all individual liberty, governing as a conquering power. English soldiers murdered, raped, arrested, assaulted, and raided the homes of their hosts with impunity." Maggie stopped to take a drink, the others silently waiting for her to resume.

"Finally, in the 1890s, Gladstone—the English prime minister—began to push for Irish home rule. But the pigheaded bastards in Parliament wouldn't pass the legislation. First the Commons defeated it, and when it was brought up a second time and Commons passed it, the House of Lords voted it down. To make a very long story short—"

"Too late," Dieter whispered.

"—the Irish got tired of waiting for the English to grant home rule and decided to kick the occupiers off their island. On Easter Monday in 1916, judging that the English would be preoccupied with a little conflict then underway in France, a group of Irish patriots attacked English outposts all over Ireland. One group of volunteers, led by Liam Mellows, attacked the Royal Irish Constabulary at Carnmore in County Galway. Two constables were killed in the attack. When the patriots withdrew to Athenry, the British sent the HMS *Gloucester* into the bay to shell their positions. Well, of course, the Irish had no armories, no rations. They were fighting only with what they could carry from their farms and villages. Mellows's force dispersed and faded back into the countryside from where it had come.

"Mellows and a couple of his lieutenants, my father being one, had bounties placed on their heads. They lay low for a few days and then sneaked out of Ireland aboard a fishing boat. Eventually, they made their way to America. Mellows made the mistake of returning to Ireland in 1922. He was executed. My father showed better judgment. He stayed in America. My mother and I joined him there in

1917. The English ran my father out of his native land because he wanted the same rights and freedoms in his country that they enjoyed in theirs.

"So, Mr. Erich Greinke," Maggie said, raising her beer bottle in a sad salute, "I hope the English get their asses kicked, whether it's by the Germans, the Irish, the Indians, or just one pissed-off redhead."

"Fruit?" Dieter asked, holding up a bunch of grapes. Elise tried not to laugh and ended up snorting, which caused Maggie to laugh, breaking the tension. Erich joined in, but he understood Maggie would never choose the English over Germany.

◆ ◆ ◆

The following day, Sunday, the German government announced that mandatory rationing of food and other necessities would begin the next day. The announcement surprised most Germans and caused concern. There had been no previous mention of rationing, and no such action had preceded the peaceful resolution of the Sudeten crisis. Suddenly, the people began to view the screaming newspaper headlines and the official diplomatic statements with heightened awareness and with growing anxiety.

That was one reason the Monday-morning line in front of Erich's passport control window was so much longer than usual. Another cause was the embassy's recommendation that Americans leave Germany in light of the increased threat of war. By the time Erich could break free for lunch, it was already nearly one o'clock. Erich pushed through the front door of the embassy and headed east along Pariser Platz. Hungry, he rapidly covered the two blocks to a small walk-up lunch counter where Hansie served Berlin's best brats. Hansie was a jolly man who had made a career of serving quick lunches to the busy bureaucrats in the many government offices there in the heart of the city. He always seemed to know what was going on and what was coming next.

"*Guten Tag*, Hansie!" Erich called out as he stepped from the sidewalk up to the counter to place his order.

"Ah, Herr Greinke! Good day to you as well!" Hansie smiled in return. Hansie was constantly in motion, moving from one task to another even as he carried on a conversation. He laid another row of wursts onto the small charcoal grill perpendicular to the counter, a light sweat already covering his face even though the day had not yet warmed up. "What's happening at the embassy of the United States of America on this fine day?"

"Everybody's waiting for the other shoe to drop," Erich replied, eyeing the slate board featuring the day's specials.

Hansie stopped and with a quizzical look asked, "The other shoe?"

"Sorry," Erich laughed. "It's an American expression. It just means we're waiting to see what happens next."

"Ah," Hansie smiled. "You and everyone else!"

Erich ordered a bratwurst and a beer. "What do you hear, Hansie?" he asked, taking a bite of the flavorful sausage.

Hansie leaned out over the counter, glancing around to ensure no one else was within earshot. "I hear the Führer is listening to the idiot Ribbentrop, who is telling him the British, and therefore the French, will back down again. Unfortunately for the foreign minister, I also hear that the British have no intention of being made the fool again. Ambassador Henderson is returning from London this afternoon with an answer from his government that may surprise Herr Ribbentrop. I'm afraid your other shoe may drop right on top of us all." Hansie smiled sadly.

Erich finished his lunch and hurried back toward the line awaiting him at his passport control window. As he passed the British Embassy on the corner of the Wilhelmstraße, he nearly collided with Clive Barnes.

Clive had just emerged from the building. He was neatly dressed, sporting an ascot instead of a tie—due to the hot weather, Erich guessed. His dark gray bowler sat squarely on his head, his rolled umbrella helping to pace his steps.

"Hello, Clive," Erich called out. "Erich Greinke," he said, extending his hand to the older, larger man. "Maggie introduced us the other evening at the Adlon Bar."

Recognition broke across Clive's face and he smiled. Transferring his umbrella to his left hand, he grasped Erich's hand in his right. "Of course, of course," he thundered in his deep voice. "I remember quite well. How are you on this lovely day? Or perhaps I should say on this sad and lovely day," he continued with less enthusiasm. "Going my way?" he asked. When Erich nodded, they continued west toward Pariser Platz.

"I had you figured as more of a night owl, Clive. What brings you out at midday?"

"The embassy has told all British subjects still in Germany to leave. I came to appeal to the better nature of the diplomats. My belief is that I can play a key role in keeping the peace given my standing among both the government here and the people back home."

"And how was your message received?" Erich ventured to ask.

"With condescension, my boy, with condescension. These, these"—Clive struggled to select the appropriate pejorative—"twits are all the second or third sons of titled gentlemen, and as such they have had no occasion in life to actually think for themselves. With Henderson out of the embassy at present, they are left witless and unable to resolve even the simplest matters."

"So, they still want you to leave?"

"Want? No! They insist that I leave!" Clive thundered again, raising his umbrella and drawing stares from other pedestrians. "The saddest thing, my young friend," he continued in a more normal tone, "is that they are packing up over there." He turned around and pointed with his umbrella back toward the embassy building. "You see that?" he asked, his eyes squinting toward the roof of the structure. Erich turned to follow Clive's stare and noted a wisp of smoke rising from one of the building's courtyards. "There. They're burning papers. Never a good sign." Clive turned and resumed walking.

"Where are you heading now, Clive?"

"I am bound for Broadcasting House, where perhaps I can do some good by prevailing on my countrymen to demand of their elected leaders a moderate approach to this crisis."

"What about the Germans, Clive? Will they be able to demand the same from theirs?"

Clive stopped walking and turned to face Erich, staring directly into the younger man's eyes. "The Germans are different, you see. They need to be told what to do. They like to be told. They are never happier than when they are directed toward some glorious cause, one that will demand sacrifice yet result in honor and victory for their Teutonic race. No, we can't expect from them that which we seem reluctant to accomplish ourselves."

By then, the pair had reached the front of Blücher Palace, which housed the US Embassy. "It seems to me that both sides are digging in their heels," Erich said. "Hitler seems ready to take what he wants, and the British and French claim they will stand by Poland. I'm afraid their maneuvering room is running out."

"Frightening times. Well, I bid you good day, sir," Clive said, touching the brim of his hat as Erich turned to enter the embassy. "Frightening times," Erich heard him repeat to himself as he continued on his way.

◆　◆　◆

"Your attention, please!" Dieter called out to the assembled staff of English Section. It was midafternoon, and he and Maggie had developed a plan for the evening's broadcasts based on fresh guidance from the propaganda ministry. "Robert," he said, looking toward the corner where Robert Hipps sat smoking a cigarette and doodling on the front page of a newspaper, "you're to stress how greedy Jewish industrialists and financiers are the only ones who will benefit from a war. All of a piece with their conspiracy to gain control of the world economy and ensure that the rich are made richer."

"Julie"—Dieter turned to Julie Clay—"you're on tonight at eleven thirty. Your audience is the American East Coast. Your angle is that this is a European conflict that is no concern of the United States. Throw in that line about European entanglements that Maggie dug up from . . ." He glanced toward Maggie. "Who was it, Maggie?"

"Thomas Jefferson," she replied quickly.

"Right. Basically, we want to convince the Americans to mind their own business. Clive"—Dieter pointed to his star performer, who, given the unfolding crisis, had been politely "invited" to join his colleagues in the daily briefing—"you will speak in your regular slot to your regular listeners. Actually, I expect you'll have more listeners than normal tonight. Maggie will go over the plan with you."

Dieter looked around the room, making eye contact with each member of his staff in turn. "This situation is as serious as it gets. The British ambassador is expected back from London later today with a reply from his government to the Führer's position. If we get word soon enough, we may make adjustments to your scripts. If we ask you to revise at the last minute, please understand it's because we have received important updates to the situation. Remember that people will be listening to you to get a more balanced perspective than they are getting from their own governments."

As the briefing ended, Maggie set to work with Clive. The Englishman seemed to realize the stakes of the diplomatic maneuvering underway. Maggie thought he was more reserved than normal—almost gloomy, in fact.

"Clive, are you all right?" Maggie asked as she pulled the last page of his script from the typewriter. "You seem awfully depressed."

Clive hesitated a moment, looking down at his hands folded across his expansive belly. "No, Maggie. I am not all right. I greatly fear where the next few days will lead us. You're too young to remember the Great War, Maggie. I was there. It was hellish." He shook his large head, his words rolling forth like a low rumble. "Death everywhere one looked. Those who weren't slaughtered outright were mangled horribly. Day after day in the cold mud. Filth piling up around you. Absolute misery. Too terrible for even Dante to describe. Too awful for one to conceive who hasn't actually survived it."

Maggie thought back to the dinner at Alois's Tearoom, when Erich and Thomas had recalled the misery and suffering they had endured in Spain.

◆ ◆ ◆

Maggie monitored the control room's London clock as it ticked toward eight o'clock. She was seated at English Section's console, where she had completed her prebroadcast checklist. She gently rapped her knuckles against the thick glass separating her from Clive Barnes in the broadcast studio, then held up her left hand and quickly opened and closed her fingers three times: fifteen seconds. Clive nodded, made one last check of the pages of his script, then returned his attention to Maggie. Both of them felt this might be the most important broadcast of his career. Maggie, keeping her gaze on the clock, began lowering a finger every second as the clock ticked to the top of the hour. She switched on the red on-air light and pointed to Clive, then sat silently, monitoring the outgoing signal through her earphones as he said, "Berlin calling . . . Berlin calling . . . Berlin calling . . .

"Good evening to my countrymen on the far side of the Channel. This is your friend in Berlin, Lord Lyon, with observations on today's news.

"This is a time of serious reflection both in Great Britain and here in Germany. Peace hangs in the balance as reasonable men on both sides grapple with complex issues. This is a time for the people of Germany and of Great Britain to recognize our historic friendship, to find common ground, and to work together—not only for peace but for a Europe where the rights of individuals are not sacrificed on the altar of political expediency.

"The Warsaw government has refused to negotiate in good faith with the government here in Berlin. Herr Hitler has even taken the extraordinary step of inviting a plenipotentiary from Warsaw to Berlin to work directly with him to resolve the situation. This, my friends, is statesmanship! But the Warsaw regime has refused to even answer this invitation, one, I daresay, which was issued out of a sincere desire to avoid conflict.

"Why do the Poles cling so to territory that is historically German? Why do the Poles cling so to a population that is of German ethnicity? Why do the Poles fall back on the tired arguments of disgraceful treaties that sought—and failed, mind you—to keep the German people down in defeat? Could it be that Poland envies the modern miracle that is present-day Germany? Could it be that Poland covets the economic success of its neighbor to the west? Could it be greed that motivates Warsaw?

"Tonight, my friends, we stand on a precipice that, if crossed, will plummet all of Europe into the very depths of a hellish existence from which, given the development of dark science and the rapidly increasing destructive capacity of man, there may be no return. Let us then set aside our differences in favor of common ground. Let the Germans work with their Polish neighbors to resolve the issues between these two great states. Let the rest of the nations stand ready to assist these neighbors. But"—he paused for effect—"let us not impose our will on either party, lest we give the impression that from our island home we seek to master the geopolitical affairs of sovereign nations.

"Pray for the guiding hand of Providence and the blessings of the Almighty. Pray that our leaders will be motivated by their love of peace and that, so guided, they will resolve differences with the turned cheek and not the raised fist. This"—the trademark pause—"is Lord Lyon in Berlin. Good night. God save the King!"

◆　◆　◆

In his daily report to Cotton at the State Department, Erich Greinke shared what he had been able to piece together from published reports, formal contacts, and informed individuals. Late on Tuesday night he wrote:

> War seems imminent. British Ambassador Henderson met with Foreign Minister Ribbentrop until nearly midnight last night. Today, he met directly with Hitler, who gave him an answer to Monday's British proposals. The Germans kept a plane waiting at Templehof to fly Henderson back to London. Instead, the ambassador simply accepted the answer and returned to his embassy. This was very disconcerting to Ribbentrop, according to my sources. It appears that Hitler has been relying on Ribbentrop during this contest and that the foreign minister has underestimated the resolve of the British. The prevailing opinion here is that Ribbentrop has allowed his boss to get boxed into a corner. He may have no way out other than to

invade Poland and hope the British (and French) are bluffing. Given the hard line apparent in Henderson's actions today, bluffing seems unlikely.

Erich finished his report and took it up to the radio room on the embassy's top floor. From there, a signals clerk encoded the message and transmitted it to Washington.

◆ ◆ ◆

"What d'ya say there, buddy boy?" Chesney Nutt called to Erich as the younger man strode into the Adlon Bar. "Can I interest you in a little libation and some titillating conversation?"

Erich turned toward the booth where Ches sat nursing his drink, curious as to how many he'd already put away. "That sounds great, Ches," he said, looking around, "but where would I find titillating conversation around here?"

"Very funny, Yankee boy." Ches smiled. "Grab us a couple of drinks and come on over here."

Erich stepped to the bar, where Georg greeted him warmly and quickly mixed two drinks. Dodging a Wehrmacht officer with a beautiful, young blonde on his arm, Erich made his way back to Ches and plopped down across from him. "So, Ches, what do you know on this pleasant Wednesday evening?" The capital had been swirling with rumors all day. Cables had been bouncing back and forth between London and the Nazi government, but the contents were unknown except to those inside Hitler's circle. Erich hoped Ches had picked up tidbits he would be willing to share.

"Oh, I know a couple of things," Ches responded, his eyes twinkling. He took a sip of his drink. "Like for instance the Poles ordered a general mobilization today."

"Shit," Erich moaned, setting his glass back down on the table even before he took a drink. He thought for a moment, then said, "They're playing right into Hitler's hands, aren't they?"

"So it would seem." Ches shook his head ruefully. "So it would seem. The propaganda boys'll be all over 'em tomorrow. They'll call the Poles aggressors. Mind you, now, the Germans have been deployed near the border for two weeks already. But, you mark my words, buddy boy, the Germans will engineer this thing so the Poles are the aggressors."

"You think it's war, don't you?"

"Oh, hell yes!" Ches snapped sourly. "Listen, how do you think the government could have announced on Sunday that rationing was going to start on Monday? You think ol' Hitler just got up Sunday morning and said well, let's put everybody on rations? You can't convert a country of eighty million people to rationing in twenty-four hours. They've been planning this for months! I'll tell you one other thing, too. I was over at Brandenburg today visiting a little friend, and there were troops all over the place. They had on battle dress, they were carrying weapons and ammo, and they were commandeering everything with wheels: delivery trucks, horse-drawn wagons, and bicycles. This thing is a go, friend. You heard it here first." Ches winked at Erich as he downed another swallow.

◆　◆　◆

Maggie hurried across the street, stepping around a young mother pushing a stroller, and turned east on the Kaiserdamm, heading toward the laundry on the corner. She had dropped off two sweaters early in the week and was eager to pick them up quickly and get back to work.

So much had been happening this week. Dieter was constantly on the phone or in meetings. Fresh guidance from the Wilhelmstraße was coming two and three times a day. It was as if no one knew what was really going on or what would happen next. Although the weather was still warm, Maggie could already tell that summer was on its way out. She had been working late—they all had—as the intensity of their broadcasting schedule had increased. Walking home late at night, Maggie had felt the crispness in the air.

"Maggie, hey, Maggie!" a voice called from behind her. She turned to find Erich Greinke jogging toward her.

Maggie gave a little wave and smiled. "What brings you to this part of town?" she said as he fell into step beside her.

"I had to deliver a couple of new passports to a Mr. and Mrs. Dale," Erich lied. "Mr. Dale is well enough connected that I had to jump. Their passports had expired and they decided that now was a good time to go home. They'd booked passage out of Bremerhaven on the first."

"That's tomorrow," Maggie noted. "That's really planning ahead, isn't it?"

"Tell me about it!" Erich laughed. "Oh, by the way, I've got something for you." He reached into his inside jacket pocket and pulled out a gray ration card. "Here, I picked up an extra one for you," he said, extending it toward Maggie.

Maggie stopped in the middle of the sidewalk and looked at the card in Erich's outstretched hand.

"Go on, take it. Quick!" he said.

Maggie hesitated just a moment and then took the card, sticking it down into her purse. When the two resumed their stroll, she asked, "Now, just where do you get extra ration cards?"

"Don't ask. And don't use that one where you use your regular card, either, or the store clerk will get wise."

"I don't know, Erich," Maggie said as she reached into her purse and began to remove the card. "This seems kind of shady to me."

Erich put his hand lightly on her forearm to stop her. "Listen, Maggie," he said. "You can trust me on this. No one will ever know you have it if you use it wisely, and I know you will. Look," he said, staring into her green eyes, "I hope there won't be a war, but if there is, it's not our fight. It's between the Germans and the British and the French. Let them duke it out if they want to. That doesn't mean we should suffer, does it? I mean, we're Americans. We have to look out for each other, you know."

Maggie removed her hand from her bag. The card stayed put. "Thank you, Erich," she said with an appraising sideways glance. "This is very thoughtful of you. I'm glad to know how resourceful you are."

"Yeah, well, you're welcome. Like I said, we have to look out for our friends. Listen, I'm glad I ran into you, but I've got to scoot. I have a whole lot of work that's been stacking up while I've been acting as Mr. Dale's private secretary. Let's have dinner some night," he called over his shoulder as he hurried away.

How strange, Maggie thought. *And how kind.* She never knew what to expect from Erich.

Erich had spent the whole day shadowing Maggie, waiting for an opportunity to make his move. Erich thought it had all gone rather well.

CHAPTER 10

Berlin, Germany
September 1939

Berlin at war was a lot like Berlin at peace, thought Maggie. The only difference was the blackout at night. Fortunately, she had a short walk to reach her apartment and few streets to cross. The curbstones had been whitewashed, which helped distinguish between street and sidewalk.

The Poles had attacked a German radio transmitter near the border town of Gleiwitz during the early-morning hours of Friday, September 1. Later that morning, Hitler had appeared before the Reichstag and vowed to defeat the Polish aggression. The British and French had protested Germany's invasion of Poland, ignoring the alleged provocation. They had demanded that Germany remove its troops from Polish territory. When Hitler failed to do so, Great Britain, on Sunday morning, had declared war.

Maggie was strolling through the Tiergarten alone, thinking. Had she made the right decision in staying? She had assumed that everything would be all right, that war would be averted just as the Czechoslovakia situation had been worked out. While she privately wondered at Hitler's decision to attack Poland, it was, after all, in response to an attack by the

Poles—and he was, after all, reclaiming what had until just twenty years ago been German territory. Would there really be fighting over Poland? There was, she believed, still time to resolve the situation. So far, neither Britain nor France had fired any shots in anger. Should she stick with it? *Well,* she thought, *if this is as bad as it gets, being on limited rations for a few weeks, it won't be too bad.* Even there, she had the advantage of the extra ration card. No, so far the war seemed very remote. Kurt and Thomas were gone—at the front, she supposed—but otherwise, there was no real change in her routine. No enemy bombers had appeared overhead, and she remembered Göring's boast that none would, "or you can call me Meier!"

Maggie continued to wander eastward, enjoying the sunny, warm Sunday. She thought of Kurt and prayed that he was safe. She thought of Thomas and hoped he was taking care of Kurt just as he had once looked after Erich Greinke. Dieter popped into her mind, and she considered his earnestness and intellect. She shook her head. Dieter was safe, out of harm's way. She prized the professional relationship she enjoyed with him. He treated her as his intellectual equal, even though she felt she wasn't. He respected her opinion and recognized that she was far more effective in managing Clive Barnes and his drinking than he'd been. Maggie smiled, remembering her first meeting with Dieter, how timid he had seemed in the presence of Herr Direktor Bauer. Yet he had proven anything but timid. His section was the most important— and arguably the most effective—within the Broadcasting Division.

Maggie looked up and realized she had reached the zoo. She stopped, then turned back toward the west. She would stay, she decided, come what may. Kurt was here. And so was Dieter Schmidt.

◆　◆　◆

"Listen, darling," Maggie said soothingly, patting Clive's beefy hand, "it's going to work out all right. You'll see." Clive had gone from depressed to jumpy over the last week. The evacuation of the British Embassy and its staff had shocked him. He had been sure that Chamberlain and Hitler would come to some kind of peaceful agreement over Poland, and yet here he was in the capital of the country with which his native England was at war!

"All this over Poland. Poland, for God's sake!" Clive cried. His eyes were bloodshot, and Maggie judged he hadn't shaved for a couple of days. His clothing was uncharacteristically rumpled. "I could be shot as a traitor for continuing to broadcast for the Germans," he wailed.

"Hung, darling," Maggie corrected, smiling sweetly.

"What?" Clive coughed.

"Hung, dear. Traitors are hung, not shot." She smiled, then took a sip of her drink. They were sitting at Clive's favorite booth at the end of the Adlon Bar. It was Friday night, very late, a week after German troops had "counterattacked" into Poland. Clive's continued heavy drinking was a concern to Dieter and Maggie. Even after the declaration of war by the Chamberlain government, Clive had remained the most popular—and therefore most valuable—of the English Section commentators. Keeping him fit to fight, or at least talk, had remained one of Maggie's chief responsibilities. "I'm sure you have nothing to fear, Clive. I don't think even the English would bear ill will toward someone who has worked so diligently and sincerely for peace."

Clive leaned back and sighed loudly. "Poland," he repeated. "We have no interest there whatsoever. Why would we allow them to drag us into another war?" He shook his broad head back and forth, his double chin covering the top of his bow tie. He became very still. In a moment, he began to snore.

Maggie stood quietly and smoothed out her skirt. She was tired; it was already past midnight. She walked to the near end of the bar and motioned to Georg. "Georg, be a dear and find someone to help Herr Barnes up to his rooms, will you?" she pleaded with a smile.

"Of course, of course! Georg will take care of it, Fräulein Maggie." Within a minute, two bellmen had flanked Clive, draping his massive arms over their shoulders, and were half carrying, half dragging him toward the elevators. Maggie collected her sweater and bag and walked toward the doors, only to be intercepted.

"Hi, Maggie!" said Erich Greinke cheerfully. "What are you doing out so late?"

"Babysitting," she yawned.

"Here, come have a drink. There's someone I want you to meet."

Maggie smiled, remembering the ration card, and said, "OK, but only one drink and only because it's you."

Erich took her by the elbow, leading her gently toward a booth in the far corner of the bar where sat a small, wiry, deeply tanned man. "Maggie, allow me to present Mr. Chesney Nutt, ace correspondent of the *Atlanta Journal*." Ches stood and smiled.

"How do you do, Mr. Nutt?" Maggie smiled, extending her hand.

"Please, call me Ches. All my friends do. So does Erich," Ches said with a wink. "Erich tells me you work in radio," he said as they sat down.

"That's right," Maggie said with more energy than she felt. "I work with the English language section of the propaganda ministry's Broadcasting Division. And you're a newspaperman?"

"All my life," Ches answered proudly.

"Ches covers Europe like the dew," Erich interjected, causing Ches to smile.

"A lot to cover these days," Maggie said, raising her eyebrows.

"So true," Ches responded.

Georg approached the table with a tray of drinks. *"Bitte sehr,"* he said, placing the drinks in front of each of them. "Whiskey neat for Fräulein Maggie, gin for Herr Greinke, and bourbon for Herr Nutt. Enjoy!" He bowed and hurriedly turned back to his bar.

"Good friends and better times," Ches said, lifting his glass to eye level. The others followed suit and took a sip.

"Tell me, Maggie," Ches began, "who's that big fella you were with just now?"

"That, Ches, is the famous—but slightly inebriated—Lord Lyon. Earlier this evening, or was it last night"—she pulled Erich's arm over to her and glanced playfully at his wristwatch—"he broadcast another plea for peace to his listeners in Great Britain, but not before downing half a bottle of gin."

Ches looked at Erich. "He might make a real interesting story, don't you think, buddy boy?"

Erich nodded. "He might at that."

"What about you, Ches?" Maggie asked. "What's your story? How come you're reduced to hanging out with Erich Greinke on a Friday night?"

"A highly perceptive question," Ches judged. "Actually, I just use Erich to meet pretty girls. It's an arrangement that seems to be working exceptionally well tonight."

Maggie jerked her head toward Erich. "What does he get out of it?"

"Why, the pleasure of my company, of course." Ches smiled and took another sip. "And, from time to time, I share certain of my keen observations and lucid insights concerning this mess we find ourselves in."

"Like what?" Maggie asked.

"Like who's whispering in the Führer's ear. What kind of success the army is having in Poland. They reached Warsaw today, by the way. They've cut through Poland like a hot knife through butter. Much faster, I think, than even they thought they could. I have a lot of contacts all over Europe, Maggie, even if I do say so myself."

"Do you know anything about German casualties?" Maggie asked, suddenly serious.

"Well, there have been some. It's a war, after all. But they don't seem to have been hit too hard. Want me to check on any particular unit?"

"Can you?" Maggie asked with surprise.

"I can try," Ches replied, staring into her beautiful green eyes.

Maggie told him about Kurt and the Leibstandarte SS Adolf Hitler. Ches promised to find out what he could.

"Sounds pretty serious, Maggie—you and Kurt," Ches observed with a twinkle in his eye.

Maggie looked down at her drink and smiled. "Oh, you never know." Then, to deflect the attention of both men, she asked, "What about you, Ches? You ever serious about a woman?"

Ches laughed and sat back, putting his hands on his knees. "Oh my, yes," he said. "As serious as a man can get. Back in '19, after the Great War, I settled down with a little French gal I had gotten to know in Paris. We moved to her family place out in the country. I thought I had died and gone to heaven! She was beautiful—dark hair, dark eyes. Just the prettiest little thing you ever saw. We had this little farm with animals and a few acres to grow things on. Since I was from the South, she figured I knew farming. Since she was French, I figured we'd have that idyllic relationship that the French are famous for: wine, cheese, poetry, lots of lovemaking. I had an old typewriter that I used to write my articles for the paper. I set that thing up on the kitchen table and began to write the great postwar novel. I wrote and wrote; she worked and worked. She'd be up before dawn milking and would work that little farm all day. And I'd be in there, writing away. She'd come in late in the afternoon and cook us a big dinner, and then she would fairly collapse. After a couple of weeks, the lovemaking stopped. She had no energy left. So, I'd stay up late and drink coffee and write. That went on for quite a while." Ches had a far-off look in his eye. "Then one day, it all ended."

"What happened?" Maggie asked, leaning forward intently.

"I ran out of paper."

Erich and Maggie burst out laughing, causing other patrons in the bar to look to their table. Ches continued to look over their heads, into the past.

"I tell you what, Maggie," Ches said, returning his focus to the present and the pretty girl sitting across from him. "How about I find out what I can about your beau, and you set me up an interview with your big buddy, the radio announcer?"

"Deal!" Maggie stated and then stuck her hand across the table. Ches shook, and the deal was sealed.

◆ ◆ ◆

"What I propose, Herr Direktor," Maggie explained, "is that we create a music program to supplement our commentaries." She and Dieter were seated in matching chairs in front of Bauer's desk. Bauer was leaning forward, his hands pressed together under his lips as though he were about to pray. "Since England has declared war, some of our listeners there have grown reluctant to tune in to our commentators. They understand we represent the enemy government's views. But if we feature music programs, we can get them listening for entertainment and then insert our propaganda. If we are smooth enough, they may not even realize it."

"What kind of music programs?" Bauer asked.

"The most popular seems to be the big band style," Maggie answered. "Also maybe some smaller jazz combos." She and Dieter had been discussing the idea for a couple of weeks, ever since the *Times* of London had reported that its readers had begun to boycott English Section's programming.

"Jazz? That's Negro music," Bauer protested. "It is not appropriate. It is completely below our standards."

Dieter, who had anticipated his boss's reaction, said diplomatically, "Of course, Herr Direktor. We would never advocate this for a German audience, but it would be aimed at British listeners. Why not broadcast to our enemy music that contains an erotic, defiling ingredient? And who would be most likely to listen to this type of music? The young—those who are also most likely to be called to military service. It would provide a pipeline right into the minds of the English fighting men."

A knock on the office door interrupted Dieter. A secretary entered quietly, handed Bauer a folded note, and withdrew.

Bauer read the note, smiled broadly, and said, "Warsaw has surrendered! Perhaps now there will be no war!"

Maggie's heart fluttered. She gripped both arms of her chair in an attempt to mask her joy at the news. Perhaps Kurt would soon be back. *If he is all right,* she thought. So far, she had heard nothing from Chesney Nutt.

"Very well, Herr Schmidt, Fräulein O'Dea," Bauer concluded, "I will take your recommendation under advisement. Thank you both."

In the corridor on the way back to the English Section office, Maggie took Dieter's arm and leaned her head on to his shoulder. "You were excellent in there, Dieter. When you started talking about erotic ingredients, I started getting excited!"

"Knock it off!" Dieter laughed. But he didn't really want her to.

◆ ◆ ◆

True to his word, Chesney Nutt was able to report that same day that Obersturmführer Kurt Engel was alive and well and still in one piece. True to her word, Maggie scheduled Clive for an interview.

"Now, no more drinking, dear, until after you're finished with Mr. Nutt. Remember, you are representing not only peace-loving Englishmen but also English Section," Maggie warned as she walked alongside Clive on the way to the Adlon. She and Ches had agreed that a comfortable, familiar setting would be more conducive for the kind of questions Ches wanted to ask and the feature he intended to write. They had also agreed that once the questions were completed, drinks would be enjoyed.

"Mr. Nutt's paper is the most widely read in the southeastern United States," Maggie explained to Clive. "Your interview is a great opportunity to solidify support among those Americans who are pro-German, or, like me, anti-British. No offense."

"None taken," Clive growled. He was in a sour mood. It wasn't that he didn't like publicity; it was balm for his bruised ego. It was just that he didn't like being cut off from his bottle for extended periods.

Arriving at the Adlon, Maggie made the introductions before settling in beside Clive in his regular booth. Ches sat across from them and asked a couple of background questions to get the conversation started. After a few minutes of Ches's friendly Southern charm, the questions began to get more serious.

"Tell me, Mr. Barnes," Ches asked in his relaxed drawl, "how do you reconcile your aversion to war with your support of the Hitler government, which has just overrun a sovereign neighbor?"

Clive shifted his bulk, casting a wistful glance toward the early-shift bartender. "An excellent question, Mr. Nutt," he began, forcing himself to focus. "To start with, it's important to recollect that Germany's foray into Poland was provoked by an unwarranted, surprise attack on a German radio station at Gleiwitz. Without the Poles taking the first aggressive action, I doubt the peace would have been broken—certainly not by Germany. Secondly, I think your readers should understand that much of what has been known as eastern Poland for the last twenty years formerly belonged to Germany. Most of the people living in these areas remained German in culture and language even after the borders were redrawn following the Great War. My experience with Americans, and here I mean no offense, is that they have very little knowledge of European geography or history. A fuller understanding of pre-1918 Europe would, I think, make some of the more recent events more logical and even appealing to your readers.

"I think we must always be hesitant to condemn what we see in others, Mr. Nutt. Take my own country: Great Britain has dominated other peoples for some centuries now, and I could argue quite effectively that it has been to the overall benefit of both those people and the civilized world. Rather than conquering and establishing colonies around the world, what the Germans have done is clear the way to unite the German-speaking peoples of Europe into one nation-state. There is a parallel of sorts in the history of your own country. Your own national government implemented progressively restrictive measures aimed at controlling your native Indian population. The eventual result was to corral these natives into controlled communities and promote the settlement of North America by Anglo-Europeans."

Ches's yellow pencil scratched notes on a pad as Clive spoke. "What about the attitude of the Nazi government toward Jews? Doesn't that raw racism concern you?"

"Yes, truly it does," Barnes replied earnestly. "It reminds me somewhat of the way Negroes are treated in your country. They are denied basic rights and liberties taken for granted by whites. It is a disturbing yet appropriate parallel. But I think it would be unwise to judge a great nation like America on this one criterion, just as it would be myopic to judge Germany solely on the basis of its Jewish policies." Maggie was impressed: Clive's answer virtually assured that the issue of Jews, much less Negroes, would be excised from Ches's article when it ran in the South's most prominent newspaper.

"Why do you continue to broadcast for the Germans even after your own country has declared war against them?" Ches asked, keeping his eyes firmly focused on Clive's.

"The answer to that, Mr. Nutt, is quite simple: England must hear a voice for peace. Like John the Baptist crying out in the wilderness, I must appeal to Englishmen to seek peace through peaceful means. The resort to armed conflict to achieve peace is one of the great cynicisms of our time. Look how miserably it failed us during and after the Great War. God cannot be pleased with us."

The interview lasted an hour, after which Ches put down his pencil and joined Clive and Maggie in picking up a glass.

◆ ◆ ◆

ENGLISHMAN BROADCASTS PEACE APPEAL

By Chesney Nutt, *Journal* Chief European Correspondent

BERLIN—The most famous radio broadcaster in England these days isn't in England these days. Clive Barnes, an amiable Englishman, broadcasts to his native country each evening from here in the enemy capital. Better known in London by his nom de radio Lord Lyon, Barnes is an unabashed voice for peace who describes himself as an English patriot and who closes each broadcast with a heartfelt "God save the King." A veteran of the Great War, Barnes remembers from firsthand experience the death, filth, and unmitigated misery of the trenches. "It is folly to fight for peace," he says in his upper-class accent . . .

Ches's article ran in the *Journal* on Sunday, October 1, and featured a picture of Clive standing in front of the vacated British Embassy. It was generally favorable, depicting Clive as sincere in his beliefs and committed in his actions. The article made no mention of Jews or Negroes. The German consulate in Atlanta clipped the article and sent copies via train to its embassy aboard that evening's Washington-bound Southern Crescent.

CHAPTER 11

Berlin, Germany
October 1939

Maggie planned a homecoming party for Kurt and Thomas for Thursday night, October 12. She had tried to book space on Friday, only to find that every suitable venue was already engaged. She settled for Thursday, reserving the same back room at Alois's where she had reunited Erich and Thomas back in April. She invited her friends from work, as well as Erich and Ches, and sent word to Kurt and Thomas to bring as many of their comrades as they desired.

Immediately after Clive said "God save the King!" Maggie grabbed her coat and waved to Dieter, whose consent for an early departure she had already secured. Maggie arrived well before her guests to check on the decorations, food, and drink. She visited the ladies' room to check her makeup, hair, and dress and to ensure that everything was just right. She wanted to look beautiful for Kurt, whom she had not seen in nearly two months.

At nine o'clock, her guests began to trickle in. Clive lumbered in, blew her a kiss, and headed straight to the bar set up in the corner of the room. Dieter, along with Elise and several of Maggie's colleagues from

English Section, arrived shortly after Clive. At 9:20 p.m., as Maggie glanced at her watch for perhaps the fifteenth time, she heard applause rippling through the main dining room. A moment later, Kurt, leading several other young officers bedecked in their field gray uniforms, strode through the door. His eyes quickly scanned the room, but froze when they saw Maggie. He stopped completely, even as his comrades surged toward the bar and the hors d'oeuvres. He smiled his handsome smile, blue eyes flashing, and tossed his cap on the closest table. He pointed to Maggie and then pointed down to the spot immediately in front of where he stood. Maggie got the message and flew to his arms. Kurt wrapped his strong arms around her waist and lifted her off the floor, laughing. He set her firmly on her feet and kissed her, as his uniformed friends cheered. Dieter watched quietly from the other end of the bar as the kiss lingered.

"Maggie," Kurt said, leaning his forehead against hers and keeping his arms around her, "you are the most beautiful girl in this room, in this city, in the whole world!"

"Oh," Maggie replied, tears of joy pooling in her green eyes, "you're just saying that because it's true!" She kissed him again.

"All right, soldier!" barked an authoritative voice. "Look smart there!" It was Thomas, juggling three beer steins. He handed one to Maggie, pecking her on the cheek, and then gave one to Kurt. *"Achtung!"* he shouted to the revelers in the room. "A toast!" He raised his glass, and the others did the same. "To the Führer, the Fatherland, and the ladies," Thomas declared, then added, "but not necessarily in that order!"— which brought laughter from all of the soldiers.

"Another toast!" Maggie responded, raising her stein to eye level and looking into Kurt's blue eyes. "To safe homecomings!"

"Hear, hear!" the growing crowd replied.

Elise began to play the old piano sitting in the corner of the room. Several of the young officers gathered around the beautiful young lady to sing and laugh. Maggie locked her arm through Kurt's and began to introduce him to her friends from work.

"That's Elise on the piano," she said, nodding toward the young Norwegian. "And this," she said with a wide smile, "is my boss, Dieter Schmidt!"

"How do you do, Kurt?" Dieter bowed slightly.

"At last, I meet the brilliant Dieter Schmidt!" Kurt laughed, shaking Dieter's hand. "Maggie has told me so much about you, and all of it good. She has such high regard for you, Dieter, that I am sometimes jealous!" Kurt said, smiling and wagging his finger at Dieter.

Dieter reddened slightly and tried to smile. "It is an honor to finally meet you, Kurt. Maggie has also told me all about you. Congratulations to you and your comrades on your great victory in Poland. Permit me, please, to buy you another drink."

"Very kind of you, Dieter," Kurt replied, still smiling, "but I must first speak with Maggie for a few minutes." Maggie shot Kurt a curious glance, but didn't let go of his arm.

"Of course. Perhaps later, then," Dieter said with a friendly nod. "It really is a pleasure to finally meet you."

◆ ◆ ◆

"Nice party," Erich Greinke shouted to Thomas above the racket.

"Ah, Erich! How's the diplomat?" Thomas replied with a broad smile. "You need a drink!" As Thomas retrieved another beer from the bar, Erich noted Thomas's deep tan and lined face. Clearly, Thomas—and from what Erich could observe, the other soldiers—had been in the field. Their faces were ruddy, the skin around their eyes creased. The civilians in the room, himself included, looked pale by comparison. Thomas motioned to Erich to join him at a table away from both the bar and the piano. Erich sat and pulled out a package of cigarettes.

"Have one?" he asked Thomas. "There're American."

"Ah yes, please," Thomas replied eagerly. "Have a beer. It's German." He smiled as he took a smoke and slid Erich's glass to him.

Erich lit both cigarettes and inhaled deeply. "So," he said after a moment, eyeing his former squad leader, "how was it?"

Thomas exhaled blue smoke toward the ceiling, then looked down into his beer. "Very, very bad. It was like using a sledgehammer to crack an egg. For the most part we just rolled right over the Poles. They were poorly armed to begin with. They have—I should say, *had*—nothing to stand up to our armor. Mongrel bastards," he added, taking another drag on the cigarette.

"Any trouble?"

"Yes," Thomas chuckled. "Believe it or not, despite our mastery of the air and our overwhelming superiority in arms, our brilliant battalion commander managed to get us surrounded on three sides by a Polish regiment. Not only were they on both of our flanks, they held higher ground!" Thomas grimaced and shook his head at the recollection.

"How'd that happen?" Erich asked, as the volume of singing from the piano intensified.

"Sturmbannführer Thyssen was adamant that we pursue a retreating Polish company right into a shallow valley," Thomas explained, "completely ignoring the advice of his intelligence officer—"

"That would be you," Erich interrupted.

"That would be me." Thomas smiled ruefully. "Of course, they weren't really retreating. They were just the bait to lure us into the trap. This they did quite well. If it hadn't been for the Wehrmacht coming to the rescue, we would have been a rare victory for the Poles."

"How come Thyssen didn't listen to you?"

Thomas lowered his voice and glanced around. "Mainly because he's an idiot. He's no more a soldier than the girl at the piano. He's a well-connected party hack. It's a minor miracle he didn't get us all killed. Fortunately, most of his subordinate commanders are much better soldiers."

"How'd the young field marshal over there do?" Erich gestured toward the table where Kurt and Maggie were holding hands. They looked to be in a serious conversation, unaware of anyone else in the room.

"Pretty well, from what I heard. Did a respectable job with his platoon. Seems to have the respect of his soldiers, and I heard his company commander say good things about him to Thyssen."

"You said it was rough?" Erich hoped to get Thomas to elaborate.

"It was brutal. Every day was like the worst day in Spain. No one was safe—old people, women, children—everyone was a target. As we got closer to Warsaw, we ran into more guerilla fighting. That's really nerve-racking. There's never a big action, but we lost as many guys to snipers and hit-and-run attacks as we ever did in a major engagement— and you never see it coming." Thomas sipped his beer. "Kurt's platoon was on our forward line, clearing out a village. They had already lost a couple of men to sniper fire. Thyssen sent me up for a situation report and to see if we could establish any patterns to the partisan attacks. So, I'm standing there talking with Kurt on the stoop of a little church and bang! A sniper takes out one of Kurt's NCOs. Fortunately, somebody saw the muzzle flash, so they were able to root the sniper out pretty quickly. By the time they brought him in front of Kurt, he only had one eye left. Kurt socks the guy in the jaw and knocks him down, then he pulls out his pistol and bam! One shot to the head."

Erich listened quietly, his cigarette continuing to burn.

"Next thing I know," Thomas continued, "Kurt has lined up five men from the village. By now his blood is up. He's really pissed off— this was only a couple of days after Thyssen got us surrounded. He makes them kneel in a line. He walks right down the line, firing one round into the back of each head. Then"—Thomas stopped, his voice catching—"then, this kid who'd been standing in the crowd watching with all the others tears loose. He's probably ten or so, skinny, wearing short pants. He walks right up to Kurt and puts his hands on his hips and says, 'God is watching you!' I see that kid every night when I close my eyes," Thomas said, shaking his head.

"What happened to him?"

"Kurt shot him through the head."

◆ ◆ ◆

By ten o'clock, Kurt was ready to leave. "Darling, you just got here!" Maggie smiled. "You can't leave yet! This party is in your honor!"

Kurt laughed and wagged his index finger toward her. "Don't tell me what I can't do! I've already met all of your friends, including your pal Dieter. You and I need some time together. Alone."

"But darling—" Maggie began again, plaintively. She was holding Kurt's hand, trying to figure out how to keep him at the party without causing a scene.

"No buts. I'm serious, Maggie. Let's get out of here and go back to your place. I haven't seen you in nine weeks. I don't want to share your company with others, at least not tonight."

"I'm not one of your soldiers, Kurt," Maggie said, trying to keep the irritation out of her voice. "Like it or not, these people"—she swept her arm toward the bar and piano, where most of the partiers had congregated—"are my guests. I can't just walk out on them."

"Sure you can." Kurt held his smile in place, but the expression of his eyes took on a more serious cast. "Get your stuff, Maggie. Let's get out of here. It's been too long and life is too short. Come on," he ordered.

Maggie hesitated. "Oh, all right, dammit!" she snapped. "Let me get my coat and try to leave gracefully." Maggie was annoyed at Kurt's selfishness and angry that he didn't seem to appreciate the effort and expense to which she had gone to throw a party for him. Her irritation was only partly mitigated by the prospect of a long night alone with him.

Erich saw Kurt pick up his cap from the table where he'd placed it less than an hour earlier. "I haven't paid my respects to the guest of honor," he said to Thomas. "Excuse me a moment." Erich took a quick swallow from his beer and headed toward Kurt, who was waiting impatiently by the door.

"Hello, Kurt!" Erich said, extending his hand.

Kurt smiled and shook. His face took on a sheepish look. "You know, Erich," he said, "that night we met, I thought you were a real prick. But I have to confess something to you."

"Yes?"

"You were right about combat. It's nothing like what I imagined. No glory in it, like we see in the cinema. Constant anxiety, random death, bloated bodies stinking to high heaven." Kurt looked down at the floor and shook his head. "And you know what?" he asked, placing a friendly hand on Erich's shoulder and shifting his focus to Erich's eyes.

"What?"

"I loved it."

"OK, Kurt," Maggie said shortly, approaching him from behind as she shoved her arm through the sleeve of her coat. "Oh"—she stopped short—"hello, Erich." Her smile returned. "I'm sorry I didn't see you come in earlier. I, well, we—"

"—really must be going," Kurt finished. "It was good to see you again, Erich. Thanks for coming." Kurt took Maggie's arm and pulled her quickly through Alois's main dining room.

Erich lit another cigarette and watched them go.

◆ ◆ ◆

The moment the door of Maggie's apartment locked behind them, Kurt pulled Maggie so closely against him that she could feel his eagerness. He leaned in to kiss her as he reached inside her coat and slid his hands up and over her breasts. He pushed the coat off her shoulders, letting it drop around her feet. With his hands on her waist, his face nuzzled her neck. Then he attacked her blouse, beginning with the top button and working his way quickly downward.

Maggie was meanwhile busy with the large buttons on Kurt's tunic. As they backed toward the bed, Kurt pulled her blouse out of her skirt. He kissed his way from her neck down to her half-exposed breasts, reaching blindly behind her to struggle with the clasp of her bra. Maggie stripped his pants off and tore at his underwear, leaving them both completely naked.

"You look none the worse for wear." She smiled. Kurt grabbed her roughly under each arm and half lifted, half tossed her onto the bed. He grabbed her arms and pinned them to either side of her pillow as he lowered himself onto her. "Kurt," Maggie began breathlessly, "you're hurting my wrists. Relax, darling."

"Quiet," he commanded. He guided himself into her, his calloused hands continuing to pin her wrists to the bed. For Kurt, it was over quickly. But it wasn't over for long.

◆ ◆ ◆

It was the bright glare that woke Maggie. The autumn sun was streaming in through her east-facing window and shining right into her face. She rolled away, bumping into the still snoring Kurt. She wasn't sure how late they had made love, but she was still groggy from fatigue when she looked at her alarm clock. *Eight thirty. Eight thirty! Damn!*

Fighting through the cobwebs in her brain, she threw the comforter off and swung her feet over the side of her bed. Kurt snorted but did not wake. She stood quickly, got dizzy, and sat heavily back on the bed. As soon as her head quit spinning, she was up again, this time into the tiny bathroom. Already late, she was going to have to take shortcuts. She pulled the shower curtain around her and gasped as a stream of cold water smacked against her shoulders. She didn't have time to wait for warm water. After a mercifully brief shower, she toweled off and pulled on a white blouse, over which she added a brown sweater. She stepped into a black skirt and hastily pulled on a pair of hose. She found the shoes she had so carelessly kicked off the night before and shoved them onto her feet. Maggie brushed her teeth for about twenty seconds, then grabbed her purse, a jacket, and a brush and scooted out the door. As she hurried toward Broadcasting House, she struggled to get her arms into the sleeves of her jacket while brushing her hair. Satisfied that her hair was passably in place, she reached into her purse, exchanging her brush for a compact and a tube of lipstick. She was trying to apply makeup and avoid running into trees, streetlights, and other pedestrians. She missed the curb and stumbled. Regaining her balance, she crossed the street and increased her pace.

Maggie strode quickly across the wide, circular parking apron in front of Broadcasting House, barely noticing the row of official vehicles lined up in the driveway. One of them, a long, black Mercedes with the top down, sported bright-red Nazi fender flags. Maggie pushed through the glass doors leading into the spacious lobby, climbed the steps, and hurried down the hallway to English Section's office. She pushed the door open, hoping to find the room empty; most of her colleagues weren't morning people.

A startled Dieter looked up as she entered. "Thank God!" he said, replacing the telephone handset into its cradle on his desk, a worried look giving way to one of irritation. "Don't even think of sitting down," he snapped, coming around from behind his desk.

Maggie had been taking off her coat and was jolted fully alert by Dieter's uncharacteristic tone of voice. He grabbed her by the elbow and half guided, half dragged her back out into the corridor.

"What is it? What's going on?" she stammered, embarrassed at being late and annoyed at the way Dieter had responded.

"Listen carefully, Maggie," Dieter said, cutting her off. "We only have a few seconds." They were heading along the corridor back toward the main stairway. "Bauer called this morning at eight thirty wanting you to come immediately to the conference room off the lobby. He said a visitor wanted to see you at nine o'clock, which"—Dieter looked dramatically at his watch—"was exactly eight minutes ago. I told him you were always in early and that you would be there with time to spare." Dieter continued to pull her as they trooped down the stairs.

"Who is it? What's it about?"

"Didn't you see the big limousine out front?" Now that they were just a few feet away, Dieter seemed to have relaxed a little. He actually seemed to Maggie to be enjoying her distress. "Minister Goebbels has come to see you, my friend."

With that, Dieter pushed open the conference room door, virtually propelling Maggie into the room. A smattering of applause broke out from the group of about fifteen people who had been waiting. Herr Direktor Bauer and Clive Barnes were standing drinking coffee with a much smaller man, a man Maggie had seen once before. He was short in stature and slightly built, but he was immaculately dressed in a brown suit with a pale-blue shirt. His face was divided by a thin nose, his dark eyes magnetic, his dark hair oiled and combed straight back from his forehead. He was obviously the center of attention—or at least he had been before Maggie's unceremonious entrance.

"Ah, Herr Minister, here is our young lady!" Bauer said with a broad smile and the delight of a proud father. "Minister Goebbels," he said, sweeping his hand toward the bewildered Maggie, "May I present Fräulein Maggie O'Dea."

Goebbels smiled, stepped forward, and gently shook Maggie's hand. "It is a pleasure to meet you, Fräulein O'Dea. I have heard many complimentary things about you."

"Thank you, Herr Minister," she replied, still completely unaware of what all the fuss was about. Joseph Goebbels was the minister of propaganda, in addition to serving as the Nazi Gauleiter of Berlin. The Broadcasting Division reported to his ministry's headquarters on the

Wilhelmstraße. He was, behind Hitler and Göring, the most popular of the Nazi leaders. He was also widely regarded as the most intelligent.

"So, this is the young lady behind that excellent article on our Lord Lyon that recently appeared in the American press." Goebbels smiled, still holding Maggie's hand. "You did not tell me she was beautiful as well as smart," he said, glancing from Bauer to Clive and drawing a chuckle from the others in the room. "Come, let us sit." He waved to the end of the conference table, where several chairs had been positioned and a coffee service had been set up. "Would you join me for some coffee?" he asked with a friendly smile. "How do you take yours?"

"With cream and sugar, thank you," Maggie replied as she was guided into a chair by Bauer.

Goebbels carefully poured a cup of steaming coffee, dropped in a spoonful of sugar, and poured in a portion of cream. Stirring it slowly, Goebbels handed the cup and saucer to Maggie and then took his seat next to her. "Now, Fräulein O'Dea, you must tell me how you arranged for such a positive article in an American newspaper. This is the essence of successful propaganda: one must use a trusted source to promote one's own message. You did so masterfully!" Goebbels was leaning forward, his brown eyes bright, his manner engaging.

"Well"—Maggie hesitated, trying to compose her thoughts—"first of all, please call me Maggie—everyone does," she said with a smile, again drawing chuckles from the around the room. "I met Mr. Nutt, the correspondent, through a friend who works at the US Embassy. I then introduced Mr. Barnes—Lord Lyon—to Mr. Nutt." Goebbels was paying rapt attention to Maggie's every word. "Mr. Barnes and I discussed some of the questions Mr. Nutt would likely ask and some of the answers we thought would properly represent Mr. Barnes's opinions. The credit really goes to Mr. Barnes, Herr Minister. He gave the interview, after all."

Goebbels laughed and clapped his hands, prompting the others to follow suit. "Brava!" he said, leaning forward, his eyes dancing. "Not only smart and beautiful but also modest! Magnificent! I think you will go far, Maggie! Thank you for your excellent work!" Goebbels stood, again taking Maggie's hand in his. "I am so pleased to have met you. I look forward to seeing you again soon. You must please excuse the brevity of my visit. These are very busy times, as you well know."

With that Goebbels bowed slightly, kissing her hand before releasing it. He shook hands with several of the others in the room, including Bauer, Clive, and Dieter, and then grabbed his leather overcoat and limped from the room, followed by his aide and his driver.

◆ ◆ ◆

"Why didn't you warn me?" Maggie asked Dieter once they were alone, climbing the stairs.

"I would have had to know to warn you. I only found out at eight thirty. If you'd been here at your usual time, it wouldn't have been such a surprise."

"Oh, Dieter," Maggie moaned, "did I come off as a complete idiot?"

Dieter stopped with one foot on the top step and turned to face Maggie. "On the contrary, Maggie," he said gently and sincerely, "anything but. You did fine. Goebbels was quite captivated by you. I've been around him a few times. He has a wicked wit and a sharp tongue. Had he been the least annoyed, you—and all the rest of us—would have felt his wrath rather quickly. Why were you so late this morning, anyway?"

"I overslept," Maggie said, looking down and hoping Dieter wouldn't see the color rising in her cheeks.

"I see," Dieter replied, choosing not to press the issue. He had noticed her early departure from the previous night's party and in whose company she had been. Despite his affection for Maggie, he could understand her attraction to Kurt. Kurt was handsome in a way he never would be, plus, Kurt had a romantic occupation: soldier in a time of war. Dieter admonished himself to control his jealousy. He still had the pleasure of Maggie's company on a daily basis, spending more time with her in the long run than Kurt or anyone else, with the possible exception of Clive. "Congratulations on that article, by the way. You really impressed Goebbels." Dieter laughed, adding, "And anything that impresses the minister impresses Bauer!"

◆ ◆ ◆

Tired from her lack of sleep and overstimulated by her unexpected encounter with Goebbels, Maggie was not her usual chipper and efficient self that Friday. Her mind drifted during the afternoon staff conference, and she had trouble concentrating on her work. Dieter noticed.

"Maggie," he said, beckoning her to his desk at five o'clock, "why don't you take off early tonight? You seem very tired. I can take care of Clive's broadcast."

"Would you?" Maggie sighed. "You are a dear! I'm exhausted, and I don't think I've done anything right all day."

"Go on," he said. "Someone as well in with the minister as you are can afford to take off early," he teased. "The rest of us will soldier on and cover for you." Maggie smiled and blew him a kiss, then grabbed her coat and headed for the door.

◆ ◆ ◆

"Hello, my sweet," Kurt said, smiling, as Maggie opened the door to her flat. He was neatly dressed in a pair of civilian slacks and a white shirt. He turned over the book he'd been reading and set it on the arm of his chair. He pushed himself up and hugged Maggie, kissing her on the lips. "I've been missing you all day!" he said. "What shall we do for supper? Would you like to fix me something, or shall we dine out?"

"Out, please." Maggie smiled tiredly. "I don't think I could manage much in the kitchen tonight."

"Saving your strength for later?" Kurt asked with raised eyebrows and a sideways grin.

"After last night, early this morning, and working all day, I haven't any strength left to save," Maggie said, slumping into a chair.

"Come, come girl, up, up," Kurt said, grabbing his jacket in one hand and Maggie's hand in the other. "Let's nourish you so you will be ready to do your duty later." He laughed.

Maggie bristled. "Duty?" she asked, a tone of anger creeping into her voice. She remained seated with Kurt pulling on her extended hand. "Let me remind you, Herr Obersturmführer, that I have worked a full day already and, having done so, have fulfilled my 'duty,' as you say."

"Ah, your professional duty, perhaps." Kurt continued to smile and pull on her outstretched hand. "But surely you must acknowledge the duty to your heart."

Maggie smiled, letting her guard down. "You were like an animal last night," she said, shaking her head.

"Come," Kurt commanded with mock seriousness. "Do not keep the Obersturmführer waiting any longer. We must eat. You still have services to perform. Then you can rest—right beside me." He winked.

Kurt and Maggie presented their ration cards to the waiter at the small corner Gasthaus. Kurt's food allowance was greater, as he was a serving military officer. They were served a simple meal of veal, potatoes, rolls, and beer, over which Maggie recounted the events of her day.

"He is so small," she said of Goebbels, "yet his presence dominates the room. He is very animated and quick. And smart. You can tell by his eyes that he is taking everything in."

"Careful that he doesn't take *you* in," Kurt warned. "He is quite the ladies' man."

"But he's married, isn't he?"

"Of course," Kurt replied, "but that doesn't matter to powerful men. Just as their duties are immense, so are their physical needs. They must be satisfied. Oftentimes, one woman isn't sufficient. Watch out for Goebbels. If he takes a liking to you, well, there wouldn't be much even I could do to protect you." Kurt's face was serious.

Maggie's eyes widened. "Do you really think he—oh, you're just teasing me!"

◆ ◆ ◆

Maggie's hips were sore, her thighs bruised from the previous evening's marathon lovemaking. But Kurt was not to be denied. He was lying on his side facing Maggie. She could see the light golden hair on his chest in the dim light of the room, feel his strong hand resting on her hip. "You must take care of me, Maggie," he explained sincerely. "It's your duty. I am a soldier and may soon have to go back into battle. You wouldn't want to feel any regrets if something happened to me."

"Listen, buster," Maggie said, squinting her eyes and tilting her head, "I feel like *I've* been in battle. Tonight we make love, not war."

"Tonight we do whatever I say," Kurt laughed, rolling on top of her.

◆ ◆ ◆

"Hi, Maggie! What's cookin'?" asked Erich Greinke. He was standing in the lobby of Broadcasting House waiting for Elise to finish work for the day. Maggie was on her way back to English Section from the cafeteria, where she had grabbed a quick bite that would serve as her supper. Kurt had reported back to his unit on Sunday night, and Maggie's days had resumed their usual routine of twelve hours of nonstop work.

"Hello, Erich." Maggie smiled, coming to a stop. "What brings you to the information nerve center of the world?"

"I'm waiting for Elise," he answered. "We're going to get some dinner. Want to come? I wouldn't mind being seen on the town with two beautiful ladies. It would be good for my reputation."

"Thanks, but I just ate."

"Say, Maggie," Erich said, "I'm glad I ran into you. You know that article you helped Ches write about Clive Barnes?"

"Oh yes," Maggie answered, "I know it well. But Ches wrote it. All I did was arrange the interview."

"Well, Ches wanted me to ask you if you had an organization chart or a directory or something that shows how the Broadcasting Division is set up. He said his editor in Atlanta really liked the piece on Clive and that their readers were interested in more articles on the German propaganda machine."

"Why doesn't he ask me himself?" Maggie asked, her brow wrinkled.

"I'm sure he would if he saw you before I did, but he's gone on some ministry press tour to Poland."

Maggie thought for a minute. Erich's request seemed harmless and, after all, it was really for Ches. She remembered how pleased Goebbels and Bauer had been over Ches's article on Clive, how positively they had viewed it. "Sure, Erich," she said, "I can get that for you."

"For Ches," he corrected. "There's Elise." Erich waved to Elise, who was approaching from behind Maggie. "Thanks, Maggie! I know Ches will really appreciate it!"

After another moment of small talk, Elise and Erich wished Maggie good night and headed out on their date. Maggie headed back to work, her mind moving ahead to the evening's broadcast.

"What good, dear listener, could possibly come from an open conflict between the armed forces of Germany and those of France and Great Britain?" Lord Lyon asked. "The situation in Poland is resolved. German lands and German people have been reunited with their Fatherland. What bloodshed there has been is regrettable, but more fighting will not change that which has already occurred, particularly if this new fighting is in Western Europe. I ask again, what good could possibly come from a battle between Germany and the western powers? None!"

Maggie sat at her console, her headset flattening her auburn hair. Since the initial days of the war in Poland, Clive had been drinking less. He was more relaxed and, Maggie thought, more effective on the air. Ches's article had been a balm to his wounded psyche. It had presented him as the peacemaker he envisioned himself to be. That it also enhanced his standing in the eyes of Goebbels and Bauer had bolstered his ego, which had been bruised by his curt dismissal at the hands of the British Embassy staff. As he came to the conclusion of tonight's broadcast, Maggie checked the clock: right on schedule.

"This . . . is Lord Lyon in Berlin. Good night. God save the King!"

As the on-air light winked off, Maggie keyed her intercom. "Nice job, Clive." On the other side of the glass, Clive nodded and smiled, grateful for Maggie's acknowledgment.

Clive put on a good show. His deep, resonant voice commanded attention. His scripts—often polished by Maggie or Dieter, but still generally the fruit of his own mind—were calculated to challenge his listeners' thinking without alienating them. Even with these talents, Clive needed frequent reassurance. Maggie made it a point to find something good to say about each of his broadcasts. That made it easier to offer constructive criticism on the rare occasions it was warranted. Tonight, it wasn't.

◆ ◆ ◆

"There you are," Erich said to Chesney Nutt, finding him in the bar at the Adlon. "How was Poland?"

"Cold, wet, and conquered," Ches replied, blowing cigarette smoke through his nose. "Georg," he called to the bartender, "another, please, and whatever Erich wants." Turning his attention to Erich, Ches asked, "How's Berlin?"

"Cold, wet, and victorious. Lots of folks around here think the war's over. What do you think?"

"I don't know," Ches replied thoughtfully. "I hear the Brits are moving troops into France and the French are keeping the Maginot Line on full alert, but I really wonder if they have the stomach for it. From what little I saw in Poland, if there's a real war in France, it's going to be much different than the last one. I hope they're prepared."

"I hear the same thing from my friends," Erich said as Georg placed their glasses on the bar before them. "They say the pace of combat and the speed of movement is tremendously greater than it was in the trenches. They say the Germans have mastered synchronized infantry, tank, and air attacks. Apparently, what we did in Spain was a dress rehearsal for what these guys did in Poland."

"I think I just might need to go to Paris and have a look, see what the French are up to," Ches said, taking a sip of his bourbon. "You ought to come with me, buddy boy. Paris is the loveliest city in the world. And the women, my God!"

"Oh, hey, I almost forgot." Erich fumbled in his coat pocket. "I got you something."

"What's that?"

"Our friend Maggie sent you this organization chart of the Broadcasting Division."

"Now, why would she do that?" Ches wondered out loud, eying his young friend suspiciously.

"Well, I guess she's hoping you'll write another article about Clive Barnes or one of the other broadcasters, or maybe do a feature on the division or something. Maybe you should ask her."

"I'll tell you this, buddy boy: I won't be writing any more articles like that one on Clive Barnes. My editor said he got an earful from some muckety-mucks up in Washington about me being in the Nazis' back pocket. Said I'd become a shill for Dr. Goebbels. You know I don't like that little bastard, and I'll be damned if I let them pull my strings like that again. No disrespect to Maggie, but you can tell her I'm not contemplating any further journalistic masterpieces on the propaganda ministry. You just keep that old chart."

"C'mon, Ches," Erich pleaded, "I'm sure Maggie didn't mean anything by it."

"Keep it," Ches repeated.

"OK, OK." Erich gave up, stuffing the chart back into his pocket. It didn't really matter to Erich whether Ches accepted the chart. What mattered was what he was able to report in his evening cable.

◆ ◆ ◆

Erich Greinke worked late that October evening to compose his daily report.

> Am finally having some success in cultivating source within propaganda ministry. Source has begun passing organizational information and may be induced to provide more sensitive material in future.

Erich covered other matters as well, paraphrasing Gino, the Italian ambassador's driver.

> Italians too occupied with their own adventures to honor treaty obligations with Germany, at least so far. Source in Italian Embassy states that Abyssinian and Albanian invasions continue to stretch Italy's resources. No thought of assisting Germans with Poland. Ambassador tells his staff no Italian leader has enjoyed battlefield success since Caesar.

Redeployment of troops from Poland to French frontier continues, albeit at slow pace. Germans hope to avoid provocative actions. Units are retraining and refitting. Correspondents report harsh treatment of Poles and minorities in occupied Poland.

This last had come from Chesney Nutt, although Erich was careful to protect the identity of his sources.

Erich reviewed his report and then began the laborious process of coding it. His messages weren't transmitted in the standard embassy code, but then, they weren't meant for just anyone at the State Department. Erich's cables were intended for an elite group of decision makers, a group that, informally at least, included William Donovan.

Chapter 12

Berlin, Germany
December 1939

"Do you know what I think?" Kurt asked. The air was cold and dry, the moon peering at them from behind the trees as they walked arm in arm through the darkening Tiergarten.

"You think Jean Harlow is beautiful and sexy?" Maggie teased.

"Yes, that's true," he said, smiling, "but not as beautiful and sexy as you!"

Maggie leaned her head against his shoulder. "That was a very good answer! I think you're more handsome than Clark Gable, too!"

"And far more virile." Kurt grinned, looking at Maggie's red nose and green eyes. It was cold in Berlin. Snow flurries had excited the city the previous evening, and now, on this early Saturday night, Kurt and Maggie were strolling home from the cinema, a full moon casting irregular shadows across their path. "But what I think is that if you quit your job, you could spend more time with me."

Maggie looked up into Kurt's blue eyes. In the dim light, she couldn't read his face, couldn't gauge his seriousness. "Well, darling," she said, casting her eyes back on the walkway before them, "how would

I support myself without a job? A job I really like, by the way." Kurt's thought had taken Maggie by surprise, spoiling the romantic moment in the moonlight. They had double-dated with Thomas and his girl, Lisbeth, who was visiting from Frankfurt. After the movie, *China Seas*, an action adventure starring Gable and Harlow, the couples had gone their separate ways. Now, Maggie was wondering if that had been part of some plan—if Kurt's idea had been the spontaneous result of an afternoon in her company, or if he was attempting to implement some greater design.

Kurt stopped walking and, turning to face her, took hold of Maggie's hand. "I will support you, of course. And you wouldn't have to worry about keeping any schedule except the one I am on."

Maggie's mind was tumbling through thoughts of what her response should be. Her Irish temper was rising, but she didn't want to let it loose on Kurt, not after a pleasant afternoon and ahead of what she hoped could still be a pleasant evening. "Why, darling"—she smiled up at Kurt—"I really love my job. I feel like I'm doing something important, something that supports what you and Thomas and your comrades are fighting for. And," she said, pulling his arm back across hers and turning as though to step off once again, "you've known from the beginning that I won't be a kept woman."

"What are you telling me, Maggie?" Kurt said, refusing to budge. An intense scowl covered his face, deepened by the harsh contrasts of the moon shadows. "What could you ever do that is more important than me? I'm the only reason you're here in Berlin to begin with. Why do you need something else to do? Am I not important enough?"

"Of course you are, Kurt!" Uncertain of where the conversation had come from or where it was heading, Maggie wrapped her arms around him. His greatcoat and her heavy jacket padded their bodies, though, making it difficult for her to reach all the way around. "It's just that you're gone a lot. I'd go crazy sitting around for days, for weeks, waiting on you. I need something to do to tide me over until you come back to me."

Kurt stared away toward the trees, his voice growing bitter. "You *need* to do what I ask of you. You *need* to focus on my needs. Do you not understand that I will soon be back in the field? Do you not understand what that means?"

"Of course I do, darling," Maggie replied, trying to keep her voice calm. She didn't know whether to be angry or frightened. Something in Kurt's tone made her uncomfortable. Suddenly, Kurt exhaled, his breath condensing in the cold night air. Maggie felt him relax.

"Never mind," he said, shaking his head and leaning down to kiss her on the cheek. "We'll speak of this another time. Come on, let's get something hot to drink."

◆ ◆ ◆

Snow was falling the Monday morning before Christmas as Maggie trudged from her apartment toward Broadcasting House. It was still dark outside, and she was again grateful that her walk was short.

Dieter Schmidt greeted her with a cup of coffee as she pushed through the door of English Section's office. Despite rationing, Dieter had been able to keep the office supplied with coffee. "Good morning," he said, smiling.

"Don't you ever sleep?" Maggie asked, removing her gloves and taking the warm mug in both hands.

Dieter's face was smoothly shaved, but dark circles gave his eyes an almost cadaverous appearance. "Not much," he replied, "at least not lately."

"Things seem to have settled down," Maggie said, pausing to take a sip. "Things are quiet in the west, aren't they? Nothing new is happening in Poland, is it? Why can't you get away from here?"

"Your fault, I'm afraid."

"My fault?"

"Yes." Dieter smiled his shy smile. "Minister Goebbels and Direktor Bauer have approved your idea for a music program."

"Oh, Dieter!" Maggie exclaimed, hugging him and spilling coffee across his newspaper. "How wonderful!" She laughed as she picked up the newspaper and drained the coffee off it into a wastebasket. "When do we start?"

Dieter was smiling, clearly enjoying her excitement. "Right away," he replied. "We have to find some musicians, which shouldn't be that complicated. Of course, we have to find some who can play jazz—not only who can play jazz but who are willing to admit it! That may make it a little tougher." He laughed.

"Oh, we can do it!" Maggie was happily pacing back and forth in front of Dieter's desk, still wearing her overcoat.

"Why don't you take off your coat and stay awhile?" Dieter joked. "You can start by outlining what we need by way of personnel to pull this off. We also need to begin to outline our programming philosophy— what we told Bauer, but in more detail. We need to identify a production assistant to work on this. You can help, Maggie, but I still need you to manage Clive."

"Of course," Maggie enthused, grateful to know that Dieter needed her. "I wouldn't want to give up dear Clive. But I'll get started right away on talent and outlining a program. When do we broadcast?"

"Christmas night," he replied. "Seven days from today."

"Gosh!" she sputtered. "We do have to move fast! No wonder you haven't been getting any sleep!"

❖ ❖ ❖

"You *what*?" asked Kurt angrily, his face flushing.

"I have to work. Tonight is the first broadcast of our new music program." Maggie had delayed telling Kurt about her holiday work schedule because she feared just this reaction.

"Well, you can't go! I forbid it!" Kurt snapped. He had been picking up torn pieces of wrapping paper from the floor. "I expect you to be with me on Christmas night."

"Kurt, darling," Maggie began in a pleading tone, "it will only be for two hours. You can come along. It'll be fun!"

"Are you being deliberately stupid?" He was angry, but calm, his blue eyes radiating menace. "I have very few days of leave left before"— Kurt caught himself—"before I have to report back. I intend for us to spend as much of that time together as possible."

"That's what I want, too, darling," Maggie replied, trying to make her voice sound soothing. "But I can't desert my job any more than you can desert yours."

"Tell them you're sick," Kurt directed.

"I can't do that," she replied, fighting to maintain control of her emotions. She had half expected this fight, but hadn't been smart enough to figure out how to avoid it.

"I'll do it for you, then," Kurt snarled, grabbing for his coat. "Where does Dieter What's-His-Name live? Does he have a telephone?"

Maggie put her hands on her hips and raised her chin defiantly. "You'll do nothing of the kind! You do your job, and I'll do my job. I would prefer for you to go with me, Kurt, but get this straight: I am going whether you do or not!"

"Not," replied Kurt, glowering at her. "Good-bye, Maggie." He headed to the door. "Merry Christmas," he said sarcastically as he slammed her apartment door.

Maggie sank into an armchair. She was shaking, and she began to cry. She chastised herself for the foolish way she'd handled the conversation. *You idiot!* she fumed to herself. *What'd you expect him to do? Damn it!*

◆ ◆ ◆

"And now, as a special Christmas treat," intoned Robert Hipps, the host of English Section's new jazz program, "we bring you the golden notes of Charlie Weber and the Swingin' Seven!"

Elise Karlsen and Maggie sat at the control console, watching through the soundproof glass and listening on their headphones as their new band leader led his cohorts through a syncopated rendition of "Mandy Make Up Your Mind." Dieter stood behind them, his hands on the backs of their chairs. Dieter and Maggie had agreed that Elise should be the production assistant for the new program.

In just seven days, with Christmas approaching, the three colleagues had managed to start the music show virtually from scratch. They had worked overtime—even by their standard—to find and employ a jazz band, set up and test a larger studio, and determine how to begin presenting their new musical program. They had settled on Robert Hipps as their emcee for the obvious reason that he spoke native English—and also for the less obvious reason that his American accent would better complement the style of music now beaming its way to Great Britain.

Dieter, Maggie, and Elise had agreed that for this first broadcast, on Christmas night, the music would be featured without propaganda. Their idea was to let Robert introduce each piece, offering some sincere-sounding holiday greetings and pulling their listeners in with a pleasant program they would later feel no guilt for having listened to. Once they built up their audience, they would begin to complement the music with a low-key political message.

As Weber and his team swung into "Dinah," Dieter leaned forward and said, "So far, so good. Robert is doing a nice job of letting the music be the focus." Maggie nodded her agreement. She was still tense from the blowup with Kurt. Her desire for a successful debut for the Swingin' Seven had only added to her anxiety.

As nine thirty approached, an hour earlier in London, Charlie and the band launched into their final selection, "Black and Blue." Robert stepped up to the microphone and said, "From Berlin, this has been

Charlie Weber and the Swingin' Seven wishing you a Happy Christmas! Join us again tomorrow night for another program of swinging jazz!" Elise watched the big clock on the wall as the second hand stepped its way up toward the twelve. At five seconds to the bottom of the hour, Elise slowly dialed the volume to zero, and the music disappeared.

Maggie flicked on the intercom to the studio where Charlie and his boys were winding down. "Well done, everyone! I predict we will have a very popular program on our hands. The English won't hear anything like that on the BBC. Robert—she paused as Robert looked her way through the thick glass—"just the right tone! Good job!" Robert smiled and waved. Maggie switched the intercom off.

Dieter bent low over Maggie's shoulder as she watched the musicians put their instruments away. "Are you OK, Maggie?" he whispered. "You seem distracted."

"Hmmm? Oh, no, I'm fine."

"Well, good job, Maggie. We never could have pulled this off so quickly without your hard work. Thanks."

Maggie's eyes began to tear up and she turned away from Dieter while muttering, "Thanks." How could she go from being chewed out by Kurt to being thanked by Dieter in just a few hours? Maggie gathered up her folder containing the outline of the broadcast and collected her overcoat and purse. She gave Dieter and Elise a quick smile and said good night, then headed upstairs, across the courtyard, and out into the cold night air.

As Maggie crunched through the frozen crust of snow on the sidewalk, she noticed a figure sitting on the steps of her apartment building. She slowed her steps, keeping her head down to watch for slippery spots and glancing up every few seconds. When she was a few feet away, the figure stood. It was Kurt.

"How did it go?" he asked.

"Fine," she said flatly. "It was fine."

"Maggie," he began tenuously, "I'm sorry for the way I acted this morning." He was looking down, pushing his right foot back and forth in the snow. "I'm afraid I ruined your Christmas." He paused. "I know I ruined mine. Please forgive me," he pleaded.

"Oh, Kurt." Maggie melted and threw her arms around him.

He kissed the top of her head. "It's just that I love you so much, Maggie, and I get to be with you so little. I don't want to miss any chance I have to be with you. You're the most important thing in my life. Sometimes I let selfishness overcome me. I'm sorry."

Maggie took him by his gloved hand and with her other hand reached into her pocket for her key. Inside the building it was uncommonly warm. Berliners had gotten used to low heat or no heat, but for this Christmas Day, the authorities had allowed heat all day long. In her apartment, Maggie faced Kurt and took his red cheeks in her hands. She kissed him once, then again. He wrapped his powerful arms around her and pulled her close.

There, Maggie thought. *It isn't such a bad Christmas, after all.*

CHAPTER 13

Berlin, Germany
March 1940

"I saw something interesting the other day," Erich Greinke said, flicking the ash off the end of his cigarette. He was seated in Chesney Nutt's favorite booth in the Adlon Hotel bar sharing drinks with the newsman.

"What would that be, buddy boy?" Ches asked, blowing smoke rings from his own cigarette.

"I was on my way to visit a friend—"

"Male or female?"

"Doesn't make any difference to the story."

"I'm a professional, Erich," Ches explained in his relaxed drawl. "I'll determine whether it makes a difference or not."

"OK, female. Anyway, I'm walking past the Hauptbahnhof and I walk right into a group of soldiers."

"You don't say!" Ches sat up and leaned forward. "A group of soldiers in a train station here in Berlin? Do you think it might have something to do with the war?"

"Shut up and listen!" Erich said, taking a sip from his drink. "I start talking to some of these boys, and find out where they're from. Guess where."

"Atlanta?"

"No, dammit! For a newspaperman, you don't seem to be very interested in this story."

"All right, all right. Where were they from?"

"Innsbruck, Kitzbühel, and a couple of other places down in the Tyrolean Alps."

"Interesting." Ches leaned back and put his thumb up under his lip. "Why would you have alpine troops in Berlin?"

"Exactly what I was wondering," Erich agreed. "So, here's the other thing. You remember Elise, the girl from Norway?"

"The pretty little thing with the big . . . eyes?"

"Right. That's the female person I was going to visit. Well, she tells me she's gotten a new assignment and that she's going away for a while, but she can't say where or for how long."

Ches stubbed out his cigarette. "And you think there might be a connection? That's mighty tenuous."

"I admit, it could be just a coincidence, but maybe it's not."

"But if they're traveling from Austria through Berlin, they're obviously heading north."

"That's why I like talking things over with you, Ches. You have such an astute grasp of geography."

"Quiet, buddy boy!" Ches growled. "Let me think. Going north. Where do you have mountains north of here? Where would you employ mountain troops?" Ches mashed out his cigarette, his lips pursed. He fixed his gaze on Erich and said, "Norway."

◆ ◆ ◆

"And so now, in the midst of a war, we have our most popular program ever!" Herr Direktor Bauer gushed as he pumped Dieter's hand. "I must congratulate you both!" he said, leaning forward to kiss Maggie's cheek. "The minister personally asked me to convey his appreciation to you for your good work!" Bauer was beaming. The music program had been an instant hit—and with the very audience English Section had been hoping to reach: younger men and women, those who had been called up in Britain's general mobilization. British audiences were still tuning in to standard BBC fare like *Band Waggon* and *It's That Man Again*, but now they were also listening to Charlie Weber and the Swingin' Seven every evening. The contemporary jazz music was attracting English listeners who could find nothing like it on the BBC. "Please also congratulate your colleague Fräulein Karlsen," Bauer said, smiling as he ushered Maggie to the door of his office. "Thank you, my dear, and keep up the good work!"

Maggie found herself alone in the waiting area. Dieter had remained inside Bauer's office. Maggie returned to English Section, stopping along the corridor to look in on Clive. He was seated behind his desk, wearing his gold dressing gown and holding a glass of gin.

"Hello, my dear!" Clive boomed as Maggie entered his private office. "I understand congratulations are in order! You have scored a rare triumph in the propaganda wars!"

"Why rare, dear?"

"Rare in that you have, so far, received credit where credit is due!" Clive explained. "All too often these petty tyrants around here, like bureaucrats everywhere, suck up all the credit for themselves when a project is successful. I understand your jazz program is the buzz of London!"

"Where do you get your information, dear?" Maggie asked, pleased with Clive's generous praise.

"I still get the *Times*," Clive said. "It's just a day later than it used to be. It now comes from Copenhagen. Neutrality has its advantages, I daresay. Promise me, Maggie, that you won't forsake me even in light of your triumph," he pleaded with mock self-pity.

"Never, darling! Why, you and I are a team. We'd never let each other down, right?"

"Yes! Too right!" Clive boomed.

Maggie smiled and ducked back out into the corridor.

"It looks like we're going to have to find another production assistant for the jazz show," Dieter said, overtaking her from behind. "Bauer is reassigning Elise to a new project."

"What project?" Maggie asked, disappointment in her voice. Elise had been a fundamental part of getting Charlie Weber and the Swingin' Seven from a concept on paper to being one of England's more popular radio programs.

"He didn't say. I didn't ask. I didn't want him to pull rank on me and tell me I had no need to know. I hate that kind of stuff."

◆ ◆ ◆

Easter came early in 1940. Kurt finagled a weekend pass, and though the weather still felt like March—cold and gray—the holiday brought people out to Berlin's parks and lakes. The government allotted a meager ration of candy for the holiday and doubled the weekly ration of eggs, from one per person to two. The holiday weekend coincided with a metal drive. Officials went from house to house on Saturday collecting copper, bronze, nickel, tin, and other metals. Batteries from nonessential private automobiles were confiscated by the army.

"This is my favorite part," Maggie said to Kurt as she snuggled closer to him beneath the blanket. The temperature in her apartment rarely exceeded fifty degrees Fahrenheit, and on truly cold days it would fall much lower. They had enjoyed a simple supper with Thomas and Lisbeth at a neighborhood restaurant, each of them presenting their ration cards. Eating out was no longer the treat it had once been. Menu choices were few, and portions were skimpy. The only real advantage, so Lisbeth said, was that someone else did the cooking and cleaning up.

Maggie and Kurt had returned to her apartment after supper. They had listened on Maggie's radio to a program of classical music performed live by Berlin's Philharmonic Orchestra; then they had made love. "It's starting to feel like there's really a war on," Maggie whispered.

"Why do you say that?" Kurt responded sleepily.

"Well, we don't get much to eat, we don't have any heat, there's only a handful of Easter candy."

"Don't worry," Kurt mumbled. "Soon it will be over."

"What's going to happen?" Maggie asked, turning her face toward his. But Kurt only answered with a snore.

◆ ◆ ◆

"Well," Dieter Schmidt said on Wednesday, April 10, "I guess now we know what Elise's new assignment is." The morning's newspapers were spread out on his desk, their headlines trumpeting Germany's successful invasion of Norway. "She must have been sent into Norway to help establish ministry control over the existing radio network there." Maggie scanned the newspaper articles and quickly identified the line to take in English Section's broadcasts that night.

"Why Norway?" Maggie asked. "I understood bringing ethnic Germans back into the Reich, but surely that doesn't apply here."

"You're right. The issue here is quite a bit different," Dieter explained. "According to the foreign ministry, the English were planning their own invasion of Norway. They intended to deprive us of key minerals and ore, materials we need to keep our industries running. And that's the story we need to tell to counter the British propaganda that will no doubt color our expedition as aggressive."

◆ ◆ ◆

"It's simply a question of free trade," Maggie explained to the team during their afternoon conference. "The British were threatening to interfere with the free exchange of goods between Germany and Norway, goods that were bought and paid for through legitimate commercial transactions . . ."

"Transactions not unlike those that built the British Empire into the power of the world," Lord Lyon explained that night during his broadcast. "What Englishman, raised on the legends of Drake and Nelson and nourished by the tales of their bravery to secure England's vital sea trade, what Englishman could doubt that the German government has the same right—nay, responsibility—to afford to its commerce an equal level of protection? Who would argue that Germany should accept the status of a second-class power? Who would contend that overseas trade is a right for Great Britain, but not for Germany? No freethinking citizen of the world!" Lyon answered his own query. "The German people do not want war. Their Führer does not want war. But Herr Hitler will not allow the greater German Reich to be squeezed by Britain, France, or any nation that simply desires to monopolize commerce. Germany is destined to lead Europe. Our neighbors to the west would do well to accept this. This . . . is Lord Lyon in Berlin. Good night! God save the King!"

"I thought his closing was a little stronger than usual," Dieter said, switching off the on-air light and disconnecting his headphones.

"That's what Herr Direktor Bauer demanded," Maggie explained, removing her own headset and smoothing out her hair. "I hope it came across all right in London."

"I hope it came across all right with Clive," Dieter said, nodding toward the glass panel separating the control room from the recording studio. Clive was still sitting at the microphone, his large head leaned forward so that his multiple chins had piled up on themselves like so many sausages. His eyes were half-closed, his thick hands resting on the desk.

"I'll go get him," Maggie said, standing and straightening her skirt. "He seemed OK earlier." She worked her way through the crowded control room. Other English-language programs, as well as those in

French, Spanish, Italian, Norwegian, and other European tongues, were still underway. Bauer's Broadcasting Division had grown to an around-the-clock operation with programming targeted at the world's great population centers. The early-evening hours, Berlin time, were still the division's busiest as its broadcasters sought to influence popular opinion in the other capitals of Europe.

Maggie rapped gently on the door to the studio and opened it. She stepped to the edge of the small desk occupied by the large man. "Clive, dear," she said softly, "are you all right?"

"No," he whispered.

"What's wrong, dear?"

"It's done, Maggie," he said quietly. "We've failed. Despite our sincere efforts, we've failed to prevent this war. Now it's really happening. We're not talking about godforsaken Poland. Now we're talking about Norway. Next maybe it will be Sweden. Then maybe France." Clive's voice had grown thick; he was having trouble speaking, tears had formed in his eyes. "One day, it will be England. Already our navies are fighting on the seas. We failed. The slaughter this time will be ruinous, ruinous. No one will survive." His voice trailed off.

"Now, Clive," Maggie consoled him, kneeling beside the desk and taking his beefy hand in hers. "No giving up, now!" She smiled. "My dear old dad always says you're never beat till you quit! And we're not quitters, you and I, are we?"

Clive turned his oversize head toward her and blinked back his tears. "Thank you, my dear." He struggled to his feet and extended his arm, which Maggie took. "Perhaps we'd both feel better after a nightcap," he said as they made their way back toward his office.

◆ ◆ ◆

Clive talked Maggie into accompanying him back to the Adlon. The capital remained blacked out, although a sliver of the new moon did its best to illuminate the cool darkness. Maggie and Clive exited their train at Unter den Linden station and made their way in the darkness to the Adlon.

The ubiquitous Georg brought them their drinks and bowed his greeting.

"You're really worried, aren't you, dear?" Maggie asked as Clive stared at his gin and tonic. He had been morosely silent on the train.

"All I've worked for since the end of the Great War, it all seems for naught. Chamberlain and"—he lowered his voice—"Hitler have completely bollixed things!" He leaned his massive body forward, his belly straining against their table. "I am beginning to wonder about Herr Hitler's sanity," he whispered. "If he had stopped with Poland, he might have been able to wait Chamberlain out. As it is, he continues to fling down one gauntlet after another. Chamberlain—for that matter, any British prime minister—had to eventually pick one up!" He took a sip with a shaky hand as he leaned back in his chair.

Maggie had started to take a sip, but now she set her glass back on the table. "You think there's no turning back now, then?"

Clive glanced around the room. It was late, and no one was seated near them. Georg was busy washing glasses, the radio over the bar was playing Strauss waltzes, and a low fog of cigarette smoke was hanging just below the ceiling. "My God, of course there's no turning back! In Poland, it was just the Germans against the Poles. Despite all the war talk from London, there was no way Britain or France could do much to influence events. Over the winter, things died down; no one really wanted to fight. Here Germany and France share a border two hundred miles long, but how much fighting has there actually been? Practically none! Yes, there were ethnic Germans in Czechoslovakia and in Poland. Do you know how many ethnic Germans live in Norway?" Clive was speaking rapidly, his eyes darting about the dimmed room as if checking for eavesdroppers. "None! So now Hitler goes and drags the Royal

Navy into it!" With his shaky hand, Clive drained his glass. "There's no turning back now. He's managed to create a direct conflict with Great Britain."

Maggie felt like she'd been sucker punched. She stared into her drink. She'd believed the Germans were acting honorably in attempting to protect ethnic Germans on the other side of their eastern borders. She believed she had been a valued accomplice in Clive's sincere efforts to preserve the peace. But Clive's blunt assessment of the Norwegian invasion was shaking her views right down to their foundations.

"Are you telling me you don't believe the British were planning their own invasion?" Maggie asked, sipping her whiskey and looking back at her colleague.

"I'm telling you it no longer matters. Hitler has now forced the British to fight. Whether they and the French would have shed blood over Poland is now moot. The die is cast." A sheen of perspiration covered Clive's forehead. His eyes were red.

"I'm worried about you, dear," she said.

"You should worry about all of us, Maggie. If you will excuse me." Clive pushed himself away from the table. "I will bid you good night."

Maggie buttoned up her coat and stepped off the curb, heading back toward the station. She was tired, and she was beginning to worry about not only Clive but also whether she'd been deceiving herself along with English Section's listeners. Did her good intentions balance the disastrous results? She was also worried about Kurt, hoping he wasn't somewhere in snowy Norway or on a ship somewhere between the Royal Navy and safety. All she knew was his unit had deployed again; she didn't know to where.

She was also beginning to wonder if she'd made the wrong decision to stay in Berlin. If Clive was right, Hitler seemed to be letting things get out of control.

"Mind some company?" asked a familiar voice as she walked past the US Embassy.

"Hello, Erich." Maggie smiled as Erich Greinke fell in step beside her. "What brings you out on this cool spring night?"

"Just looking for a little fresh air after a day spent watching over the affairs of our native land," he joked. "And here I am with Berlin's most beautiful citizen all to myself! A rather pleasing end to a long day! Hey," he said, shifting to a tone of concern. "You look a little down. Everything OK?"

"OK, I guess," Maggie replied. Then, laughing, she said, "Just don't get too close. I've used up my soap ration already."

"That reminds me," Erich said, reaching into the pocket of his overcoat. "Here." In the darkness he held out a ration card. "A small gift from your government. Unofficially, of course."

Maggie took the card and shoved it into her pocket. "How do you do that, Erich?"

"You just have to know the right people and know how to keep your mouth shut. And you have to have something to trade."

"Well, that lets me out," Maggie said. "I haven't two coins to rub together."

"Oh, you've got something to trade," he said through the darkness.

Maggie felt the fine hair on her neck bristle. "I'm not that kind of girl." She laughed nervously, attempting to strike a light note.

"I'm sorry, Maggie," Erich replied as they continued to walk. "That came out all wrong. I was referring to information. You know a lot about what's going on inside the Broadcasting Division. You know who the decision makers are and what's coming up. You probably know a lot about how the ministry makes decisions, too. Information is pretty valuable in our little world right now."

They walked on a few steps in silence as Maggie weighed her response. "You sound like a spy, Erich."

Erich laughed. "Nothing so dashing. No, our job at the embassy is simply to help President Roosevelt and his lieutenants better understand how the Nazis govern. We collect information and pass it back to Washington. Just like the Germans back in Washington report to Berlin."

"I'm not a spy, Erich. I'm in love with a German soldier, for God's sake. I certainly wouldn't betray him."

Erich stopped walking and laughed again. "I'm sorry, Maggie," he repeated. "I'm doing a terrible job tonight. I would never expect you of all people to do something disloyal to Kurt or Dieter or any of the people you work with. By the way, have you heard from Elise?"

"No. I suspect she's either back in Norway, or soon will be."

"Yeah." Erich rubbed his chin with his gloved hand. "Yeah, you're probably right." They resumed walking. "Listen, I respect the fact that you've worked hard to promote peaceful solutions, Maggie, although I didn't always agree with the way you were doing it. I think the president has the same objective. It seems pretty clear that he's going to run for a third term. He's worked hard to maintain our neutrality, but he also wants to stop the fighting before it goes too far. If we could provide greater insight to how the Nazis are thinking, maybe we could help him step to the table and broker some kind of peace deal." Erich paused. "I would never ask you to share information of a confidential nature. I promise I wouldn't do anything to put you or your job at risk. Well, here we are," Erich said as they reached the stairs leading to the train platform. "And that little gift"—he reached over and patted the pocket where she'd placed the ration card—"it comes with no strings attached. Think about it, OK?"

Maggie nodded.

"Good night then," Erich said, turning to head across the river toward his flat. "I'm glad I ran into you."

Maggie watched Erich recede into the darkness. Could she trust him? Could she trust anyone right now? *Oh, that's right, Maggie girl,* she answered herself. *Why trust a man who keeps giving you extra ration cards—cards with no strings attached.* All he wanted was information he could probably get from reading the newspaper anyway. Why was she suspicious?

Maggie shook her head, trying to clear away the phantom debaters. What was she worried about? The war continued to go well for Germany. No bombs were falling, no enemy armies attacking. *Lighten up, old girl,* she chided herself as she stepped onto the westbound train.

CHAPTER 14

Berlin, Germany
May 1940

The sun was laboring to dry up puddles left by the morning's rain showers. The cool spring air was scented with the fragrance of blooming flowers that spilled out of window boxes decorating the buildings along Unter den Linden. Erich had left his raincoat at the embassy, betting that the rain was over for the day. The warm sun felt comforting on his face as he strolled along the tree-lined boulevard.

"Now, this is the way May is supposed to feel," he announced to Chesney Nutt, who was walking alongside him. The two made an odd pair: Erich, tall, handsome, young; and Ches, short, wiry, wrinkled.

"Reminds me of April on Peachtree Street," Ches agreed.

Erich and Ches arrived at Hansie's lunch counter. Only two patrons were in front of them, both of whom appeared to be office workers from the nearby government buildings. "Quiet around here," Ches muttered through the side of his mouth.

"*Guten Tag*, Hansie," Erich said, stepping forward and resting his elbows on the counter. *"Wie geht's?"*

"Not so good, Herr Greinke." Hansie smiled ruefully. "What for you today?"

"A bratwurst, potato salad, and a beer, please." Erich reached into his pocket and pulled out a Reichsmark coin. "Where are all your customers today?"

"*Ach!* That's why I am not so good," Hansie replied, leaning on the counter from the opposite side. "No business today! And such a pretty day!" He turned his palms up and shrugged.

Erich reached back and pulled Ches forward by the shoulder. "Hansie, meet Herr Nutt. He's a great newspaperman from America."

Hansie shoved his beefy hand across the counter to shake Ches's. "You would like to eat, yes?"

"Yes!" Ches laughed. "I'll have what he's having." He jerked his thumb toward Erich.

Hansie served up bratwursts and beer, checking off Erich's and Ches's ration cards. "Bon appétit!"

They took their food and sat on a bench under a shady linden tree. "I know where his customers are," Ches volunteered, stuffing a bite of the tasty sausage into his mouth. "Some of them, anyway."

"Oh yeah?" Erich licked yellow mustard off his thumb. "Where?"

"Well, a lot of soldiers and ministry of war types that are usually hopping around here have deployed to the west," Ches said, cocking an eye toward Erich.

"You mean they're getting ready to attack? The *Sitzkrieg* is over?" Erich used the popular term the German public had coined to describe the war in which neither the Germans nor their western antagonists had fired more than a few harassing shots. Literally translated, it meant "sitting war," and it rhymed with the German word for "lightning war," *Blitzkrieg*, which had so accurately characterized the German attack on Poland.

"Listen, buddy boy," Ches said as he chewed, "I was out near Dortmund two days ago following up on a rumor coming out of a little town called Bielefeld. The whole place was crawling with soldiers: Wehrmacht and SS both."

"Really? A group of soldiers? Here in Germany?" Erich said, repeating the line Ches had used on him at the Adlon. "Do you think it might have something to do with the war?"

"Shut up and let me finish," Ches growled. "I was following up on a story there in Bielefeld and the place was just covered up. Men, trucks, tanks, artillery: just sitting everywhere. Some of it was hidden in barns, but most of it was pretty much out in the open. You can't hide that many troops and all the support units it takes to feed 'em and supply 'em. They're getting ready to go, buddy boy. You mark my words."

"Go where?"

"West, buddy boy, west. If they go in a straight line, they'll come out in Holland. If they head south, France. But there's just too many of 'em to be an exercise, and they can't keep that many men in the field for long without all hell bustin' loose."

Erich sipped his beer. "Why'd you go to Bielefeld in the first place?"

"I told you: I'm working on a story."

"What's it about?" Erich pressed.

"Too soon to say, buddy boy." Ches shook his head. "It's dark, though, if it's true. I've still got some work to do. If I turn anything up, I'll let you know."

◆ ◆ ◆

There was still a glow in the western sky, although the sun had set. Erich leaned against a useless streetlamp on the corner of the Kaiserdamm and Soorstraße. He hoped to intercept Maggie on her way home. It was nine thirty and he was tired, but he judged it would be worth his effort if he could talk to her, if only for a minute.

After another fifteen minutes, Erich discerned a familiar figure crossing the boulevard. Even in the near darkness, he could make out

Maggie's figure and confident stride as her open raincoat flapped in the breeze. He straightened up at her approach.

"Maggie!" he called as she stepped up onto the sidewalk. Hearing her name brought Maggie to a halt. She glanced toward him, then seemed to relax when she realized it was Erich.

"You startled me!" she said, exhaling.

"Sorry," he said, smiling as he walked over to her. "I didn't mean to scare you. I have some information for you. Ches says that Kurt's unit has deployed to the west. He says an attack is imminent."

"Oh God," she groaned, looking away.

"I just thought you'd want to know, Maggie," Erich said, keeping his hands in his pockets. "I'm sure it's hard for you not to know where he is or what he's doing."

Maggie looked back at Erich. He could see tears in her eyes. "Thank you, Erich," she whispered.

"Yeah, well, we have to stick together," he said. "You'll be all right?"

"Yes," she said with more conviction than she felt. "Let me know if you hear anything else, will you?"

"Sure, sure." Erich nodded in the darkness. "You do the same, OK?"

They didn't have to wait long for news.

The blow fell in the west on Friday morning, May 10. Hitler's forces rolled into the Netherlands, Luxembourg, and Belgium, overwhelming the smaller countries with coordinated attacks by armor and infantry formations supported by artillery and aircraft. Ches's information had proved correct. The Germans had moved west, hoping to swing through the rather lightly defended Low Countries and then pivot to the south, behind France's renowned Maginot Line of defensive fortifications.

Ches had joined a pool of foreign reporters being escorted toward the front by officials of the foreign ministry's press office. Erich was making the rounds of his contacts, starting with the foreign press corps and working his way back through more informal contacts like lunch counter owners and ambassadors' drivers. Despite the breaking news, Berlin's residents seemed calm. But not everyone was handling the news so well.

"I've already stolen two open bottles from his office," Maggie hissed to Dieter through gritted teeth. "I swear, if I don't check him every five minutes, there's no telling what condition he'll get himself into!"

Dieter listened. He'd had his share of challenges keeping Clive Barnes sober and on-air ready. "I'm sure you will handle it with your usual skill and aplomb, Maggie," he said, trying to stifle a smile. He hoped Maggie hadn't noticed how much he was enjoying her annoyance. "Here," he said quickly, trying to move the conversation back to the business of their evening broadcasts. He shoved a typewritten piece of paper toward Maggie. She stopped pacing and took it, standing with her other hand on her hip.

"Self-defense?" she asked, looking up at Dieter. "That seems pretty thin, doesn't it? I mean, Germany really isn't threatened by Luxembourg, is it?"

"Maggie," Dieter said, peering at his colleague from under arched eyebrows, "it's not like you to question the direction we're given from the ministry. Nor is it a wise course of action."

Maggie bit her lip. "It's just that in the past, I guess I could always rationalize what we were being told. It always made sense on some level. But this . . ." Her voice trailed away.

"This is no different," Dieter said, moving around his desk to stand beside her. "This is the same. Hey," he said, placing a friendly hand on her shoulder, "look at me. I know you're worried about Kurt, but this is self-defense, really. Why should our troops sit and wait and give the English and the French the initiative? The English have been sending troops over for months, and the French army was already in the field. It's better if we're calling the shots, not our enemies. It was only a matter of time until they attacked us. You see? This really is self-defense."

"The Dutch, Dieter? The Belgians?"

"It's a war, Maggie. What can I tell you? Bad things happen. It's better than being defeated, I can tell you that." Dieter gently patted her shoulder. "Better get back to Clive. Lord Lyon needs to be on the top of his game tonight. He's got to be sincere, logical, and likeable. We don't have to persuade, necessarily, but we must keep the English listening. And the Americans, too."

Maggie stood still, staring at the sheet of paper in her hands, the warmth of Dieter's hand on her shoulder moderating her doubts. "Of course. You're right." She forced a smile. "I'll start working up something for Clive."

Maggie returned to Clive's office with the ministry's guidance in her hands. Clive was seated behind his desk.

"There you are," he said as she entered. "Be a dear and hand me that pitcher of water, will you?" Clive pointed to a pitcher on the small side table.

Maggie grabbed it and set it squarely in front of the big man. "All right, dear," she said, pointing to the pitcher. "Stick to that for the rest of the afternoon. We have to get things just right for tonight!"

Clive smiled and nodded, filling his glass. "As you say, Maggie."

It was not until after the staff conference on that momentous day that Maggie realized she'd been duped. The pitcher of "water" wasn't water at all. Clive had decanted a full bottle of gin into the container between Maggie's visits to his office. As she worked away trying to write a script that wouldn't make them all look like bald-faced liars, Clive had worked away at completely numbing his mind—and perhaps his conscience. By the time Maggie figured out his game, Clive was barely coherent.

"Dieter!" Maggie said, panting, having run the long corridor from Clive's den to English Section's office. "I need help! He's been sucking down gin all afternoon right under my nose, the fat old bastard!"

Dieter would have laughed, but he quickly and correctly determined that Maggie's anger was real, and he was determined to stay in her good graces, if possible. He followed her back to Clive's office. Sitting on the edge of Clive's desk was the nearly empty pitcher.

"I have a little coffee left," Dieter said. "I'll get it while you try to wake him up."

"What do you suggest?" Maggie asked, her arms crossed and an angry frown on her face.

"Cold water!" Dieter replied, stepping back into the hallway.

He returned just in time to see Clive sputtering and spitting, his head and shoulders dripping wet. "Damn, damn, damn!" Clive's voice increased in volume with each word. "What are you doing!" he shouted to no one in particular, his eyes squeezed tightly shut.

"We're getting you ready for your broadcast, Clive!" Dieter snapped, grabbing a towel from the hook on the back of the door. He had almost reached Clive when Maggie let fly with another cascade of cold water. Dieter jumped back. Clive gasped and started, his chair creaking at the sudden shifting of his mass.

"What the hell are you doing?" he boomed.

Dieter took a step forward, then thought to look over his shoulder at Maggie. She was unarmed, having emptied both her fire buckets on her obese colleague, a smile of grim satisfaction now in residence on her face.

"Come on now, Clive," Dieter said, toweling off the big man's shoulders and head. "We've got to get you up and moving. Here," he said, shoving a cup of hot, black coffee into Clive's hand. "Drink up!"

Clive cracked his eyes open. *"Owww!"* he wailed as the light assaulted his pupils. He slammed his eyelids closed again. *"Agggh!"* He retched as the coffee attacked his taste buds. He set the mug unsteadily down, sloshing its contents onto his desk. "What are you doing to me?" he cried.

Dieter motioned to Maggie to come around to Clive's other side. Together they began to lift the big man, trying to bring him to his feet. Clive whimpered, but finally he stood, extending his arms in an effort to maintain his balance. "Stand still, you two!" he commanded. Dieter and Maggie exchanged worried looks. He took an unsteady step toward Dieter, his left hand planted on his desktop to provide balance. "Get me my jacket," he ordered. Maggie stepped across the room to the coatrack and then held the jacket up behind him, helping force his trunklike arms through its limp sleeves. "I think I shall forgo my necktie this evening," Clive slurred as he reached for the door handle—and missed. Dieter yanked it open.

"Grab the script," Dieter said to Maggie as he wedged his shoulder up under Clive's arm. Dieter pulled and tugged Clive through the doorway. He glanced at his watch. They had only fifteen minutes before airtime and still had to maneuver through the corridor, down the stairs, across the courtyard, into the basement, and through the control area to the broadcasting studio. Dieter was beginning to wonder if they would make it when Maggie, script in hand, grabbed Clive by his other arm and began supporting him as Dieter steered.

The stairs were tricky, but when they got outside to the courtyard, the fresh air seemed to jolt Clive awake. He began to walk more steadily, as if the evening air helped clear his senses.

"How're you feeling, Clive?" Dieter asked, panting and sweating as he continued to pull his colleague along.

"I'm very tired, Dieter," Clive said, slurring his words. "So good of you to help."

"Hurry!" Maggie called, holding the door to the basement open. "We're cutting it really close!"

Down the steps the ungainly trio made its way. "Maggie, take Clive into the studio and get him ready," Dieter panted. "I'll get things set up at the control console."

Maggie nodded, shifting her shoulder up under Clive's armpit. "Come on, Clive," she said, "just a little bit farther." With her free hand, she reached out and pulled open the door to the small broadcasting booth. The clock on the wall indicated two minutes until airtime. She pulled Clive through the door and shoved him toward the chair. On the other side of the glass, she could see Dieter adjusting dials and pulling on his headphones. Dieter caught her eye and motioned to his watch. He held up his index finger: one minute.

Maggie guided Clive into the chair. She pulled the script out of her pocket and smoothed it out on the table in front of him. "Ready, Clive?" she asked, her gentle voice masking her tension.

"Ready, old girl," Clive burped with a smile.

Dieter rapped on the glass and with his eyes on the clock, flashed the fingers on his right hand: fifteen seconds. Maggie pulled the microphone over into position so it would capture Lord Lyon's sonorous voice for his audience six hundred miles away, then stepped back, her attention focused on Dieter's raised fingers. They began to fall, one by one, as the second hand approached the top of the hour. Maggie turned toward Clive and watched helplessly as he slowly leaned forward until his forehead hit the table with a dull thud.

He wouldn't be broadcasting tonight. Dieter glanced away from the clock and pointed to Clive. The red light came on.

◆　◆　◆

"Berlin calling . . . Berlin calling . . . Berlin calling . . ." Dieter was on his feet, staring openmouthed into the broadcasting studio. Behind him, at his raised control center, Herr Direktor Bauer was also standing, watching with a mixture of concern and anticipation as Maggie delivered the customary greeting to Lord Lyon's listeners.

"This is—" Maggie hesitated, unsure of how to proceed. Obviously, she wasn't Lord Lyon. In her moment of hesitation, calmness descended upon her. She knelt down by the microphone, next to Clive's massive, unkempt head, and picked up the script. "This is . . . Betty from Berlin, greeting all of my friends across the Channel," she said.

"I'd like to talk tonight to the women of Great Britain," she continued, focused now on the script. Dieter wondered if she would be able to revise it as she talked, to present it from a woman's perspective. "What a heartbreaking day this has been for all of us with loved ones serving in the armed forces! I know you're worried for your husbands, brothers, and fathers, just as we here in Germany are concerned for our loved ones. Let us pray that peacemakers will prevail and that this frightening war can be swiftly halted before we once again find ourselves mired in a horrible, bloody stalemate."

Dieter continued to watch, motionless, as Maggie spoke. She was already off the script, which had centered on the defensive aspect of Germany's attack. "We women," she continued, her voice pleasing, friendly, and intimate rather than deep and sonorous like Clive's, "have an obligation to speak the truth as we see it. And, as will come as no surprise to you, we see it from a much different perspective than our menfolk. For us, truth is found in the laughter of children, the embrace of our husbands, the warmth of our hearth and home. These are the things that matter. Yet these are the very things that are now at risk!"

Dieter sat down slowly. He adjusted the volume on the control panel, amplifying Maggie's gentle voice.

"Our children need their fathers. Our farms need our sons. And we—well, even though we don't always like to admit it—we need our men. We need them to provide for us, to care for us, to help us raise our children. We need them to love us! We need them to come home!

"Women must unite. We must make our voices heard—our voices for peace, our voices for family. Won't you join me for a moment of prayer: Almighty God, ruler of all nations, we beseech thee to soften the hearts of those who seek war, of those who seek to bend others to their will through force. We pray that you, O wise and powerful God, will create wisdom in our leaders and will create in them hearts for peace. Though we acknowledge our differences, Lord, help us find the common ground that binds us together in these hours of fear and darkness. Help us emerge from this night of tragedy into the bright light of your love and a future of peace between our peoples. Guide us to follow the example of Jesus, who said 'blessed are the peacemakers.' Amen.

"Together, let us work for peace. Thank you for listening. I look forward to visiting with you again soon. This is Betty from Berlin, good night."

Wide-eyed, Dieter wound the volume down to nothing and switched off the microphone. He flipped the on-air light off. Maggie, still on her knees, looked up and met his eyes. She smiled meekly, her forehead bathed in perspiration. Dieter switched on the intercom. "Maggie, please come out here."

Maggie disappeared through the door in the rear wall of the studio. She emerged into the control room a few moments later. Bauer and Dieter stood side by side, their faces expressionless.

"I did the best I could under the circumstances," Maggie began, her voice catching.

"My dear," Bauer said softly, taking her hand in his, "you did superbly!" He smiled. Dieter smiled. Maggie smiled, tears forming in her eyes. "Herr Schmidt, I believe Maggie needs a drink. As my presence is needed here for the next several hours, you will please see to it. Maggie," Bauer said, redirecting his attention toward her, "you are indeed an amazing woman!" He bowed slightly and then to Dieter said, "Off with you!"

Dieter gently took Maggie by the arm. "What about Clive?" she asked softly.

"Let him sleep. He'll probably be there until tomorrow morning, anyway. Relax now," Dieter said as they passed through the transmission room and headed back up the stairs. "You're trembling."

"Oh, Dieter, I've never been so frightened in my life! I didn't know what to say!"

Dieter closed the door behind them and pulled aside the blackout curtain. He led Maggie out into the starlit courtyard. "You were incredible, Maggie," he said softly, turning to face her, gripping her hand in his. "You were soothing, gentle, personal. You were all the things that Clive is not, could not be even if he wanted. You are amazing! And you're still trembling," he said, pulling her to him.

Dieter leaned into Maggie and kissed her. To his delight, she kissed him back. "It's not a mistake this time, Maggie," he said, kissing her again.

"No," she replied, losing herself in his embrace.

◆ ◆ ◆

Dieter took his time undressing Maggie. He kissed her lips and worked his way around her, pulling off her coat, then her sweater, then her bra. Standing behind her, he slid his hands up and down her torso while he kissed and nibbled her neck and shoulders.

Maggie spun around. "You're taking too long!" she giggled, causing Dieter to laugh. Facing her, Dieter unclasped her skirt and let it fall to the floor. She rolled off her stockings.

"You're beautiful, Maggie," Dieter gasped softly. He kissed her again, his hands roaming over her breasts as she unbuckled his belt and his trousers. She quickly unbuttoned his white shirt and he pulled it off.

"Um, Dieter," Maggie began, "do you have a bed in your apartment?"

He laughed and took her by the hand. Dieter was gentler and more patient than Kurt. He attended to Maggie's pleasure first before yielding to his own desire.

"I have a confession to make," he said afterward. "I've been in love with you since the first month you came to Broadcasting House. I thought that first day, when Bauer brought you to our office, that I would never be able to concentrate on my work with someone as beautiful as you around. But then I saw how you jumped in, even on that first day. I saw how you earned everyone's respect through your competence and your pleasant manner." Dieter laughed again, a sound Maggie found so comforting. "And how you managed Clive! Even if I was permanently distracted by your looks, it was worth it to see you handle Clive. You're like a circus trainer with her elephant!"

Maggie rested her head on Dieter's shoulder, her left arm across his lean body. "Oh, you're just saying that because it's true," she giggled.

The war was completely out of her mind now. She was relaxed and at peace in Dieter's embrace.

"I love you, Maggie," he said, kissing her on the forehead.

The Mercedes touring car moved slowly along the Kaiserdamm, heading toward the center of the city. Maggie couldn't remember her last trip in an automobile. The batteries of most private cars had been confiscated for military use, leaving the wide boulevard free from all but a few army vehicles and the random taxi. The warm morning sunshine beamed down on her, the fresh air adding to her feeling of contentment. Dieter sat beside her, unobtrusively holding her hand. In the front seat, next to the driver, sat Herr Direktor Bauer. The Netherlands had surrendered within five days of the German invasion. The Belgians, French, and

British were reeling before the German *Blitzkrieg*. And Maggie was on her way to the Ministry of Public Enlightenment and Propaganda for an interview with the minister himself, Joseph Goebbels.

Maggie had been an instant hit. Her spontaneous substitution for Lord Lyon had touched a nerve with the English, particularly with English women. Listenership, impossible to measure from Berlin, had been widely reported in the London papers, including the *Times*. Subsequent, scripted talks had also been well received: Maggie's talks differed from the propaganda the English had become accustomed to. Rather than representing the official position of the Nazi government, Maggie seemed to strike a more informal, personal tone with her listeners. According to the newspapers, which were received through still neutral Denmark or Switzerland, Maggie had enjoyed a rapid ascent of popularity, surpassing even Lord Lyon himself.

"When we arrive"—Dieter leaned over and spoke quietly as the car continued toward the Brandenburg Gate—"our driver will hold the door first for Herr Direktor, then for you. Wait until he opens it before you stand up. We'll go into the ministry through the Wilhelmstraße entrance and will be escorted to the minister's chambers. He will be happy to see you, the newest star in the foreign broadcasting constellation." Dieter grinned. "It's usually best to let him initiate and direct the conversation. He can be charming, but he can also attack with wicked sarcasm."

"I'll be fine, Dieter," Maggie said, taking a deep breath of the fresh air and enjoying the luxury of riding through the Tiergarten in an open car. "Minister Goebbels was quite the gentleman when I met him the first time." Maggie recalled her minor triumph over Clive's profile in the *Atlanta Journal*.

"Yes, well," Dieter continued in a whisper, "just make sure he remains a gentleman!"

The car pulled up in front of the stately Ordenspalais, a sturdy structure with a peaked tile roof that dated back to the 1730s. Maggie's party was met at the car by an aide who escorted them into the building and down the ornate corridor to the minister's private suite of offices.

A secretary in Goebbels's outer office stood as Maggie, Dieter, and Bauer entered. He bowed and greeted them, ushering them to seats and inquiring if they would like coffee. Goebbels had the reputation for keeping his guests waiting. It had the effect of heightening their anticipation. After fifteen minutes of waiting and sipping coffee, the massive wooden door to Goebbels's inner office swung open, and a different secretary approached.

"Herr Direktor." He bowed his head to Bauer. "Herr Schmidt, Fräulein O'Dea. If you please, the minister will see you now." He turned on the thick carpet and led them into Goebbels's lair.

The office was huge. A massive desk, trimmed in red leather, sat opposite a large fireplace. In the chair, speaking rapidly into a telephone, was Joseph Goebbels. A larger-than-life portrait of Hitler gazed over the minister's shoulder. Goebbels stood, nodding to his visitors. Still talking into the handset, he waved the trio toward heavy, red leather chairs arrayed in a semicircle in front of his desk. *"Ja!"* he said. "Heil Hitler!" He returned the phone to its cradle.

Goebbels's aristocratic face was split by a wide smile. "So, we meet again, Maggie!" he said as he limped from behind his desk. "How pleasant to see you!" He took her hand and lifted it gracefully to his lips. He turned his attention next to Bauer, shaking his hand, and then to Dieter. "Please, sit, sit!" he said, waving toward the luxurious armchairs.

Goebbels backed up to his desk and leaned on its forward edge. Maggie noticed how neat everything was—from the desktop, with its pads and pencils aligned in neat rows, to Goebbels himself. The minister was wearing a light-brown suit with narrow blue pinstripes over a blue silk shirt and a red necktie. His face was lean, divided by a long, straight nose. He had brown eyes set above high cheekbones and a charming smile.

"Well, Maggie," he said, clapping his hands together, "once again you have represented our ministry with distinction. I simply had to see you again to tell you how impressed we all are and to tell you personally how grateful I am for your good work. Our information from England is that people there, especially women," he added, "are thoroughly enchanted by your forthright views on this unfortunate conflict. You have, I believe, even exceeded the audience of your mentor, Herr Barnes." Goebbels glanced at Bauer, who nodded in confirmation. "How delightful!" Goebbels was almost gleeful with this latest victory of his propaganda machine. "Tell me how you felt when you were thrust into the breach, as they say."

"Well, Herr Minister," Maggie answered, attempting to keep the nervousness from her voice, "I didn't feel I could come across very believably by reading Clive's script. I had no rapport with the audience. I thought the best thing to do was to simply say what was in my heart. It seems to have worked."

"*Wunderbar!*" Goebbels gloated. "I was with the Führer last night, and I shared with him your successes, first with the newspaper article and now with your radio broadcasts. Do you know what he said to me?"

Maggie shook her head. "No, Herr Minister."

"He said we must continue to sensitively present the facts to the English people, whom he greatly respects. He was fascinated by your approach, and he encouraged me to encourage you!"

"Thank you, Herr Minister," Maggie replied, though she couldn't deny that her satisfaction in the skillful performance of her job was being undermined by her growing doubts in the German cause. But what was she supposed to *do* with such doubts? Walk away from her position? Leave Germany—and the man she loved? And based upon what? What did she really *know* about what was happening outside of her bubble in the ministry? It seemed to Maggie that the best thing to do was hope that the pace of events slowed, that peace could somehow, against all odds, be regained. She wished that didn't feel like such a flimsy hope.

"Now, Maggie," Goebbels said as he stood and walked around his desk, "I must ask one small favor, may I?" He reached for the switch on his intercom.

"Of course, Herr Minister."

"If you will indulge me, I would like our photographer to take our picture!" He flipped the switch and ordered in the photographer, who had obviously been waiting just beyond the great office doors. After several shots of Maggie with Goebbels, with Goebbels and Bauer, and then with Goebbels, Bauer, and Dieter, the minister brought the interview to a close.

"Thank you, my dear, for visiting with me today! Perhaps you will join us again some evening for a more relaxed visit. In the meantime," Goebbels said, holding Maggie's hand and guiding her toward the door, "please keep up the excellent work you are doing. Our troops are enjoying great success on the battlefront. We can hasten their victory through the continued, skillful application of our message." Goebbels bowed and stepped back into his office, the huge doors swinging closed as if pushed by some invisible hand.

Maggie exhaled. "Wow!" she said, her doubts momentarily suppressed. "Sometimes you get so caught up in your work that you don't realize the impact you have."

◆ ◆ ◆

Erich Greinke sat in his embassy office, his cigarette's blue smoke drifting out the open window into the pleasant May afternoon. He stared at the picture on page four of the *Völkischer Beobachter*, the Nazi party's daily newspaper. In the picture, Propaganda Minister Goebbels was smiling broadly and shaking hands with a lovely young lady while two other smiling men looked on. The accompanying article presented an embellished account of Maggie's brilliant and extemporaneous substitution for Lord Lyon, whom the story reported had become ill only moments before his scheduled broadcast. According to the paper, Maggie's impromptu debut had been so successful that she was now broadcasting to England on a regular schedule. Fortunately, the article continued, Lord Lyon had sufficiently recovered to return to his regular broadcasting schedule as well.

Erich's eyes shifted from Maggie's happy face to Goebbels's and back. He whistled softly. "Careful, Maggie girl. Be very careful."

◆ ◆ ◆

"I have to ask you a question, Maggie," Dieter said, staring at the ceiling. "I'm sorry to be so insecure, but what happens to us when Kurt comes back?" Dieter felt Maggie's body tense as the words fell from his mouth. He had fallen hard for Maggie, had in fact been falling for her these many months. Yet he was worried that the attraction might be more one-sided than he would like.

"Oh God!" Maggie pulled her hands from under the sheet and rubbed her eyes. "I don't know . . ."

"Listen, I know I'm not like Kurt," Dieter began. "He's more athletic, stronger . . ."

"But he's not you, darling!" Maggie interrupted, turning to face Dieter and laying her finger across his lips. "Kurt is—was—wonderful in his own way. But with you, it's different! There's a depth to my feelings for you that goes beyond what Kurt and I shared. You treat me so tenderly, yet you treat me as an equal. Kurt, as much fun as he was, tended to treat me like a possession."

"I love you, Maggie. Do you know that?" Dieter asked softly. He pulled himself up on his right side, facing her, his head propped up by his hand. With his finger, he gently stroked her cheek. "So, how do we handle Kurt?"

Maggie rolled back over on her back. "I'll handle it," she said. "I'll just have to think of the right way. It has to be done in person. I can't break things off with him in a letter."

"I don't want you to face him alone," Dieter said, stroking her pale shoulder. "I'll be with you."

"Let me think," she replied. "I'll come up with something."

CHAPTER 15

Berlin, Germany
June 1940

By the end of the first week in June, the British Expeditionary Force was encircled at the Channel coast town of Dunkirk. The collapse and surrender of the Belgians had compromised the British flank, allowing General Heinz Guderian's XIX Panzer Korps to surround the British and drive them back to the Channel's edge. As the British prepared to evacuate the continent, Goebbels and his staff prepared a shift in the propaganda war—a shift expressed each evening by Broadcasting Division's commentators.

"You know, Betty," Lord Lyon said into his microphone, "the nature of modern war is so vastly different than in the war of 1914–18. The destructive capacity is so much greater, and the speed with which the battles are now joined has enabled German forces to race across the Low Countries and France at a pace that in the past one could only dream of."

Sitting across from Lyon and facing a microphone of her own was Betty from Berlin. English Section was testing a new, less formal format on this night. Lyon and Betty were carrying on a conversation as if between friends—and hoping that many would eavesdrop.

"You're right, Lord Lyon," Betty responded, according to her script. "And I am afraid of the fearful toll that the Battle of France has taken on the brave, but poorly led, boys in the BEF. Once again, we've seen the flower of Great Britain's manhood pitched unprepared onto the continent to fight France's battle."

"And now," said Lord Lyon, picking up the narrative, "we've seen how complex modern war is, especially when dealing with a multinational alliance. Obviously, the British and their French ally were ill prepared for this battle. There was no unity of command, no coordination of action or effort. The result is that our politicians and generals have allowed the burden to fall on the shoulders of our courageous boys once again."

"I'm saddened by the ordeal they've had to endure," Betty responded. "And now they are backed up to the water's edge, under constant artillery fire and air strikes. These brave young men, many of whom were holding hands with their girls or bouncing their children on their knees just six months ago—now they may be killed, maimed, or captured. Oh, but it doesn't have to be this way. If only the mothers, wives, and daughters of Great Britain would rise and take a stand against Mr. Churchill's warmongering friends. If only they would say, 'Stop! Enough is enough!'—why, this foolish war could be brought to a speedy end."

"Yes, Betty, you are right. It is time for people of conscience to stand together. What more have the British people to gain from the ruin and slaughter of our men? France is lost. The continent is lost. Now is the time for rational thinking. Now is the time for peacemakers to step forward. Now is the time for the people to demand peace! This . . . is Lord Lyon in Berlin. Good night. God save the King!"

"Good night," Betty added.

The red light blinked off, and Dieter, observing from the control console, switched on the intercom. "What do you think?" he asked Clive and Maggie. "How did that feel to you?"

Clive looked at Maggie and gestured toward her with his beefy hand. "Ladies first."

"It felt a little stilted to me," Maggie said, glancing between Clive and Dieter. "It didn't feel like a normal conversation."

"I concur, as usual, with my esteemed colleague." Clive smiled. "I'm afraid it sounded just as it was: a scripted conversation."

"Perhaps so," Dieter said, his voice tinny through the speaker. "Maybe we can solve that by going back to talking points rather than scripted responses. And maybe rehearsing a bit more before airtime. At any rate, I think it's good that we continue to employ new formats for presenting our views. As Maggie's number one fan, Minister Goebbels, says, we must present a continued, skillful application of our message." Dieter grinned at Maggie through the glass.

"Why, Dieter," Maggie said with a wink, "I thought you were my number one fan!"

◆ ◆ ◆

Maggie was brooding, sitting in the English Section office poring over the morning's newspapers, haunted by the question Dieter had asked her. How would she break things off with Kurt? How could she, without feeling guilty for having fallen into the arms of another man even as Kurt was on the battlefront? True, Kurt had been different since his return from Poland. He had been more demanding, less considerate of her feelings and her independent nature. When he had wanted something, he had expected Maggie to comply with his wishes, almost as if she were one of his soldiers. Maggie wondered which Kurt would return from France—if he returned at all. The obituary pages in the newspapers had seen an ominous increase in death notices placed by the families of soldiers who had died in service to the Führer or the Fatherland. Maggie continued to light a candle for Kurt at least weekly at Saint Canisius, where she prayed for his safety. But she no longer looked forward to his return. Her relationship with Dieter had blossomed into something far more fulfilling, on an intellectual as well as physical level.

The loud jangle of the telephone startled Maggie from her thoughts. "English Section, Maggie here," she said, holding the black handset to her ear.

"Hello, Maggie? It's Erich. Have you got time for a quick lunch today?"

"I think I can work you in," Maggie replied playfully. "You going to be out my way?"

"Yes, and I know a place where you can get a good lunch on the cheap!"

"Is that all I'm worth, a cheap lunch?"

"Oh, of course not," Erich laughed. "It's just that as a humble civil servant I have to carefully marshal my limited resources for when an equally beautiful, but more available, young lady comes along!"

Maggie laughed and agreed to meet Erich at one o'clock at a small Biergarten in Westend, a short walk from Broadcasting House.

Maggie stepped through the gate of the fenced Biergarten. Picnic tables and benches were lined up in neat rows, most of them occupied by Berliners on their lunch breaks. To her right, she noticed Erich standing and waving to her. Maggie smiled, returning the wave, and threaded her way through the rows of tables to where he stood.

"I see you found it." Erich greeted Maggie with a smile, motioning her to the bench opposite his. "Thanks for meeting me on such short notice."

"Anything for a free lunch," Maggie replied, smiling. "What brings you out west?"

"Just some routine errands." Erich raised his hand for the waiter, and the two placed their orders after showing their ration cards. "You should try the strudel here. It's the best in Berlin!" Erich said as the waiter waddled back to the kitchen. They were seated beneath the shade of a tree, the warm sun casting a mottled shadow on their table. "I came across a couple of interesting pieces of information the other day," Erich said, looking into Maggie's green eyes. "Things I thought you'd like to know."

Maggie leaned forward. "Go ahead."

"First, Ches was on a tour of the battlefield sponsored by the Foreign Office last week. He got as far as Saint-Venant, about thirty miles from Dunkirk, where there had apparently been some pretty heavy fighting. He asked his guide, a fellow who works as a liaison with the army, about Kurt's battalion. The guy said he didn't know anything about individual units, but the next day, he tells Ches that Kurt's unit had been in that same area. He also reported that Kurt was OK. Ches thought you'd like to know."

Maggie felt her stomach flip. She was pleased, but unnerved at the same time. Erich's well-meant message forced her to once again confront her Kurt conundrum. "Please thank Ches for me when you see him," she said, forcing a smile. The return of the plump waiter carrying their food on a tray saved her from further comments about Kurt.

"And the second thing you thought I'd like to know?" Maggie glanced up at Kurt, poking her potato salad with her fork.

Erich took a sip of beer to wash down a mouthful of potatoes. He set his fork down, staring at his plate and then lifting his eyes toward Maggie's. "I was reading the paper the other day and I came across a very interesting picture. It was a picture of a friend of mine with a high-ranking member of the government. She was being recognized for some particularly outstanding work—which I might add is nothing unusual for my friend. She is very talented." Erich dropped his gaze back down to his plate. "Maggie, I hope you know that I admire your independence and your ability. I think I understand the reason for your animosity toward the British"—he smiled at the memory of Maggie's scathing lecture in the park—"but, as your friend, I have to caution you: you're getting much too close to some very bad guys."

Maggie stared at Erich as he pushed his veal around on his plate. "Is this an official or unofficial warning?" she asked.

"Purely personal, Maggie," Erich replied softly. "I like you, and I would hate to see you get so mixed up with these guys that you can't get away. They can be kind of like the Tar Baby in that old story."

Maggie chewed a forkful of potato salad before answering. "Listen, it isn't that I don't appreciate your concern. I do, really. It's just that I don't see this as any big deal. It's pretty much doing what I was doing before, only now I'm doing it on air." Maggie felt the color rising in her cheeks. She was torn between appreciation for Erich's concern, embarrassment at his apparent disapproval, and the gnawing feeling that maybe Erich had a point.

"Yeah," Erich replied. He took another sip of his beer, weighing his words carefully. "It's just that at some point, I think this thing widens. Do you understand what I'm saying?"

"Not really." Maggie put down her fork. "The French are finished, Paris has fallen. What's left of the BEF either sailed across the Channel or got captured at Dunkirk. The Germans have conquered five countries in seventy-five days! Who's left to get into this 'thing,' as you call it?" Maggie was struggling to keep her voice low and even.

"Here's all I'm saying, Maggie." Erich again looked her in the eye. "The Nazis are the aggressors"—he held up his hands, palms facing her—"regardless of the position you take on the radio. Luxembourg, Belgium, the Netherlands—none posed a threat to the Third Reich. They were weak countries that had declared their neutrality. And they got steamrolled. Look at the last two years, Maggie. Austria,

Czechoslovakia, Poland—do you see a pattern here? These guys aren't nice guys. Yes, I like Dieter and Clive Barnes and Elise, wherever she is, but the guys making the decisions aren't nice guys, and I'd hate to see you get too mixed up with them."

"Thank you, Erich," Maggie said, willing herself to stay calm and take another bite. "I think I have shown that I am quite capable of making my own decisions."

Erich smiled. "Indeed you have, Maggie, which is why I felt, as your friend, that I should make sure you had all the facts. Now, having done my friendly duty, let's enjoy the rest of our lunch, shall we?"

It was always this way with Erich: always smiling, friendly, then something she didn't want to hear, something generally unpleasant to think about. Yet she truly believed he was motivated by a genuine concern for her well-being. He was a little too paternal in his advice, but he seemed to trust her to make her own decisions.

"Thank you, Erich," she said after a few minutes.

"You're welcome." He smiled.

Chapter 16

Berlin, Germany
July 1940

"I've never seen anything like it, buddy boy," Chesney Nutt drawled, waving his half-finished cigarette in the air.

He and Erich were seated at a small table in a sidewalk café off the Kurfürstendamm, Berlin's main retail district. It was a Thursday, just past midday, and the newspaperman and his younger friend had just finished lunch. While there were plenty of shoppers in the area, there wasn't much shopping. Nearly everything was rationed and in short supply. In addition, heavy surtaxes to help finance the enormous cost of war left the general public with little more than a subsistence wage.

"I saw more burned-out vehicles and dead horses in a one-mile stretch of road near the French-Belgian border than I saw the whole time I was in Poland," Ches said, exhaling blue smoke. "From what we saw, it looked like the Germans put an old-fashioned ass-whippin' on the Brits and the Frogs."

"Sure," replied Erich, "but didn't you just get to see what they wanted you to see?"

"An astute question," Ches said, cocking his head to the side. "You surprise me," he teased. "But you're right. We only saw what they wanted us to see, for the most part. We had very little freedom of movement outside the group. Still, I've seen battlefields before, and this one looked like a pretty one-sided affair."

"The outcome was certainly one-sided," Erich agreed as a heavyset woman wearing a white blouse and a straw hat adorned with a feather pushed past him to take a seat two tables away. The weather was sunny and warm, and although most of the men in the café and passing by had doffed their jackets, they continued to keep their sleeves down and their ties tight.

"Well, then we went down to Paris. I used to live there, you know." Ches stared off into the distance, remembering. "They drove us right down the Champs-Elysées, and there was the biggest, reddest Nazi flag I ever saw hanging under the Arc de Triomphe. I almost cried, buddy boy, I almost cried."

"Did you get any good stories out of your trip?"

"The usual stuff. Big German victories. Gallant German soldiers. A lot of it was true. But Dr. Goebbels's boys also tried to feed us some crap that seemed a little far-fetched. They were pitching us tales of atrocities by the French. 'Course they didn't have any evidence, just some alleged 'witnesses' who all told the same stories, right down to the color of the bad guys' eyes. I just didn't buy it. Besides, our readers aren't too interested in atrocities by the country that just got the shit kicked out of it by the Nazi war machine. I did get one interesting story, but I can't print it, least not yet," Ches continued.

"Why not?" Erich asked, noticing the fat lady shifting uncomfortably in the warm sun.

Ches mashed out his cigarette and leaned forward. In a quieter voice he said, "Well, I did get one atrocity story that rang true, but it was allegedly perpetrated by the Germans."

"Tell me," Erich said, locking his eyes on Ches's weathered face.

Ches stared down at the remnants of his lunch while he fished in his pocket for another cigarette. Erich pulled out his lighter and lit the smoke for his friend. Ches took a long, deep pull, leaned back in his chair, and stared into the blue sky. "It seems that while the British were awaiting evacuation at Dunkirk, they left some fellows south of there as a rear guard. One of these units got overrun by a German regiment, the Leibstandarte SS Adolf Hitler."

"That's Kurt's regiment," Erich interjected. "You remember, Maggie's friend?"

"I remember Maggie." Ches's eyes twinkled. He exhaled, looking toward the neighboring tables where the fat lady sat staring at the two Americans. He nodded to her and resumed his story. "Well, the Germans capture a bunch of these Tommies and a few French soldiers manning a supply depot nearby. They take them to a farm on the outskirts of a little village called Wormhoudt and shove them all into a little tiny barn. Then the brave German lads throw in about five grenades—boom!" Ches flexed the fingers on both hands to simulate an explosion. "Then they drag out the ones who aren't dead—bang!" He made the shape of a pistol with his thumb and forefinger. "Coup de grâce, right in the head. That kind of stuff gives war a bad name."

Erich had stopped looking around, his attention focused solely on Ches's story. "How many did they kill?"

"About eighty is what I was told."

"Who told you all this?" Erich had seen murders in similar situations in Spain, but never on such a scale, and not between uniformed forces.

"Well, you see, they gave us a tour of a field hospital set up in a French school. The Germans wanted us to see how advanced their medical setup is and how well they're taking care of their wounded. Not coincidentally, they also wanted us to see them taking care of enemy wounded. You know, they wanted that whole humanitarian angle in our dispatches—how they're really the good guys, even though they stomped on their helpless little neighbors. Anyway, I see some British boys in the back of this hospital, but I'm not allowed to talk to them. So, using my flawless German," Ches said with a smile, "I start talking to the medics and orderlies. This is a couple of weeks after the heavy fighting has died down, mind you, so these boys aren't too busy; they're actually kind of bored. And that makes them kind of talkative. One of 'em told me this story."

"C'mon, Ches!" Erich interrupted. "Why would a German tell you a story that makes his comrades out as murderers?"

"Well now, that's two astute questions in one afternoon, Erich. That puts you, let's see"—Ches put his finger to his lips and looked skyward as though he were calculating—"two over your quota." Erich shook his head. "Actually, he told me the story so I would know about the gallant actions of the German soldiers who discovered the survivors. These were Wehrmacht boys, of course, regular army, not the SS thugs. Anyway, they find about fifteen of these guys, all in pretty sorry shape physically. Their medics administer first aid, and then they transport these poor boys to the hospital. It just goes to show that there are still some good Germans—just not in the party."

"And this was the Leibstandarte? Hitler's body guard?"

Ches nodded. "So I'm told."

"Do you know which units were involved in the killings?"

"Second battalion is what I heard."

"Any names?"

"No," Ches answered, shaking his head.

The fat lady, apparently too hot in the July sun, stood and made her way through the maze of tables. She stopped at Ches and Erich's table.

"You are speaking English," she stated in German. Ches and Erich nodded. "You are American?" she asked.

"Yes, ma'am," Ches answered with a friendly smile.

The lady swung her purse in a wide, high arc, slamming it into the side of Ches's head. She began shouting curses as she pulled her arm back for a second swing. The maître d' came running through the tables, nearly tripping over an empty chair as the dumbfounded Ches threw his skinny arms over his head to ward off the blows.

"Meine Dame!" the maître d' shouted, waving his arms and inserting himself between the attacker and her victim. *"Bitte!* These gentlemen are my customers!"

The woman was speaking fast and loud, condemning America and Americans and cursing President Roosevelt. The maître d' managed to arrest her swing. Fighting the flying purse with his left arm, he glanced over his shoulder toward Erich. "Go!" he shouted. Erich reached into his pocket for money and started to drop some coins on the table. The maître d', now with help from another waiter, was pushing the woman away from their table. "No, *mein* Herr! You do not owe anything. Just go!"

Erich shrugged and grabbed Ches by the elbow. "C'mon, let's get out of here," he muttered, keeping an eye on the belligerent woman whose insults chased them out onto the sidewalk. Ches hadn't said a word throughout the attack. "You all right, pal?" Erich asked, placing his hand on the shorter man's shoulder.

"Sure, sure. Just a little startled, that's all. That old bitch was loud, but she didn't really hit that hard." He laughed, smoothing down his rumpled hair. "By the way, Erich, happy Fourth of July!"

◆ ◆ ◆

Erich returned that afternoon to the embassy, where all but a skeleton staff had taken off for the holiday. In the peace and quiet that had descended on the massive old building, he set about composing his regular cable to Mr. Cotton in Washington.

> In addition to widely reported official announcements from the Nazi government condemning the president's pledge to sell war materials to the British and the

French, the general public is beginning to shed its long-standing admiration and affection toward Americans. I personally observed a harmless but ominous attack on an American national at a café today. Other Americans have reported rude treatment from Germans in restaurants, cafés, and bars as well. The average German does not understand why the president is willing to sell surplus munitions to the British. This is, quite naturally, perceived here to be against Germany's interests. Most Germans think it is natural that Germany should be the most powerful continental state and don't understand why others might hold a different view. The relative ease of their recent victory in France has emboldened both Hitler's government and the population at large.

Next Erich reported on military movements he had observed, which had slowed to a trickle. Most forces were still in the field in France, where, no doubt, many would remain on occupation duty. A short update on rationing and the public availability of goods came next. Then Erich dropped in his bombshell. He proceeded to relay the story Ches had told him, adding some additional information from his own records.

Highly reliable source reports German executions of British and French POWs near village of Wormhoudt in France. Source reports atrocities committed by Second Battalion, Leibstandarte SS Adolf Hitler. Battalion commander believed to be Wilhelm Mohnke. Leibstandarte regimental commander is Sepp Dietrich, personally very close to Hitler for many years. Will attempt to obtain fuller accounting of incident as witnesses are identified.

Erich's report of the murders was the first to escape now-occupied Europe.

◆　◆　◆

"Thank you, ladies and gentlemen, for coming today," began Theodore Williams, the embassy's first secretary. "I promise that we will not keep you long, but there are sentiments in play here in Berlin, as well as in other German cities, I'm told, that you simply need to be aware of."

Williams was pacing back and forth in the embassy's formal reception room, the largest room in the building. Nearly two hundred Americans, including Chesney Nutt and Maggie O'Dea, were in the audience, which was seated in neat rows of wooden folding chairs. Many of them were fanning themselves with folded papers, the July weather in the capital warmer than usual. American citizens living in and around Berlin had been invited to attend one of a series of embassy-sponsored briefings on the evolving political situation within Germany.

"Recently," Williams continued, "we have received reports of increasing hostility toward Americans by the German public. We attribute this to German disappointment at some recent statements by President Roosevelt as well as a resurgent nationalism on the part of the general population here." Williams gestured emphatically with his hands as he moved back and forth in the front of the room.

"Although the fighting appears to be over for the time being, we think it is unlikely that the Churchill government will be willing to negotiate any type of peace settlement with the German government. We have no official knowledge, of course, but we think it is possible that parts of Germany may be subject to air attack by the British. For that reason, and to do all that we can to ensure your safety, we are once again suggesting that you consider returning to the States if your presence here in Germany is not essential." This brought forth mumbles and worried looks from some in the audience.

"For those of you who insist on staying in Berlin, we suggest you follow a few simple rules. First, when you go out in public, go with other Americans. There is less likely to be trouble if you are with a group. Second, if you are able, speak German. Even if you don't speak it well, most Germans will appreciate your effort and will respond with greater friendliness if you are speaking their language. Third, keep a low profile. Don't flaunt your nationality. We would never counsel you to deny your citizenship, but obviously when tensions are running high you should use discretion when you are out in public. As always, cooperate fully with police or government personnel, and don't hesitate to contact us here at the embassy should you encounter any difficulty. We are here to assist you in any way we can."

Erich Greinke watched from the back of the room as Williams fielded questions, his eyes scanning the crowd, making note of the faces he recognized. Among the audience was one face that was not American, but an Italian national who collected "information" for his government. Erich was glad Williams had stuck to the script, which was pretty vague and contained no incendiary statements. No doubt the content of Williams's briefing would shortly be common knowledge in the chancellery and at the ministries lining the Wilhelmstraße.

As the formal briefing ended and the attendees began to trickle out, Erich caught Maggie's eye and waved her over. He also grabbed Ches by his skinny arm as the reporter strolled by. "How about a quick lunch, you two?"

◆ ◆ ◆

"If you didn't know there was a war going on, you'd never be able to tell, would you?" Maggie asked no one in particular. She, Erich, and Ches were seated at an umbrella-shaded table under the linden trees on the main boulevard cutting through Berlin's government district.

"What are the barricades for?" she asked, pointing toward workers positioning wooden barriers between the sidewalk and the street. The disheveled workmen were dressed in gray coveralls distinguished by orange armbands emblazoned with the letter *P*. The armband marked them as *Polskis*, Polish workers shipped into the capital to perform manual labor.

"They're setting up for the parade tomorrow," Erich said, munching on a bite of sauerkraut. "Supposed to be a big victory parade right through the Brandenburg Gate. All the government offices are getting half a day off so their staffs can attend.

"Have you heard from Kurt?" he asked, raising an eyebrow. "I thought maybe he and Thomas might be back to march in the parade."

"No," Maggie answered without making eye contact. "I haven't heard from him." *Nor do I want to,* she thought. She dreaded confronting Kurt, still unsure how she was going to break the news that their relationship, like the peace, had ended.

"Tell me, Maggie," Ches said, joining the conversation, "how's your broadcasting career coming along? Erich told me you'd made quite a splash."

Maggie was glad to take the conversation in this new direction. "Well, it certainly pays better than a producer's salary." She laughed. She relayed the circumstances of Clive's collapse and the details of her on-air debut as Ches listened and chuckled.

"Maybe I should write a feature on you, my dear," Ches smiled, reaching for his beer.

Erich shot a warning look at Maggie, but he needn't have worried. "No thanks, Ches," Maggie replied. "I think I prefer to labor in anonymity." Again, that smile. "So, what's behind these briefings, Erich?" she asked. "I haven't seen anything like what Mr. Williams alluded to."

"I'm afraid there's some basis to it," Erich responded, relating Ches's encounter with the purse-swinging matron a couple of weeks earlier.

"Yep," Ches elaborated, "we were just having a nice, quiet lunch, and next thing I know, *whammo*, this bi—uh, this lady—is trying to knock my block off!"

"Did the lady know you were Americans?" Maggie asked.

"She heard us speaking English, and that's what set her off," Ches answered, smiling.

"What Williams said today is pretty good advice, based on our experience," Erich interjected. "We were just having a quiet conversation about what Ches saw on his trip up to the front. We certainly weren't boisterous or anything, were we, Ches?"

Ches shook his head.

Maggie eyed the correspondent. "What did you see, Ches?"

"Lots of dead bodies, burned-out vehicles, and slaughtered livestock. The regular nastiness of war. Looks horrible, smells worse." Before Erich could stop him, Ches plunged into the story of the Wormhoudt massacre.

"I'm not sure Maggie should hear this, pal," Erich said before he'd gotten far, with an emphasis on the word *pal* that he hoped would get Ches's attention.

"Why not, Erich?" Maggie asked, turning toward Erich. He always seemed to think he knew what was best for her—and usually expressed that belief without any input from her.

"Maggie, as I've mentioned to you before, you're working with some pretty ruthless guys. I don't mean Dieter or even Bauer, of course, but above them . . ." His voice trailed off and he shrugged his shoulders. Erich stuck his fork into a paper-thin schnitzel, trying to keep his tone of voice matter-of-fact. "I think anybody who knows this story, especially foreign nationals like us, takes on additional risks. This kind of story, if it ever got out, would do serious harm to the Germans' reputation."

Ches snorted derisively.

Erich continued, "And I think it could also prompt retaliation against anyone who might be suspected of reporting it." Erich shifted his gaze between his two companions. "Both of you—actually all three of us—need to be very careful with information like this."

Maggie hesitated. "I think I can handle it, Erich. You may remember that I know a little something about Germany's reputation. I help burnish it every night." She turned to Ches. "Tell me what you know."

Ches repeated the story in detail, even identifying the unit involved.

Maggie fell silent. She dropped her gaze to her plate, unwilling or unable to maintain eye contact with either Ches or Erich.

Having proven unable to stop the telling of the story, Erich attempted next to shift the conversation to another subject. "Ches, before Mrs. Max Schmeling clobbered you with her handbag, you mentioned there was another story you were working on."

"Oh yeah, I almost forgot that one," Ches said, waving to the waiter for another beer. Ches leaned forward across the table, signaling that the information he was about to impart was of the highest sensitivity. "It seems the Nazis have gone into euthanasia."

"Where's that?" Erich asked.

"Not where, buddy boy, what," Ches replied with a grimace.

"OK, what's that?"

"Mercy killing," Maggie answered flatly, her eyes locked onto Ches's face.

"Right you are, my girl. Erich, you remember I told you I'd been up around Bielefeld?" Erich nodded. "Well, I went up there to investigate a story I'd heard about an asylum for feebleminded children. It's called Bethel, and the place is run by a fellow named Bodelschwingh. From what I could learn, everybody around there holds this fellow in pretty high regard. He's a Protestant pastor, but the Catholics up there like him, too. Anyway, the Nazis direct Bodelschwingh to start turning his patients over to them for special 'research.' Only he won't do it without the family's permission, and who in his right mind would trust the Nazis with a family member who couldn't take care of himself? My source says the Nazis have laid out a master plan to kill mentally retarded patients in order to eliminate weakness from the master race."

Erich noted that Maggie's face had turned pale. She had listened quietly, intently, to Ches's story. "Has this Bodelschwingh given in to the Nazis?" she asked, her attention riveted on Ches.

"Not so far," Ches replied. "It'll be interesting to see how long he can stand up to them."

"He can't do it for long," Erich opined.

"My God!" Maggie said excitedly, causing both Ches and Erich to flinch. "How can you say that? He has to protect those poor people. They've done nothing wrong. They aren't responsible for their condition!"

"Quiet down, Maggie!" Erich said, keeping his voice low but his tone emphatic. "Remember, we don't need to call attention to ourselves."

"Erich, somebody needs to do something! The government has to stop this, this despicable business."

"The government's behind it, my dear," Ches said. "Why, this is Herr Hitler himself, along with that bunch of thugs around him: Goering, Hess, Goebbels."

"I know Goebbels." Maggie shook her head. "He's not like that!"

Ches and Erich exchanged uncomfortable glances.

Erich reached across the table and gently laid his hand on her forearm. "Maggie, please stay out of this. Ches doesn't even have enough solid information to write a story. That means he can't prove it. If you took this to Dieter—or, God forbid, to Goebbels—the results would be disastrous for you, Ches, and maybe even this Bodelschwingh guy. The Nazis would think nothing of erasing you two to cover up a story like this. I'm telling you, they don't play nicely, Maggie." Erich pulled his hand back, glancing around at the other tables nearby. No one seemed to have noticed Maggie's burst of emotion. "At the very least, let's wait until we know something definite."

"Then what?" Maggie asked, a frown on her face.

"Then, maybe we pursue a diplomatic approach. We can hide behind the anonymity of the State Department."

Maggie thought for a minute, staring down the broad, tree-lined boulevard. Maybe Erich was right. He seemed to have thought the issue through much more rapidly than she had. One of the traits she recognized in Erich was his ability to think two or even three steps ahead. Whereas she sometimes let her emotions determine her actions, he seemed to proceed from step to step based on some internal logic.

"Maybe you're right." She nodded after another moment. "But you"—she pointed to Ches—"you promise to keep me informed!"

"Yes ma'am," Ches agreed, clearly taken aback by Maggie's command.

Although Ches was startled, Erich was pleased. Maggie's strong reaction had put him one step closer.

◆ ◆ ◆

Erich and Ches watched the victory parade from a third-story window in the embassy. Thirty feet above Pariser Platz, they had an excellent view of the long columns of gray-clad, goose-stepping soldiers who trooped through the Brandenburg Gate. The afternoon had been declared a holiday, and government as well as factory workers had turned out to cheer the conquerors. Leading the parade was Hitler's bodyguard, the battle-tested Leibstandarte SS Adolf Hitler.

Erich nudged Ches with his elbow. "See anybody you recognize?"

"No, not really," Ches replied, lazily puffing on a cigarette, one hand against the casement of the raised window. It was hot and humid, a rare sultry day in Berlin. Even from a distance, observers could make out the sweat trickling down the tanned faces of the marching soldiers. "The only boys I got really close to were the medical orderlies and some of their wounded. I never had any contact with real combat troops."

"Well, those guys right there," Erich said, pointing to the lead formation, "they're as real as it gets. My guess is that some of these guys were involved in that massacre." Erich scanned the rows of helmeted soldiers, looking for Kurt Engel or Thomas Müller.

Thousands of happy Berliners ringed Pariser Platz, outlining the route of the march east along Unter den Linden. Vendors worked behind the crowds on either side of the square, some selling popcorn or summer apples, others handing out small Nazi flags. The whole event had a festive, celebratory air. It was if the war was won, as if the war was over. Maybe it was.

◆ ◆ ◆

"Now would seem the best chance for us all to stop this madness of war," Betty from Berlin said into the table microphone. "No longer are British and German troops fighting one another. No skirmishes are underway. Germany and France are now at peace. Why not the same for Great Britain and Germany? Today, before the German Reichstag, Herr Hitler has again offered peace to Mr. Churchill; peace with no strings attached. Peace that would end the need for British boys to risk life and limb; peace that would spare English hearth and home; peace that would permanently void the specter of invasion; peace that seems imminently sensible and honorable after the continental carnage of these last two months.

"We should seize whatever opportunity we have to avoid further, pointless bloodshed—to spare our husbands, fathers, and sons the physical and emotional destruction caused by war. Now is that opportunity! Now is the time to stand up for peace. Now is the moment to examine all sides of this issue and to demand a halt to senseless cruelty, violence, and death. Spare your families. Spare your homes. Spare your country. I pray with you that wise and peace-loving leaders will prevail. This is

Betty from Berlin. I look forward to visiting with you again soon. Good night from Berlin." The red light blinked off.

"I'm beginning to sound like a scratched record," Maggie said as she and Dieter left the studio area and headed back upstairs through the courtyard and into the main building.

Dieter smiled in the summer twilight. "Remember what Minister Goebbels says: propaganda must be simple and repetitive."

"Yes, but it needs to be interesting also. I'm afraid our peace talk goes in one ear and out the other. I don't think it's making much of an impact with our listeners. Certainly we can see no difference in the attitude of the British government."

"What do you suggest?" Dieter asked as they made their way to the commissary for a late supper.

"Maybe it's time to shift more of the message to the musical program. Let Charlie Weber and the Swingin' Seven play popular tunes and we give them new lyrics: funny, you know, but with an edge to them." Maggie's enthusiasm was growing as she talked. "We could get the most popular American records from Switzerland and then rework the musical arrangements and write new words. That'd get the stodgy old Brits to listen!"

Dieter slid his tray along the counter, pointing to a piece of chicken and a bowl of cooked apples. "We can't just go stealing their music, though, Maggie," he warned. "We have to observe copyrights. We're not at war with America."

Maggie waited until they sat down to eat, then leaned close to Dieter. Quietly, she said, "You mean to tell me we can attack one neutral nation after another, lay waste to them, occupy them, and take over their countries—but we can't violate a copyright law?"

Dieter smiled patiently, chewing his food. "Let me see what can be done."

"Thanks, darling." She smiled and leaned over to kiss his cheek.

When she'd finished eating, Maggie grabbed her handbag from the seat next to her and stood. "I'm bushed," she said. "I'll see you in the morning."

"Good night, Maggie," Dieter said, smiling and half standing. As she strode from the dining room, Dieter wondered at her seemingly endless ability to come up with new ideas. *It must be the American influence,* he thought, as he returned his attention to the chicken on his plate.

◆ ◆ ◆

"There you are!" called a familiar voice as Maggie stepped out into the lobby of Broadcasting House. Maggie flinched, then tried to smile as she came face-to-face with Kurt Engel. He reached around her, juggling a flower bouquet, and gathered her in a bear hug. He leaned down to kiss her lips, but Maggie turned her head just slightly, causing his lips to fall on her cheek. "Is that any way to greet a conquering hero?" Kurt laughed, his eyes twinkling in the fading light of the evening.

"Welcome back, Kurt," was all Maggie could think to say. She looked into his bright-blue eyes and could see the first signs of confusion there. Her stomach felt like it was twisting into a pretzel. "It's good to see you in one piece."

Maggie stepped back. Kurt's smile faded from his face.

"Well," he began, forcing a grin, his brow furrowed, his eyes uncertain. "You don't seem as pleased to see me as I am to see you." He labored to keep his tone friendly.

Maggie looked down at the floor, then slowly raised her gaze back to Kurt's face. "I'm sorry, Kurt. I guess I'm not." She saw Kurt's shoulders sag. Despite hours of nagging, gnawing thought, Maggie had never really figured out how to tell Kurt their relationship was over. And now, here he was, demanding—deserving—an explanation.

"What's this all about, then, Maggie?" he asked, puzzled.

"Kurt," she started, then hesitated, looking around the empty lobby. "I've—we've grown apart . . ."

"No, Maggie." He shook his head vigorously from side to side. "No, we've *been* apart, but that's not the same as growing apart." The bouquet hung down from his left hand.

"You're different," Maggie resumed. "You're demanding. You think you own me, like you own a dog or a horse; that I exist only to please you, to serve your needs."

"C'mon, Maggie!" Kurt barked. "I've been fighting for my country, counting on you to be here, thinking of you every night, praying to God that I would make it through in one piece so I could hold you again, and you tell me I'm different?" Kurt's voice rose as his anger became more apparent. "Damn right! I spent most of the last few months getting shot at every day. That changes a man. But you wouldn't know about those changes, because we haven't been in the same country!"

Maggie attempted again. "You changed after Poland, Kurt."

"It didn't seem to stop you! You didn't complain when I was servicing you every night! You didn't whine, 'Oh, Kurt, we're growing apart!'" he mimicked her. "You seemed to like things just fine. Now I come back from months on a battlefield and all of a sudden this—this pathetic greeting!" Kurt leaned toward her, subconsciously slapping the flowers against his thigh, petals dropping onto the lobby's shiny floor. Maggie was frightened. She had seen his temper before, but now it was directed at her. Her face was burning; she was on the verge of tears. She had imagined a nightmare scene like this, and now she had it. Her only consolation was that no one was around to witness it.

Kurt's body was tense, a sneer had replaced his beautiful smile, pain registered in his eyes. "You know I loved you, Maggie. I would have made the rest of my life with you. You owned me body and soul. But now I see. You're no different than those French whores all my men chatter about."

His eyes narrowed to slits. "You're sleeping with somebody else, aren't you? You're just another American slut! Growing apart? Sleeping apart! How many, Maggie?" He let loose an ugly laugh. "I should have known. You were too eager from the day we met!" He drew his hand back and Maggie flinched again.

"No." He lowered his hand. "No, you're not worth it. Now I see who you really are. Thank God," he said, lifting his eyes toward the heavens. "Thank God I now see the real Maggie."

He turned on his heel and started to walk away, then stopped and turned to face her again. "It's your little friend Dieter, isn't it?" he sneered. "I'll take care of him." He closed the distance between them, leaning his face down to hers. "Yes," he whispered menacingly, "tell your sweetheart that I will deal with him. Then I'll come back and deal with you, you cheap *Schlampe*!"

Kurt spun around again and marched across the lobby, his boots echoing off the tile floor. As he reached the double glass doors leading to the street, he tossed the flowers into a waste can.

Maggie sobbed, tears coursing down her cheeks, her body trembling.

"Here, here. What's all this?" came a voice from behind her.

Maggie wiped away her tears with the back of her hand and turned to find Herr Direktor Bauer.

"What's the matter, my dear?" he asked, reaching out and placing a hand on her shoulder.

"I . . . I just had a rather unpleasant encounter with an old boyfriend," Maggie confessed. She couldn't come up with a better answer than the truth at that moment.

Bauer pulled her into a paternal hug and gently patted her shoulder. "These things do happen. Best to learn what we can and move on. Try not to dwell on it. That's always been my policy," he said in a soothing voice. Then, more loudly, he called out, "Herr Schmidt!"

"Herr Direktor?" Dieter answered, crossing the lobby from the other corner. As he approached, Dieter registered that Bauer was holding someone and that that someone was Maggie. He had no idea what was going on, but he knew it would be better for Bauer to tell him than for him to ask.

"Herr Schmidt, would you be so kind as to escort Fräulein Maggie home and see that she is safely in for the night?"

"Of course, Herr Direktor," Dieter answered, pleased with the task he'd been given.

◆　◆　◆

As they walked toward her apartment building, Maggie described her encounter with Kurt. At the Kaiserdamm, Dieter paused and scanned the area.

"What are you doing?" Maggie asked, a note of panic in her voice. "You don't think he's still out there, do you?"

"Relax," Dieter replied. "I just don't want to step out in front of a truck in this blackout."

"He called me a French whore," Maggie said. As she did, she found herself weeping again.

Dieter placed his arm around her and pulled her close. "No, Maggie," he consoled her. "You're not like that, not at all." Maggie unlocked the front door and Dieter walked up the stairs with her to her flat. He smiled at her. "I will admit that you're beautiful, that's certainly true. And yes, you are brilliant. Of course you know how to work with people. I've seen your successes, from Clive to Goebbels. But no, you don't have the skills of a French prostitute," he said, looking into her green eyes and trying not to laugh. "Of course, I will do everything I can to assist you in developing these and any other skills you may desire . . ." Dieter ducked as Maggie swung at him. He backed away, smiling broadly as Maggie advanced.

"I don't want to laugh!" she said, but she was already losing the fight. Dieter caught her by her right arm, stopping her punch and pulling her toward him. He kissed her on her forehead as he pulled her tighter.

"I don't want to laugh, either," he said, smiling. "I just want to hold you for the rest of my life."

◆ ◆ ◆

Erich squeezed himself into the narrow, wooden booth in the back corner of the Sword & Stirrup, a pub on the north bank of the Spree River frequented by military officers. "Hello, old comrade," he greeted Thomas Müller.

Thomas peered over the rim of his beer, taking a gulp and then setting his glass down on the wooden table between them. The tabletop was the victim of a thousand knives. Each, it seemed, had carved the initials of its owner, or perhaps those of his lover.

"Well, Mr. Diplomat." Thomas smiled. "How nice to see you again." From the tenor of his speech, Erich judged Thomas's beer wasn't the first of the evening.

"How are you, Thomas? You look well for someone who's just conquered France and the Low Countries."

"Ah, never better, never better. How about a beer?" Thomas raised his arm and gestured to the waiter. Catching his attention, he held up his thumb and forefinger, signaling for two more glasses.

"So, tell me," Erich said after the waiter had placed the two foaming drinks on the table, "how was it this time: better or worse?"

Thomas leaned back, at least as far back as he could within the confines of the booth. He placed both his hands on the table, one on either side of his beer. "It's always worse. You should know that by now." He shook his head, but kept eye contact with Erich. "In some ways it was easier than Poland. Maybe because we expected it to be so much harder than it turned out. But still, you know, it's war. Shitty business."

"Yeah," Erich agreed, glancing around the restaurant. Most of its patrons seemed engrossed in their own drinks and conversations. "Here." He pushed across a package of Lucky Strikes. "Here's a little coming-home present."

"I wish we got to stay home for a while," Thomas said, sliding the cigarettes off the table and sticking them into the pocket of his uniform trousers. "We're off again tomorrow, back to France."

Erich saw his opening and charged through. "But I hear Paris is beautiful in the spring." He laughed.

"It's summer, you idiot," Thomas grumbled. "Besides, we aren't going back to Paris. We're going to the Channel coast to work on fortifications. They're going to turn us into engineers."

"Building instead of destroying." Erich cocked his head as if considering a new thought. "That should be a challenge for an old soldier like you. You'll have to learn new skills." He leaned forward, his head halfway across the table. "Can I ask you a couple of questions?"

"Go ahead," said Thomas, lifting his glass.

"I heard a story about a place called Wormhoudt. Like maybe somebody got careless with some British prisoners and they all ended up dead. You know anything about that?"

Thomas was suddenly completely alert, his eyes clear and locked on to Erich's. "No," he paused. "And you don't either. Drop it."

"Sometimes I hear things, Thomas. I guess maybe some people want to tell me things that are bothering them—you know, share their confessions with me."

Thomas snorted. "You're no priest! I fought beside you, remember?"

Erich laughed. "Of course not, but people tell me things just the same. Things they wouldn't normally repeat."

"This would be a good thing not to repeat. Let it go."

"I can't. My conscience is burdened with this information. If I can look into it and learn it's just a story, that there's no truth to it, then I can be relieved of the burden."

Thomas sighed. "The burdens of a passport clerk. I had no idea."

"What happened?"

Thomas looked down at his half-empty glass and slowly shook his head. "Forget it."

"Just answer a couple of questions, then."

"No."

"I'll keep you out of it," Erich promised. "No one will know what I know, so no one will be able to trace anything back to you." Thomas just shook his head, avoiding his friend's face.

"OK, just do that."

"Do what?" Thomas asked, his red-rimmed eyes focusing on Erich's.

"Just shake your head if I'm wrong. Don't do anything if I'm right. You don't even have to say anything." Thomas stared at him as if trying to will himself to another place. Erich pushed ahead. "Was it Second Battalion?" Thomas stared at him. "Was Mohnke the battalion commander?" Thomas remained impassive. "Were you there? Did you see it?" Thomas sat still, then slowly moved his head from side to side in a barely perceptible motion, his eyes remaining on Erich's. "Was Engel involved?" Thomas sat still.

Thomas broke his silence with a whisper. "I don't know where you heard this story, but if you repeat it, you're putting your life at risk. And mine. Don't call me again." He pulled himself out of the booth and reached into his pocket. He dropped two coins on the table and pulled his cap off the hook on the side of the booth, then walked unsteadily between the tables and out the front door.

Erich sat silently and reached for his beer.

CHAPTER 17

Berlin, Germany
August 1940

The lights burned late at the Reich Chancellery, Hitler's official government office. From what Erich could piece together, Hitler's chief lieutenants were busy drafting the plans for the invasion of Great Britain.

"The Italians will fight like lions!" Gino assured Erich as they munched wursts together at Hansie's lunch counter. Gino was the driver for the Italian ambassador. He was only twenty-five years old, ruggedly handsome with dark eyes and dark hair that he combed straight back. He enjoyed Erich's company because Erich was generous with two things: American cigarettes and American magazines. Gino's English had gotten progressively better under Erich's informal tutelage so that now it rivaled his German. "*Il Duce* will command the invasion himself," Gino boasted. "We will fight like animals!"

"Like you did in Abyssinia?" Erich teased.

"Oh, that was different, Erich, so very different. Now we have a noble, courageous ally in the Führer and the German people. They have a great military that will support Italy's valiant attack against the

English." Gino smiled his handsome, white smile and wagged a mustard-smeared finger at Erich. "You will see!"

Erich concluded that while invasion planning might actually be underway, neither Gino nor the Italians would have any role in it.

◆ ◆ ◆

Maggie retired fairly early on Sunday night. The weather had remained warm into late August, much like it had been the previous year, when the world had waited to see what would transpire between Germany and Poland. Now, of course, it knew.

She raised her windows, hoping for a cooling breeze, and lay down under a sheet. She wanted an early start on Monday morning. She felt whatever ability she had enjoyed to influence popular opinion in England was on the wane. Whereas her initial broadcasts had been met with favorable reviews from the English press, Maggie knew she had been ineffective in promoting a peaceful counterpoint to the stubbornness of the Churchill government. What she needed was a fresh approach that would signal an end to Hitler's appetite for additional territory, a time-out that would stop the fighting and offer a time for renewed negotiations. Perhaps, she thought, Dieter would have some news on how to use popular songs to send the right message to the English. She slipped off to sleep, thinking of Dieter.

Maggie was awakened by the mournful wail of the air raid sirens coming to life around the western end of the city. The unusual sound was disorienting. Within a minute, Maggie heard doors opening inside her building, heard muffled voices and footsteps. She rolled out of bed and moved toward her window, where her lace curtains hung limply in the light from the quarter moon. She looked outside and could just discern movement in the shadows, people heading toward the shelters.

Whump! Whump! Maggie heard flak guns firing. She guessed the firing was coming from the northwest. She looked up into the starry sky, searching for the enemy bombers, but from her window she could only look to the east. Between blasts from the flak guns she began to hear a steady drone, like the buzz of a hundred bees. The blasts grew louder, closer. The drone grew deeper, closer. Maggie remembered the statement in the previous week's papers from Göring, head of the air force. He had said Berliners needn't go to their shelters at the sound of the sirens, but only when they heard the firing of nearby antiaircraft guns. *How nearby?* Maggie wondered.

Maggie pulled on a pair of slacks, a cotton shirt, and some shoes. She tugged her apartment door closed behind her and descended the stairs, coming out the west-facing front of the building. Her assigned shelter was half a block south, toward the Kaiserdamm. From the sidewalk, Maggie could see a spectacular light show in the western sky. Bright-orange bursts of light punctuated the darkness, followed a few moments later by a crisp report. Streaks of green light raced into the black night as the tracers searched for targets. Wide, white columns of light from distant searchlights hunted the sky for enemy bombers.

Maggie stood entranced, her senses taking in the colors, the lights, the dull thump of the guns, and the sharper racket of their exploding ordnance. Standing on the sidewalk, Maggie could tell the bombers were passing to the north of her—over Templehof, she guessed. A large flash of yellow light threw shadows toward her. She felt the concussion of a large explosion and then heard it. She couldn't tell how far away it was, only that it wasn't very close. Another flash, another concussion, another explosion. Then another and then more and more, coming so rapidly she could not count them. A glow lit the sky to the northwest, reflecting off low clouds of smoke, turning the night orange. Maggie looked up and down Soorstraße. She was the only person in sight. The buildings, trees, and lightless lamp posts were all tinged an ochre hue.

Gradually, the drone faded away, the hammering of the flak guns slowed, and the glow in the northwest diminished. The sirens wailed out the all clear, and people began to emerge from their cellars and shelters. Maggie stood and watched and listened as the mostly pajama-clad residents of Soorstraße walked back to their buildings. The dying light of distant fires provided enough illumination to keep them from running into one another.

"That fat Herr Meier has some explaining to do," one older man grumbled, referring to Göring's boast that no enemy bombers would break through Berlin's defenses. He gripped his wife by the arm, both of them wearing bathrobes above their dress shoes.

"It's like having a baby in the house," a woman said in the darkness, "getting up in the middle of the night."

"Yes," agreed her companion. "Let's just hope it's over in three months and then the baby sleeps all night!"

◆　◆　◆

"Bomber Command's visit to Berlin last night caused little damage, except for the garden shed that was destroyed," Betty from Berlin reported in her August 26 broadcast. "Unfortunately for some families—wives, children, and parents—fifteen bombers were shot down during the raid. Sadly, many of the pilots and crew were killed as they dropped bombs on German houses, schools, and churches. Fortunately, the valiant Luftwaffe fighter pilots and antiaircraft gunners demonstrated that skill, daring, and might will protect our capital. Not a single Berliner was killed during last night's bombing."

Really laying it on thick tonight, old girl, Maggie thought to herself.

"Our German flyers have standing orders to bomb only military targets and to ditch their bomb loads in the Channel if they can't avoid damage to civilian areas. The distinction between the terror bombing strategy of the Churchill government and the strategy of the honorable crews of the Luftwaffe could not be more evident.

"And now to the boys in Bomber Command: How many missions will you last, with a casualty rate of nearly sixteen percent? Math was never my strong suit, but I think the answer to this problem is pretty simple—not many. Somewhere between your sixth and seventh visit to Germany, your wife or sweetheart is going to get a knock on the door from the King's messenger. I think it would be wise to make sure your will is up to date. Or, better yet, just stay home. If you do decide to come back, we'll have a warm welcome waiting for you. This is Betty from Berlin. I look forward to visiting with you again soon. Good night."

"That was good, Maggie," Dieter said over the intercom.

Bauer had returned from his daily ministry briefing red-faced and agitated. Goebbels had been outraged at the British attack. Hitler, he said, was furious—furious with the British for striking the capital, and furious with Göring and the Luftwaffe for allowing the bombers to get through. As a result, Goebbels had dictated a change in the tenor and tone of the propaganda message beamed toward England.

"It certainly feels like we've taken the gloves off," Maggie replied, her voice sounding tinny to Dieter over the small speaker. "How much of that about their losses was true?"

Dieter snapped off the intercom, hoping no one from the other consoles, or Bauer, had heard Maggie's question. He motioned to her through the studio glass to meet him in the corridor.

"What did I say?" she asked, her brow wrinkled.

"Come with me," Dieter responded. Once up the stairs and into courtyard, Dieter answered her. "Don't ever question the information we get from Bauer or the ministry, Maggie. Ever! Accept it as the gospel truth. Don't ever give them"—he didn't identify *them*—"a chance to question your loyalty or dedication. As an American, it's especially important that your commitment be above reproach. If they say British losses were one hundred percent, that's what we have to report. If they say not even a garden shed was damaged, that's the way it is."

"Even if we know it's not true?"

"Well, first of all"—Dieter stopped and put his hands on his hips— "I don't know it's not true. For all I know, it's completely accurate. Do you know differently?"

Maggie heard the irritation in his voice and answered cautiously. "I heard the planes. I felt the bombs. I saw the fires. And I was two miles away, according to the papers this morning. There's no way those bombs didn't cause some kind of damage."

"What got damaged, Maggie? Who got killed? How many planes were shot down? Did you see it? How do you know?" Dieter's questions came rapid-fire, so that Maggie had no chance to answer. "Listen," he said, lifting her chin with his fingers, "Bauer and Goebbels are aware of a much bigger picture than you can see from your sidewalk. They have information you and I don't have. They see how all these pieces fit together. We have to trust them, OK?"

Maggie stared into Dieter's eyes. She knew he was sincere. She was less confident about Bauer and, based on her conversations with Erich Greinke, had serious doubts about Goebbels.

◆ ◆ ◆

"The Gestapo ordered his arrest," Ches told Maggie. They were sitting in the warm sunshine on a bench in the Tiergarten. Erich had arranged the Sunday-afternoon meeting so Ches could personally relate this latest update on Pastor Bodelschwingh. "He still refuses to surrender his patients."

"He must be a very good man," Maggie said, tears forming in her eyes. Erich stood in front of the bench, listening to the conversation and ensuring they weren't overheard. "Did the Gestapo take any of the patients?"

Ches nodded slowly. "I'm told they carried away fourteen Jewish patients with varying degrees of feeblemindedness. I promised to let you know what I know, Maggie, and that's pretty much it."

"Are you going to pursue the story?" she asked, hoping for an affirmative answer.

Ches leaned forward and studied his hands. "Well, I'm not sure, Maggie. There's not much I can do with some stories if I want to stay in Berlin. Your boss, Dr. Goebbels, takes a dim view of any story that reflects poorly on the government. This most surely would. This war's the biggest event of my life—anybody's life, really. I couldn't cover it nearly so well from London or Washington. This is where the action is likely to stay for a while. I'd kind of like to stay here, too. If I run afoul of Goebbels, he'll stick me on the next train to Switzerland." Ches looked away from Maggie.

"Isn't there anything we can do?" Maggie shifted her attention to Erich. "Those poor children. They're so helpless and this is so . . . so evil." She dabbed at her eyes with a handkerchief.

Erich shrugged, flicking ash from the end of his cigarette. "I'm not sure. I can speak to Mr. Kirk, the chargé d'affaires at the embassy. I'm not sure he's in a very strong position with the Nazi government right now. With the president promising to supply the Brits with war materials, he may not even be able to get an audience with the foreign minister."

Maggie was disconsolate. "There must be something, some way we can stop this."

Erich decided the time had come to make his pitch to Maggie—but not in front of Ches. He waited until Ches, who seemed embarrassed by his lack of enthusiasm to pursue the story, wandered a few yards away to light a cigarette. Erich knelt down in front of Maggie and gently took her hand in his. Looking up into her green eyes, he said, "Tomorrow you're going to get a phone call from the embassy. You will be told to come in with your passport, that we are conducting a census of all Americans in Germany in light of the war situation and the danger of aerial attacks on German cities. Do as you are told and come at the appointed time. Between now and then, I'll see if—and it's a big if—the State Department is willing to intercede. I won't promise anything except that I will ask a question. Agreed?"

Maggie stared into his eyes and nodded.

◆ ◆ ◆

Maggie slept fitfully that night. She dreamed of her sister, Maureen, snuggled in her lap as they sang nursery rhymes together. Maureen was wearing her hand-me-down nightgown, the one with little pink sheep on it that Maggie had once worn. Kurt, holding a bouquet of wilted flowers, came and sat beside them, reaching out for Maureen, coaxing her onto his lap. Maggie moved in slow motion; she tried to stop Maureen from leaving the safety of her embrace, but she couldn't, nor could she speak a warning. Maureen laid her head on Kurt's shoulder as he smiled at Maggie. Clive lumbered up on a wobbling bicycle, somehow balancing a tray holding two shot glasses. He offered her a drink, but before she could reply, Clive's face was replaced by Erich's, darkened with a wicked smile. Erich laughed and said, "I told you so!"

Maggie jerked awake at five o'clock entangled in her sheets, wrestling with phantoms, trying to protect her sister. She was too keyed up to go back to sleep, so she got up and made a simple breakfast of bread and jam.

As soon as she judged the morning editions would be out on the streets, she was dressed and out the door. She bought three papers from a newsstand on the Kaiserdamm and walked the remaining block to Broadcasting House. She was surprised to find the English Section office vacant. Usually Dieter, who never seemed to sleep, was there drinking coffee and waiting with news highlights. Maggie removed her light jacket and spread her newspapers across her desk. She carefully scanned each page, looking primarily for any stories about the Bethel asylum or Pastor Bodelschwingh. Nothing.

Shortly before ten o'clock, Dieter strode through the office door. "Hello, Maggie!" he called out.

"Good morning, Dieter." Maggie forced a smile. "You're late," she said with more humor than she felt.

"A long briefing this morning at the ministry," Dieter replied, dropping his newspapers on the desk and shrugging off his suit coat. "The British keep flying their nighttime bombing raids and they keep hitting civilian targets. It's really indefensible!" Color was rising in Dieter's normally calm face. "They're dropping their bombs on residential areas, churches, even schools. Last night there was a raid on Hannover. The Luftwaffe attacked and damaged several of the British bombers. They think one of them jettisoned its bombs over Bielefeld. They struck an asylum for the mentally infirm."

A jolt of adrenaline surged through Maggie. She fought to appear calm, beads of sweat breaking out on her forehead. "Were any of the patients . . . hurt?" she asked, struggling to keep her voice under control.

"Yes," Dieter said, looking into her eyes. "Apparently fourteen of them were killed. Needless to say, this has to be included in our broadcasts tonight."

"Fourteen? *Precisely* fourteen? I, um, I don't know if I can do it," Maggie stammered, blinking back tears, a lump rising in her throat. The fourteen Jewish patients being led away by the Gestapo—had they sung nursery rhymes as they went?

"Why can't you do it?" Dieter paused. "Oh, Maggie, I'm sorry. Your sister . . . I didn't think." Dieter stepped over to Maggie. He gently placed his hand on her shoulder. "I'm really sorry, darling. I should have been more sensitive. Of course you don't have to broadcast this. I'll give this to Clive."

Maggie shook her head. "No," she said, her voice barely audible. "I'll do it." The doubts she had had about the necessity of attacking Belgium and Holland and her skepticism over the reported losses of the British bombers raced through her mind like floodwaters, churning her thoughts and leaving a muddy film on her conscience. How much, she wondered, had been a lie? How many falsehoods had she helped spread? There was no escaping that she'd been the mouthpiece for lies; the question now was at what cost? Had her desire to tweak the nose of the English bulldog prolonged the peace—or hastened war? Erich had tried to warn her, but she'd arrogantly dismissed him. Now she realized that Erich had been right all along. She *had* been working for "bad guys." As Dieter hovered over her with a concerned expression on his face, all Maggie could think of was how to get out of this mess—a mess she'd helped create.

"You're sure you want to do it?" Dieter's question brought her back to the present. "I can give it to someone else." He was making the offer, but he was clearly hoping Maggie would give voice to this atrocity.

"It's OK," she answered finally, looking him in the eye. "It's actually a story I want to tell. They have to pay for this." She didn't say who *they* were.

◆ ◆ ◆

Shortly before lunch, Maggie received a phone call from the US Embassy requesting that she pay a two o'clock call on the passport control officer, Mr. Greinke. Maggie told Dieter that the caller, a secretary at the embassy, explained that the State Department was conducting a census of all Americans living in Germany. The action was necessary in light of the war situation and the increased risk of aerial attacks on German cities.

Two o'clock found Maggie in front of Erich's passport window off the embassy's lobby. "Well, hello, Miss O'Dea!" Erich greeted her formally. "Thank you for coming in on such short notice."

"Oh, it was no problem at all." Even though she was smiling, Erich noted the seriousness in her eyes.

"If you would please step down the hallway to your right and knock on the second door, we'll review your passport and make sure everything is in order." Erich smiled pleasantly, pointing down the corridor.

As she reached the second door, Erich opened it from inside. "This way, Maggie," he said, turning and leading her toward an inner office. Once inside, Erich motioned to a wooden armchair in front of a non-descript wooden desk. "Please sit down." He closed the door, leaving them alone in the room.

"Here's my passport, as requested," she said, handing over the gold-embossed booklet.

"Thank you," Erich said, taking the passport and dropping it into a large brown envelope. "Take this form with you," he said, handing over an official-looking document. "You'll need to fill it out and bring it back. How about tomorrow afternoon?"

"Why don't I just finish it now?"

Erich pressed his lips together and shook his head. "The form is just an excuse, Maggie. It's simply a cover for you to have to come back to the embassy."

"Tomorrow afternoon is fine," Maggie agreed.

Erich sat down behind the desk and leaned forward, his hands folded in front of him. He fixed Maggie with a steady gaze. "I wanted to update you on my conversations with Mr. Kirk. Unfortunately, his response was sort of what I expected. He said our government could not afford to intervene in the Bethel situation without a great deal more information and hard facts—facts that we don't presently possess," Erich lied. He had neither seen nor spoken with Kirk since his conversation with Maggie in the Tiergarten. "The problem, of course, is that we have no way to investigate the situation, and our correspondent friend is unwilling to reveal his sources."

Maggie's response reflected the intensity of feeling that Erich was counting on. "We can't let the Gestapo murder innocent children!"

She struggled to keep control of her voice. "Somebody's got to do something!"

Erich looked down at his folded hands as if trying to work out a solution. "We can't take on the Gestapo, Maggie," he said finally. "They enjoy this kind of thing. If they even suspected we knew about this, they'd kill us."

She tilted her head to the side, offering a skeptical look to her host.

"I'm serious, Maggie. I've told you before, these aren't nice guys." He paused again. *It's now or never, pal,* Erich told himself. He plunged ahead. "There's only one way I know to fight back."

"How?"

"Work with us. Be our eyes and ears inside the propaganda ministry. Feed us information on what's happening—who's going where, who's giving advice to Goebbels, anything that comes your way."

"Who is *us*?" Maggie asked cautiously.

"The United States. More specifically, the State Department. Most specifically, me." Erich sat back. He had set the hook. Now patience was required to land the fish.

"Why me? I'm not on the inside. Besides, I'm an American. They'll never trust me far enough to let me know any secrets."

"We're interested in information, Maggie. We don't expect you to tell us secrets, but if you know some, that would be just fine." Erich smiled. "From what Dieter has told me, you already have his confidence and that of his boss. And then, of course, according to the *Völkischer Beobachter*, you're part of Goebbels's inner circle already." Erich smiled again, spreading his arms apart with his palms up. Again he waited on Maggie to take the next step.

"If the Nazis are as ruthless as you say they are, Erich, won't this be dangerous?"

"Not if we do it right."

"And how's that?"

"Are you in or out, Maggie?" he asked quietly. He realized he was holding his breath. Months of effort came down to Maggie's answer. She stared into Erich's eyes. He could tell she was weighing her decision carefully. Erich hoped he hadn't frightened her away. He'd worked steadily to plant seeds of doubt in Maggie's mind, to convince her that while she might have liked her colleagues, she was playing ball for the wrong team.

Maggie thought. Erich waited.

"In."

"Excellent." Erich breathed again, careful not to show his excitement. "Is there anyone in the States with whom you regularly correspond?"

"My father. We exchange letters every couple of weeks or so."

"Tomorrow, when you come back," Erich directed, "bring me two of his letters." He glanced at his watch. "You've been here long enough," he said, pushing back from the desk and standing. "Tomorrow, we'll go over a few things to help you communicate with us."

"Why don't I just come and tell you?"

"This isn't a game, Maggie." He walked around the desk and put his hand on the door handle. "From now on, you and I will never meet publicly except when you are here on embassy business. We'll create some other ways for you to pass information to us. That's how we keep you safe. We have to look out for our friends, you know."

Erich escorted Maggie back to the hallway and through the lobby of the embassy, pausing just inside the double doors that opened onto Pariser Platz. "Do you like apples, Maggie?" he asked, digging into the pocket of his trousers.

"Sure."

Erich handed her a ten-Pfennig coin. "Buy some on the way home."

◆ ◆ ◆

"I would tell you that the perpetrators of this barbaric act, this murder of innocents, should be hunted down like the criminals they are," Betty from Berlin lectured that night in her broadcast to England. After her visit to the embassy, Maggie had returned to Broadcasting House to prepare her script. True to her word, she had insisted on telling the Bethel story, even though Dieter had again offered to assign it to one of the other commentators.

"No, thanks," Maggie had said. "It's a story I think I'm supposed to tell." Now she was telling it.

"I would tell you they should be hauled before the bar of justice to stand trial for this heinous act of cowardice, or perhaps that they should be made to appeal for mercy to the families of their helpless victims. But the sad fact of the matter for these terror fliers—these bombers of civilians, of churches, of schools, and now of hospitals—is that retribution will come from the gallant knights of the Luftwaffe's fighter squadrons. As I mentioned recently, the odds for any pilot or crewmember run out after seven missions. With the weather so poor in England tonight, I suppose many of Bomber Command's boys have tuned in. Just look around your briefing hut tomorrow afternoon, fellows. Count how many of your comrades have been around for more than five, six, or seven missions. Not many.

"Even if, through some combination of skill and luck, a crew survives ten or even fifteen missions, the odds that they will live to see the end of this war are, well, not very promising. So, if you are going to continue to fly, to drop your bombs until you yourself are dropped from the sky, at least be so honorable as to drop them on military targets, not poor, helpless children in a place like Bielefeld.

"This is Betty from Berlin. I look forward to visiting with you again soon. Good night."

As he walked with her out of the building that night, Dieter asked, "Shall I walk you home?"

Maggie stared down at the sidewalk in front of her, watching for the whitewashed curb. "Thanks, darling, but I need to be alone tonight."

"Of course." He stopped at the corner as Maggie turned north on Soorstraße and watched in silence as she disappeared into the blackout.

◆ ◆ ◆

"I heard part of your broadcast last night," Erich said, showing Maggie back to the inner office the following afternoon. She had returned with her completed form just as he had directed during her first visit. "You really put the wood to those RAF boys."

"Imagine what I would have said if I really thought they were the guilty party." Maggie smiled ruefully. "I can't understand the mind that would kill mentally deficient children. What could be the point of such cruelty? Don't you think people would figure out what was going on? Wouldn't there be an outcry against it?"

"No offense, Maggie," Erich replied with a hard look as he took his seat behind the desk, "but you and your colleagues spend your days and nights revising and modifying the truth so that the public hears and sees only what you want them to. As to an outcry: I don't think so. How many Germans have you seen standing up for the Jews?"

"Point well taken," Maggie agreed. "I guess that's why I'm here, isn't it? I have to do something. I can't sit back any longer. I bought the party line on Czechoslovakia and Poland. I thought we were working for peace after that. I could even sort of understand Norway. But the attacks on Belgium and Holland—well, that just seemed like naked aggression to me. I'm fairly certain we've been overstating RAF losses and underreporting the Luftwaffe's losses over England. And then this Bethel thing comes along." Maggie shook her head. "You said the Nazis were bad guys. I guess you've been right all along, Erich."

"Believe me, Maggie, I get no pleasure from being right about this. Believe this, too: we appreciate your willingness to help us." Erich took

Maggie's form and placed it in the same brown envelope that held her passport. "Tomorrow, I will need you to come back again. Our cover this time will be to take new passport photos. We will do that here so we will be able to spend some additional time together going over communications procedures. Speaking of which, did you bring the letters from your father?"

"Yes, here." Maggie handed over the two most recent letters from home, both in their opened envelopes.

Erich quickly glanced at them and set them aside. "Did you buy an apple yesterday?"

"Yes, two," Maggie answered, puzzled. "Tell me why I bought apples."

"We're beginning to establish some habits in your life that will assist you in communicating with us. The apples are part of it, and so are your father's letters. I'd like you to begin eating lunch outdoors on sunny days. There is a small park just to the west of Broadcasting House. You know it?"

"Adolf Hitler Platz?"

"Yes, that's it. There's a bench in the southeastern corner of the park. I'd like you to start eating lunch on that bench in nice weather. I'd like an apple to be part of your lunch."

"OK," Maggie said with a smile, still puzzled. "But tell me why."

"The bench has six horizontal slats that form the seat. We've hollowed out the left end of the third slat from the front and capped it with a piece of wood that blends right in. You can't tell unless you're looking for it. From time to time, we'll leave things there for you to pick up. Likewise, you will leave things for us."

"What kind of things?"

"Notes, papers, whatever you think will be useful. Put whatever you have in this." Erich slid a small wax paper envelope across the desk. "Stick your notes in this envelope; put it in the bench. It will protect your notes from moisture. If we need information about a specific item, we'll let you know that, too, so you can be on the lookout."

"What if someone else accidentally finds what I've left for you?"

"Good question. We'll be watching the drop site in case anyone intercepts your messages. My suggestion is to bring a newspaper with you to lunch. That will give you some cover if you have information to leave for us. Use the newspaper to shield your hand from view while you make your drop. In essence, you'll be hiding behind the propaganda your boss puts out."

"It sounds simple enough," Maggie said. "So, tell me, what's with the apples?"

"We'll go into that in detail tomorrow, when you come back to have your passport pictures retaken. In the meantime, start taking your lunch, including the apple, in the park. Take a newspaper. Watch what's going on around you. Watch for familiar faces and see who shows up day in and day out. We're going to try this for a while before we attempt any exchanges of information. Any questions?"

"Lots," answered Maggie, "but they'll wait for tomorrow. I need to get back."

Erich stood and moved to the door. "Maggie, this is important work. I'll help you develop the skills you need to do it safely. At some point, as I've told you in the past, I think the United States is going to be sucked into this war. If we do our jobs well, we may be able to put that day off. Maybe, if we're lucky, we might be able to avoid it altogether."

"I hope so." Maggie nodded, standing. "I can't think of anything sadder than going to war with the Germans. The Nazis I don't like so much, but I really love the Germans."

Particularly one, Erich thought to himself.

CHAPTER 18

Berlin, Germany
September 1940

Adolf Hitler Platz was just a short walk from Broadcasting House, and on this pleasant late summer day Maggie was delighted to take her lunch break there. A large, circular central plaza dominated the roughly rectangular park, which was encircled by a tangled network of roads. Within the park were several young trees, shrubbery, and walkways—along with benches that sat back around the perimeter of the park.

Maggie picked the bench in the southeast corner of the park, closest to Masurenallee, and sat down with her lunch and her newspaper. The sun was warm, and the lunch was simple: a cheese sandwich, a bottle of beer, and an apple. As she munched, Maggie read the newspaper, digesting her food along with the latest news—or at least the latest news sanctioned by her employer, the minister of propaganda. Sitting on the left end of the bench, Maggie held the paper with her right hand, letting the newsprint fall across her lap and her left hand. Glancing around, Maggie slowly moved her hand beneath the paper and felt for the loose end cap on the third slat. She wiggled it loose and, carefully keeping it hidden under the paper, felt inside the slat. There was nothing there, but then she hadn't expected anything. She slid the end cap back in place and shifted her attention back to the news. She read about the Luftwaffe's latest successes over England, where German flyers were enjoying such good hunting that the invasion would be uncontested. As she read, she frequently looked around, noting who else was in the park. A mother and two small children were playing some kind of game in a grassy area. Two Wehrmacht officers were strolling and smoking on the far side of the plaza. To her right, two foreign workers in dirty, gray overalls were sweeping the walkway. They wore orange armbands emblazoned with black *P*s. Maggie took a bite of her apple, tart and sweet at the same time—sort of like life in Berlin, she thought. Maggie pondered the events that had brought her out to the park on this sunny afternoon: her affair with Kurt; that first, unpromising impression of Dieter; Clive's on-air collapse; Erich Greinke. Where was she headed now, with this first step along a different, more treacherous path?

◆　◆　◆

"Ah, Herr Nutt! How do you do?" exclaimed Joseph Goebbels as he climbed into the back of his Mercedes limousine and settled his slight frame next to Chesney Nutt.

The propaganda ministry's foreign press office had notified Ches earlier in the evening to stand by to accompany the minister. When the British bombed Berlin, Goebbels, in his role as Gauleiter, toured the damaged areas, coordinating firefighting, repairs, and relief. Ches had waited in the well-appointed lobby of the Hotel Kaiserhof, Goebbels's official residence, from about eight o'clock on. Around ten o'clock, the air raid sirens had begun to blare, beckoning the city's residents to their shelters. As a foreign correspondent, Ches had elected to remain aboveground, listening first to the approaching drone of the British bombers and then to the warm reception they were given by the capital's air defense gunners. Tonight's bombs had fallen to the north of the

Spree River, allowing Ches to relax on the lobby's comfortable leather sofa, focus on his bourbon and water, and review his notes on the Bethel story.

Once the drone of the bombers had begun to recede and the concussions from the bombs had faded away, Ches had been escorted to Goebbels's car, which had been brought around to the hotel's main entrance. A second car for the minister's staff sat just behind. Goebbels had appeared quickly once the immediate danger had passed, trailed by aides and assistants. Goebbels moved deliberately despite a leg deformed by childhood illness. Now, as the cars pulled away from the Kaiserhof and turned onto the Wilhelmstraße, the minister turned to his guest.

"Like a pinprick, isn't it?" Goebbels smiled as his driver steered the open-topped car toward the north, where the sky glowed a pale orange.

"A pretty loud and dangerous pinprick, Minister," Ches replied. Goebbels was one of the few men Ches had ever been around who made him feel big. Yet the force of Goebbels's personality—his charisma—enabled him to hold his own in the company of larger men like Hitler and even the corpulent Goering.

Goebbels held his smile. "You will see, Herr Nutt, how ineffectual the British bombing is. It is designed merely to terrorize our citizens through its randomness. There is no military advantage to be gained from the bombing of homes and schools and churches. No, the British are simply trying to destroy morale. You will see in a few moments how badly they are failing."

"So, you're saying, Minister"—Ches pulled out his battered notepad—"that the English aren't attacking military targets? That they are bombing only civilian areas of the city?"

"Precisely!" Goebbels agreed enthusiastically, the orange glow of the approaching fires reflecting off his narrow face. "And you will see the incredible bravery and stamina with which our Berliners are responding to this despicable tactic!"

Shortly, the car was brought to a halt by a policeman waving a torch. Goebbels quickly dismounted from the car, leaving Ches scrambling to catch up. The driver stayed with the Mercedes, but two aides from the trailing car followed along with Goebbels and Ches as they picked their way around a collapsed wall of bricks and mortar. Ahead in the next block, a building was blazing, a pumper truck gallantly spraying streams of water into the inferno in what looked to Ches like a losing battle. As Ches watched, men continued to appear from the darkness and join the fight. Ches guessed that they had emerged from their shelters only to find that their neighborhood had received the heaviest damage of the night's raid.

"What building is that, Minister?" Ches asked, pointing to the fire. Large sparks floated skyward amid the flames and thick, black smoke, hiding the stars that had been visible earlier.

"It is, or was, an apartment building," Goebbels answered, his brown eyes never leaving the fire. "According to Herr Rolf there"— Goebbels indicated one of the firefighters with whom Ches had seen him speak—"there was a stationer's store and a butcher's shop on the street level and then four apartments above."

"And the occupants?"

"Thankfully, all safe." Goebbels turned to Ches and smiled. "You see, Herr Nutt, our system of civil defense is quite sophisticated. We have our early-warning network and strong air defenses. We protect our citizens from the few random bombers that do get through by sheltering them in our extensive network of bunkers."

The heat from the fire was turning the firefighters' stream of water into steam and warming Ches to the point that he untied the belt holding his overcoat closed. A small crowd had gathered to watch the firemen. Goebbels, like any good politician—and he was one of the best—strode over and began to shake hands. Ches watched from several yards away as the faces in the crowd brightened, then cracked into grins and smiles. Soon he heard laughter, as Goebbels bucked up their spirits with his sarcastic barbs at the British. "Yes," Goebbels replied to an elderly woman clutching a blanket about her shoulders, "we will have a relief van here shortly. They will assist you in finding new rooms. I am sorry for the loss of your flat. Look at it as your contribution to beating the English!" He put his hand on the woman's shoulder and gave it a gentle squeeze. "We are taking the best they have and we will return it to them with interest!" he called out to the crowd, which responded with cheers and applause.

"*Jawohl*, Herr Minister!" The old woman smiled, shaking her fist.

As word spread that Goebbels was in the neighborhood, the crowd began to grow. Ches was impressed that these Berliners cheered the Gauleiter even as the fire continued to burn, continued to warm the chilly night. Indeed, Ches thought, their morale seemed unaffected by the bombing of their homes.

After several minutes, Goebbels bade the still growing crowd good night and moved away to speak again with Herr Rolf, whom Ches determined was leading the firefighting efforts. Ches watched as Rolf, sweat streaming down his face, nodded and gestured toward the still burning building. When Ches tried to move in closer so he could hear the exchange, one of Goebbels's aides intercepted him. "Not safe. Too close," he warned, holding up his hands and stepping into Ches's path.

By the time Goebbels returned to his car, the crowd had begun to dwindle. Those who still had homes returned to get what little sleep they could during what remained of the night. Those whose possessions had been destroyed or damaged lined up behind a government van to register for new accommodations and clothing.

"Look around you, Herr Nutt," Goebbels said as the car began to back away from the scene. "What you see is a purely civilian area bombed by the British warmongers. Do you see factories here? No," Goebbels answered his own question. "Do you see supply depots? No. Railyards? No. I ask you, Herr Nutt, as a neutral observer, do you see anything of military interest in this area?"

"Only you, Herr Minister. Only you."

Goebbels laughed.

◆ ◆ ◆

As the black Mercedes crossed the Spree on its journey back to the Kaiserhof, Ches felt the air cool. He pulled his overcoat closed and shifted in his seat to have a better look at Goebbels.

"May I ask you a question on an unrelated topic, Herr Minister?" Ches ventured.

"Of course. On any topic, Herr Nutt. I respect your objectivity and the fairness of your reporting. Your feature on Herr Barnes last year is a good case in point."

"Thank you, Herr Minister." Ches was almost facing Goebbels in the back of the car. "I've been picking up some rumors about a government program that euthanizes the mentally infirm," Ches said, closely watching for Goebbels's reaction. "What do you know about it?"

"Nothing, of course," Goebbels responded confidently. "A program such as you describe would be under the purview of the ministry of health—if it existed."

"So, you're saying it doesn't?"

"Not to my knowledge," Goebbels replied. "Perhaps I could make some inquiries for you. Where did you hear these rumors?"

It was Ches's turn to laugh. "Now, Herr Minister, you know I can't reveal sources."

Goebbels smiled again. "Of course not. I was merely offering my services. As I said earlier, I have complete confidence in the fairness of your reporting and would not wish to interfere in any story you are developing. Just know that I am at your service should a need arise. Well, and here we are!" Goebbels said as the limousine pulled into the circular driveway of the Kaiserhof. "Home again and none the worse for our trip!"

Goebbels's driver was quickly out from behind the wheel and holding open the rear door for his minister. Goebbels leaned forward as if to step out of the car, then paused. He glanced over his shoulder at Ches. "Remember what you saw tonight, Herr Nutt. Remember the indiscriminate bombing of civilian areas. Remember the valiant Berliners bombed from their homes yet fortified by their belief in their Führer. That's not a story founded on rumors, but one you witnessed with your own eyes." He smiled again. *"Gute Nacht!"*

"Good night, Herr Minister," Ches said as Goebbels climbed out of the car and headed through the double doors into the lobby.

◆ ◆ ◆

Although she had grown accustomed to her regular broadcasts, Maggie was nonetheless nervous on this late September Thursday. Tonight, the Swingin' Seven were scheduled to broadcast a new program featuring popular American tunes—with new lyrics. Maggie and Dieter had devoted even more hours than usual to choosing the music and writing the new words—words with a decidedly pointed message. Maggie had also visited several Berlin nightclubs searching for a singer to provide the vocals. She had discovered Traudle Lange, a large woman with a deep, creamy voice.

Traudle and the band had practiced together for a couple of hours that afternoon. Now, with just two minutes until airtime, Maggie was worrying that it had not been enough. Space was tight in the studio, with the band, instruments, music stands, and paraphernalia. Add in Maggie and an overweight singer, and Maggie just hoped they wouldn't be tripping all over one another.

Maggie's role was mistress of ceremonies. Her job was to introduce the program, the band, and Traudle, and to provide the transitions between pieces.

A gentle knock on the glass window of the studio pulled Maggie back to the moment. She stared through the glass at Dieter as he raised his right hand and slowly ticked off the seconds. The red light flickered on, and Dieter pointed to Maggie.

"Good evening, friends," she began. "This is Betty from Berlin calling. Tonight we offer a special music program featuring Traudle Lange and the Swingin' Seven. We hope you enjoy this first piece. It's a tune you all know, and it's dedicated to the doomed boys in Bomber Command." Maggie nodded briskly to Charlie the bandleader, and the group broke into "Nothing Could Be Finer." As the first verse ended, Traudle stepped up to the microphone. The band continued playing, rolling smoothly into the second verse, and Traudle began to sing.

> Nothing could be better than some moonlit
>   bombing weather in the morning
> Nothing more satisfying than to watch civilians
>   dying in the morning
> Dropping bombs on Berlin, watching them
>   explode,
> Seeing those bright fires turning the night to
>   gold.
> Flying over Berlin with a load of high explosives
>   in the morning
> Dodging flak and fighters dropping bombs on
>   you poor blighters in the morning
> If we all live through it, if we all get home, we'll
>   start off again tomorrow from our aerodrome
> Nothing could be better than some moonlit
>   bombing weather in the morning.
>
> Nothing quite like killing from a twenty-thou-
>   sand-foot ceiling in the morning
> Churchill keeps us flying, we keep dealing death
>   and dying in the morning

German fighters rising up into the night sky,
 they'd like to turn the tables and make us the
 ones to die
Nothing could be better than some cloud-free
 bombing weather in the morning
Dropping high explosives making Germans into
 toasties in the morning
Wish the senseless slaughter could be brought to
 a stop, but that would take an order from the
 big man at the top
Nothing could be better than some cloud-free
 bombing weather in the morning!

Traudle sang as the band played through three more songs, each with new lyrics approved by the ministry and designed to convey the villainy of the British bomber forces. Happily for Maggie, the broadcast was relatively error free. She was relieved when the moment came for her customary signoff. "This is Betty from Berlin. I look forward to visiting with you again soon. Good night."

As the musicians packed away their instruments, Dieter met Maggie at the recording studio's back door. "I thought that went remarkably well. Once again you have added a weapon to our propaganda arsenal." Dieter smiled. "I love beautiful and intelligent women!"

"How many do you know?" Maggie teased. "I was a little worried, but Traudle and the band seemed to work well together. She has a great voice for radio."

"And a great face for it, too," Dieter agreed, drawing a playful punch from Maggie. "Seriously, Maggie," Dieter began as they stepped out into the cool night air of the courtyard, "your good work—of which there has been no shortage, by the way—has continued to draw the attention of my superiors."

Maggie linked her arm through Dieter's. "You have no superiors, darling."

"True. Let me rephrase that: my seniors." Dieter smiled. "My seniors have noted your professionalism and talent, dear Maggie. Herr Direktor Bauer and Dr. Goebbels have you in mind for a new position."

Maggie stopped and turned toward him. She was both excited and conflicted. To be recognized for good performance was certainly gratifying. To be entrusted with additional responsibility was likewise heady stuff for a young woman. But, she cautioned herself, what price might she pay for the new opportunity? "What type of position?"

"Well, it seems pretty clear that we aren't going to win the war by inciting the English to rise up and overthrow Churchill. Our best chance is to isolate Great Britain politically. Without allies, even the British Empire isn't strong enough to stand against Germany. Goebbels is considering a shift in strategy, a shift that involves you."

"What kind of shift?"

"I think you need to hear the rest of it directly from Dr. Goebbels."

"Tell me," Maggie pleaded, holding Dieter's hands in hers. "I'll reward you!" she promised with raised eyebrows and a smile.

Dieter laughed. "Why, Maggie, simply being in your presence is reward enough for a simple man like me."

"Oh," Maggie said with a grin, "you're just saying that because it's true."

◆ ◆ ◆

Maggie exited the A Line train at Stadtmitte station, eager to get away from the odor of so many bodies, so rarely washed, packed so tightly together. Without her illicit ration card and the extra soap it provided, Maggie knew she would be one of the unclean as well. She silently gave thanks for Erich Greinke's largesse.

Under a pleasant morning sun, Maggie walked northwest six blocks toward the headquarters building of the propaganda ministry. She had plenty of time before her scheduled 11:45 a.m. appointment with Goebbels, and she enjoyed the morning air and the sunshine. Dieter had refused to tell her more about why Goebbels wanted to see her. He had said only that she had an appointment with the minister and Herr Direktor Bauer the following morning, and that under no circumstances should she be even one second late.

Maggie strolled north along the Wilhelmstraße, passed through the security checkpoint, and entered the ministry through its main entrance. From her previous visit, she remembered the location of the minister's office and had no trouble finding her way there. At 11:35 a.m., she was shown to a seat by one of Goebbels's undersecretaries. She sat nervously in the straight-backed chair, anxious to learn about her potential new assignment.

At 11:50 a.m., the large wooden doors to Goebbels's office opened a crack, and a well-dressed man stepped out. "Fräulein O'Dea"—he bowed in front of Maggie—"I am Herr Oven, the minister's secretary. Dr. Goebbels will see you now. Please follow me." Oven was courtly, but not friendly. He led Maggie toward the large doors, pulled one open, and stepped to the side to allow Maggie to pass.

As she stepped inside, Maggie felt the door close behind her. To her front was the same massive desk she remembered from her previous visit; behind it, the same small man. A larger man, Direktor Bauer, was seated in one of the large, red leather armchairs arrayed in front of the desk.

"Ah, Fräulein Maggie!" Goebbels exclaimed, a welcoming smile on his lips. "Won't you please come and have a seat?" He stood and gestured toward one of the chairs. "Herr Direktor Bauer and I were just discussing you."

"Good morning, my dear." Bauer smiled weakly, offering his hand. Maggie noticed Bauer was far less comfortable in the minister's office than he was on his own turf at Broadcasting House.

Goebbels remained standing behind the desk as Maggie took her seat and Bauer resumed his. "I have decided to transition our English-language propaganda to a new strategy. Herr Direktor Bauer concurs with this change, of course." *I'll just bet he does,* thought Maggie. "It is no longer reasonable to believe that our propaganda efforts can bring about a change in Britain's leadership. We must continue to weaken the will of the English to fight, but we must shift our efforts to a more important objective. That's why we have asked you to join us this morning." Goebbels's intense brown eyes were locked on to Maggie's face, almost as if he was in a trance.

Maggie wondered how a man so meticulous and so conscious of appearances had not perceived that his cavernous office and massive desk accentuated his small stature and slight build. The office was larger than the control room at Broadcasting House. The furnishings were oversize. Even the twin portraits of Hitler and Frederick the Great were larger than life.

"So, Fräulein Maggie, what do you say?"

Maggie realized she had allowed her mind to wander. She feared she had missed the main point. "Herr Minister, I am honored that you would consider me for a position of responsibility," she said, attempting to cover her lapse.

"*Wunderbar!* I knew we could count on you!" Goebbels spread his hands apart, as if to catch something dropped from the sky, a smile spreading across his face. "Now, let us get to details, as they say. You will become chief of American section in the Broadcasting Division. You will be responsible for creating a broadcasting program directed not at the English, but at America. You will report through Herr Schmidt and Herr Direktor Bauer to me and will attend our weekly staff meeting. We must coordinate your broadcasting message with our other propaganda outlets and with our foreign press office."

"Herr Minister." Maggie was completely alert now. It was as if a thousand tiny needles were pricking her skin. "What is the objective of our new program?"

Goebbels looked from Maggie to Bauer and back, a slightly puzzled expression on his face. "Why, to keep America out of this war, of course!"

◆ ◆ ◆

"So, he said, 'To keep America out of the war,'" Maggie mimicked Joseph Goebbels as she recounted her visit to Chesney Nutt in the Adlon Hotel bar late that night. They were sitting at his favorite corner table, Ches with his bourbon and water, Maggie with her whiskey neat. She had contrived to accompany Clive Barnes back to his residential suite at the hotel, hoping to "accidentally" run into Erich Greinke. She was mindful of Erich's admonition that they should no longer meet in public, but she wanted to personally share her new assignment with him since they still hadn't established the means to communicate surreptitiously.

"Very interesting, Maggie," Ches said after considering her story for a moment. "You realize, don't you, that this puts you working at odds with your native country? How you gonna feel about that?"

"But that's the thing, Ches," Maggie protested, "I'll be working *for* the best interests of my—of our—country! Keeping us out of this war has to be the right thing to do."

Ches just sat and stared at her for a minute. He shifted his gaze to his drink and lifted the glass to his lips. "You know, Maggie, your friend Clive once told me the same thing. Look at him now." Clive had continued to drink heavily since the fall of France. "I'd hate to see a pretty, young thing like you get broken up over this thing."

"OK, Ches, you tell me how it's not in America's best interests to stay out of this thing; how I wouldn't be serving my country to help keep us out of it." Maggie was intense, color rising in her cheeks, her eyes locked on to Ches's.

"Well, here's a scenario, my dear." Ches threw back the rest of his drink and wiped his mouth with a cocktail napkin. "Suppose, just suppose, that our friend Dr. Goebbels and his boss, Herr Hitler, and their merry band hope to pick off the great powers one by one. Start with England, an island nation. Blockade it with their U-boats. Strangle shipping, cut off their lifeline, and starve the British into capitulation. Then, after a few months of R-and-R, maybe they turn their thoughts and their considerable war machine on the good old US of A. Maybe they start with their friends in Mexico or South America. Slowly they consolidate their gains, strengthen their allies, and before you know it, they're crossing the Rio Grande. By keeping America out of it, as you say, you may just be lulling our citizens into a state of false security. Didja ever think of that?"

Maggie looked away, counting the patrons at the bar. When she looked back, Ches was smiling.

"I'm not saying that's the Nazis' grand plan, Maggie. I'm just saying that you can't trust Herr Hitler and company. You've seen how ruthless they are. You even know how they think; hell, you see it every day. By the way, Maggie," Ches continued, lighting a cigarette, "I had a little face time with your boss the other evening. We went tooling around in his big old official car to inspect the response to the bombing up north of the river. On the way back, I asked him if there was an official euthanasia program."

Maggie froze, her glass halfway to her lips. Slowly she lowered it back to the cloth-covered table. "And?"

"He denied it, of course. But he did offer to help me track down my sources. That was real kind of him, don't you think?" Ches smiled genially.

"Aren't you taking a big risk asking Goebbels a question like that?"

"A calculated risk," he answered. "I didn't make a big deal out of it, didn't push him or anything like that. I just wanted to see how he'd respond." Ches blew a cloud of blue smoke toward the ceiling. "He's a pretty cool customer, that one. But I still don't have enough to make a story."

"Ches," Maggie said with pleading eyes, reaching across the table to place her hand on his forearm, "do me a favor, will you?"

"Sure I will."

"Tell Erich to get in touch with me."

◆ ◆ ◆

"Of course you should do it!" Erich Greinke said two days later in the back office of the embassy's passport control section. "It's really a lucky break!" He was pacing back and forth, rubbing his hands together, trying to control the excitement he felt at having heard about Maggie's new job. "You'll be closer than ever to Goebbels's inner circle. This should really help us, Maggie."

"But won't I be in danger of being seen as a traitor?"

"Is Lindbergh considered a traitor? The America First Committee hasn't got a stronger voice than Colonel Lindbergh. Some people may disagree with him, but no one considers him a traitor. Besides, Maggie"—Erich stopped pacing and perched himself on the front corner of his desk—"what better cover could you possibly have?"

Ostensibly, Maggie had been summoned back to the embassy to pick up her new passport. With the swelling tide of refugees attempting to escape from Europe, the United States, through its passport control offices, was improving the security of its documents in order to increase the difficulty of forgery.

Once the issue of Maggie's new job was settled, Erich spent twenty-five minutes instructing her on communication techniques. Maggie reported that she had followed Erich's instructions on eating her daily lunch, including an apple, in the park. She had accessed the cavity in the third slat of the bench and felt confident that she could deposit messages there without arousing suspicion.

Erich instructed Maggie in the use of ciphers and secret writing. *So, that's what the apples are for,* Maggie mused. Erich also told her how to signal that a message was ready for pickup and how he would communicate with her on a routine basis.

"Since face-to-face meetings are risky," he began, "I'll communicate with you by letter. Remember those letters of your father's that I asked you to bring me?"

Maggie nodded.

"Within the next few weeks, you'll get a letter from your father telling you about an old friend of his who has moved to Switzerland. The letter will include the friend's address. Not long after that, you'll receive a letter from the friend in Switzerland." Erich reached back to the top of the desk and pulled a piece of paper from a plain envelope. "Here," he said, handing it to Maggie. "This is the background on your father's friend, including your relationship, past contacts, et cetera. Memorize it, then burn it. Don't leave any traces. This is part of your cover story should anyone ever question you." Erich's veiled warning frightened Maggie, but she was committed now, and her pride wouldn't let her back out.

"Once you begin receiving letters, we want you to reply to them, using the return address. It's actually a letterbox in Switzerland that our people will service. Use the techniques we've practiced, including the code we talked about."

"We talked about how to use a one-time pad," Maggie said, referring to the key to their cipher, "but you haven't given me the pad you want us to use."

"I was hoping you'd ask." Erich smiled. "You just passed your first test." He stood up and stepped back behind the desk. He bent down and pulled a well-worn book from a drawer. "Here you go." He handed the book to Maggie. "This is your one-time pad."

"*Lady Chatterley's Lover*? Are you kidding me?" Maggie asked with wide eyes. She noticed Erich's ears redden. "I'm not sure this is the kind of book a lady of my new status should have around her flat."

"Yeah, well, it's the only book I have that I've got two copies of, so it's the one we'll have to use."

Maggie hesitated for a moment, then laughed and stuffed the tome into her handbag. "Fine," she snapped, shaking her head. "We'll just make do."

"That's the spirit, Maggie." Erich glanced at his watch. "You've been here long enough. Any questions?"

"What should I report and how often?"

"To begin with, just tell us what your routine is and what you see and hear going on at Broadcasting House and at the ministry. As things move along, we'll send you any specific requests for information in our letters."

Maggie stood up, smoothed her skirt, and picked up her book-laden bag.

"Got your passport?" Erich asked. She held it up by her face. "Off you go, then. Good luck, Maggie. Remember the routine if you need to contact me in a hurry. And remember this, too: our objective is the same as Dr. Goebbels's—to keep America out of this war."

CHAPTER 19

Berlin, Germany
November 1940

Maggie had received the first letter from John Reilly near the end of October. The letter had been postmarked in Bern, Switzerland, and had been informal in tone, as would be appropriate for a letter between old friends. Of course, Maggie and Reilly weren't old friends; in fact, Reilly didn't even exist. He was simply the mechanism Erich Greinke had created to allow unfettered communication between himself and Maggie.

Reilly's letter included references to Maggie's father and stepmother in the States as well as details about Reilly's work at Nestlé, the Swiss chocolatier. Reilly expressed the hope that Maggie would respond to his letter. Indeed, she would.

Dieter lingered in her doorway as Maggie kissed him good night. He turned to leave, then turned back and pulled her close once again, pecking her on the forehead. "Good night, Maggie O'Dea," he said quietly.

Maggie stood with the door cracked open and watched Dieter descend the darkened steps. She heard the building's front door shut. She pushed her own door closed and latched it. She had fallen for

Dieter. His gentleness and desire to please her, along with his treatment of her as an intellectual and professional equal, was a combination Maggie had not experienced before. She found herself laughing at his silly jokes, admiring his judgment, and envying his physical stamina. One reason he rarely spent the night with her was that he never seemed to want to sleep, even when Maggie could no longer hold her eyes open.

On this particular rainy November night, however, Maggie found her energy renewed with the bolting of her door. She had selected this Saturday night to write her first letter to John Reilly. She hung up her robe and redressed, pulling on a wool sweater and light jacket along with some heavy slacks. It was too cold in the apartment for more comfortable attire.

Maggie moved to her small kitchen, grabbing an apple from a bowl on the counter and picking up a small paring knife. She sliced the apple as thinly as she could without cutting herself, piling one slice on top of another into a small bowl. Once she was done with the slicing, she took a pestle and began to mash the apple pieces into a mush. She then poured the juice off into a glass and portioned a measure of water into it.

Next, Maggie took a plain piece of paper and laid it out on the hard countertop. Using a dry dish towel, she gently brushed the paper from corner to corner. Working by the light of twin candles, Maggie picked up a wooden stylus given to her by Erich Greinke. It looked something like a toothpick, only larger, but with the same pointed end. Maggie turned the paper at an angle, dipped the stylus into the liquid, and wrote the number ten at the top of the page. Within seconds, the writing disappeared.

Good, Maggie thought, *it's working as advertised.*

This number would serve as the key to the one-time pad that John Reilly—whoever he was—would use to decipher the message Maggie was about to write. It told Reilly what page of the pad—in this case, *Lady Chatterley's Lover*—to use. Specifying the page was critical, as each subsequent letter to John Reilly would use a different page for encoding, and there was no guarantee that letters would be received in the order they were written and sent. Erich had impressed upon her that under no circumstances should a page be used more than once. That, he had said, would defeat the security of the one-time pad.

Maggie then took her message, which she had written out by candlelight the previous evening, and began to encode it. She and Erich had agreed that the page number, in this case page ten, would not only signify to the receiving party the page number in the novel that would serve as the key to the cipher but also provide the multiplier for the letters to be included in the message. Maggie's eyes had glazed over at this and later stages in Erich's description of the process, but he was patient with her. With ten as the multiplier, an *A*, the first letter in the alphabet, would be written as eleven, a *B* as twelve, and so on. Using the word *Berlin* as an example: once Maggie had converted her plain text message into the "multiplied" text by adding ten to each number, the values for the text would be:

B E R L I N
12 15 28 22 19 24

Since that alone wouldn't provide a very robust code for this six-letter word, there was an additional step, which again involved the use of the novel, their one-time pad. Maggie would turn to her "key" page and find the first six letters—say, *t-h-e-w-o-m* if the first words on the page were *the women*—and give those letters the same treatment, once again applying the "multiplier" ten to the plain text values of its letters:

T H E W O M
30 18 15 33 25 23

Then she would add the corresponding values together to determine the final coded values for the word *Berlin* to be written with the apple juice:

B E R L I N
42 33 43 55 44 47

If the next word to be coded consisted of four letters, Maggie would use the next four letters on the page for this step and so on.

John Reilly, or whoever deciphered the letter on the receiving end, would note the page number written on the letter, turn to that page in the novel, and then work backward to arrive at the plain text values for each of the message's coded words. By using a page only once, the code was, theoretically at least, unbreakable.

Once she had become familiar with the one-time pad procedures, Maggie found that the actual work went fairly quickly. After fifty minutes or so, she had filled the page, although to the casual observer, it appeared blank again. Maggie waited several more minutes to be sure the apple juice solution had completely dried. Then she straightened the paper and began her reply to the "real" John Reilly. She briefly described her job and told her correspondent about life in wartime Berlin. She was careful to use descriptions even Dr. Goebbels would approve of. She closed with the hope that Reilly would continue their fledgling correspondence.

At midnight, she blew out the candles and collapsed on her bed. The rain, she hoped, would guarantee a bomb-free night—and sound sleep.

◆ ◆ ◆

By the end of the following week, Erich Greinke in Berlin was reading the letter Maggie O'Dea had mailed to John Reilly in Bern. He was most interested in the invisible portion of the letter, which he coaxed to light through the careful application of steam from a small tea kettle. As he passed the letter back and forth above the kettle's spout, the apple juice characters began to reappear as brown numbers on the page.

Next, Erich took out his copy of Lawrence's scandalous novel, turned to page ten, and began to decode the message. Writing it letter by letter on a lined tablet, Erich marveled at Maggie's seemingly intuitive skills of observation. She had condensed a description of Goebbels's daily routine from the time he arrived at his office in the morning (8:20 a.m.) until he left in the early evening. Erich shook his head slowly, a grin spreading across his face. It seemed that Maggie approached her unofficial duties with the same skill and determination her professional responsibilities demanded. Erich was well pleased.

◆ ◆ ◆

Maggie's report on Goebbels's routine was based in part on her own observations. Goebbels had insisted that Maggie, a rising star within his ministry, accompany Bauer and Dieter to his daily eleven o'clock department head meeting. Here, broad strategies were reviewed and specific tactics discussed to ensure that the entire Ministry of Public Enlightenment and Propaganda spoke with one voice, whether that voice spoke English, French, Norwegian, or one of the dozens of other languages the ministry employed to inform the world of the glorious achievements of the Third Reich.

Maggie was at first captivated by her seat at this table of power. She listened carefully and spoke only when asked a question. Slowly, the men around the table began to accept her presence, despite their underlying suspicions of a woman functioning at their exalted level. In barely two years, Maggie had fashioned herself into a propagandist first class. And, if she didn't always understand the Nazi culture or philosophy, she knew how to convey the right message to her listeners in North America.

Maggie still presented her personal commentaries twice a week. She was still popular in Great Britain, where she was considered a more reasonable, friendlier voice than some of Dieter's other broadcasters, and she was slowly gaining popularity in the United States, where she was known only as Betty from Berlin. Targeting America meant a change in her broadcasting hours: the United States was five hours behind

London, six behind Berlin. Her work rarely ended now before three or four o'clock in the morning. Her days started later as well. Where she used to hustle, often without success, to beat Dieter into the office, now she had to defer, usually arriving just in time to catch a ride with Dieter and Bauer on their way to the Wilhelmstraße headquarters for the morning conference.

In addition to her own broadcasts, Maggie supervised the production of the music programs featuring the Swingin' Seven, provided script direction and review to the other English-language commentators targeting North America, and fed a constant stream of new programming ideas to Dieter. As head of English Section, Dieter was still Maggie's nominal supervisor. She continued to report through him to Bauer. But Maggie's presence at Goebbels's daily meetings reflected the importance the Nazis placed on her American mission and their confidence in her.

Maggie's new schedule, and her increased workload, meant her time to be with Dieter was mostly limited to weekends. So was her letter writing.

◆　◆　◆

"Who are you writing?" Dieter asked one Sunday afternoon as he looked up from his book, *Gone with the Wind*. It was a bestseller in Berlin, and Dieter liked to imagine Maggie in the hoopskirts and crinoline of its heroine.

"A friend of my father's who's been transferred to Switzerland," Maggie replied without looking up. She had completed her coded message the night before, an outline of Goebbels's new strategy on America. Now, she was writing her cover letter to John Reilly. She had decided that letting Dieter know she was writing would make her relationship with Reilly less suspicious should it ever be discovered by someone else.

"What's he doing in Switzerland?"

"He works for Nestlé, the milk and chocolate company."

"How do you know him?"

"He was an Irish immigrant, like my father," Maggie explained, pleased to have the opportunity to practice the cover story under Dieter's gentle questioning. "He was in the dairy business and used to take out loans from my father's building and loan."

"How'd he get to Nestlé?"

"An excellent question." Maggie smiled. "I think I'll ask him!" She resumed writing, posing the very question Dieter had asked. Dieter resumed his reading.

◆ ◆ ◆

The British bombers stopped their raids on Berlin. The weather turned colder, the nights longer. Germans settled in for the winter, a treaty with Russia securing their eastern borders and the English Channel protecting them in the west.

CHAPTER 20

Berlin, Germany
March 1941

"That damn Jew-lover!" Goebbels was so worked up that he spat out his words. His face was flushed, and the veins in his neck and temples were bulging. Maggie had heard stories about the minister's temper but had never personally witnessed such an outburst. From his public performances, Maggie knew he possessed great oratorical skills, but there he was under control, following a script, seeking to persuade his listeners. Here he came across as furious, a loose cannon about to smash through the gunwales of this ship of state. His rant came back to the point.

"That damn Roosevelt! He claims that America is neutral and demands that we respect the neutrality of his shipping even while he works to pass this, this miserably hypocritical law that lets him flaunt his personal bias under the cover of legality!" The *this* in question was the new Lend-Lease Act that the president had signed into law, making it legal to supply belligerents with arms and munitions on a cash-and-carry basis. Lend-Lease allowed Great Britain, with its far-flung empire, to provide the United States long-term leases on British military bases in exchange for war matériel. Germany saw the new law as a street lawyer's tricky maneuver around America's long-professed neutrality.

"Fräulein Maggie!" Goebbels thundered, turning to focus his entire attention on his American section chief. "How do we combat this blatant partiality?" Goebbels paused to catch his breath and regain his composure as now every eye around the large conference table focused on Maggie.

Maggie stood slowly, smoothing out her skirt and tugging at her sleeves. "Herr Minister." She began by looking Goebbels directly in the eyes. She could see perspiration on his forehead. "We begin by realizing that although Roosevelt was reelected last year, it was his narrowest margin of victory yet. There is a large minority of Americans who do not hold to his views about intervention in the war. We must sharpen our focus on this core group."

"Yes, yes." Goebbels waved his hand impatiently. "This I know. How do you propose to do so?" His patience was short, his anger on display. Maggie was intent that it not be directed at her.

"Forty-five percent of the voters in last November's election voted for Mr. Wilkie, Roosevelt's opponent. We appeal to that forty-five percent by highlighting Roosevelt's bias and by attributing it to greed and corruption."

Goebbels's appearance had calmed, but the grip of his hands on the back of his chair indicated that he was still agitated. "Details!" he snapped. "How do you implement these tactics? What does it sound like?"

Maggie paused, looked down at some notes on the pad in front of her. She looked back up at Goebbels. "Something like this, Herr Minister." Maggie adopted her radio voice. "The president has signed into law the Lend-Lease Act, which will allow the shoe factories he owns in New York to sell boots to the British army at greatly inflated prices. But where else are the poor British to turn to shoe their homebound soldiers?"

Goebbels paused, staring at Maggie. Then he smiled. He wagged a finger at her and laughed. He turned his attention to the men seated around the large table. "There!" he chuckled. "There is a propagandist!" The others joined in the laughter, thankful that Maggie had provided an answer to break the minister's foul mood before it was turned on them.

◆ ◆ ◆

"Mr. Roosevelt's shoe factories will make a nice profit selling boots to the British army. But be careful, friends: don't let America get stuck once again fighting England's war. That the president wants to make a little money on the side shouldn't be justification for sending American boys to die for the British Empire. If we're not careful, America could get sucked into this war just as surely as Dorothy was pulled into that Kansas twister! America is a great country because Americans have always looked at both sides of the story. Look hard at this story. Don't let an elitist government with strong ties to big business and manufacturing send your boys off to do some other country's dirty work. This is Betty from Berlin. I look forward to visiting with you again soon. Good night."

Maggie had worked right up until airtime to get the tone of her commentary just right. She wanted to avoid the harsh, strident note struck by some of her colleagues. She wanted to keep a friendly relationship with her listeners in the belief that an adversarial approach would only push them away. She'd leave that approach to Robert Hipps or Julie Clay or one of the others.

"Well done, my dear," said Herr Direktor Bauer as she emerged from the broadcasting booth. With the greater recent emphasis on reaching America, Bauer, too, was staying later at Broadcasting House. "Exactly what Dr. Goebbels expected. Your commentary was recorded so it can be rebroadcast in three hours to reach the West Coast cities."

Already it was three thirty in the morning (eight thirty in the evening New York time). "You look tired, my dear. Are you quite finished for tonight?" Bauer asked in a paternal voice.

"Yes, Herr Direktor."

"Schmidt!" Bauer called out authoritatively. "Be so kind as to escort Fräulein O'Dea to her home."

Dieter crossed the control room quickly. "With pleasure, Herr Direktor," he replied, stealing a wink at Maggie.

◆ ◆ ◆

"You look somewhat tired yourself, darling," Maggie observed as she and Dieter walked carefully along the darkened street. "Not that I can actually see you, of course," she added with a laugh. Although a light rain was falling and the cloud cover lessened the risk of air raids, the blackout was still in effect. With no traffic on the roads, Dieter and Maggie were walking in the street, using the whitewashed curb to guide them.

"I don't need much sleep," he said, yawning. "But don't think I'm saying that just to get you to ask me up. I won't accept."

"And why not?" she asked with mock indignation. "Is something wrong with me?"

"Of course not!" He was grinning in the early-morning darkness. "It's just that Herr Direktor Bauer is correct, for once," he chuckled. "You need some rest. My chief American deputy must be at the peak of performance. She must have a rested mind and clear judgment so she can continue to meet my high expectations of her performance."

The pair reached the front steps to Maggie's apartment building. As she pulled the key from her purse, Maggie turned to Dieter. "Sure you won't come up?"

"I'd love to," he replied.

Chapter 21

Berlin, Germany
June 1941

"What say there, buddy boy?" Ches asked with a smile as Erich slid onto the bench across from him. Ches was working on his second bourbon while he scratched out notes on a ragged yellow pad. The Adlon Bar was less crowded than usual. With the air raids of the previous autumn, many correspondents had packed up their typewriters and gone home. Not Ches. He was at home wherever there was a story—and at present Berlin was the best story going.

"Did you see the article?" Erich asked, waving to Georg at the bar. Georg smiled and nodded.

"Yeah, I saw it." Dr. Goebbels, in his regular column in the Nazi party newspaper, the *Völkischer Beobachter*, had written that the invasion of England could begin at any time.

"Well? What'd you think?" Erich paused as Georg set a gin and tonic in front of him. "*Danke*, Georg."

"*Bitte sehr, mein Herr!*" Georg smiled and returned to the bar.

Ches thought for a moment while his finger fished around the inside of his pack for the last cigarette. "Well, buddy boy," he said, slipping the unlit smoke between his chapped lips, "it seems awfully ballsy to me. But, you know, it sort of follows their game."

"How so?" Erich asked, leaning forward with his lighter.

Ches took a pull on the cigarette and leaned back, keeping his eyes on his young friend as he blew smoke from the side of his mouth. "Well, remember how they started things off in the Sudetenland? It was sort of like, 'Hey! Here we come!' Then Poland was kind of the same thing. Not very subtle. These fellows just sort of line up and charge straight at you, and if you aren't smart enough to get out of their way, why, they just run right over you."

"So, you think they're about to invade?"

Ches paused and scratched the back of his ear, the cigarette dangling from his lips. "No, I didn't say that. Can't say that. I just don't know. None of my usual sources is talking."

"Why don't you just ask your pal the good Herr *Doktor*?"

"Oh, I dare not," Ches chuckled. "Ever since I asked him about his euthanasia program he's been rather cool to me—even though I wrote a pretty flattering piece about our ride together to inspect the bombing damage. Yep, I think old Dr. Goebbels is peeved with me."

"I tried to find some more copies of his article, but the papers were already gone."

"That's right. They had a crew of folks rushing around collecting them back. They even pulled 'em out of the press club lounge. Said there had been a printing mistake. Mistake, my ass!" Ches spat, his cynical grin fixed in place. "Those boys are up to something."

"Yeah, but what?"

◆　◆　◆

On her way home through the early-morning darkness, Maggie fished in her jacket pocket for the thumbtack and pulled it out, concealing it in her left hand. She stopped in front of an oak tree, the third one in front of her apartment building. While bracing herself with her left hand, she adjusted her shoe as though to dislodge a pebble. At the same time, she stuck the thumbtack into the bark of the tree just at eye level. Then she continued walking toward her apartment.

Maggie had continued to write letters to John Reilly in Bern. She hoped the information, mostly about the inner workings of the ministry and whatever else she could pick up about Goebbels, was useful, but she received no feedback or even acknowledgment. She didn't even know if her letters were being received. One of the problems with her letters, a problem Erich Greinke had identified to her in their sessions in the passport control office, was that they were a relatively slow means of communication. Urgent information would have to be dealt with in a more expeditious manner: the dead drop.

Erich and Maggie had agreed on a simple signal to let the other know that information had been left in the third slat of the park bench: the thumbtack. By placing the tack on the sidewalk side of the third tree from her building, Maggie was signaling that the drop needed to be "serviced," or picked up. A tack in the last tree on the block, placed at knee height parallel to the curb, was a signal for Maggie to pick up information from the bench. Maggie had no idea who watched for the signal or who serviced the dead drop; Erich had told her she didn't need to know.

Maggie had been awake the previous morning until almost six o'clock encoding and writing the message she would leave in the park later this afternoon. For now, she was anxious for sleep. Entering her apartment, she checked that the east-facing window was completely covered by the blackout curtain—not to keep the light in, but to keep the sun out when it rose in just a couple of more hours. Maggie stripped quickly, pulled on a cotton gown, and slid beneath the sheets.

◆ ◆ ◆

Her attendance at Goebbels's daily staff meeting had changed Maggie's routine. She now reported to work around ten in the morning for a quick scan of the headlines. Then she caught a ride with Dieter and Bauer to the ministry headquarters on the Wilhelmstraße. If there was no official car in which she could hitch a ride, Maggie took the A train from Adolf Hitler Platz to the Stadtmitte station. After her meeting at the ministry, Maggie returned to Broadcasting House and began her day's work. She usually took her lunch break in midafternoon, around three o'clock.

On this warm, late-spring day, Maggie strolled toward her favorite park bench, the sun on her face. She carried her lunch—a cold bratwurst, a portion of potato salad, and an apple—in a small bag, along with a newspaper under her arm.

Maggie set her lunch on the bench beside her and opened her newspaper. As she appeared to scan the headlines, she covertly examined the park, looking for anything or anybody who appeared out of place. On pretty days, there were more children in the park, more young lovers holding hands and strolling, and more dog lovers with their animals leading them around by their leashes. Maggie noticed workers from nearby offices with the same idea about lunch that she appeared to have, as well as the foreign workers who were busy raking the paths and keeping the park clean.

Satisfied that she was not drawing undue attention, Maggie carefully pulled her message from her purse. Holding the newspaper with her right hand, she let the other side of the newsprint fall across her lap—and her left hand. With her hand covered, she wiggled loose the end cap of the third slat and slid the wax-wrapped paper into place. She quickly replaced the end cap, leaning forward as though she was concentrating on a particular article. She held the pose for several minutes, forcing herself to read and then reread an article in the unlikely event someone should actually question her about the paper. When she finally looked back up, after what seemed like several minutes, she noted that everything was the same as it had been before. The only difference was that the foreign workers had moved closer with their raking and pruning.

Maggie remained a few more minutes. She felt light perspiration on her forehead and was certain those closest to her, a pair of secretaries from Broadcasting House and an elderly couple walking their dachshund, could surely hear the hammering of her heart. Finally, she collected the remnants of her lunch, her purse, and her paper and stood. She tossed the leftovers in a trash barrel and headed the two blocks back to Broadcasting House.

Making the drop had been nerve-racking, but she hoped to an observer that this lunch would have appeared just like the dozen or so others that had preceded it. She also hoped Erich Greinke would find her latest report of interest.

◆ ◆ ◆

At about the same time Maggie was preparing to broadcast to the East Coast of the United States, Erich Greinke was unwrapping the parcel from the bench at Adolf Hitler Platz. It had been relayed to him by several sets of hands, only the last of which would he recognize.

While he waited for his kettle to boil, Erich pulled out his copy of the novel that served as the key to Maggie's code. Once the kettle began to steam, he gingerly held Maggie's letter over its spout until the brown numbers appeared. He used the first set of numbers to identify the page Maggie had used and opened the book to that page. Within thirty minutes Erich had decoded the message.

"Wow." He whistled, sitting back from the tablet on which he had deciphered Maggie's work. He rubbed his eyes and checked his work; he wanted to be sure he had gotten the message right.

> Goebbels gleeful. Article in *Völkischer Beobachter* indicating imminent invasion of England was hoax designed for consumption of foreign press. Copies

of *Beobachter* withdrawn from circulation as soon
as neutral press saw article. Goebbels publicly repri-
manded, but apparently all a trick to focus attention
on England and away from something else.

Erich had seen the article himself. He and Ches had discussed it
over a drink. Maggie's report suggested the article was part of a propaganda misdirection plan. Erich included Maggie's information in
his cable to the State Department. He wondered what the Nazis were
up to.

◆ ◆ ◆

He didn't have to wait long to find out. On June 22, the Germans
attacked the Red Army in eastern Poland, opening up the second
front.

"Now we know," Ches drawled. He and Erich were walking along
Unter den Linden, the early-summer sun filtering through the leaves of
the trees lining the boulevard. "Geez, you'd think that even these dim
bulbs would know better than to open a second front!"

Ches fanned himself with a folded newspaper as they walked. They
made an odd couple, the slightly built, older man in his rumpled jacket
and the younger, taller man in his business suit. Berlin seemed pretty
normal. No special precautions had been taken. No additional security
measures were in place. Even with the German army now deployed in
the east, no one expected any threat to the capital from the Russians.
What air force they possessed was badly outclassed by the battle-tested
squadrons of the Luftwaffe.

"Maybe that's why we didn't see it coming," Erich replied after a
few steps.

"Shit"—Ches spat into the street—"you'd think at least one of these
birds had read *Mein Kampf!* Old Hitler warns against the second front

repeatedly, and here he goes off and does this!" He shook his head in bewilderment. "What is he thinking?" he asked, mostly to himself, then squinted at Erich. "Did you and your State Department boys know this was coming?"

"What do you mean?"

"You know damn well what I mean, buddy boy," Ches retorted, an edge in his voice.

"I didn't know. I can't speak for the State Department. What do you hear from your sources?"

They reached the end of the block and crossed Friedrichstraße. "Well, it's pretty clear that this is why they clammed up on me. Now that it's out in the open, they say they're cutting through the Russians like a scythe through wheat. Caught 'em flat-footed, complete tactical surprise. You will recall that I have seen the German army in the field. It's pretty damn good, all that Teutonic discipline and all. They beat the crap out of the British and the French in a month, and those folks were more or less ready."

"Yeah," said Erich, "but there're a whole lot more Russians, and if they can hold the Germans off until winter . . ." His voice faded away, as if he wasn't convinced himself that the Russians could stand up to their invaders.

"Well, from what I'm hearing, the Red Army will be wiped out by winter at the rate our German friends are moving."

Erich glanced over at his friend. "What's eating you? You seem angry. Let me rephrase that: angrier than usual," he added with a laugh.

"That little bastard Goebbels has apparently told his stooges not to allow me to leave Berlin. I can't get to the front, so I can't apply my keen skills of observation and can't in lucid, insightful prose report to my dear readers what is truly happening in the biggest story in the history of the world. But other than that I'm just fine, dammit!"

"You ought to talk to Maggie. She's in tight with Goebbels. Maybe she can get you permission to go to the front."

"I may just do that, buddy boy," Ches replied sourly. "I may just do that."

◆ ◆ ◆

"Herr Minister?" Maggie inquired as the staff meeting was breaking up. Already Goebbels's secretary had gathered the minister's pads and colored pencils, carefully stowing them in the proper pocket of the leather briefcase that would accompany the minister throughout the remainder of his official day. Goebbels paused and, smiling, turned toward Maggie.

"What can I do for you, Fräulein Maggie?" he asked, taking a step toward her.

"Herr Minister, one of my friends—well, he's really more of an acquaintance—is Chesney Nutt, the American newspaperman. He's the one who wrote the very favorable article about Lord Lyon that appeared in the American papers."

"Yes, yes, of course. I am familiar with Herr Nutt and his work," Goebbels replied, the smile slowly fading.

"Well, Minister, to keep this brief, as I know your time is limited," Maggie forced herself to continue, "Herr Nutt is dying to get to the front to report on the campaign against the Russians, but for some silly reason, he believes he's been restricted to Berlin. He can't get a travel pass to leave the city. I told him, based on the good articles he's written about our cause and our people, that I would make an inquiry for him." Maggie took a deep breath.

Goebbels stared at Maggie for a moment. His intensity in one-on-one conversations made her uncomfortable. She felt as if his brown eyes were trying to read her thoughts. She wanted to look away, but forced herself to wait, to focus on Goebbels as though nothing else existed. Finally, he seemed to relax. "Very well. Of course he must have credentials if he is to continue the favorable reporting he has so far presented." Goebbels snapped his fingers loudly, drawing the immediate attention of his secretary, Oven. "Please be so kind as to arrange immediately for credentials and a guide for the American Herr Nutt. He may travel where he wishes, so long as he does not put himself or others in danger." Oven nodded and quickly left the room to carry out the minister's orders.

"I'm sorry to bother you with such a trivial matter, Minister," Maggie apologized. "It's just that he's been quite sympathetic to us in several articles and he is widely read in the States. If he sees the might of the Wehrmacht in action, well, I think his readers will have another reason not to want to get involved in a fight they can't win."

Goebbels's smile returned. "I am sure you are quite right, Maggie." He reached out with his slender hand and took Maggie's. He placed his other hand on top, holding her hand briefly and continuing to stare into Maggie's green eyes. "Thank you for bringing this matter to my attention." He paused, smiled again, and released her. He quickly limped from the room, exiting through the side door that led back to his suite of offices.

Maggie exhaled slowly. It was as if Goebbels could read her mind, as if his powerful, charismatic personality sapped the energy from her body simply by concentrating on her. Maggie had felt a hypnotic attraction to the man, much like the masses must feel in one of his party rallies, she thought. She shook her head, picked up her notes, and headed back to Broadcasting House.

◆ ◆ ◆

Unlike radio commentators, whose stories first had to be approved by censors from both the military and the propaganda ministry, newspaper reporters merely needed a telephone line to dictate stories to their editors back home. Once committed to paper, the stories were then sent via telegraph to the paper's home office, where some overpaid, under-worked editor—in Ches's opinion, anyway—would painfully butcher the soaring prose of his dispatch.

Still, as Ches read the eight-day-old Sunday edition of the *Journal,* he couldn't help but feel pride at seeing his byline, his story above the fold on page one.

EXCLUSIVE EYEWITNESS REPORT FROM RUSSIAN FRONT! trumpeted the headline. JOURNAL SPECIAL CORRESPONDENT ACCOMPANIES GERMAN WAR MACHINE ON RACE THROUGH RUSSIA! *Not bad,* Ches thought. Not a bad headline at all. Made his name really stand out.

WESTERN RUSSIA, July 27—Mechanized war assaults and quickly overwhelms the senses. Your ears are the first sentries to alert you to the chaos of combat. They start by attempting to sort out the various explosions, gunshots, and the grinding machinery of war. But your ears can't keep up. They cannot cope with the tidal wave of sound that washes over them.

Your nose deserts you next. It is overpowered by the wet aroma of sweat and the swirling clouds of dust. The scents it gathers become more powerful as you approach the scene of battle. Engine fumes and the tang of sulfur mingle with the stench of slaughtered animals and dismembered corpses. Your nose hasn't got a chance.

Perhaps worst of all are the sights that greet your eyes: flaming wrecks, the heat from which threatens to singe your brows as you ride by on the narrow pig track of a dirt road; the newly orphaned children standing in the bare yard of the shack

that previously housed their family, its thatched
roof ablaze; the bloodied or blackened bodies of
the dead: soldier, civilian, man, woman, child. Your
eyes cannot bear the cold efficiency with which
mankind now delivers death, nor its indiscriminate
application.

Ches's story described his two weeks tagging along with General
Heinz Guderian's Second Panzer Army as it knifed its way into Russia,
racing to link up with the Third Panzer Army and encircle 180,000
Red Army soldiers. It detailed the largest tank battle ever fought as the
Russians counterattacked with seven hundred tanks—only to be driven
back by the air superiority of the Luftwaffe. Ches ended his story by
reporting that the Germans were halfway to Moscow and warning that
the Wehrmacht appeared invincible.

◆ ◆ ◆

"I owe it all to Maggie," Ches said, dropping the paper on the desk in
front of Erich Greinke. Two weeks in the field with the swiftly moving German army had been enough for Ches. He had taken leave of
Guderian's headquarters and returned to the capital, where communications facilities were more readily available. Not to mention bourbon.

Erich picked up the paper and turned it over, his eyes immediately
drawn to a small map that illustrated the German advance described
by Ches's article. "So," Erich said slowly, his eyes scanning the typeset
page, "what you saw is pretty much what they've been reporting in their
domestic press."

"And why not, buddy boy," Ches replied, slumping into the chair
opposite Erich's desk. "They are kicking old Ivan's ass and using both
feet to do it! Why wouldn't they want to share the good news with the
rest of us? I thought France was a walkover, but this"—Ches shook his

head—"this beats anything I've ever seen. These boys moved several miles per day! Per day!" he repeated. "Any organized resistance they met would be bypassed and then leveled with artillery and air support. The tanks would just keep rolling on by. The only thing that slowed 'em down was their fuel supply. Not even the Germans' logistical efficiency could keep pace with their rate of advance. I tell you, buddy boy, this is the best fighting force I've ever seen—and I've seen a bunch."

Erich shook his head. From Maggie's letters to John Reilly, Erich had known the propaganda ministry's objective had shifted to convincing Americans of the unstoppable might of the German war machine. He just hadn't realized how good Maggie would be at implementing the Germans' new strategy. Maggie had skillfully played both Goebbels and Ches—the first for travel passes, the second for an article that would contribute to the overall picture Maggie and her colleagues were trying to paint. And neither knew he had been manipulated.

"So now that you've been to the front," Erich began, taking a sip from his drink, "what's your next story?"

A knowing smile spread across Ches's face as he leaned back and stretched, putting both hands behind his head. "Well now, buddy boy," he said, winking, "I just might have me a good enough source on that elusive euthanasia story. Yes sirree!" Ches seemed very pleased with himself.

"Better go easy on that one, pal," Erich warned. "Just because you give them a good story like this"—he jabbed his finger at the folded paper—"doesn't mean they'll look the other way if you try to cross them. You'd better be really careful."

"Oh, don't worry about me, buddy boy." Ches took a sip of his drink. He licked his lips and then smiled again. "I know how to take care of myself."

CHAPTER 22

Berlin, Germany
September 1941

The capital and its inhabitants had been enjoying peaceful nights. Britain's Bomber Command, achieving little in the way of damage— and that only at a very high cost in terms of air crews and aircraft—had shifted its nighttime attacks to less heavily defended targets closer to Britain's bomber bases. Following the air raids of the previous summer, Berliners had once again grown accustomed to nights of uninterrupted slumber. So when the British bombers returned on the night of Sunday, September 7, Chesney Nutt was eager to see what was happening. He defied civil defense regulations and, instead of waiting out the bombing in an underground shelter, raced toward Potsdamer Platz for a firsthand look at the damage.

Maggie joined the other occupants of her building as they huddled in its cellar. Even there, the concussions of the bombs could be felt and the shattering explosions heard. Fortunately, on this particular night, the bomb damage was contained around the Potsdamer Bahnhof, several kilometers southeast of Maggie's Soorstraße apartment block.

In the heart of the city, Erich Greinke was also defying the authorities. He was standing on the roof of the embassy, smoking a cigarette and watching the explosions and the growing fires some three kilometers to the south. The rapid firing from the antiaircraft batteries in the Tiergarten caused his ears to ring, but the spectacular light show of tracer rounds and searchlights entranced him. He could not force himself to look away from the hypnotic display of power the capital's defenders were throwing skyward. Erich took a drag on his cigarette and wondered if the British were causing any damage worth the expense of man, machine, and matériel.

The following morning, a cloud of dust and smoke covered much of the city center. As was her custom, Maggie left her apartment earlier on Mondays, eager to get a head start on the week ahead and mindful that the most productive hours were those when no one else had yet arrived at the office. She stopped at the newsstand on the corner of the Kaiserdamm and purchased copies of the early editions. Maggie tucked the papers under her arm and walked the remaining block to Broadcasting House.

She greeted the morning guard as she crossed the expansive lobby of the building and mounted the stairs. She walked down the long corridor, past Clive Barnes's private chamber and into her office. She pulled her arms out of the sleeves of her sweater, plugged in the hot plate, and started some water to boil. As she waited for the water to heat, she began to scan the papers, starting with the *Völkischer Beobachter*. There was a small article on page one about the previous night's bombing. It was the usual official release saying that no military targets had been hit and that only civilians and their private property had been damaged. There was no mention of deaths or injuries.

Maggie continued to flip the pages. She almost missed the small article on page four. Her eyes strayed to page five before her mind registered the small headline: CORRESPONDENT KILLED. Maggie let the page fall back to the table and read the two-column-inch article.

The only confirmed casualty in last night's raid on civilian residential areas in the city was an American newspaper correspondent, Chesney Nutt. Mr. Nutt was employed by the *Journal* of Atlanta in the American state of Georgia and was highly regarded for his fair and accurate reporting. Ironically, Mr. Nutt had just returned from Russia, where he braved the front lines to report firsthand on the gallant efforts of our forces. He reported on the army's victory at Smolensk, where an unprecedented number of Russian troops were surrounded and captured.

Mr. Nutt was apparently killed when a British delayed-fuse bomb detonated as he passed nearby. Funeral arrangements will be announced by the embassy of the United States.

Maggie felt tears forming in her eyes as she stared at the paper. Ches had been a good friend. He had helped obtain news of Kurt, back when she'd cared. His article on Lord Lyon had been the catalyst for Maggie's first promotion and had brought her to Goebbels's attention. He had shared the awful story of the asylum at Bielefeld. Maggie supposed that story, the source of which Ches had never revealed, had died with her friend. She brushed away her tears and tried to move on to the next page, but she just sat and stared. She had forgotten about the boiling water.

◆ ◆ ◆

Erich Greinke had lost a friend and a valued source. He had others, to be sure, but none with the freedom of movement, network of contacts, and level of access that Ches had enjoyed. And none quite so colorful, either.

It had rained during the small funeral at Berlin's Ausländer-Friedhof, the cemetery for foreigners. The service had been attended by Ches's American friends and by Clive Barnes, Dieter Schmidt, and official representatives of both the foreign ministry and the propaganda ministry. Maggie had also attended, wearing her most somber gray dress and holding a black umbrella over her head. She had greeted Erich with a handshake as he spoke to the propaganda ministry's press chief. That was the limit of their conversation. Security demanded that their contact be kept to a minimum. That suited Maggie just fine.

◆　◆　◆

Maggie continued to exchange letters with John Reilly. On the surface, her letters were chatty and filled with details about Berlin in the fall and how its citizens were bravely coping with the hardships of bombardment and rationing. The underlying messages included any tidbits Maggie could pick up from Broadcasting House, such as program schedules and frequencies, along with information from her frequent trips to Goebbels's headquarters. She reported on his travels, though this was usually after the fact, as Maggie was not privy to his itinerary. She also conveyed the growing confidence in Goebbels's ministry and elsewhere that the German army would make short work of the Russians. Maggie found that her skill at encoding her messages had improved. She could now finish the coding in minutes instead of the hour it had taken when she had first begun writing with apple juice.

◆　◆　◆

"What's the matter?" Dieter asked, gently rubbing the backs of his fingers across Maggie's cheek. She snuggled closer to him beneath the quilt on her bed. It was cold in her apartment. Heat and hot water were limited to the weekends. Dieter was warm, though; that was one of many things Maggie liked about him.

"I'm just a little sad, that's all." She attempted a smile in the darkness. "I'm sad about Ches. He was funny and helpful, and I liked him." Dieter continued to caress her cheek. "He always seemed to know what was going on, and if he didn't, he could always find out."

"I heard from a friend of mine that he was a little reckless," Dieter said. "My friend said Nutt seemed fearless, and that he didn't seem to care that there were bullets and bombs flying around. He just wanted to get to the story. Maybe that's what got him killed."

Maggie nodded in the darkness. "Maybe, but I liked that about him, too. He was going to do whatever he could to get his story. His death just seems so, so random." She wanted to tell Dieter about Bielefeld and the asylum, but she thought better of it. Best that he not know, she decided. That way the story couldn't do him any harm if it ever came out.

◆　◆　◆

Maggie continued to eat her lunch in the park on pleasant days. She continued to check a certain tree for thumbtacks. She continued to work very hard and quite effectively, frequently testing new techniques with the hope that these would help keep American public opinion opposed to intervention in what was essentially a European conflict.

In early October, Maggie received an invitation to a party to be held at Alois's Tearoom. The party was in honor of Erich Greinke, who had been reassigned, and was being hosted by some of Erich's embassy colleagues. On the evening of Friday, October 17, Maggie and Dieter arrived at Alois's shortly after ten o'clock. Maggie had arranged the week's broadcasting schedule so that Traudle and the Swingin' Seven were America's main entertainment for that evening. Even though rationing had reduced the availability of most goods, including many foods, Alois's always seemed to be well stocked. Maggie didn't know if that was due to family relations or the fact that the party was being hosted by a neutral embassy—nor did she care.

The back room at Alois's was already crowded with revelers determined to give Erich a memorable sendoff. A thin cloud of blue smoke hung above the tables, filtering the already dim light. A pretty, young secretary from the embassy was seated on the piano bench next to a sweating, round-faced man who was pounding on the keys, inexpertly playing "Blue Moon." Dieter checked their coats as Maggie scanned the room for the guest of honor. Before she could spot him, she heard a familiar voice from over her shoulder.

"Hello, Maggie."

Maggie turned and her eyes widened with surprise as she saw Thomas Müller seated at the table closest to her. "Thomas!" Maggie smiled, genuinely pleased to see Kurt's old friend. "What a nice surprise! What brings you to the party?" she asked, approaching the table.

Thomas slid his chair back and stood. Momentarily losing his balance, he shot out his hand and grabbed on to the back of his chair, shifting his weight. Maggie reached out and grabbed his other arm, steadying him. "Are you all right?" she asked with a laugh. "I can see you've already been partying."

Thomas smiled his wide, friendly grin. Maggie noted his deeply lined face, the crow's-feet wrinkles around his large, blue eyes, and the dark pouches beneath them. Thomas lowered himself awkwardly back into his seat. "Ah, Maggie," he said, smiling as he sat, "I'm not the man I used to be!"

"Well, it's early," Maggie teased. "You just haven't gotten your second wind yet."

Dieter arrived, and after Maggie introduced him to Thomas, he excused himself to get their drinks. "How are you, Maggie?" Thomas asked.

"Fine, dear. And how are you?"

"I'm not the man I used to be," Thomas repeated, shifting in his chair and swinging his leg out from under the table. As if knocking on a door, Thomas brought his knuckles down on his thigh. A hollow, thumping sound resulted. Maggie felt a jolt of recognition as Thomas continued. "I lost my leg in Russia, near Minsk. That's why I'm a little unsteady—not the beer." Thomas smiled ruefully, raising his half-empty mug with his right hand and tipping it toward Maggie in a mock salute.

"Oh, Thomas," Maggie gasped. "Oh, Thomas, I'm so sorry. I didn't know."

"Of course you didn't." Thomas smiled again. "It's OK; I'm slowly getting used to it. They have a school to teach us how to use our artificial limbs now. I'm one of the lucky ones, really. So many of our soldiers are just given a set of crutches, a pension, and a pat on the back. At least they kept me on duty."

"What will you do now?" Maggie asked, unsure of how she should respond.

"I've been reassigned to the Reich Security Main Office. They'll find some fulfilling and meaningful work for me there, I'm sure," he said, a hint of sarcasm in his voice. Thomas let his eyes wander across the room.

"Of course they will," she agreed. "But you never answered my question," she said as cheerfully as she could. "What brings you to the party?"

"You've forgotten? Erich and I fought together in Spain."

"I remember now." Maggie nodded. "Where is Erich? I haven't seen him yet."

"He's somewhere near the bar, holding court," Thomas said. "You really hurt him, you know."

"Hurt him?"

"Kurt. You really hurt him." Thomas stared into her eyes.

"You saw how he'd become, Thomas," Maggie said, trying to keep the defensiveness out of her voice. "Things weren't right between us anymore. Kurt was demanding and possessive. He began to frighten me. I suppose he's at the front now?"

"I suppose so." Thomas continued to stare, holding her gaze. "I guess Dieter is the man in your life now?"

"Yes." Maggie was uncomfortable. She was embarrassed that she'd made fun of Thomas's balance, and now she was embarrassed by the direction of the conversation.

"Well," he said, seeming to sense her uneasiness, "I hope he's a good man, Maggie, because I still consider you a friend. We have to look out for our friends, you know." He looked away again and nonchalantly reached for his beer.

"Thank you, Thomas. I consider you a dear friend, too." Maggie was elated when Dieter finally returned with their drinks. "I think we should go find the guest of honor," she said with more enthusiasm than her encounter with Thomas left her feeling. Thomas smiled and shook Dieter's hand, but he didn't attempt to stand again.

◆ ◆ ◆

Maggie and Dieter threaded their way between the tightly packed and occupied tables, the hubbub of their occupants drowning out any attempt at conversation. The piano player had moved on to "Daisy Bell," but he was mangling it with the same relish with which he had tortured "Blue Moon."

Erich raised his hand in greeting as Maggie and Dieter approached the far end of the bar, where he stood surrounded by friends and colleagues. His dark tie was loosened, and the top button of his shirt was undone, but he still wore his suit coat. He shook Dieter's hand and pecked Maggie on her cheek. He motioned her to a table in the back corner of the room, while one of his coworkers intercepted Dieter and engaged him in a conversation at the bar.

"Congratulations on your transfer, Erich," Maggie began with a smile. "Where are you going?"

"Bern, in Switzerland. Listen, I don't want to talk for long," he said abruptly. "Our means of communication don't change: letters for routine stuff, dead drop for urgent matters." Maggie nodded. "Same signals for pickups, same address for the letters. Follow the procedures you've been following. They'll keep you safe."

"OK," Maggie said. Erich's mood was intense. She had expected him to be relaxed, to enjoy the evening and the sendoff from his friends. "Erich," she said, searching his face for a crack in his professional façade, "I'm sorry about Ches. I know you and he were very close friends. His death was so random. I keep wondering what would have happened if maybe he'd been just a few yards farther away from that bomb. Anyway, I'm sorry. I didn't get to say that to you at the funeral."

Erich stared at her for a moment as if she were a child. Then he spoke. "Ches wasn't killed by a bomb, Maggie. I saw his body. He was shot in the back of the head." Erich leaned forward and gripped her forearm tightly. He lowered his voice, the cacophony of the party drowning out his words to all but Maggie. "They found out about Ches and Bielefeld, Maggie. They found out he was going to write the story. Ches wasn't killed by a bomb. He was executed by the Gestapo or the SS or somebody. Listen, Maggie: be careful. Don't take chances. If you ever feel you're in danger, put out the signal and use the dead drop. I'll get word and we'll get you out. Do you understand?" Maggie nodded her head wordlessly, her eyes clinging to Erich's, trying to comprehend what she'd just been told. "Right," Erich continued, releasing her arm, "back to the party with you. Act like you're having a good time. Laugh or something." Erich smiled and took a sip of gin.

CHAPTER 23

New York City
December 7, 1941

It was cold at the Polo Grounds, a good day for football. In his private box, William Donovan pulled the velvet collar of his overcoat up around his neck. Donovan had been working slavishly, as was his custom. But, instead of focusing on his law practice, he had been toiling to set up his new office as President Roosevelt's director of central intelligence. He had set aside this Sunday afternoon to relax by taking in the Giants' contest against their crosstown rivals, the Brooklyn Dodgers, in the final regular-season game for both teams.

The Giants, with an eight-and-two record, had already won the NFL East title. They were looking forward to playing the Chicago Bears in the league's championship game scheduled for December 21. The Dodgers, entering the game with a six-and-four mark, were out of the playoffs. Now, early in the second quarter of a scoreless game, Brooklyn's Pug Manders broke through the center of the Giants' line and raced twenty-nine yards to New York's three-yard line. In spite of the roar from the crowd, Donovan heard the public address announcer call his name: "Attention, please! Attention! Here is an urgent message.

Will Colonel William Donovan call operator nineteen in Washington, DC." Donovan stood to leave, watching as Manders charged across the goal line for the Dodgers' first score of the game. For Manders, it would be a memorable day. He would score twice more, once by returning an interception sixty-five yards. The Dodgers would win 21–7. But Donovan wouldn't be there to see it.

Donovan climbed into his chauffeured limousine for the drive back to his office. He looked out the window as the car headed down Broadway, covering the length of Manhattan quickly in the light Sunday-afternoon traffic. Back in his office, Donovan placed his call to operator nineteen.

"One moment please, Colonel," the operator said in her pleasant drawl.

"Colonel? This is James Roosevelt," came the voice from the capital two hundred miles to the south. Roosevelt, the president's son, worked in Donovan's fledgling intelligence organization. "The Japanese have attacked the Pacific Fleet in Hawaii. According to our reports, the attack has caused extensive damage. How fast can you get to Washington?"

Donovan paused as his energetic mind weighed the ramifications of Roosevelt's message. "I'll be on the next plane out of the city. I'll get there tonight."

"Very good, sir. The president would like a briefing as soon as possible."

"Yes, I understand. I'll call when I reach Washington." Donovan hung up and exhaled. Although he, as well as many others, had feared this day would come, he had hoped against hope that it could be avoided, that a strengthening America and an expanding military would deter aggressors. Donovan switched on his intercom and directed a secretary to call the airport and hold a seat on the next plane to the capital. His Sunday wouldn't be relaxing, after all.

◆ ◆ ◆

Erich Greinke had adjusted quickly to life in Bern. Here there was no rationing, no blackout, and no threat of British bombings. Here, good food, wine, and even liquor were in abundance. The streets were filled with traffic, the stores with goods, the people with goodwill. It was a pleasant change from the dreariness of wartime Berlin. Strolling back to the house on the Herrengasse, Erich enjoyed the cold night air and the reflection of the city's lights in the waters of the Aare River.

The river carved its path through the city, forming a steeply sloping peninsula that stuck out into the curve of the river like a man's thumb. The slope leading up from the river to the Herrengasse was covered in vineyards. The road ran from east to west along the spine of the peninsula. The house where Erich lived and worked sat just off the street with a commanding view of the river and the snow-covered mountains beyond.

Erich entered through the front hallway of the house and climbed the stairs to his two-room suite. One room served as his living area, with a simple sofa, a small writing table, and a couple of chairs. The other was his bedroom. The toilet and shower were off the hall and shared with the other residents of the house. A spacious kitchen on the ground floor was available for the residents and was also used for office functions.

Erich unlocked the door to his rooms and stepped inside. He pulled off his coat and his sweater. Here was another advantage over Berlin: heat. He flipped on a lamp and turned on the tabletop Grundig radio. As it warmed up, he checked his calendar to see what was scheduled for Monday. It would be Erich's turn to pick up the mail from the post office and his turn to cook supper as well. Erich rather enjoyed working with a team again after the solitary duty in Berlin. In Berlin, there was no one in whom he could confide, no one with whom he could share his triumphs—or his failures. Here, everyone was in on the work. While they didn't all know one another's sources and contacts, at least they all understood the game they were playing.

Erich stopped, his attention drawn to the voice on the radio. Its volume was growing as the set's tubes warmed. ". . . apparently inflicting serious damage. American commercial radio reports the attack began shortly before eight o'clock this morning Hawaii time. That would be seven in the evening here in Switzerland, a little more than two hours ago."

There was a rap on Erich's door. "Are you listening to the news?" asked Peter Fisher as he opened the door and let himself in. Peter was one of Erich's new colleagues in Bern. Like Erich, Peter had been raised in a German-speaking household. He had grown up in Cincinnati and attended Princeton, where he'd studied economics.

"C'mon in," Erich said, bending over the radio and adjusting the volume. "I just turned it on. What's the story?"

"The bloody Japanese bombed Pearl Harbor!" Peter exclaimed. "Destroyed the whole Pacific Fleet. They're on their way to California!"

"Where the hell is Pearl Harbor?" Erich asked, annoyed that Peter seemed to know more than he did.

"It's in Hawaii. You know where that is, right? They taught geography at Moo U, didn't they?"

Erich wasn't in the mood for jokes. "Where's Billy?" he asked, referring to the officer in charge of their station. "Does he know this is going on?"

"I don't know. I haven't seen him since this afternoon."

"Well, go find him!" Erich snapped. His tone penetrated Peter's excitement.

"Sure, right away, Erich," said Peter, turning quickly and leaving the room.

"Holy shit," Erich muttered.

◆ ◆ ◆

Maggie heard the pounding on the door and rolled over to look at her clock. In the darkness, she could see it was shortly before midnight. At first she thought it was another air raid, but the wailing of the sirens was noticeably absent. *What now?* she wondered. Whatever it was, it had ruined the good night of sleep she had been counting on. Maggie could rarely fall back asleep once awakened.

She threw back her covers and grabbed the robe from the foot of her bed as the pounding continued. Everybody in the building was going to be awake in a minute, Maggie thought, as her bare feet crossed the cold wooden floor.

She opened the door to find Thomas Müller and two other men standing in the corridor. One of them shined a flashlight in her face. "Thomas? What's all this? It's the middle of the night!" Maggie said, mustering what dignity she could in her nightclothes.

"I'm sorry, Maggie," Thomas replied. "We're here on official business. Please get dressed immediately. We will wait here with the door open." There was no familiarity in Thomas's greeting, none of his friendliness or warm smile.

Maggie tilted her head, annoyed. "For what purpose? I am an employee of the propaganda ministry. I am on Dr. Goebbels's staff. Can't this wait until morning?"

"Fräulein O'Dea," Thomas answered in an official voice, "the Gestapo doesn't give explanations. You are a foreign national living in the Third Reich and are subject to its laws." Thomas paused, then continued in a less formal tone. "You must come with us now, Maggie. Please get dressed."

Maggie hesitated a moment, searching Thomas's face for some hint of what was going on, then turned and disappeared into the darkness of her flat. Thomas pushed the door the rest of the way open. The man with the flashlight directed its beam up toward the ceiling, away from where Maggie was dressing. The ceiling reflected just enough light that Thomas could tell where Maggie was in the room. After several minutes, a fully clothed Maggie reappeared in the doorway. She was wearing her overcoat and had her purse in her hand. She stepped into the corridor to join her three escorts and turned to lock her door.

"Allow me," Thomas said, taking the keys from her hand. He quickly locked the door and then handed the keys back to Maggie. "Fritz." He nodded and the man with the flashlight led the way down the stairs. On the street, Thomas opened the door of a Mercedes coupe and held it while Maggie climbed in. He climbed in behind her, forcing her to slide across to the far side of the backseat. Maggie noticed that Thomas had grown accustomed to his new leg. If she hadn't known, she would never have suspected. Fritz climbed into the front, the other man at the wheel.

"Where are we going?" Maggie asked as the car began to move through the deserted streets of the capital.

"Don't talk," Thomas whispered through clenched teeth. "Just cooperate and answer the questions you are asked."

"Can't you tell me what's going on, Thomas?" Maggie pleaded softly. She was frightened. The Gestapo knocking on her door in the middle of the night? What good could come of that? A rush of adrenaline jolted through her system as her mind raced to the letters she'd sent to John Reilly; to her dog-eared copy of *Lady Chatterley's Lover*; to her lunch routine in the park; even to the extra ration cards Erich had provided. Could all this be about that?

The car crept slowly through the darkened Tiergarten, its shaded headlamps illuminating only small patches of asphalt. Maggie stared out the window, trying to think of a pleasant ending to this threatening predicament. The street widened, and Maggie saw the Brandenburg Gate looming ahead in the darkness. The car slowed and turned to the right as it entered the Pariser Platz, coming to a halt in front of the sturdy double doors of the US Embassy. A platoon of gray-clad soldiers had taken up positions surrounding the building. They were restacking the sandbags that had been placed around the structure to protect it from stray British bombs.

The man in the front passenger seat opened the car door and stepped aside. Thomas climbed out, motioning for Maggie to do the same. "Here we are," he said, reaching back to help her out of the narrow backseat.

"I still don't understand what this is all about, Thomas," Maggie said, letting a hint of annoyance come through.

"Didn't you listen to the radio this evening?"

"No. I wrote some letters and retired early. I have—had—an early start planned for this morning. Why have you brought me here?" Looking around, Maggie noticed for the first time other cars and a truck also delivering Americans to the embassy.

"We have to look out for our friends, Maggie," Thomas said. "I wanted to make sure you got here safely. All Americans living in Germany are to be interned."

"What?" Maggie gasped. This was ludicrous! "But why? This makes no sense whatsoever. We're not your enemy; England is."

"Our heroic allies, the Japanese," Thomas began sarcastically, "bombed an American naval base Sunday morning. Now America, you included, is in this war as a participant, not a spectator."

Maggie's knees nearly buckled. Standing in the cold night air in the dim light from the hooded headlamps of the vehicles dumping American citizens in front of their embassy, Maggie's mind raced through all her efforts to keep America out of the war. She considered the risks she had taken to supply Erich and "John Reilly" with information, risks undertaken to no avail. Here she was, a foreigner among friends, standing in the darkness in the heart of the enemy's capital. *Well,* she thought, *if I can no longer keep America out of the war, maybe I can find a way to help America win it.*

CHAPTER 24

Berlin, Germany
August 1943

Greer Garson and Walter Pidgeon were singing a hymn when their son stepped across the center aisle of the small English church to join the grandmother of his martyred wife. A proud smile flickered across the faces of the cinematic parents, the hymn reached its crescendo, and the screen faded to black.

"Marvelous, simply marvelous," Goebbels said as he clapped his slender hands. "That is real propaganda: message, emotion, story—all wrapped together seamlessly! What a shame we can't do work like that!" he added, now standing and facing his guests. Although he had banned American films from German theaters early in 1941, Goebbels had nonetheless invited Maggie, Dieter, and several others to his lakefront home north of Berlin for a private Saturday-evening showing of *Mrs. Miniver*, the Oscar-winning film chronicling an English family at war. The film had been a huge hit in America, capturing the Academy Award for Best Picture as well as a Best Actress Oscar for Greer Garson.

"Everything we do appears so heavy-handed next to work like that," Goebbels lamented as the projectionist began to rewind the film.

"Maggie," Goebbels called out, "maybe I should put you in charge of film production!"

Maggie smiled. "All I know about movies, Herr Minister, is that I enjoy watching them." She was sitting next to Dieter, and she leaned into his shoulder.

"As do I, my dear," Goebbels replied, drawing a chuckle from his other guests. "No matter." Goebbels waved the subject away. He stood before his guests, who still sat facing the now blank screen. Goebbels was typically expansive after an evening of film. It energized his creative mind. "With the Führer's leadership and our superiority in science and engineering, we will soon regain the initiative. Our engineers are working on a number of startling new weapons that will give us remarkable advantages on the battlefield!"

"Secret weapons?" Maggie's face brightened, as if she had been promised an extra serving of ice cream for dessert. For her to continue her work passing information to Erich Greinke, it was important that she appear an eager apostle for the Nazi regime. "Can we include any details in our broadcasts, Herr Minister?"

"Of course not!" Goebbels laughed, wagging a slender finger at her in warning. "All in good time, my dear," he said, then added, "but not yet!"

A year and a half had passed since Maggie had been dragged to the US Embassy in the middle of the night. During that time, Germany's fortunes had soared. In the east, German forces had laid siege to Leningrad and advanced to within sight of the Kremlin's towers. Rommel had ruled North Africa, capturing Tobruk. In the Crimea, the Germans took Sevastopol, ending Soviet resistance in the region.

But, only eleven months after Pearl Harbor and Hitler's declaration of war on the United States, things began to turn away from Germany's favor. The Allies invaded North Africa. The Germans surrendered at Stalingrad. More German cities came under attack from the heavy aircraft of Bomber Command and the US Eighth Air Force. Because of unsustainable losses, U-boat operations in the North Atlantic were suspended. Sicily was invaded, and the German forces there evacuated to Italy. Mussolini was arrested, and a new Italian government was established to negotiate peace with the Allies.

Maggie had had to think and talk fast to avoid internment with the other Americans caught in the Third Reich after December 7. She knew that if she was returned to America, she would have little hope of atoning for her prewar naïveté. She had pointed to her record of loyal service to the Nazi regime over the previous three years. She had pointed out the quality of her work and the fact that it had earned her repeated promotions. Dieter had come to her assistance, both professionally and personally, seconding her contributions to the Reich's propaganda efforts while supporting her decision to stay in Germany.

Under questioning from Thomas and his Gestapo colleagues, Maggie had maintained a dignified bearing, only to tremble when she was later released back to her apartment. She thought it miraculous that her accommodations had not been ransacked or at least searched, as were the quarters of other Americans. When the train of American internees had finally pulled out of Berlin's Anhalter Bahnhof on a cold winter day several weeks later, Maggie had breathed a sigh of relief that she wasn't on it. She had work to do, she told herself—work to do on two levels.

Maggie had felt the extra scrutiny. For months she was kept away from ministry headquarters on the Wilhelmstraße. She noticed that her papers and files at work were constantly rearranged. Her scripts were now more carefully vetted, not by Dieter, but by both military and foreign ministry censors, who maintained offices at Broadcasting House. But Maggie continued to do her work with the same dedication, talent, and flair that had initially gotten her noticed. And it worked again.

By spring, Maggie had worked her way back into the ministry's inner circle. She once again accompanied Dieter and Bauer to the daily staff meetings and always seemed ready with a disarming answer when Goebbels began to show his temper. With nineteen hours of daily programming ranging from swing music to news reports to commentary critical of the Grand Alliance, Maggie's American division was the busiest in Broadcasting House. And she had climbed back into Goebbels's favor.

On the drive back to the city, Maggie sat nestled against Dieter in the back of one of the ministry's chauffeured limousines. "It might be fun, you know," she said.

"What might be fun?" he asked.

"Making movies!" Maggie laughed. "You could be the handsome star! I would be the director, of course, telling you what to do, how to say your lines, how to kiss the girl."

"What girl?" Dieter asked drowsily. Goebbels usually kept his guests late.

"Traudle, of course!"

"Ha," Dieter said. "Very funny."

◆ ◆ ◆

Maggie had kept up her letter writing. She could still buy apples, the only fruit readily available in Berlin. She had been allowed to send an occasional letter to her father through the Red Cross, but most of her mail went to John Reilly at a post office box in Bern.

The day after her visit to Goebbels's estate, she wrote:

> Goebbels often references secret weapons. No details. He refers to several scientific and engineering break-throughs that will yield battlefield advantage. Have probed lightly for more information. He says "not yet." Not clear if he has firsthand knowledge of any such weapons.

Maggie hoped John Reilly would find this information of interest. Most of what she was able to pass on seemed rather mundane. When she could, she would report on Goebbels's travels or his nocturnal visits to supervise firefighting and relief to heavily bombed areas of Berlin. Still, none of what she was able to pass along seemed very important.

◆　◆　◆

There was constant traffic through the house on the Herrengasse in Bern. In addition to the Swiss, there were Italians, representatives from the Vatican, and even the occasional German. You never knew who you might bump into. The house was well positioned for clandestine visitors: the steep slope leading down to the river was covered by a vineyard. Visitors could easily float down the river, pull into the bank, and hike up the hill under the cover of the leafy vines.

The summer weather made for warm, sunny days with pleasantly cool nights, and the proximity of the house to the river meant that a refreshing dip was never far away. That was, of course, if one had time for swimming. For Erich Greinke, the last few months had been packed with activity. After Pearl Harbor, he had been dispatched to Vichy, France, to assist with the arming and supply of partisan cells. He had traveled twice to Spain, working with contacts there to encourage Franco's continued neutrality. He had already made one trip to Italy to assess the capabilities of guerilla groups there that were willing, they claimed, to engage in espionage on behalf of the Allies. Erich had learned quickly that while enemies of the Germans were his friends, they often had objectives far different than those established by Donovan and the allied high command.

In spite of his tireless pace, Erich looked forward to his regular trips to the Swiss Post to check John Reilly's mailbox. He enjoyed reading letters from those who had remained in Berlin. He especially enjoyed getting mail from Maggie. He would imagine her sitting and writing, and in his mind once again enjoy her pretty smile, her flashing eyes, and her pleasing figure. The information she had so far been able to pass along had been rather routine—not unimportant, as it helped Erich's analysts piece together a fuller picture of the inner workings of the Nazi government, but not terribly meaningful on its own.

On this midsummer afternoon, Erich carefully held Maggie's letter over the spout of a steaming kettle, watching as groups of brown numbers began to appear on the page. Erich immediately set about decoding the numbers, using his copy of the novel that served as the key. The words *secret weapons* caught his immediate attention. The Allies had been hearing about frightening new weapons almost since the war began. There had been rumors of superbombs that could level whole cities; of new types of faster, more maneuverable aircraft; and of long-range artillery that could reach from continental Europe into the streets of London. So far, none of these had materialized, but it was the job of the Office of Strategic Services, or OSS, to find out about these weapons, if in fact they existed, and to uncover the truth if they did not.

Now, here was Maggie's letter with a reference from a highly reliable source, Goebbels himself. Erich felt in his gut that it was unlikely Goebbels would fabricate secret weapons from his own vibrant imagination just to share with his staff. Erich felt it was more likely the master propagandist would use the hint of mysterious weapons to curry favor with the war-weary German public and to sow seeds of worry among the Allies through the daily radio broadcasts. Erich reasoned that there was something behind Maggie's scoop.

Erich sat at the kitchen table with a pad, a pen, and the cipher key. He wrote quickly, keeping his message short and on point. He encoded it rapidly, double-checked it, and prepared it for dispatch.

◆　◆　◆

Three days later, as Maggie walked to work, she saw the thumbtack. It had been placed in the last tree on her block, at knee height on the side of the trunk parallel to the curb. She felt a surge of excitement. Erich had a message for her. Although she had been faithful in taking her lunch in the park on pretty days, the routine of it had become boring, right down to having to eat an apple each day. Oh, she liked apples well enough, and she'd always believed they were good for her, but it had gotten a little monotonous. Now, her mind raced through the possibilities of what her summons might mean. What could be so important as to risk utilizing the dead drop?

Maggie's mind wandered as the morning slipped into midday. She had reviewed a commentary idea with Dieter concerning Anglo-American unity in Italy, where two Allied armies—the US Fifth Army, under Lieutenant General Clark, and the British Eighth Army, under General Montgomery—were battling entrenched German defenders. Dieter had offered a few constructive thoughts, as he always did, without seeming to notice Maggie's frequent glances at the clock on the wall.

Finally, at one thirty, Maggie grabbed her lunch and slipped out of the office. She walked the short distance to Adolf Hitler Platz under a bright sun and blue sky, light perspiration forming on her forehead. She crossed the nearly empty street and entered the park, where she noticed immediately that her favorite bench was occupied by an elderly woman accompanied by a small brown dachshund. Maggie hesitated for a moment, then began to stroll around the park's perimeter. She hoped that if she walked slowly, leisurely, the woman and her dog would be rested and on their way by the time she completed her circuit. After all, her only reason to be in the park was to sit on that bloody bench and see what had been left there. Maggie walked, trying to enjoy the afternoon warmth and remembering Erich's instructions to observe who and what else were in the vicinity. She saw two workers in the coveralls with the orange *P* on their sleeves. They were repairing part of a gravel walkway. A short, heavyset man in a gray suit was sitting on a bench on the north side of the park, sweating in the sun. Maggie tried not to look too often or stare too long at "her" bench as she ambled around the park. As she came within thirty feet of the bench, the lady finally stood to leave, picking up the dachshund and gently setting him on the gravel path, cooing to him the whole time. Taking the leash in hand, the woman slowly walked away with her dog, her heels crunching in the gravel.

Maggie exhaled in relief and took her place on the end of the bench. She slowly unpacked her lunch, then opened her newspaper. The front page was highlighted with stories of military successes in Italy and Russia. Maggie began scanning the inside pages as she nibbled at her lunch, another cheese sandwich. She skimmed Goebbels's weekly column and let her eyes skip to the headlines. Air raids in Cologne, again. Heroics in Italy. A successful counterattack in Russia. Holding the paper with her right hand, Maggie let her left hand drop to her side. Using the newsprint as a cloak, she carefully tugged on the end of the third slate of the bench. Once it wiggled free, she reached her fingers inside the cavity and smoothly extracted a small bundle wrapped in wax paper. She pulled it into her lap, beneath the newspaper. She held the wooden end cap and reached slowly down to her left to slip it back into place—and dropped it. Maggie held her breath for a moment, glancing around surreptitiously. She picked up her bottle of beer and took a swig. Carefully, she slid just far enough to her right to leave space on the end of the bench where she could set the bottle. Deliberately, she set the bottle on the edge of the slats, ensuring that it would also fall to the ground. Maggie immediately feigned distress, quickly snatching up the now foaming bottle and the end cap in one smooth motion. With the bottle in her right hand and her left hand down to her side, Maggie sat back down, her legs now hanging off the end of the bench and her skirt providing the cover needed to replace the end cap. Maggie chuckled to herself and shook her head, as if to assure anyone watching that she felt foolish for carelessly spilling her beer. She gathered up the remnants of her lunch, including her uneaten apple and the small wax-wrapped bundle, and folded it inside her newspaper. On her way back to Broadcasting House, Maggie would slip the parcel into her purse, saving it until she returned to her apartment in the wee hours of the following morning.

From the roof of a building across Thüringerallee, a man in a dark suit watched as Maggie left the park. He had been amused when she spilled her beer. She was such a pretty woman, he thought.

◆ ◆ ◆

"It's such a shame to see the blood of these valiant, young men shed simply because their leader has no ability to successfully plan, much less lead an attack. All he knows to do, it would seem, is to throw your boys piecemeal into the teeth of veteran, entrenched, and well-equipped German defenders."

While it was becoming more and more obvious to Maggie that her section's propaganda was making little impact on American morale, it was imperative that she maintain her reputation as a committed propagandist. She had to be above suspicion in order to continue her work for Erich—and to protect Dieter and her other colleagues. Were she to be discovered passing information to the Allies, she was confident hers wouldn't be the only head to roll. Tonight, Maggie was trying something new: letting Clive Barnes broadcast not to London, where his influence was now practically nil, but instead to America, where he was little known. The idea of an English voice denigrating the abilities of an American general had appealed to Maggie. She had run the idea past Dieter, who had concurred. Now, Clive was letting Fifth Army commander Mark Clark have it! "There will always be casualties in war," Lord Lyon carried on, "such is the nature of this beastly business. But to fling these poor boys against a solid front of steel is to revert to the outdated tactics of the Great War or even those of your own revolution! Surely, better field leadership would result in fewer deaths, even if your objective is hopeless. I'm afraid your American generals just don't have the, shall we kindly say, experience of our English chaps. I hate to see them gaining it at the expense of your sons and husbands. This . . . is Lord Lyon in Berlin. Good night. God save the King!"

"Well done, Clive," Maggie said as the on-air light switched off. "That ought to put mothers and sweethearts in an uproar and rattle the bonds of Anglo-American cooperation. We may do some more of this. We may recast you as a retired general, a military expert uniquely qualified to comment on strategy, tactics, and leadership," Maggie mused.

"Well," Clive wheezed, "I was a soldier, right enough."

"Thanks, darling." Maggie pecked the big man on his cheek and left the studio to find Dieter.

Maggie was tempted to rush back to her apartment to decipher her message once Clive's broadcast was over, but Dieter had discovered a new underground nightclub that he was eager for her to visit. So, at three o'clock on Saturday morning, following a full day of work, he led her down a set of musty stairs into the cellar of a block of nondescript buildings north of the river. Maggie could feel the thumping rhythm of drums and the muffled strains of jazz floating up from somewhere in the bowels of the building. Dieter led her by the hand through a labyrinth of darkened corridors before finally stopping before a heavy, black door.

"How'd you ever find this place?" Maggie asked.

Dieter knocked twice on the door, waited a moment, and then knocked once. A bolt slid back, and the door cracked open. Dieter nodded at the man on the other side, and the door opened wider. Maggie followed Dieter into a crowded, noisy cellar filled with people dancing, drinking, and smoking. Hot spotlights bathed the small stage in a yellow glow, the lights glinting off the brass instruments of the six-piece band blowing Dixieland jazz. Three of the musicians were black, sweat streaming down their faces and into their collars. The other three appeared to be German, though Maggie wasn't sure.

It was hot in *Die Schwarze Katze*, The Black Cat, as Dieter had called the club. Dieter pushed his way through the crowd thick with soldiers and young women, claiming a small, two-seat table by a cinder-block wall and motioning to a harried waiter. He was a young man with a scrawny mustache and a cigarette dangling from his lips. Dieter shouted to him over the competing racket of the dancers, the talkers, and the band. Maggie guessed he had ordered their drinks. She watched as the young waiter shook his head and said something she couldn't hear. Dieter nodded and reached into his pocket, taking out a folded Reichsmark note. The waiter puffed on his cigarette as he unfolded the bill, eyed Dieter, and nodded, turning away. Dieter sat opposite Maggie.

"Some place, isn't it?" he shouted over the noise.

Maggie nodded. She was already tired and rather anxious to read the message she had retrieved from the park, but she felt to rush home on a Friday night would require an explanation, and she didn't want to fabricate one, certainly not for Dieter.

"Who's the band?" Maggie shouted, but Dieter had turned away, watching the small ocean of dancers as it swayed back and forth. It looked to Maggie as though the dancing couples would have to move with the group: as it surged toward the tiny stage, everyone would have to flow with it; as its tide receded, the same would be true. There simply didn't seem to be any room to wedge another body into the throng.

The band wound down a set, the musicians setting their horns and drumsticks aside and pushing their way through the crowd to a doorway to the left. The partiers slapped them on the back and hoisted their drinks as the band members passed by. Taking a break, having a drink, Maggie guessed. With the music silenced and the dancers now milling about more in pairs than en masse, Maggie made another attempt at conversation.

"Great band!" she said loudly.

Dieter nodded, "Yes, they're quite good. Two of the Negroes are from New Orleans. They married German girls." He smiled. "Dr. Goebbels tolerates this place because it caters to soldiers on leave—but he hates the Negroes and their music!"

Maggie had noticed the many soldiers. Except for Dieter and the waiter, the only other young men in the club were in uniform. *Or mostly in uniform,* she thought as her eyes danced over a soldier and his girl groping each other on the now less crowded dance floor. Someone had started a phonograph that was playing jazz records.

"How did you ever find this place?" Maggie asked again.

Dieter waved to the waiter, who was struggling through the dancers trying to balance his tray. He finally squeezed past the last couple and set the drinks on the table. Dieter palmed another Reichsmark note and slipped it to the waiter, who nodded and gave a quick smile before plunging back into the crowd.

Dieter pushed Maggie's whiskey neat toward her and lifted his gin and tonic. *"Prosit,"* he said, clinking his glass to hers. Each took a sip, then Dieter set his glass down and smiled. Maggie thought he was most handsome when he smiled. It made him look younger, less serious. "I asked the boys in your band where to find the best jazz in Berlin, and this is where they sent me. I'd say they're right."

Maggie nodded. Her eyes swept the room, but the low ceiling hidden in a cloud of blue cigarette smoke and the low lighting prevented her from seeing much beyond the stage. A cheer went up from the revelers as members of the band emerged from the side room and made their way back toward the stage.

In the very back of *Die Schwarze Katze*, at the end of the narrow, wooden bar, a man sipped his beer. He had to shift frequently to keep Maggie in sight.

◆　◆　◆

Streaks of orange highlighted the eastern sky as Maggie and Dieter walked down Soorstraße. Dieter had accepted Maggie's invitation to come up. As badly as she wanted to read the message from the park, Maggie knew Dieter expected an invitation; and, by now, she was too tired to go through all the steps to decode the note, anyway. It was Saturday, a day off for both of them. They had no broadcasts scheduled, and their production assistants would see to that evening's schedule of programs. *No,* Maggie thought, *I'll sleep and get to it later.*

◆　◆　◆

Dieter had departed shortly after noon. Maggie was somewhat rested, but her eyes were still red from the fatigue and smoke of the previous night. She put some water on to boil, cut up an apple, and retrieved the wax-wrapped note from her purse. As the kettle began to steam, Maggie unwrapped the small package and removed a neatly folded piece of paper. She held it carefully by the edges and moved it back and forth over the kettle. Groups of brown numbers began to come into focus.

Maggie removed *Lady Chatterley's Lover* from the drawer of her desk and flipped open the pages. Quickly and efficiently, she moved down the rows of numbers. Within a few minutes she was converting numbers to letters, letters to words.

> Get more aggressive re secret weapons. High priority.
> Need details re facilities, locations, types, capabilities.
> Convey information expeditiously.

Maggie sat back in her chair and munched a piece of apple. She had only one source for information about secret weapons: Goebbels.

◆　◆　◆

Maggie's opportunity came the following Wednesday, as Goebbels's staff meeting with his division chiefs and key lieutenants was breaking up. "Herr Minister?" Maggie asked as Goebbels limped toward the conference room door that led back to his office.

Turning, Goebbels's face brightened and broke into a smile. "Hello, Maggie," he said, reaching out to shake her hand. "And how is the chief of our American section today?"

"I'm very well, thank you, Herr Minister," Maggie answered, reflecting his smile with her own. "Thank you so much for inviting Dieter and me to watch the film last week. We both enjoyed it so!"

"Wunderbar!" Goebbels exclaimed as his secretary, Oven, caught up carrying his briefcase. "It is a good thing I'm a married man," Goebbels teased, his brown eyes dancing over Maggie's face, "or I would give young Schmidt a run for his money!" He was still holding her hand, and now he patted it with his left hand. From what Maggie had heard, Goebbels didn't consider his marriage a hindrance to extracurricular affairs. She was suddenly more grateful for Dieter's affections than she

had realized. "Now, what is on your mind, my dear?" Goebbels asked. "I'm afraid I have a rather full day ahead." Oven had already left the conference room. He stood waiting just inside Goebbels's connecting office.

"Of course, Herr Minister," Maggie began. She had practiced this next line, but was still apprehensive now that she stood in front of Goebbels. She lowered her voice to barely above a whisper. "The other evening, you mentioned new weapons. Is there anything about them that we could use to unsettle our listeners? We are already questioning the leadership ability of their top officers and probing for cracks in their alliance. If we could start rumors about powerful new weapons that were about to be unleashed, it might further chip away at their morale."

Goebbels paused and laid a slender finger across his lips in a thoughtful gesture. "Perhaps, Maggie, you could prepare a brief on this strategy for me. No more than one page"—Goebbels turned to go—"by Friday. Get it to Herr Oven," he called over his shoulder as he stepped into his office.

"Of course! Thank you, Herr Minister!" Maggie called as Oven closed the heavy door.

◆　◆　◆

On Friday, Maggie was back at the ministry's headquarters on the Wilhelmstraße. With her, concealed in an unmarked envelope, was a one-page outline for the use of information concerning new weapons. Without specific knowledge of the weapons and their capabilities, Maggie's outline was very general. Even though both Dieter and Herr Direktor Bauer had initialed their approval, Maggie was concerned that it would be too shallow for Goebbels.

Maggie entered the large outer office of the minister's suite. Oven sat at his desk, working quietly, transcribing dictation notes. At her approach he glanced up and, recognizing her, stood immediately with a smile. "*Guten Morgen,* Fräulein."

"Good morning, Herr Oven," Maggie replied. "As requested, I have brought a paper for the minister's review. May I see him?"

Oven smiled again and, in the way of bureaucrats in every government, displayed his importance as Goebbels's gatekeeper. He picked up a neatly typed single sheet from his desktop and examined it officiously. "I am sorry, Fräulein," he said. "You are not on the minister's schedule for today."

Maggie put on her most crestfallen face. "But Herr Oven," she protested, "this is the paper he specifically requested concerning the new weapons program." She had lowered her voice at the words *new weapons.*

Oven set the schedule down again and held out his hand, his smile still in place. "I am afraid the minister is out of the city for the day. Of course, I will put it with his papers and make sure that he gets it upon his return. He may be interested in it now more than ever."

Oven turned away from Maggie and carefully placed her envelope in a leather case containing letters, dispatches, and other documents. Clearly, these would all be presented to Goebbels upon his return. As Oven attended to the briefcase, Maggie craned her neck forward, attempting to read the upside-down schedule. She scanned the page quickly, noting the words *Anhalter Bahnhof . . . Peenemünde.*

As the secretary turned back around to face her, Maggie smiled broadly. "Thank you, Herr Oven, for your help. Please ensure that the minister knows that the paper was delivered as requested."

"With pleasure." Oven nodded and smiled at the pretty, young woman.

◆ ◆ ◆

That night, in the darkness on her way home from Broadcasting House, Maggie quickly placed a thumbtack in a certain spot on a particular tree. Although tired from a typically long day and late night, Maggie was exhilarated as she sat down at her desk and by candlelight encoded the most urgent message she had yet sent to Erich Greinke. Based on Oven's comment and what she had been able to see of Goebbels's itinerary, Maggie proposed a link between Peenemünde, wherever that was, and the secret weapons program. She finally felt she was sending information of some value.

She scratched out the apple juice numbers and watched while the paper dried and the figures disappeared. Next she got out her fountain pen, the nice one Dieter had given her for Christmas, and began to write a cover letter on top of her invisible coded message. Just like her letters to John Reilly, any notes for the dead drop had to have cover in the event they were discovered by someone else. Maggie and Erich had agreed that the cover for these messages would be communications between illicit lovers. Such lovers would require "secure" means to communicate, and if the notes were found, the discoverer wouldn't suspect they were anything more sinister than love letters. Or so they hoped.

CHAPTER 25

Berlin, Germany
December 1943

The bombers had returned in late August. In the past, dozens of bombers had flown over the city, dropping their bombs and causing only moderate damage. The animals in the Berlin Zoo had taken the heaviest casualties, but, for the most part, civilian deaths had been few. Since the resumption of the bombing, the British by night had ratcheted up the intensity of the raids, now dispatching hundreds of heavy bombers and vastly increasing the bomb tonnage unleashed on the capital.

While the ministry continued to deny the effectiveness of the raids in disrupting manufacturing and transportation, there was no mistaking their effect on civilian morale in the capital. Over one million had been evacuated to the countryside, including most of the children. Schools had been closed. The raids disrupted sleep, leaving a grumpy and fatigued workforce. Berliners, instead of wishing their neighbors *"Gute Nacht,"* now wished them *"eine bombenlose Nacht"*—a bomb-free night.

Maggie sat huddled in the basement of Broadcasting House with Dieter, Clive, and many others whom this air raid had caught working the nightshift. Clive had been determined to finish his broadcast to America, again commenting on American generals' strategic short-comings, when electrical power to the building was interrupted, extinguishing the lights on the control panels and plunging the building into darkness. Flashlights were quickly produced, and the technicians, producers, and on-air talent proceeded to the bomb shelters. Even underground, Maggie could hear the distant wail of the warning sirens.

She heard and felt the dull whump of exploding bombs. They sounded as though they were to the west of Broadcasting House, but she couldn't be sure. In the darkness, with the power out, it began to get cold. Maggie wanted to snuggle closer to Dieter, but they'd become separated, and she was unsure where he had ended up. The booming explosions grew louder, as though the bombs were walking across the landscape above, closing in on Broadcasting House. As the detonations grew closer and more frequent, Maggie heard sniffling beside her. She reached out her hand and felt an arm, then a hand, which she grasped. Perhaps it was Marta, one of the younger production assistants. Whoever it was, she held tightly to Maggie's hand.

The building shuddered, its walls and foundation absorbing the concussion of the nearby explosions. Maggie caught herself holding her breath. The bombs felt closer than ever before. A huge blast shook the building, rattled their teeth, caused grunts of discomfort and muffled curses. *The Brits are laying it on heavy tonight,* Maggie thought. *They must not realize I'm down here.* She smiled to herself. Another explosion, then another. Maggie felt that Broadcasting House itself must surely be the target of the raid. *They're trying to knock us off the air.* She flinched as more explosions beat on her eardrums and shattered the cold night air.

The next explosions seemed a little less close, as though the bombs had walked past them in the night. The concussions grew less uncomfortable, the report of the exploding ordnance less sharp. *Breathe deeply, old girl,* Maggie told herself. *Maybe the worst is over.* She noticed that her hand was still being squeezed tightly and that a hand was also gripping her upper arm. Maggie smelled smoke. Without power to the building, the sophisticated air-conditioning system used in the underground broadcasting studios didn't work. Maggie wondered if the building was on fire—and if so, how much time she and the others had to escape.

A flashlight switched on, its beam dancing among the huddled refugees. A battery-powered lantern was turned on, casting a dim, yellow light around the cellar. The bombs continued to recede, leaving their lethal footprints across the city. Maggie looked to her left to find Marta holding tightly to her hand and arm, a grim look of determination on her pretty face. Maggie tried to smile. She hoped it was reassuring, that the fear she felt didn't show.

"Maggie!" The beam of the flashlight landed on her face. "Come on, let's get out of here." It was Dieter. He stepped over outstretched legs and reached out for Maggie's hand. "I think that's the worst of it," he said. "Let's go see what's left."

Maggie turned to Marta and cupped her hand to her cheek. "Are you all right, dear?" she asked in a voice more soothing than she felt. "I think everything's OK now." Maggie stared into the frightened girl's eyes. Marta blinked back and nodded. She brought her hand up and patted Maggie's hand and smiled weakly.

"*Ja,*" she said. "*Danke*, Maggie."

Maggie stood up and brushed herself off as best she could. Cracked plaster had fallen to the floor, and dust continued to swirl in the flashlight's beam. She grasped Dieter's hand, and they began to make their way toward the cellar door as the others began to stir. Dieter slid the bolt back and pushed open the door. He flashed his light up the stairway. "All clear, I think," he said, and, pulling Maggie by the hand, began to climb the stairs.

They emerged into the large courtyard between the spokelike wings of Broadcasting House. Smoke hung low over the building, reflecting the flames from a thousand fires. Cold wind whipped through the yard. Windows were cracked, shattered, or missing. Shards of glass, chunks of metal, and shreds of paper littered the ground. "When the windows were blown out," Dieter explained as they picked their way carefully across the yard, "the wind from the fires and explosions sucked all the loose paper right out of the offices. Careful!" Dieter gently pulled Maggie to the left. "That," he said, pointing with the shaft of light, "is shrapnel from the antiaircraft guns. I sincerely hope we made the Brits pay!"

With no power in the building and little likelihood that it would be restored before morning, there was no point in remaining at the office. Clearly, there could be no more broadcasts tonight. Dieter and Maggie continued through the lobby of Broadcasting House and out on to Masurenallee. Once outside, they witnessed a hellish scene of fires reaching to the sky, shattered trees, crumbled buildings. Fire and rescue units were just beginning to arrive, but Maggie wondered where they would begin. A quick sweep of the block revealed no fewer than ten separate fires, ranging from the small flames of a burning delivery truck to the massive conflagration of nearby buildings. Miraculously, Broadcasting House, except for its shattered windows, seemed relatively undamaged.

"C'mon," Dieter said, switching off his flashlight and pulling her by the hand. They had plenty of light by which to find their way. Dieter took off his overcoat and turned north toward the Kaiserdamm. The heat from the fires was more than sufficient to warm up the December night. As they walked, Maggie could feel the heat on the back of her head, even as her nose and cheeks, facing away from the fire, felt the nip of the air. They walked north, the orange glow lighting their way. Every few minutes, another fire truck and crew raced past them in the night, rushing to join the battle against the inferno.

As they crossed the river, the smoke began to dissipate, and the acidic smell of the high explosives diminished. Maggie recognized the area, and before long, she followed Dieter down another set of steps and into the corridor leading to *Die Schwarze Katze*. The doorman recognized Dieter and his beautiful companion and pointed them to a table along the wall. The club was practically deserted compared with the first time Maggie had come. It was the middle of the week, for one thing, not to mention the massive air raid.

Even in the midst of the war economy, Dieter and Maggie had found that good food and drink were available for a price if one knew where to look. *Die Schwarze Katze* was one of those places.

The same scrawny waiter appeared at their table, a cigarette again hanging from his sardonic lips. Dieter ordered food and drinks, then turned his attention back to Maggie as the waiter sauntered away. "Whew," Dieter exhaled dramatically. "That's the worst one I've been through. The bombs felt like they were falling right on top of us."

Maggie nodded. "And they were a block away. Can you image what it's like to be sitting in your cellar when one of those bombs falls really close?" She shook her head and noticed her hands trembling slightly, the release of pent-up fear.

Dieter noticed, too. He reached out and held her hands. "I love you, Maggie," he said.

Maggie looked down at the stained white tablecloth. "Why?"

"I love the way you looked out for that girl in the basement. She was clinging to you as if you were a raft on a stormy sea. I could tell you comforted her."

"Go on," Maggie said, glancing up, a smile playing at the corner of her lips.

Dieter smiled. "I love the way you do your work. Your professionalism. You don't have to be here, and yet you endure all of this." He waved his hand toward the ceiling, indicating the aboveground Berlin they had only just fled. "And then, of course, I love your smile and your laugh and certain of your, shall I say, physical features."

Maggie was staring at his dark eyes, smiling. What a difference half an hour and a few city blocks made, she thought.

"Maggie," Dieter resumed, "what about after this war? What are you going to do?"

"I thought I might apply to be the propaganda minister for some small developing country," Maggie quipped. Dieter grinned. She looked down at their hands and said, "I suppose a lot depends on what happens here. I'm not sure I'd be welcomed back home. Staying here sort of burned some bridges." She shifted her focus back to Dieter's face. "And part of it depends on my offers here."

The waiter arrived with sandwiches and beer. *"Meine Dame,"* he said, setting a plate in front of Maggie. *"Mein* Herr," he repeated for Dieter. He lingered for a moment, enjoying the sight of Maggie, until Dieter thanked him politely. He slunk away.

"And what about you?" Maggie asked before taking a bite. She hadn't realized how hungry she'd gotten. "What are you going to do?"

Dieter smiled. "Depends on my offers." A more serious expression replaced his grin. "I'm very worried, Maggie. We're losing ground in Italy and in Russia. Your Americans are building up forces in England. Berlin is getting pounded from the air several times a week—and it's not just us. So are the other cities. If the Russians get here first," Dieter said, lowering his voice, "none of us will be doing anything after the war."

"What do you mean?" Maggie asked, still chewing.

"They're absolutely brutal," Dieter replied, staring directly into her eyes. "A friend of mine at Goebbels's headquarters just returned from a tour of duty in Russia. He said the Russians are savages. They kill soldiers, prisoners, women, children, animals. He says it makes no difference to them. Everyone and everything is a target."

Maggie stopped chewing. "Do you think we're losing?"

"Yes, we're losing!" Dieter whispered. "It may take another two or three years, but the noose is tightening already. What happened tonight is becoming more and more common. That means the Luftwaffe either can't or won't protect the cities anymore. My guess is that they can't attack England, either. If the Allies control the air, they will invade. Then we're surrounded. Once that happens, our only options are defeat or negotiation."

"But Roosevelt says he won't negotiate."

"He won't. At least not with Hitler. Neither will Churchill or Stalin."

"Then why are we going through all this?" Maggie asked. "Do we really have some supersecret miracle weapon about to appear?"

Maggie doubted Dieter knew any more about secret weapons than she did, but here was a chance to find out.

He didn't.

CHAPTER 26

Berlin, Germany
March 1944

Maggie exited the train and made her way up the stairs to the street above. She was still more than a mile from the propaganda ministry's Wilhelmstraße headquarters, but the A Line's tracks had been cut by a heavy bombing raid the previous weekend and the damage not yet been repaired. In addition to disrupting public transportation, the raid had been ominous for other reasons as well: it had occurred during the daytime, and had been flown by the Americans.

The nightly bombing by the British had been bad enough. Now the threat existed day and night. There was no rest for the war-weary Berliners. They had coped as best they could by working harder, going to sleep earlier, and resorting to humor. As she walked through a bombed-out block, Maggie passed a windowless storefront. A wag had scrawled on the door in chalk, JETZT OFFEN TAG UND NACHT: Now open day and night. The grim humor reflected Maggie's own mood as she headed toward an appointment with Goebbels. She was unsure why she had been summoned, only that Dieter had told her to present herself to Oven at eleven o'clock.

Work crews were still busy cleaning up from the weekend's raids, sweeping sidewalks and stacking bricks that just days before had been walls. There were no civilian vehicles on the capital's streets. Instead, pedestrians, some in uniform, strode purposefully toward their next appointments. Even though battered, Berlin retained an air of purpose mingled with the dusty refuse of the bomb damage.

Maggie reported for her scheduled appointment, and Oven escorted her into Goebbels's large inner office. The minister was busy reading something at his oversize desk, so Maggie and Oven stood silently facing him.

When he glanced up, Maggie noticed large, dark circles beneath his brown eyes. "Good morning," he said curtly.

"Good morning, Herr Minister," Maggie replied.

"I have reviewed your concept paper on the propaganda value of secret weapons and I am authorizing you to implement this strategy. Herr Oven has a written directive to that effect. Do you have any questions?" he concluded, looking back down to his papers.

"Just one, Herr Minister," Maggie ventured, though somewhat shaken by the absence of any of the charm and friendliness he had exhibited during their previous encounters. Goebbels looked up again. "What shall I say about the types of weapons? Are there any characteristics I should emphasize?"

Goebbels pursed his lips and looked toward the ceiling for a moment. "These are military secrets, of course. You will simply report the existence of weapons with great new killing powers; weapons developed by German science and perfected by German engineering; weapons that will tip the balance of power in our favor. I will leave the details up to you. Now, please excuse me." Goebbels nodded to Oven, who led Maggie back out of the office.

◆ ◆ ◆

Because Erich had placed a high priority on any information concerning new weapons, Maggie decided to risk leaving a letter in the park. Although she could offer no details, she felt the go-ahead from Goebbels was an acknowledgment at least that a secret weapons program existed. In addition to that fact, she included a regular update on the local economy—what was not available and what was, and at what price. Coffee, for example, which had cost eighty marks per pound two years earlier, was now fetching more than 400 Reichsmarks—if you could find it. Food rations were miserly; an adult got only ten ounces of meat per week. Bartering was becoming more prevalent as consumer goods were generally unavailable in stores. One might trade a pair of scissors for a flashlight, for example.

It was rainy and cold, so Maggie had to wait several days before the weather and her schedule cooperated enough to allow for lunch in the park. This time her drop was completed without any complications. This time the watcher stood in the doorway of a ruined building across the street, smoking a cigarette. His view wasn't as complete from the doorway, but one had to adapt. His rooftop perch had been destroyed—along with most of the rest of the block—during the all-too-frequent Allied bombings.

◆ ◆ ◆

"Here," Maggie said, handing Dieter the first draft of the script on secret weapons. Her concept was for Clive to present the commentary to both English and American listeners. Having repositioned Clive as an expert on military issues, allowing him to break the news about the new weapons might lend some gravity to the situation.

Dieter quickly scanned the typewritten, double-spaced pages. "Let me look it over this afternoon, Maggie," he said. His desk was strewn with papers, ranging from technical data on frequencies and wavelengths to program schedules and other scripts. "I like the idea of

Clive reading it." Dieter's eyes were red and puffy, his face creased with wrinkles.

"You look tired, darling," Maggie said, placing her hand lightly on his shoulder. "You are sleeping some, aren't you?" she teased.

Dieter attempted a smile. "Some," he replied. "I'm just waiting, like the rest of us, for the Allies' next move."

"What do you mean?"

"The invasion. It's coming." Dieter glanced around the room to ensure no one else was within earshot. "And no matter how valiant our soldiers, we aren't going to be able to stop it. Not unless some of this"— he held up the script in his right hand—"turns out to be more truth than propaganda for a change." He offered a sarcastic smile. "Check back with me later this afternoon, OK?"

"Will do," Maggie replied, giving his shoulder an affectionate squeeze.

When she returned at five o'clock, Dieter was nowhere in sight. She checked Clive's office, but it was empty. She didn't find either of them until shortly before airtime, when she took her place next to Dieter at the control console.

"Hi there." Dieter smiled. "Sorry I couldn't get back to you on the script. I got called into a meeting with Bauer. Everyone's getting nervous. They think spring is the season for invasion."

Maggie nodded and noticed Clive seated on the other side of the window a few feet in front of them. He was attired in his blue pin-striped suit with a red-and-white-polka-dot bowtie over a white shirt. Maggie had yet to get over the irony of the lengths to which Clive went to dress for radio. Dieter glanced up at the wall clock as the second hand climbed toward eight o'clock. He rapped gently on the glass, and Clive nodded back at him. Dieter held up his fingers and counted down to the top of the hour. The red light went on. It would be Clive's last broadcast.

◆ ◆ ◆

"These wonder weapons are the terrible fruit of German technology, the products of brilliant scientists and engineers. Their use on the battlefield will ensure the survival of Europe and will help beat back the godless Slavs who even now threaten the cradle of Aryan culture."

"Think of it!" Clive continued, his deep voice rising. "Rocket planes too fast for Allied fighters to catch, too nimble for your aerial gunners to target. Bombs delivered by rockets, their lethal payloads accurately diving to destroy targets in London, in Manchester, even in New York or Washington! Long-range aircraft that are invisible to your radio direction-finding and that can cross the ocean to bomb America, bringing the war of terror to your cities just as you have attempted to deliver terror upon innocent women and children here in German cities. Invisible submarines firing torpedoes that are guided to their targets by sound. The list of these wonder weapons and their capabilities is quite long.

"I must add that we are not here discussing gases or biological weapons, which Germany long ago agreed not to use in war—but which we are prepared to defend against! No, these are weapons with tremendous destructive power that will be brought to bear against any and all invaders. You will not hear them coming. You will not see them coming. You will only feel the horrible destruction they deliver.

"You cannot defend against these weapons. You can only die—die by the hundreds, die by the thousands, die by the tens of thousands, die by . . . well, I am sure you get the picture, as our American friends like to say."

Clive reached the conclusion that Dieter had painstakingly drafted during the course of the afternoon. "Now is not the time to attack Fortress Europe. Now is not the time for a futile attempt to counter the capabilities of these amazing weapons against which you cannot defend. No nation, no army, certainly no man can stand up to them. Rather"— Clive switched to a more conciliatory tone—"now is the time to once again search for peace; to approach the conference table; to negotiate an end to this madness of war. Now is the time for the Western Allies to come to their senses and avoid the fearsome cost of blood and lives that would result from an invasion of Europe. Now is the time to reach out the hand of brotherhood and to conclude hostilities with a plan that ensures the future of Western civilization. This . . . is Lord Lyon in Berlin. Good night. God save the King!"

◆　◆　◆

Oven pushed open the door to Goebbels's office and stepped inside. In his left hand, he carried the case containing the official dispatches from overnight. In his right hand, he held a single piece of paper.

"What is the news this morning?" Goebbels asked, settling into his oversize chair, a blue pencil at the ready.

"I think Herr Minister will wish to see this first," Oven replied, holding out the single page. Goebbels took it impatiently and quickly identified it as an official letter from Ribbentrop, his idiot counterpart at the foreign ministry. Goebbels scanned the letter, then glanced up at Oven. He leaned back in his chair and, holding the letter in his slender hands, reread it more carefully.

"Incredible!" Goebbels said with more self-control than Oven had expected. "Absolutely incredible. Have the car brought up, and then call Bauer and tell him to wait for me in his office."

◆　◆　◆

Bauer's secretary stood behind her desk. She was certain she could see the door to his office vibrating as the shouting penetrated to the outer office. She had never, in her thirty-five years, heard such a tongue-lashing as Bauer was enduring from Goebbels. The minister had limped through her outer office so fast she had barely had time to stand. His eyes had been like burning embers as he jerked open the door to Bauer's private office and slammed it behind him before she could even say good morning.

Her phone rang, causing her to jump involuntarily. She snatched up the receiver. "*Ja*, Herr Direktor," she said, trying to sound composed. She acknowledged his instructions and quickly placed another call.

◆　◆　◆

The phone on Dieter's desk in English Section rang. Julie Clay was walking past and picked it up. "Dieter," she called out, "it's for you."

Dieter stepped around Julie and took the phone. His pale face became paler. "Yes, of course," he said into the handset, then settled it in its cradle. "Maggie"—Dieter motioned to his colleague—"our presence is requested in the Direktor's office."

Maggie pulled on her suit jacket, picked up a pad, and followed Dieter into the hallway. "What's up?" she asked as they turned toward the staircase.

"It's time for consequences," Dieter replied, looking down at the tile floor.

"What do you mean?" Maggie hesitated. Dieter stopped and reached back, pulling her forward by the arm.

"Listen carefully, Maggie. I don't have much time. Goebbels is in Bauer's office. I didn't let you find me yesterday to review Clive's script for last night because you can't be involved in this."

"In what?"

"Just listen!" Dieter snapped. "I put all that stuff in about negotiation. I added that after you gave me your initial draft. We have to send a message to the Allies that we understand we can't win and we have to get them to agree to negotiate a settlement. Otherwise Germany will be destroyed. When we get in there, play it smart. Agree with what I say—don't attempt any heroics. You're still an American, don't forget. If any of this sticks to you, well, I don't want to think about it."

"What about you?" Maggie exclaimed, her eyes wide with fear.

"Play it smart, Maggie," Dieter repeated as he opened the outer door and stepped inside.

"*Guten Morgen*, Herr Schmidt, Fräulein O'Dea," Bauer's secretary said nervously. She was still standing. "You are both to go straight in."

Dieter knocked on Bauer's door and entered, Maggie trailing behind him. A grim-faced Bauer was standing behind his desk. Goebbels was standing opposite the doorway with his back to the wall.

"Herr Minister," Dieter greeted Goebbels. "Herr Direktor." He nodded toward Bauer.

"What is the meaning of this?" Bauer glared, holding up a copy of the previous night's script. "Who authorized this inexcusable breech of judgment?"

Dieter quickly surmised that this was to be Bauer's show, that Goebbels had vented his displeasure and now Bauer's performance in disciplining his subordinate would determine the Direktor's immediate future.

"I and I alone, Herr Direktor," Dieter replied with as steady a voice as he could muster. Maggie stood mutely to Dieter's side, her eyes tempted to look from Bauer to Goebbels, but the latter was too far to her left and she could not see him around Dieter.

Bauer dropped the script to his desk, the rustle of the paper the only noise in the room. "Why?" he asked.

Dieter swallowed hard and answered, "Because it is clear that we can no longer win this war unless something changes—quickly."

"And you, Herr Schmidt, you are he who decides what this something is to be?" Goebbels asked quietly, still standing against the wall. "You, a midlevel civil servant? You, with your vast experience in foreign affairs? You, with your history of diplomatic successes? You, Herr Schmidt?" Goebbels's voice was soft, carefully modulated, dripping with sarcasm. "Would you not say, Herr Schmidt, that decisions such as an offer to negotiate peace should emanate from the chancellery, or at the very least from the foreign ministry? Would you not say that these are matters for the leaders of the government, not a junior official of that government such as yourself?"

Goebbels pushed himself away from the wall and came to stand in front of Dieter, his brown eyes squinting, his face a mask of intensity. His eyes drilled into Dieter's, his thin lips drawn tightly. Goebbels turned his head to the left, taking in Maggie with an appraising eye. "And what of you, Fräulein O'Dea, our American representative? What is your role in this treasonous fiasco?"

"Maggie had no role, Herr Minister," Dieter interjected. "She wrote the script on our new weapons as authorized and turned it in to me. I added the passage about negotiations and presented it to Herr Barnes. He read it just as I wrote it. He and Fräulein O'Dea are blameless."

Goebbels continued to stare at Maggie. "Do you expect me to believe this?"

Maggie dropped her eyes and stared at her toes. *Play it smart,* Dieter had told her. "Yes, Herr Minister. It is as Dieter has told you." She immediately felt she had done the wrong thing. She felt she was abandoning her lover, yet she was doing so at his own direction. She began to tremble. "I turned in the script in the early afternoon. We were to review Dieter's revisions later, but when I went to look for him, I couldn't find him. It was only as Clive was speaking the words that I realized there had been a change of substance."

Goebbels turned his attention back to Dieter. Bauer stood silently behind his desk, sweat now rolling down his pudgy cheeks. Goebbels stared at Dieter for what seemed several minutes. Then he turned his head toward Maggie. "You may go." Maggie reached out to touch Dieter's sleeve. "Go!" shouted Goebbels.

Maggie turned and left the room. As she reached the outer office, she began to sob. Bauer's secretary came around from behind her desk and offered her a handkerchief. The phone on her desk rang shrilly and she reached across to answer it.

"*Ja*, Herr Direktor," the secretary answered, "right away." She put the phone down and then, looking at Maggie, picked the receiver up. "I'm sorry, Maggie," she whispered. Then into the handset she said, "Connect me please with the Gestapo."

◆ ◆ ◆

Maggie knew she shouldn't wait, but she couldn't force herself to leave. She loitered in the corridor, questioning the answers she'd given Goebbels. *There must be something I can say to change things,* she thought. *I must do something to help Dieter.* She tried to reason through a solution, something logical that would take Dieter off the hook. Or maybe she could come up with that old propagandist's tool: the big lie. Maybe that would work. She continued to pace back and forth, her mind stumbling over its emotions, but failing to find any answers.

She heard the steps before she saw them. As they turned the corner and came into sight, Maggie immediately recognized Thomas Müller at the head of the Gestapo contingent. Thomas made eye contact with her as he turned to go into the office, offering her a barely perceptible nod of his head.

◆ ◆ ◆

Maggie was too upset to return to work. *The hell with it,* she thought. *The others will have to figure out the content for tonight's broadcasts.* She wandered through the lobby of Broadcasting House and stumbled out onto the sidewalk. The day was overcast, and a cool breeze swept down the nearly empty boulevard. Maggie turned and started walking, pulling up the collar of her suit jacket. *I denied him,* she thought, *just like Saint Peter denied Jesus. I left him for the wolves. I should have done something, said something that would have changed their minds. I should have defended the idea of negotiations.*

Sure, old girl, she told herself. *Put yourself in the middle of this and you'll spend the rest of your very short life in a Gestapo jail. Besides, there was nothing you could have done to get Dieter off the hook. He's a big boy. He knew what he was doing.*

But did he?

Maggie continued to walk, crossing the nearly empty street and entering Adolf Hitler Platz. She lifted her head and looked around, habit taking control of her behavior. She stepped onto the gravel path and walked to her bench, sitting on the left end.

Why didn't you see this coming, stupid? she asked herself. *You could have headed it off last night. You could have prevented all this!*

Maggie's mind wandered as the sun made an unsuccessful attempt to penetrate the low clouds. She remembered her first day at Broadcasting House, her meeting with Bauer and her assignment to English Section, where she had been less than impressed in her first encounter with Dieter Schmidt. She recalled how, on that first day, Dieter had offered her a chance to prove her ability, and how her work had impressed him. *That's all it took,* Maggie thought. After that, Dieter treated her as an equal, something Kurt had never considered.

She wasn't sure how long she'd been sitting on the bench when she heard the crunching, uneven footsteps on the gravel and felt someone sit down on the other end of the bench. Maggie pulled her mind back to the present and glanced to her right. Thomas Müller's hand was inside the pocket of his leather overcoat. He pulled out a crumpled pack of cigarettes and shook one loose. He stuck it between his lips and returned the pack to his pocket. He dug in his other pocket and produced a lighter, which he shielded from the breeze with both hands while he lit his smoke.

"I thought I might find you here," he said without looking at Maggie.

"Why?" she replied, staring at him.

"You seem to like this spot," Thomas said, exhaling smoke. The wind whipped it away. "You come here a lot."

"How do you know that?"

"We have to look out for our friends, Maggie."

"Why did you follow me?"

"I didn't follow you. I just knew where to find you. There's a difference," Thomas replied evenly.

"Fine," Maggie retorted, clearly annoyed. "Why did you come here?"

"To find you."

"Why?" she repeated.

Thomas blew out another small stream of smoke. "I thought you'd want to know about your colleague, Herr Schmidt." Thomas finally looked at her. "Do you?"

Maggie hesitated. "Yes."

"He's being sent to the front. He's been offered the chance to serve the Fatherland as a soldier, to fight the unwinnable fight. Apparently Bauer has a soft spot for Schmidt, and he talked Goebbels into giving Schmidt an honorable way out."

Maggie sighed deeply and looked down at her folded hands. She was relieved, to be sure, but an assignment to the front might be more dangerous than imprisonment. At least Dieter wouldn't be considered a traitor, a criminal.

"Your other friend, the fat man"—Thomas continued shaking his head—"not so fortunate. As a British citizen, he can't be offered the same opportunity. He's on his way to Prinz-Albrecht-Straße." Gestapo headquarters.

"But why?" Maggie asked plaintively, turning toward Thomas. "Clive didn't do anything wrong! All he did was follow the script he was given!"

"He's the scapegoat, Maggie; the sacrificial lamb. Somebody has to pay for this fiasco. Ribbentrop was furious. He and Goebbels hate each other anyway, and Schmidt gave Ribbentrop lots of ammunition for going after the propaganda ministry. Goebbels had to do something to demonstrate his firmness and prevent the whole issue from landing on Hitler's desk. He had to sacrifice Barnes to keep this little crisis at the ministerial level. Your man Barnes is English, he's mostly ineffective anyway, according to our sources, and he's much more visible than Schmidt. He's the perfect scapegoat." Thomas mashed out his cigarette on the side of the bench and put the butt back in his pocket.

"How can you play with people's lives like that?" Maggie felt her face flushing, her Irish temper beginning to burn.

Thomas shifted on the bench, turning to face her. "I'm not the one playing with lives, Maggie. That was your lover's doing," he said scornfully. "Besides," he continued, pushing himself forward and standing unsteadily, "we're all puppets here. None of us is in control. I think that was the point of Herr Schmidt's little rebellion, wasn't it?" Thomas stood looking down at her for a second, the wind ruffling his hair. "Be careful, Maggie," he warned as he turned and walked away.

Maggie screwed the top back on her fountain pen. You couldn't buy them on the open market anymore. The metals used to manufacture them were now exclusively earmarked for the war effort. You couldn't get lots of things in Germany these days. Cosmetics were out; so were permanent waves for women. Even the children sacrificed: no more toys were being produced.

Maggie folded her latest letter to John Reilly and placed it in the envelope. So far, she'd received no acknowledgment of the information she had forwarded about Germany's secret weapons program. *Perhaps,* she told herself, *that's because I haven't been able to turn up any details.* Her latest letter, which she would mail at the Reichspost the following day, included details about Dieter's negotiations ploy and his subsequent arrest and reassignment to the army. Maggie also included the news of Clive Barnes's incarceration.

She had returned to work the day after the arrests. Her colleagues had embraced her and she had jumped back into the work with her characteristic dedication, but she found her mind wandering. She would be reading the morning papers and find that she'd been staring at the same page, the same article, for several minutes without any idea of what it was about. When she walked from English Section's offices to the broadcasting studios, she would listen for Dieter's voice. Once, she caught herself just as she was about to knock on the door of Clive's private office.

I should have stopped it, she told herself.

CHAPTER 27

Berlin, Germany
May 1944

Maggie's recovery had gone slowly. Everything she saw reminded her of Dieter. Bauer had yet to replace the chief of English Section, and Dieter's desk sat empty, a constant reminder of his absence. Maggie had not returned to ministry headquarters, nor had she regretted her lack of contact with Goebbels. Instructions were now communicated to her by Bauer, with whom she met most days. When she had scripts that needed vetting, Maggie would make an appointment with the Direktor and sit patiently while he reviewed and revised them. She promised herself that no one else would pay for her mistakes. She would make sure she knew and understood what was going on the air. Whether she needed to or not, Maggie ensured that her on-air commentators noted the approval stamped on the corner of their scripts and initialed by Bauer. No one ever said anything to her about Clive's fate, but they appreciated knowing it wouldn't be delivered upon them.

◆ ◆ ◆

"I'd like to see Herr Barnes," Maggie said to the SS clerk at the desk. She had come to the Reich Security Main Office on this Saturday morning to visit her jailed colleague. The building on Prinz-Albrecht-Straße was large, filling nearly the entire block. It had once been a school, but had been commandeered by the Nazi Party shortly after Hitler came to power. These days, it housed the state's security apparatus, including the Gestapo and the People's Court. The clerk was young and except for a permanent sneer would have passed for handsome. His desk sat in the ground floor lobby between the building's entrance and the corridor. Maggie supposed that he was the gatekeeper.

"Why do you want to see him?" the young SS man asked.

"He's my friend, a former colleague."

"A pretty girl like you shouldn't have friends in here," he replied, letting his eyes wander over Maggie's figure.

"Oh, but I do," Maggie replied, leaning forward over the desk and smiling flirtatiously. The guard smiled back until Maggie added, "Including Sturmbannführer Müller. Perhaps if I call him you will treat me with the respect I'm due."

The guard frowned. "That won't be necessary." He silently reached into his desk drawer and withdrew a notebook containing a visitors' log. "Fill this out and sign here," he said curtly, pointing to a box with his finger.

Maggie leaned over and signed as instructed. The gatekeeper motioned to another guard. "Take this lady to number fifteen," he said. The guard nodded and held out his hand, pointing toward her purse, which Maggie surrendered for inspection. Satisfied, the guard handed it back and led Maggie down a long corridor, then turned right and unlocked a heavy wooden door with a small window covered by a metal grate in its upper half. Once Maggie was through, the guard turned and locked the door behind them, returning the ring of oversize keys to his belt. Maggie followed the guard down another hallway, this one more brightly lit, that led into an open room with several small wooden tables and chairs.

"Sit here," the guard said, indicating the closest table. Maggie sat down. The guard left the room, leaving Maggie alone. She looked around the room. Two large windows let in light from outside; their bars made sure nothing from inside would escape. The tile floor was white and clean, the tables arranged in orderly rows, the chairs shoved up beneath them. Everything seemed in perfect order. But the room was cold. *What am I doing here?* she asked herself. *They could leave me in here and no one would ever know what happened to me.*

After a few moments of uncomfortable, silent waiting, the guard reappeared, guiding Clive by his right elbow. Upon seeing him, Maggie stood and stepped forward to meet the big Englishman. "Oh, Clive," she said, trying to keep the quiver from her voice, "it's so good to see you!" She attempted to hug Clive, but the guard intervened.

"No physical contact," he directed, staring at Maggie. "You sit here"—he pointed to the chair she had just left—"and you sit here." He pushed Clive toward a chair on the opposite side of the table. With that, the guard retreated several paces, crossed his arms over his chest, and stood silently watching.

Clive began talking even before they were seated. "You are a dear, brave girl, but you shouldn't come here," he whispered. "I truly appreciate it, you understand, but you needn't put yourself at risk."

"What risk, dear?" Clive had aged five years in the weeks he'd been in residence in the prison. His eyes drooped, and Maggie guessed he'd lost thirty pounds by the way his clothes hung so loosely on his large frame. Several days' growth of whiskers covered his gray face.

"Maggie," Clive leaned forward, keeping his voice low, "the Germans believe every prisoner in here is guilty. They view with suspicion anyone who visits a prisoner. As grateful as I am to see you, it isn't safe for you to come here."

"I don't care, Clive!" Maggie whispered in return. "You shouldn't be here! You've done nothing wrong. I'm worried about you."

Clive attempted a smile. "You are a dear, sweet girl, Maggie O'Dea. But don't worry about me. As bad as this is"—he waved one of his large hands toward the barred windows—"it beats the hell out of the trenches." Maggie's face fell and she turned away. "I've somehow said the wrong thing," Clive said. "I'm so sorry, my dear, please forgive me."

Now it was Maggie's turn to attempt a smile. "No, it's all right," she said looking back at Clive's sagging cheeks and watery, blue eyes. "It's just that they sent Dieter to the front, to the trenches, as you say."

"That's better for him, Maggie. He'll regain his honor there. Dieter is a good man, and he'll adapt to the army. You'll see."

"Of course," Maggie replied, unconvinced. "What about you? What do you need? Can I bring you something?"

Clive smiled gently. "My passport?" he quipped, drawing a genuine smile from his visitor. "A blanket would be nice. A bottle of gin would be heavenly. But, no, I think a blanket would suffice quite nicely—if you insist on returning."

"I do, dear, and I will."

"Your time is up!" the guard barked, startling Maggie.

"The high command believes the Allied invasion could come within the next few weeks," Bauer said, pacing back and forth behind his desk, his hands clasped behind him. Maggie believed the Direktor had lost weight. *Who wouldn't, on present rations?* she thought. "We need to sow seeds of uncertainty and fear among enemy soldiers and among the folks back home."

Maggie was one of several section leaders arrayed in folding chairs in front of Bauer's desk. His message was primarily to English Section and its American department, but also for South Africa, India, Australia, New Zealand, and other German enemies.

"I would like your ideas on a radio drama that would create doubt and weaken enemy resolve," Bauer went on. "Ideally, with minor changes, it could be adapted for use in different languages. Questions?"

Maggie glanced around the office, but saw no hands go up.

"Very good," Bauer resumed. "Be so good as to have script outlines to me by this coming Friday. Thank you," he added by way of dismissal.

◆　◆　◆

Maggie placed the thumbtack in its signal position that night on her way home. It was a starry, cool night, but definitely spring. She wondered why there had been no bombing raids for several weeks. It was as though the Allies were waiting for something. *The invasion?* she wondered.

The following day was sunny and warm. Maggie took a late lunch in the park, depositing her message in the key slot of the bench seat. She reported what Bauer had said in the briefing, that the German high command expected the invasion soon, and offered a recap of Bauer's instructions. She placed the message without incident and returned to the office.

◆　◆　◆

"It's basically a radio play in two acts," Maggie explained as Bauer held the outline he'd requested. "Act One, Scene One follows two soldiers in their encampment in England waiting for deployment for the invasion. Scene Two takes us to the American heartland, where we listen in as a mother and father discuss the upcoming invasion. The mother worries about her son, the father about American generalship. You will recall, Herr Direktor, that this is a continuing theme in our America commentaries."

"Quite so." Bauer nodded, still looking at the typewritten pages.

"Act Two starts with the actual invasion, which, due to the employment of the new weapons we have been warning the Allies about, turns into a disaster. The end of the act, and the drama itself, occurs as the family back in the heartland learns of their son's death. With the proper effects, which I think we can pull together, we should be able to send just the message you requested."

Bauer smiled, looking up from his outline. "Very good work, Maggie," he said. "I think it might be effective for your soldiers in Act One to discuss the secret weapons program that they've heard about. That might add to their anxiety."

"An excellent suggestion, Herr Direktor," Maggie agreed. She felt a twinge of guilt every time the discussion turned to the wonder weapons program. Was there any truth to it, she wondered? Or was she simply adding to the considerable anxiety that must surely be the lot of Allied soldiers preparing for the invasion?

"And what is the title of your drama?" Bauer asked.

"*Blood on the Beach*."

◆　◆　◆

The next day, Maggie returned to Prinz-Albrecht-Straße, a wool blanket under her arm. She had bartered for it, swapping her weekly meat ration. Maggie's salary was much higher than the average German's owing to her prized linguistic abilities as a radio commentator. At 2,500 Reichsmarks per month, she could afford to buy food on the black market. Blankets, clothes, and other fabric items were much harder to acquire. Maggie felt lucky to have found a willing trader.

Maggie entered the security headquarters through the same ground floor entrance as before, crossed the same tiled lobby, and stopped in front of the same desk. To her relief, the gatekeeper was different, a blond-haired youth of no more than eighteen, Maggie guessed. He sat with his arms crossed on the top of the desk and asked, "May I help you?" in such a pleasant manner that Maggie momentarily forgot where she was.

"I'm here to see Herr Barnes," she explained to the smiling youth, "one of your guests."

"Let's see," the gatekeeper said, opening the drawer and removing the notebook. "Barnes." He placed his finger on the page and slid it down, scanning each name. "Barnes, you say?" he asked, glancing up into Maggie's green eyes.

"Yes, Barnes." Maggie smiled, hoping to keep the young man in a helpful mood. "I think he is in number fifteen," she recalled from her previous visit.

The SS man returned to the book, flipped a page back and then two pages forward. "I'm sorry, *meine Dame*," he said, looking up. "There is no Barnes here."

"Why that's ridic—" Maggie caught her Irish temper before it flared. "That's really puzzling. He was here just last week. Would you please check again?" She smiled sweetly.

The guard smiled and did as he was asked, but his second search was as fruitless as the first. "No Barnes," he reported, pressing his lips together and cocking his head to the left. He really hated disappointing this beautiful woman. "Sometimes they're transferred to other facilities," he added helpfully.

"How can I find out?"

"I have no idea." The young man smiled, leaning forward. "I'm new here."

Maggie thought for a moment. "Can you direct me to Sturmbannführer Müller's office?"

"Oh, I'm afraid he's out," the gatekeeper replied. He winked and leaned forward again. "They tell us to say that about everybody," he whispered. "They"—he tilted his head toward the corridor behind him—"don't want any visitors. Sorry."

Maggie nodded and turned, walking back through the lobby. She paused outside on the sidewalk and looked back up at the building. She couldn't get to Thomas's office, but perhaps she could reach him by telephone.

◆ ◆ ◆

"I'm frightened by these reports in the newspapers about Germany's secret weapons," Julie Clay read from her script. It was Thursday, May 25, and Maggie's radio drama was being broadcast live to Great Britain. It was also being recorded for retransmission later that night to America. There had even been some discussion of retransmitting it again later in the week, depending on the initial reaction from listeners on the other side of the Channel and the other side of the Atlantic.

"Yes," replied Robert Hipps, playing her husband and the father of their son. "I understand the Germans now have unmanned weapons aimed at likely invasion beaches and that they can defend Fortress Europe, as they call it, without having to commit their own soldiers to battle. I'm not sure our generals know how to fight a battle like that. I hope Johnny's smart enough to keep his head down . . ."

Maggie followed along on her copy of the script, each page of which had been approved and initialed by Bauer. This was the most ambitious live broadcast English Section—and, for that matter, Broadcasting Division—had ever attempted. In addition to the live performances of Julie, Robert, and several other English-speaking actors, Maggie had written in interludes and musical segues by the Swingin' Seven and multiple prerecorded sound effects to simulate a battle on the beaches. Crashing waves would mingle with small-arms fire and heavy artillery, swooping aircraft, and even the unfamiliar sound of rockets. No sound recording of rockets was readily available, so Maggie and one of the division's sound engineers had created a whooshing sound from scratch.

The cast, including the sound effects man and the entire band, had been moved into one of the larger studios for the broadcast. Maggie was seated in front at a small desk, from which she could make eye contact and direct the players, musicians, and technicians. Bauer and one of the many production assistants were seated at the control console on the other side of the studio's glass window.

At precisely twenty-four minutes and forty seconds into the performance, a knock came on the front door of the imaginary Midwestern farmhouse. Julie Clay answered.

"Why, yes, this is the Smith residence," she said in a flat voice.

"Telegram for you, ma'am," a male voice responded.

"Oh no, no!" Julie replied dramatically.

"What is it, Mother?" Robert's voice sounded distant and was succeeded by rapid footsteps, as though a man was running to her. Julie began to cry. Listeners heard the crinkle of paper.

"Here," she sobbed.

"Lemme see that." The sound of a telegram being snatched and unfolded. "Oh my God!" Robert cried. "Johnny! Our boy!"

Maggie gestured to the bandleader, who lifted his baton and started the solemn music that would close out the show. Beneath the rising music, Julie and Robert continued to sob. Maggie nodded once more and the music faded in volume.

Maggie began to speak into her microphone. "Every death is a tragedy. Especially the death of a beloved son . . . or husband . . . or father. And especially when these deaths are so senseless. You can't reverse the status quo. Germany is too strong, our defenses too stout, our weapons too terrible and efficient. Don't risk the lives of your loved ones. Don't risk your own life. Don't be deceived by the grandiose plans of your generals or the cynical rhetoric of your politicians. Don't run like the lemmings to certain death and unparalleled disaster. Remember always that we are waiting for you"—she paused—"waiting to spill your blood on the beach." The music rose, the drums beat, the music faded. The on-air light blinked off. Silence.

"Great job, everybody!" Maggie called out, drawing a deep breath and allowing herself her first smile of the evening. She turned to look through the studio window and found Bauer's beaming face staring back. He joined his hands together and waved them over his shoulder like a champion prizefighter. Maggie acknowledged the compliment with a nod of her head. Once again, she knew she'd done a good job sending the "right" message. Once again, she knew the message would fall on deaf ears.

CHAPTER 28

Septeuil, France
June 1944

"Drop your bag there," SS *Scharführer* Walter Huber instructed his new squad member, pointing to a corner of the cellar. The small house in which Huber's squad was billeted sat on the edge of the village of Septeuil, about fifteen miles west of Paris. The whole area around the village had been designated as the assembly area for Sepp Dietrich's Sixth SS Panzer Army, which was to serve as the western front's mobile reserve in the event of invasion. Huber was proud of the fact that his squad had such pleasant accommodations when most units were sleeping in the nearby forests in tents and trucks. But then, he always took pride in looking after his men, in finding the best quarters, and in requisitioning the best food—by the book when he could, by force when needed. This house had been acquired by the latter.

Huber liked the looks of his new man. He seemed intelligent, and if he didn't have any soldiering experience, his fluency in English would no doubt come in handy working in the battalion's intelligence section.

"Follow me," Huber directed, "I'll take you to meet *Obersturmbannführer* Wiersema, our commander." They climbed up the short ladder leading out of the cellar and directly into the yard of the house. Huber kept his eyes up, scanning the skies for enemy aircraft, especially the low-flying fighters. "Watch and listen," he called over his shoulder. "The enemy flies low, and if they catch you without cover, they'll rip you open like a can of beets."

Huber turned left onto the next road and walked up the three steps of the third house on the right. Black wires ran out of every ground floor window, tangling together, then scattering in every direction. The wires connected the battalion headquarters located in the house with its higher and lower commands.

Huber walked down the short hallway, his boots adding to the mud that had accumulated on the floors. He stopped at what had been the small dining room and knocked on the frame of the open door. "Excuse me please, Herr Sturmbannführer," he said to the back of an officer bent over a table studying a map. The officer held a grease pencil in one hand, a soiled handkerchief in the other. "This is *Oberschütze* Schmidt, here to meet the commander." Huber swept his hand toward Dieter and stepped to the side. Dieter entered the room.

The gray-clad officer straightened up and slowly turned around, a wry smile on his face. "Well, well," he said. "If it isn't the famous Dieter Schmidt!"

Dieter's heart somersaulted. He stood face-to-face with Kurt Engel.

Maggie fidgeted. She was waiting, the phone held against her ear. In the background, she could hear conversations, an occasional shout, phones ringing, and the rhythmic *tack-tack-tack* of typewriters. She had called Thomas Müller's office again on this Tuesday morning and thought that perhaps luck was finally on her side.

The three previous times she had called, Thomas had been out—or at least that was what she'd been told. Now, on this early June morning, the man who answered the phone had admitted immediately that the

Sturmbannführer was indeed in. Maggie wondered if it was the same pleasant young man who had greeted her on her previous attempt to visit Clive.

Maggie heard the clattering sound as someone on the other end picked up the receiver. "Hello!" she called out. "I'm trying to reach Sturmbannführer Müller!" She was fairly shouting into the telephone.

A new voice: "*Ja*, one moment, please." The noise in the background persisted. *At least they haven't hung up*, Maggie thought.

"Müller." It was Thomas.

"Hello, Thomas! It's Maggie!"

"Hello, Maggie," Thomas answered, impatience in his voice. "What can I do for you?"

"I was hoping you would be a dear and help me track down Clive Barnes. He was at your headquarters there until a week or so ago, and now he's been moved."

"Maggie," Thomas began, "I really can't help you with this right now. I suggest you let bygones be bygones. He's probably been moved to one of the camps."

"But can't you at least tell me which one? C'mon, Thomas. For old time's sake?"

"Maggie, you need to drop it. I'm talking to you as a friend. It won't look good for you to chase him down. Leave it be."

"You would never turn your back on Kurt if he were in trouble, would you?" Maggie asked, desperation mixing with anger.

"Listen, Maggie," Thomas replied, an edge in his voice, "I'd like to help you, but I'm too busy to make these kinds of inquiries."

"Oh, really? And just what is so damned important that you can't do this one little favor for me, Thomas?" The desperation had surrendered to anger.

"The invasion started this morning, Maggie; or at least the preliminary diversion. We're trying to sort it all out. I'm sure you'll understand that my priority is defending my homeland, not slogging through the bureaucracy to track down some overweight Englishman! Good-bye, Maggie!" Thomas jammed the phone back on its cradle.

Maggie held the phone away from her ear. The invasion! For a moment, all thoughts of Clive were swept from her mind. For a moment, Maggie imagined the blood-bathed beach her radio drama had described. Would the secret weapons—if they actually existed— really wipe out her countrymen attempting to liberate Europe? She felt a strange mixture of excitement and worry. Her mind jumped to Dieter, wondering where he was and praying that he was safe. The invasion! If her propaganda was right, it would be the end of the Allies. If Dieter was right, it would be the end of Germany.

◆ ◆ ◆

"Come on, Schmidt! You've got to move more quickly!" called Kurt Engel with a smile.

The battalion headquarters was loading up to move west, toward Caen, to reinforce the defenders there against the expansion of Montgomery's beachhead. Dieter had never worked so hard in his life. He was accustomed to the intellectual work that came with his duties as intelligence clerk, but the physical labor of soldiering was more than he was used to. Plus, he had to keep up with his field gear, cleaning his weapon, and standing guard—new and tiring endeavors. Nor was he used to spending so much time outdoors. He found that he was never comfortable; too hot in the daytime, too cold at night. And the spring showers were a daily nuisance as well. Fortunately, he still managed to get by on relatively few hours of sleep each night.

Kurt was constantly in motion, shouting orders, slapping men on their backs, and offering encouragement as he organized the convoy that would carry the headquarters toward the front. Despite the fatigue all of them felt and the tension of preparing for battle, Kurt remained energetic and enthusiastic, as though preparing for a soccer match. He was clearly in his element, enjoying the camaraderie and authority, anticipating—even craving—the danger and the combat.

Dieter climbed in behind the wheel of the gray Opel truck. His vehicle was fourth in a column of ten trucks. Behind him, in the middle of the convoy, was a light armored car that mounted a single 7.92 mm MG 34 machine gun to serve as defense against Allied fighter planes.

Clouds of thick, black smoke belched from the exhausts of the trucks as the convoy prepared to move out. Men who had been scattered around the edges of the formation now scampered to climb aboard. Dieter watched as Kurt marched down the left side of the convoy, calling out to the drivers, pumping his fist, waving, a smile fixed on his face. Kurt turned sharply and threaded his way between Dieter's truck and the one in front. He turned right, stepped up on the running board, and swung open the door.

"I think I'll ride with you for a while, Oberschütze Schmidt!" Kurt laughed, dropping into the passenger seat. He leaned his head out the window and peered at the vehicles behind them as the convoy slowly began to roll out of Septeuil. "Take a good look, Schmidt," he shouted over the roar of the engines and the grinding of gears. "We won't be back here again!" Kurt sneezed and pulled his handkerchief from his pocket to wipe his nose. "I love France in the springtime"—he shook his head—"but the pollen is hell on my allergies." He glanced over at Dieter as the convoy left the quiet village and turned onto the main road. Only a hint of his smile remained in place. "I know we have something of a shared history, Dieter," Kurt began, "but we are both here as soldiers. We have important jobs to do. Focus on that. Nothing else really matters. We are in the death struggle now. Not only for you and me but also for Germany."

Dieter slammed the truck into the next gear. They were rolling through the countryside now, passing fields and the occasional farmhouse. "May I speak freely, Herr Sturmbannführer?" he asked.

"By all means, of course," Kurt answered, staring out the window at the blue sky.

"Do you still believe we can win?"

"Pull to the right, quickly!" Kurt shouted as he reached across Dieter's right arm and slammed his fist down repeatedly on the truck's horn. Dieter spun the wheel to the right, following his officer's command without understanding why. In the next moment, the vehicle in front of him burst into flames and Dieter's windshield cracked into a vision-blocking web of broken glass. Dieter's left front bumper caught the right rear of the burning truck ahead, jarring Dieter and shoving his truck toward the roadside ditch. Kurt had his door opened already, holding on to it with one hand while trying to keep the enemy fighter in sight. Dieter wrestled with the steering wheel, attempting to control the truck as its right front tire slipped into the ditch. Kurt jumped and Dieter lost sight of him as he struggled to keep the truck from plunging into the shallow ditch. The vehicle lurched forward, teetered for a moment on its two right wheels, and then fell over, landing on its side. Dieter held on to the wheel to keep from being tossed across the cab. He held on tightly until the truck rocked back to a full stop, and then he killed the engine. He was only a few meters away from the burning truck, the heat tanning his face, the smell of spilled fuel stinging his nose.

Dieter heard the airplane coming in for a second run. He heard the deep-throated roar of the big radial engine. He heard the staccato firing of the machine guns and felt his truck jerk as the bullets punched through its engine, sending shards of hot metal ricocheting through the cab. Dieter let go of the wheel and covered his face with his hands and arms. He found himself sitting on the inside of the passenger's door, a cut on the back of his right hand. He felt the heat from the fire that had ignited in the truck's cargo bed.

"Give me your hand!"

Dieter looked up to the driver's window and saw Kurt Engel's arm reaching down from above. Dieter grabbed it and pulled himself up, kicking with his feet to find a toehold on the seats, the dash, the steering wheel, anything. He pulled his chest even with the frame of the window. Kurt, now kneeling on the outside of the door, grabbed Dieter by the back of his belt and heaved. Together, they toppled off the upended truck and onto the dusty roadside.

"Up! Quickly!" yelled Kurt, grabbing Dieter by his collar and shuttling him across the road and away from the burning trucks. They slid into the opposite ditch, along with dozens of soldiers from the strafed convoy. Thick, black smoke spiraled skyward, clearly marking the spot of the Allied pilot's success.

Kurt looked Dieter in the eye, smiled, and pointed his finger at him. "Stay right here!"

The plane was wheeling low over a field of wheat, preparing for a third run at the convoy. Kurt sprinted to the armored car and leaped into the back of the vehicle. He yanked back on the charging handle of the MG 34 and checked the belt of ammunition feeding into the chamber. The fighter—Dieter made it out to be an American Thunderbolt with wide white and black stripes on its wings—leveled out of its turn and came roaring right at Kurt and his machine gun. Kurt opened fire at the same time the Thunderbolt pilot let loose. Flashes winked from the ugly snouts of the airplane's wing-mounted machine guns. The noise was deafening, the smoke and dust blinding. The Thunderbolt's bullets ripped huge chunks of dirt and pavement loose, but missed Kurt's mount. As it passed over, Kurt swiveled his machine gun and fired again. This time the plane climbed higher, tipped over into a steep turn, and headed back toward the west and England.

By now, the soldiers were climbing out of the ditch and straggling back to their vehicles. Two had been destroyed by the strafing fighter. Two more, including Dieter's, had been wrecked. The rest appeared still to be drivable.

"All right, Schmidt?" Kurt asked loudly, reappearing from out of the smoke.

"Yes, Herr Sturmbannführer!" Dieter replied automatically.

"Come along then! Let's get this mess straightened out and get back on the march. We have a lot of ground to cover, and it looks like that may take a while."

Dieter assisted as best he could, his ears still ringing from the explosions and the firing, his eyes stinging from the smoke of the tiny, insignificant battle he'd just been a part of. Cargo was salvaged and reloaded, including personnel. The seriously wounded were left beneath an apple tree in the care of a medic. The two dead were left for the graves registration unit, their bodies respectfully covered.

Having lost his vehicle, Dieter jumped up into the bed of another truck, his legs hanging off the back. As the convoy resumed its journey west, Kurt swung up onto the back of the truck next to Dieter. "Can we win?" Kurt lit two cigarettes and offered one to Dieter. "There's your answer," he said.

◆ ◆ ◆

"Germany will continue to fight and Germany will win!" exclaimed Betty from Berlin on a late June evening. "Those 'doodlebugs,' as you call them, will continue to rain down on London and your other cities. Here in Germany, we don't compare them to harmless insects. We don't make light of their deadly cargo. Here we call them *Vergeltungswaffen*. That means vengeance weapons. And that's exactly what they are: revenge for the thousands of tons of bombs British and Americans have dropped on our women and on our children; revenge for the schools, churches, and homes you've destroyed."

A week after the invasion, an ecstatic Goebbels had called an emergency meeting of his department heads. Maggie had not been invited, but from Bauer's enthusiasm she could tell the meeting had been extraordinary. He had at once called together Broadcasting Division's section chiefs to share the news.

"The Führer has unleashed the wonder weapons we have been hearing about," Bauer said, smiling broadly. Around the room, Maggie saw answering smiles break out. "We have begun to bombard London with pilotless aircraft, rockets really, launched from northern France and western Belgium. So far, several have been fired and have hit the center of London. According to English radio broadcasts, they are creating quite a panic!" Bauer chuckled. "Herr Doktor Goebbels refers to these as *Vergeltungswaffen*, and we are to use that name in all our broadcasts." Maggie raised her hand. "Yes, Maggie." Bauer pointed at her.

"Herr Direktor," Maggie began. "Will the new weapons be aimed solely at London, or will other cities also be targeted?"

"For now, London. We must quickly break the Britons' spirits so they will halt their buildup of forces in France. Besides," Bauer added, "the rockets' range can't reach too deeply into England from their launch sites along the coast." Maggie had made a mental note of Bauer's unguarded reference to the launch sites and the limited range of the new weapons.

"Which is greater now," Betty asked her radio audience, "your shame at the tactics of your terror fliers or your fear that now the hand of retribution visits the same calamity upon your cities, upon your homes, and upon your children? The *Vergeltungswaffen* that have been unleashed so far are but a meager fraction of our arsenal. Now we will destroy London, and then Birmingham and Manchester and . . . well, you get the picture. And we'll do so without sacrificing so many of our young heroes of the air. You see, it doesn't take us ten men to deliver one payload, ten men who may never return from the unfriendly skies. Our rockets guide themselves. But you've already seen that, haven't you?

"I've tried to warn you about our secret weapons, about our scientific and technological superiority, but you haven't listened. That's so unfortunate for you . . . and for your loved ones," Betty added ominously. "Don't think that our *Vergeltungswaffen* are the only tricks up our sleeves. We have more surprises in store. You'll see. This is Betty from Berlin. I look forward to visiting with you again soon. Good night."

◆ ◆ ◆

Maggie was eager to get home after the final broadcast of the evening. She was eager to place the thumbtack in the tree signaling that she had important information to be retrieved. As she and Erich had agreed so long ago, the frequent use of the dead drop was to be discouraged. It was more dangerous than sending innocuous letters through the mail to John Reilly. But Maggie recognized that the information Bauer had shared was of an urgent nature. If London was about to endure a second Blitz, Maggie would do whatever she could to make it as short—and as harmless—as possible.

Maggie reached the steps of her apartment building and put her key in the outer door. She stepped into the dark central hallway and quickly checked her mailbox. Inside was one wrinkled and smudged envelope. She couldn't determine who it was from in the dark, so she stuck it in her purse and trudged up the steps to her flat. Inside, she carefully checked her blackout curtains, then lit the candle on her desk. She draped her jacket over the back of her chair and walked over to the sink, grabbing the apple that she kept on hand for occasions such as this. Efficiently, she set about slicing it into thin pieces and grinding then them to a juicy pulp using her mortar and pestle.

With the mortar in hand, she returned to her desk, sat, and pulled a sheet of paper out of her drawer. Setting her copy of *Lady Chatterley's Lover* on the desktop next to the candle, she began to compose and encode her message. She worked quickly, holding the wooden stylus in her right hand and using her left index finger to help her keep track of the fading numbers on the page. When she was finished, she held the paper up, examining it carefully in the candlelight. Satisfied that the apple juice had dried, Maggie began to write her cover note to her imaginary lover, Gino. Her love letter was neither long nor particularly lucid, but Maggie judged that it would serve its purpose—if needed.

Maggie wrapped the letter in wax paper and stuck it into her purse. In her eagerness to write down the latest information on the secret weapons, Maggie had forgotten the letter from her mailbox. Now she pulled it out, looked at the return address, and gasped. It was from Dieter! Maggie's fingers fumbled at the envelope, careful not to damage the return address. She pulled the letter out and held it up behind the candle.

10 June 1944

Dear Maggie,

I can't write much because we haven't got long. We are somewhere in France and have been under attack almost constantly since the invasion began. I am in a headquarters section, so I am not on the front lines, but we are still on the receiving end of enemy artillery and aerial bombardment.

I am fine, although dirty and always tired. We don't eat often, but one of the advantages of being in France is that we can occasionally eat well.

You will find it humorous (I hope) that your old friend Kurt is the officer in charge of our headquarters. Don't worry; he treats me (and all of our comrades) well. He is a good officer, competent and respected.

I love you, Maggie. I miss you. I long to see your green eyes and your dazzling smile. Best to all at English Section,

Affectionately,

Dieter

Maggie held the letter in her hands and read it again and again. She copied down the return address and then, weary after a long day and night, she carefully folded Dieter's letter and placed it beneath her pillow.

◆ ◆ ◆

The following day, in the early afternoon, Maggie returned to Adolf Hitler Platz. The day was sunny and warm, with a bright-blue, bomber-less sky. It had been nearly three months since the last air raids of any consequence. Berliners were again enjoying full nights of sleep. Roads were open. Trains were on schedule. Without constant bomb damage to clean up, the city even looked better.

Maggie walked to her bench, enjoying the weather and observing who else was in the park and what they were doing. A distinguished-looking man in a business suit sat on a low wall nearby, reading the *Völkischer Beobachter*. Two thin men in overalls were repairing one of the benches on the west end of the park. A young mother sat on a blanket playing with her curly-haired toddler. Small children had become uncommon in Berlin during the heavy bombing of the previous winter, as many had been evacuated to the countryside.

Maggie arranged a cheese sandwich and a bottle of beer on the bench next to her apple and opened her newspaper. Dropping her left hand beneath the newsprint, she quickly pulled the end cap off the slat, stuck her folded note inside, and replaced the wooden end piece. She brought her left hand casually back up to the newspaper, holding the page still while she reached over with her right hand to pick up her sandwich. As she took a bite, she glanced around the park. *All in order,* she thought.

Chapter 29

Berlin, Germany
December 1944

The flow of troops, tanks, trucks, artillery, and even horses through the capital would have alerted the most casual observer that something was up. The traffic continued for several days, both by road and by rail. Everything seemed to be moving in the same direction: from east to west.

Maggie had no trouble striking up conversations with the soldiers passing through. After all, who wouldn't enjoy chatting up a beautiful young woman after spending a couple of years in the field? They told similar stories: they'd been pulled out of the line in Poland or Estonia or Latvia and shipped back to the capital. Their officers mentioned defense of the homeland, but isn't that what they'd been doing? At any rate, they were happy to be back on German soil and happy to be out of the mud and misery of the front lines. Through her conversations, Maggie was able to identify several divisions, both infantry and Panzer.

She had received infrequent letters from Dieter, whom she now believed to be in western Germany. In one letter, he had enthralled her with his daring escape from encirclement by the Allies. He, Kurt, and a handful of others from battalion headquarters had dodged American patrols and aircraft by slogging up creek beds and traveling only at night. They had suffered through several close encounters with the enemy, but after a week of evasion they had reached the reconstituted German lines. It was clear from the letter that Dieter's admiration for Kurt had grown. *How ironic,* Maggie thought with a wistful smile. In his last letter, which Maggie regarded as an early Christmas present, Dieter had, in careful language, implied that his unit was almost constantly on the defensive:

> I don't know how much longer this struggle will last, Maggie. What I do know is that I love you and long to hold you again. Because in this current disarray, firm plans seem the refuge of fools, let's make a simple pact. Let's plan to meet at the Brandenburg Gate on the first day of summer. I'll bring you a rose.
>
> Love,
> Dieter

And how she missed Dieter! She never tired of replaying in her mind his words of encouragement or the first time he'd kissed her. She missed the warmth of his body next to her on these cold nights. She felt again the pain of regret at her silence on the last day she saw him. Maggie wondered if what she was about to do would count as a second betrayal.

◆ ◆ ◆

Thomas Müller exhaled deeply and pushed himself away from his desk. It was already one o'clock, and he was long past the point of hunger. "I'm taking a break for lunch," he said to his aide. "If I'm not back in"—he glanced at his watch—"two or three days, call off the war."

"*Jawohl,* Herr Sturmbannführer!" his aide answered with a chuckle.

Thomas grabbed his leather overcoat off the rack and headed out into the hallway and down the stairs. For Thomas, the late summer and fall had been filled with work—dirty, unpleasant work. Following the attempted assassination of Hitler in late July, Thomas and his Gestapo colleagues had worked around the clock rounding up suspects, unraveling networks, and closing down conspiracies. For several weeks it had seemed that the only sleep Thomas got was in the car on the way to the next interrogation or arrest. Although the worst of it was over, Thomas hoped, he was still tired, and today he promised himself a more enjoyable task: making his periodic observation of Maggie O'Dea.

Maggie quickly placed the small bundle inside the bench's third slat. She was working more quickly today than usual, not because she was in a particular hurry, but because the weather was uncooperative. She would have preferred to wait for a nicer day, but felt the information she was passing along might be needed quickly, too quickly to wait on the post. The wind whipped her newspaper, making it more difficult to conceal her hands. The gray sky threatened rain. It was hardly the type of day one would enjoy spending in the park. Even the two workmen in their coveralls were huddled in the lee of one of the park's stone walls.

Maggie lingered for a few moments, then purposefully became annoyed with her wild newspaper and theatrically folded it and stuffed it under her arm. She grabbed her purse, and with an exasperated expression, stuffed the remnants of her lunch inside. She leaned into the stiff, cold breeze and headed back to Broadcasting House.

Thomas Müller watched from the bombed-out building across the alley as Maggie picked up her things and turned to go back to her office. He was disappointed her lunch was over so quickly. Usually, she stayed for at least half an hour. Of course, in this weather, he didn't blame her. Even in his overcoat, Thomas felt the cold air and the brisk wind.

His eyes followed her as she left the park and crossed the nearly empty street. He would have liked to sit down and visit with her, but he knew that wouldn't do. As Thomas turned to leave, his attention was attracted by new movement in the park. One of the workmen, the taller of the two, had walked over to the bench Maggie had vacated. Thomas watched as the man knelt beside the bench, his back to Thomas, his body shielding his hands from view. As the man stood back up, Thomas saw him slip something into his pocket. Thomas glanced back to the right. Maggie was still walking, now on the sidewalk. He returned his attention to the workman. He was walking away from the bench, away from Thomas, back toward his colleague.

The two men were too far away for Thomas to hear them, but he could clearly see them exchange words. Then, the two of them left the park, heading north.

Thomas waited a moment, then crossed the alley and entered the park. He walked down the pathway, the gravel crunching under his feet, until he came to the bench. He stopped and stared for a moment, taking in every detail. He looked at the soft ground to the left of the bench where he'd seen the workman kneeling just moments ago. He replayed in his mind the times he'd watched Maggie eat lunch at this very spot; usually on warm and sunny days, rarely on a day like this. She always ate lunch. She always read the paper. She drank a beer. No beer today, Thomas thought. But still, she ate lunch, she read the paper.

He sat down on the bench. The newspaper in Maggie's hands throbbed in his mind like a pain that couldn't be identified. Thomas began to mimic her motions with the paper. She couldn't read it, he thought, because she couldn't hold it still in the wind. So why did she let go of it with her left hand? Why did the workman kneel next to the bench? Thomas swiveled his body to the left. He ran his hands along the slats that formed the back of the bench. Nothing. He thought again of the newspaper, how it hid Maggie's left hand, a left hand that could then slide along the bottom of the bench. Thomas raked his hand along the bottom of the bench, leaning his head far over for a better look. As he did, he noticed a slight crack on the end of the third slat. He picked at it with his hand and the end cap came loose.

◆ ◆ ◆

Dieter Schmidt pulled the collar of his greatcoat up around his neck and shoved his hands under his armpits. He was happy to be dry, but he was still cold. It was dark, though he judged that the sun should have been well up by now. Heavy snow covered the ground and blanketed the boughs of the fir trees with white trim. Thick, gray fog limited Dieter's view to only about ten meters in any direction. The Schwimmwagen's canvas top was up, but the side curtains had been lost, and it was cold in the front seat. Dieter would have preferred to run the little car's heater, but Kurt had prohibited the running of the engines of any vehicles that weren't on the move—and they definitely weren't on the move right now. Kurt, who now commanded the battalion, had issued strict instructions on conserving petrol, and Dieter knew better than to disobey Kurt's orders.

Dieter tugged his watch cap over his ears. *Sure, it's cold,* he thought, *but I'm dry and I'm full.* The headquarters section had feasted on a generous breakfast of real eggs, bacon, potatoes, and bread a few hours earlier. Kurt had acquired the food—Dieter didn't know by what means—from a local farmer. That was like Kurt, Dieter thought: able to endure any hardship in combat, but willing to secure comforts for his men when possible.

He had lost track of how long he'd been sitting in this traffic jam of tanks, half-tracks, trucks, and other vehicles trying to snake their way along the narrow, snow-covered tracks cut through the

Ardennes Forest. Kurt had walked forward some time ago, disappearing into the fog, to assess for himself the delay. They'd been attached to Kampfgruppe Peiper, the sharp point of Hitler's winter offensive, to divide the Americans from the British and capture the port of Antwerp. The attack had started early that morning. According to the plan, *Standartenführer* Peiper's Tiger tanks would punch a hole through the thinly held American lines, and Kurt's battalion would race through, scattering the Americans and securing a crossing over the Moselle River. Speed was critical: Peiper's forces had to move fast to keep the Allies off balance and to frustrate their counterattack. Any delay would give the Americans and British time to redeploy their overwhelming superiority of forces.

For the past three hours, Dieter had heard the sounds of battle from up ahead. He'd heard the sharp report of tank guns mingled with the muffled pop of small arms and the rhythmic clatter of machine guns. Now he heard new sounds as the tanks to his front belched thick, black smoke, their engines grumbling to life in the cold. Kurt emerged from the fog like an apparition and swung his athletic figure into the passenger seat, a cigarette dangling from his lips.

"We've got a gap in the lines up ahead!" Kurt shouted over the growing racket of the tanks. "We're ready to punch through. Stay close to Gruber!" Kurt gestured to the tank commander standing in the open hatch of the Panther tank immediately ahead. Kurt's face was red from the cold, his bright-blue eyes wide with the anticipation of battle.

Dieter started the car and slipped it into first gear. Slowly, the caravan began to move ahead, the tank throwing great chunks of snow against the front of the car. "No worries about fighters today," Kurt shouted, smiling and looking up to where the fir trees disappeared into the fog.

Since their narrow escape from Allied encirclement in France the previous summer, Dieter had served as Kurt's driver and runner. It was a relationship that seemed to work well for both men. For Dieter, who had slowly adjusted to life as a soldier, it had meant staying alive long enough to learn how to survive. He'd followed Kurt through more than one close encounter with the enemy, and through Kurt's skill, intuition, and luck, they had helped slow the Allied advance while avoiding death or capture. For Kurt, Dieter's presence provided an escape from the daily routines of life in the field. In Dieter, he had at least one comrade with whom he could discuss literature, music, and even, on rare occasions, politics.

"We've got to hit them hard and move fast," Kurt said, exhaling a cloud of smoke. "We can't give them any time to regain their balance!" He turned to Dieter and slapped him on the shoulder. "Now we put the *Amis* on the run for a change, eh?" He smiled.

"*Ja*, Herr Sturmbannführer!" Dieter smiled in return. Despite their rivalry over Maggie—a rivalry, Dieter reminded himself with satisfaction, that he had in fact won—Dieter valued his camaraderie with Kurt. In fact, it was this camaraderie with Kurt and the other members of his unit that made life in the field, and especially in combat, survivable. Without this loyalty to his comrades, and theirs to him, Dieter doubted he would have survived his six months in uniform.

Kurt flipped his spent cigarette out into the snow and tugged a folded map from his pocket. The sky, still overcast, was lighter now. "We should be coming to a highway up ahead. We'll turn right and head toward Baugnez. Peiper's switching routes to keep us on better roads. We'll be able to keep our speed up. From what he told us about an hour ago, we caught the Americans with their drawers down. They're disorganized and on the run. Speed, speed, speed!" He pounded his fist against the side door, grinning.

Within a hundred meters, the leading tanks turned right onto a hard-surface road and headed north. The forest bordered the road on the right, but fields were visible through the thinning fog to the column's left and front.

Dieter jammed on the brakes as the tank in front slowed. A loud blast from just ahead caused Kurt to jerk his head up from the map. At the *bap-bap-bap* of a tank's powerful machine gun, Kurt leaned over and stuck his head out of the car, attempting to see around Gruber's tank. Gruber turned around in his open hatch on top of the turret and waved Kurt forward. "Pull around him," Kurt ordered his driver.

Dieter eased the Schwimmwagen into first gear again and let out the clutch, keeping as close to the lumbering tank as possible and inching forward carefully to avoid dropping a tire into the snow-filled ditch alongside the road. In front of Gruber's tank was the lead Panther, commanded by Edelman, its cannon still smoking. Now Dieter could see what Edelman had fired at and what had halted their column: a convoy of American trucks! The lead vehicle was blazing, its cab destroyed, dead and wounded soldiers spilled on the road beside it. Soldiers from the remaining trucks were diving into the ditches on either side of the road as Dieter pulled in behind Edelman.

The driver of the last truck in the American convoy was trying desperately to turn his vehicle around. The tank's machine gun ripped the air, startling Dieter as Kurt leaped out of the car and clambered up on the turret. Through the windscreen, Dieter could see his commander shouting above the firing to Edelman, who nodded. The tank fired another round from its main gun and the last truck in the American convoy exploded, a plume of flame momentarily dissipating the fog.

Now they're really stuck, Dieter thought, as burning hulks at the front and the rear of the column trapped the four remaining trucks on the narrow road.

The machine gun fired again, this time at the enemy soldiers who had sought cover in the ditches. The rounds walked across the road and through the ditch, ripping into bodies and pitching them backward.

Kurt turned around and signaled Dieter to join him. When Dieter had jumped from his vehicle and scaled the back of the tank, Kurt grabbed him by his lapels and shouted instructions, his face just inches from Dieter's, his eyes intense, his orders clear and concise. He released Dieter and slapped him on the back as Dieter jumped down onto the snowy road.

Dieter raced back to the half-tracks just behind the Schwimmwagen and relayed instructions to the young Obersturmführer in charge of the Panzergrenadiers, the infantry assigned to support the tanks. His men dismounted and sprinted to the two lead tanks. Meanwhile, Edelman's machine gunning had achieved the desired effect: the Americans had thrown down their rifles and thrown up their hands.

Kurt waved the infantry forward. Within minutes, the Americans were standing in the snowy field to the left of the highway, their hands in the air, bewilderment on their faces. Quickly, the Panzergrenadiers took up positions along the side of the field, forming a picket line between the Americans and the road.

Kurt, who was still standing behind Edelman, shouted new orders to the tank commander and jumped down. The big tank groaned and its tracks dug into the snow as it resumed its journey northward, shoving the still burning lead truck into the drainage ditch. Gruber's tank followed, and Kurt's column began moving again.

Kurt strode over to the Panzergrenadier officer. Dieter, who had sprinted back to the Schwimmwagen as the column resumed its march, now pulled the car alongside his commander. Kurt turned away from the Obersturmführer as the column passed by and motioned to Dieter. "Get out," he said. "We've got some work to do."

At that moment, the Panzergrenadiers opened fire on their field of prisoners, the rattle of their weapons punctuating the rumble of the advancing spearhead. Dieter flinched and then froze at the sight of the firing weapons, the falling men, the blood-spattered snow.

The firing stopped as quickly as it had begun. The mournful moans of wounded and dying men replaced the sharp sounds of firing.

"Let's go," Kurt said, pulling Dieter by the sleeve.

Dieter stumbled into the field behind his commander and watched as Kurt pulled his pistol from its holster. He walked up to a soldier writhing in the snow, blood oozing from a wound in his shoulder. Kurt aimed and fired one shot into the soldier's head, stilling him. "You take that one," he said to Dieter, pointing to a terrified American a few feet away. Dieter hesitated. "Quickly! We can't afford to waste time!" Kurt moved on to the next wounded man and fired again.

Dieter slowly pulled his pistol, chambered a round and moved toward the American.

"No, no, no!" the man pleaded. He'd been shot in the leg, but now he tried to crawl away, leaving a crimson trail in the snow, his eyes locked on Dieter.

Another shot came from behind Dieter as Kurt fired again. "Hurry up, Dieter!" he shouted angrily.

Dieter raised his pistol, took a deep breath, and fired.

"I want to send a special greeting out to the boys of the 101st Airborne Division in Bastogne," Betty cooed to her radio audience two days before Christmas. "This song is dedicated to you." She pointed her finger at the sound engineer, who released the turntable. The deep, melodious voice of Bing Crosby drifted over the air singing "I'll Be Home for Christmas." Maggie checked the clock and glanced at her script; right on schedule.

The Germans finally had some good news. Their surprise offensive in the west had caught Eisenhower and the Allies flat-footed. German Panzer units, aided by fierce winter weather that was keeping Allied air power on the ground, had made significant territorial gains and destroyed entire American divisions.

Entire American divisions. Before her own country's troops were involved, she'd been able to speak and think in such general terms without her heart being fully engaged. Now she was wearing down. Now it was hundreds, perhaps thousands of boys like the ones she grew up with in High Glen—quite likely, some of those *very* boys— being torn to shreds on the battlefields, the hearts of their families and other loved ones forever ravaged along with them. There was no side left for her to pray for, since she was as sick with worry about those boys as she was about Dieter (and even, despite their last bitter meeting, Kurt). The victory of one side now meant only laying waste to the other.

It was Dieter above all whom Maggie thought of as she listened to the Crosby song. She wondered where he was and if he was safe. Part of her wanted him to stick close with Kurt, who seemed to have not only a warrior's skill but also a healthy measure of luck. Part of her wanted Dieter far away from Kurt, whom she still didn't completely trust with the best interests of her lover.

Crosby came to the conclusion of the song—"if only in my dreams"— and the music faded out.

"That's right, boys," Betty resumed, "only in your dreams. We had thought about playing 'White Christmas' for you, but we guessed you already had all the snow you wanted. Normally, I'd tell you I was looking forward to talking with you again on Christmas Day. But I don't think that's going to happen. You see, the German Wehrmacht is closing in on Bastogne at this very minute. You're already surrounded. They're tightening the noose. In fact, this will be the last time most of you poor boys hear my voice."

Maggie was right, but not for the reason she thought.

◆　◆　◆

Life had evolved into one long workday, Thomas Müller thought that gray December morning as he grabbed his overcoat and hat off the rack in this office. "Come along, wake up." He nudged *Oberscharführer* Weiss, who had fallen asleep across his desk.

Weiss blinked sleepily, cleared his throat, and replied, "*Jawohl*, Herr Sturmbannführer." Weiss got slowly to his feet and pulled the coat and scarf off the back of his chair.

Thomas stepped across the dimly lit corridor and signed out of the office with the holiday duty officer. The man looked up from a book just long enough to note Thomas's presence and his departure.

Together with Weiss, Thomas walked down the stairs, then along the mezzanine-level main hallway of the Reich Security Main Office building. From there, they took another set of stairs down two more levels to the basement. Thomas nodded to the guard on duty, a stocky man in a soiled uniform and greatcoat. Even though they were still inside the headquarters building, down here in the basement it was so cold they could see their breath.

"Which number, Herr Sturmbannführer?" the guard asked, standing, keys at the ready.

"Twenty-two," Thomas replied. He had reached the delicate point in his investigation, and he was eager to put it behind him. The guard trudged along the cement floor, the only illumination from bare bulbs hanging from the ceiling. He stopped in front of a heavy wooden door set into the concrete wall and fumbled for a moment with the keys. Selecting the right one, he turned the lock and swung the door open. Thomas stepped around the jailer and into the cell. Weiss stood silent watch from the doorway.

"So, my friend," Thomas began, staring at the solitary figure huddled in the corner, "what have you decided to share with me?"

The man sat shivering, perched on a small wooden box and wrapped in a thin blanket. His left eye was swollen nearly shut, and a colorful bruise covered his cheek. "Only what I told you yesterday, Herr Sturmbannführer." The man's voice cracked with hoarseness. "I was paid to pick up the messages. I would leave them under a stone in the sidewalk of Herbststraße. The next day, I would return and collect five Reichsmarks from the same spot. I never knew who the messages were from, or who they were for."

"Stop lying to me!" Thomas shouted, taking a step forward. The man flinched, turning his swollen face away from Thomas. "You know exactly who left the messages and to whom you delivered them. And now I want to know also."

"I swear to you, Herr Sturmbannführer, as God is my witness, I don't know!"

"Tell me this, then, my unfortunate friend," Thomas continued, "how did you know to pick up and deliver these messages in the first place?" Thomas stood silently waiting for the answer.

"It's been a long time, Herr Sturmbannführer, since I had any water to drink."

"It's likely to be much longer if you don't answer my questions quickly and honestly," Thomas growled. "Who hired you for this little courier job?"

The man shifted on his crude chair and pulled the blanket more tightly around his shoulders. The end of his nose was red from the cold, his exposed hands pale. "It was a long time ago now," he began haltingly. "An Italian man came to the park one day and said he needed help to pass notes along to his lover. He said he couldn't take the risk of his wife catching him. You know how the Italians are, Herr Sturmbannführer. The only thing they seem to be good at is affairs of the heart." The man smiled weakly.

"Describe him," Thomas ordered.

The prisoner shrugged. "An Italian. Dark hair, dark eyes, olive skin. What more can I tell you?"

"A name." Thomas felt his impatience rising. "You can tell me a name."

"Oh no, Herr Sturmbannführer; no names were ever used. Just money. Twenty Reichsmarks up front and then five more for each delivery." He sniffed and used the corner of the blanket to wipe his nose.

"How long since you saw this Italian?"

"Three years perhaps. But the five Reichsmarks were always paid, always the day after a delivery."

"What did the messages say?"

"I never looked, Herr Sturmbannführer. My interest was in the delivery fee, not the contents."

Thomas thought for a moment. "How did you know when a message had been left?"

"I worked in the park daily, Herr Sturmbannführer. I would check the bench. If there was a message, I delivered it."

"But you saw the woman, yes? The woman who left the messages. You knew she was the one leaving them, right?"

"Yes, Herr Sturmbannführer."

"Let me ask you this: Did the Italian guy look like a man who would be with a woman like that?"

A smile creased the prisoner's face. He chuckled and shook his head slowly from side to side. "Oh no, Herr Sturmbannführer, I don't believe so."

The man's answer confirmed Thomas's suspicion. Maggie wasn't involved in a tryst; she was passing information to someone. Thomas mentally kicked himself for not realizing what he himself had witnessed the day Maggie spilled her beer. *Idiot!* She had been passing a note. And then he'd seen her do it a second time, just a few days ago. *Fool!* He should have arrested this man the day he observed him servicing the dead drop. If he had gotten hold of the message, he would have had a much better idea of what was going on. Now, the only proof he had was a letter Weiss had intercepted from Maggie to a John Reilly in Bern. A very curious letter at that. Thomas looked over his shoulder at Weiss and nodded. He turned to leave.

"Herr Sturmbannführer?" the prisoner asked. Thomas looked back at the pitiful inmate. "Might I have a drink of water? It is Christmas, after all."

◆ ◆ ◆

They exited into a cold, gray morning with a light snow falling and walked to the end of the street, where Weiss had parked the Mercedes. Weiss slid behind the wheel, and Thomas eased himself into the passenger's seat. His leg hurt more in cold, wet weather. It hurt more when he was tired, too.

Weiss made a U-turn and headed west. He turned right on Stresemannstraße, and as he accelerated on the deserted street, the back of the car fishtailed for a moment. "Be careful," Thomas warned. "I wouldn't want you to have to buy the Reich another car."

"As if one was available," Weiss muttered.

After a fifteen-minute ride, Weiss pulled the car up to the curb. Thomas swung his legs out and cinched the belt of his overcoat tighter. The wind had picked up, and he envied Weiss's scarf.

"Shall I stay with the car, Herr Sturmbannführer?" Weiss asked hopefully from the driver's seat.

"I think not. I think today it would be best that you accompany me."

Thomas opened the outer door of the building, and with Weiss in tow, climbed the stairs, pulling on the handrail to lessen the strain on his aching leg. When he reached the apartment, he rapped loudly on the door. He heard footsteps on the other side.

Maggie opened the door. "Thomas!" she said, smiling her beautiful smile, her eyes wide. "This is a pleasant surprise! Merry Christmas!" Maggie reached out to take Thomas's arm. She saw Weiss standing just behind. Her smile faded.

"I'm afraid we're here on official business, Maggie," Thomas said flatly. "And I'm afraid you will have to come with us."

Maggie forced a laugh. "I know you didn't come to take me to the embassy." Her eyes searched Thomas's face for some indication of what this was all about.

"No, not the embassy," he replied grimly. "Wear something warm, Maggie. It's cold where we're going."

◆ ◆ ◆

Maggie was tired of peeing into a bucket. She was tired of the stink, tired of the filth, tired of the indignity. It seemed that whenever she needed to relieve herself, the guard picked that moment to peer into her tiny cell. Most of all, Maggie was tired of the fear that constantly gnawed at her mind.

The nights were the worst. Although most activity in the cellar stopped at night, there was the constant and irritating sound of dripping, the scurrying of the rats, the sounds of men moaning, sniffling, and weeping. The mind-numbing cold made sleep intermittent at best, and what sleep she could find was interrupted by vivid, frightening dreams of dirty, foul-smelling attackers pursuing her terrified, shrieking sister, Maureen.

The rats, the guards, even the other prisoners scared Maggie. The guards never hesitated to abuse the prisoners. Maggie still hadn't grown accustomed to the sound of grown men crying from beatings that seemed to occur daily.

And then there were the air raids. The Allied bombings had resumed in August and had continued day and night, interrupted only by bad weather. In her basement cell, Maggie was safe enough, she knew, from anything other than a direct hit, but the guards all left to seek shelter during the raids, and Maggie feared being trapped in her cell in a burning building with no way to escape.

In truth, air raids were the least of her problems.

As she paced, Maggie worked on her story. She anticipated the questions she would be asked and pondered her responses. She knew that even the tiniest mistake on her part would end up getting her killed.

She blew into her chapped hands. It was always cold in the basement of 8 Prinz-Albrecht-Straße. According to Thomas, she would normally have been transferred to the women's jail at Alexander Platz, but things were mostly shut down due to the holiday. She'd been fingerprinted and photographed, measured and cataloged. That had been five days ago.

Maggie knew the sands in her hourglass were running out, that soon the footsteps in the corridor would stop at her door, that the stomach-churning sound of the jailer's key would click in her lock and that she would be dragged upstairs to interrogation. From what little Maggie could see from the feeding slot in her door, prisoners were invariably in noticeably worse condition upon their return—if they returned at all.

She expected her interrogation to begin at any time, and she knew that she was in grave danger just by being here. What she didn't know was how much the Gestapo knew—and how far they would go to find out.

A dark thought popped into Maggie's mind.

Well, maybe I'll find Clive after all.

CHAPTER 30

The bright lights hurt Maggie's eyes. She had been in the basement cell for most of the past two weeks, let out only twice to wash. She was dirty and hungry, and her body ached from the cold. Two guards had walked her up four flights of stairs to a small room on the ground floor. Inside was a single chair, next to which sat a small table. In front of the table was a lamp with a directional shade that allowed the light to be focused toward someone or something.

Maggie stood just inside the closed door, enjoying the relative warmth of the room. Outside, she could hear the occasional grumble from the guards as they moved another prisoner to interrogation.

She was hungry but doubted she could eat. She was frightened. She guessed that she had been brought here for interrogation, and she feared that, at some point, her story would begin to unravel. She knew she had to put on a convincing performance to buy time, but for how long?

She heard footsteps approach the door and turned to face it. The door swung inward and she stepped back. Thomas walked in, accompanied by the same man who had driven them here on Christmas Day. Maggie was relieved at the sight of Thomas, but only a little.

"Hello, Thomas." She smiled uncertainly.

Thomas nodded. "Maggie." He held a thick, well-worn folder under his arm. "Go ahead and sit down," he said. "I don't believe I ever properly introduced you to Oberscharführer Weiss," he continued, nodding in the direction of the other man.

"How do you do, Oberscharführer?" Maggie smiled at Weiss.

"Fräulein," Weiss acknowledged.

"Would you be so kind as to get me a chair?" Thomas asked Weiss, who nodded and disappeared through the doorway. "Please"—Thomas gestured at the chair next to the small table—"sit down."

Maggie took off her overcoat and folded it, setting it on the small table, then sat.

"You look none the worse for your little vacation here," Thomas lied. "Perhaps this place agrees with you."

"I don't think so," Maggie replied with a grin. She wanted to keep the conversation as light as she could for as long as she could.

Weiss returned with a wooden chair and placed it directly in front of Maggie, about six feet away. Thomas put his hand on the back of the chair, eased himself into the seat, and situated his prosthetic leg with a practiced movement. "Thank you, Oberscharführer," he said. Weiss moved back to the door and closed it, then turned to watch Thomas and Maggie, standing silently, his arms crossed over his chest.

Thomas cleared his throat and opened the file on his lap. "I suppose you know why you're here." It was as much a question as a statement.

"Did I say something I wasn't supposed to?" Maggie asked innocently. "I made sure that all of my scripts were approved, and I never deviated from them."

Thomas continued to flip through the file, greeting her answer with silence. Finally, he looked up, directly into Maggie's green eyes. "Maggie, we're friends," he started. "I'd like to help you, but you're going to have to help me, too. I'd hate to have to throw you in with the Ukrainian prisoners. They're rough on pretty girls. Do you understand?" Thomas kept his eyes locked on Maggie's.

"Sure, Thomas," she replied, trying to disguise the dread she felt. She wondered if this was how it had started with Clive—some dire, unthinkable threat—and where he was now.

"Now, I need to ask you some questions, and I need you to tell me the truth." Maggie nodded. "When did you first come to Germany and for what purpose?"

"I arrived in the summer of 1938 to study German language and culture at Heidelberg," Maggie answered confidently.

Thomas made a note in the margin of a page and asked his next question. "When did you come to Berlin?"

"In July of that same year."

The questioning continued with Thomas posing nonthreatening questions and Maggie giving truthful answers about where she lived, where she worked, and who her friends were. Maggie described her time at Broadcasting House, how she had started as a clerk and worked her way up to producer and then how she'd been thrust onto the air. Thomas asked about Kurt, about Clive, and about Dieter.

Maggie interrupted her questioner. "Where is Dieter now, Thomas?"

He glanced up from the file. "At the front, I suppose. Would you like some water, Maggie?"

"Yes, please."

"Oberscharführer Weiss, would you please bring Fräulein O'Dea some water?" Weiss nodded and left the room, pulling the door closed behind him. Thomas resumed his questioning. "You mentioned that your scripts are approved in advance. Has that always been the case?"

"Yes."

"How then did Dieter Schmidt get his plea for negotiations with the West out over the air? Why didn't someone stop him?"

Maggie exhaled quietly. If this was just residue from Dieter's folly, she was in the clear; she'd had nothing to do with it. "Dieter had script-approval authority," she explained.

"So, Dieter could, in essence, approve his own script. He could say whatever he wanted to?"

"Correct."

"But you couldn't, even though you were his equal as chief of the American section," Thomas stated matter-of-factly.

"No, not exactly. I was still Dieter's subordinate. My section fell under his general supervision. Plus, as a foreigner, I was never granted script approval."

"You had a personal relationship with Dieter also. Is that correct?"

Maggie swallowed. "Yes," she said, looking directly at Thomas.

"How is it then that you didn't know what he was putting Barnes up to on the night of his last broadcast?"

Maggie recounted the script approval process and that Dieter had deliberately avoided her that night. The door opened and Weiss returned. He set a tin cup of water on the table next to Maggie and a cloth bag next to Thomas's leg, then resumed his post inside the door. Maggie took a sip of the cold water, then another. *Funny,* she thought, *how one takes a drink of water for granted—until it's no longer available.*

"So, you're telling me that you had no foreknowledge of Dieter's plan and no knowledge of what was in the script Barnes read that night?"

"That's correct. I was surprised when I heard it, but I assumed that since it had come from Dieter, it was the official position of the government." Maggie felt the pinprick of guilt as she once again did the *smart thing*, as Dieter would have put it. Maggie's eyes strayed to the cloth bag beside Thomas. *What's in there?* she wondered.

"And have you had any further contact with Dieter since he enlisted?"

"Oh yes!" Maggie's eyes brightened and a smile broke across her face. "I received a couple of letters. Believe it or not, he's in Kurt's battalion! Isn't that ironic?" Maggie detected surprise on Thomas's face; he hadn't known this tidbit. She wondered what else he didn't know—and more important, what he did.

Thomas leaned over to his right and loosened the drawstring on the bag. He reached in and grabbed something, but his arm blocked Maggie from seeing what it was. She heard a clinking sound and then saw her mortar and pestle placed on top of the file in Thomas's lap. "Tell me, Maggie," Thomas said. "What is this exactly?"

"It's a mortar and pestle. It's used for grinding and mixing in the kitchen."

"What do you mix in it?"

"Oh, you can mix spices or crush things. You could make juice with it if you could get fruit. Mash potatoes, you know, things like that."

Thomas raised an eyebrow. "You like to cook, Maggie?"

"Yes, I love to cook, but with just a hot plate, it's pretty hard to do much. I really don't use that very often"—she pointed to the mortar—"simply because I don't cook much."

Thomas scrutinized the bowl and the pestle, holding them at eye level as though trying to imagine Maggie cooking. He reached back into the bag and pulled out a wooden stylus about five inches long. "And this?" he asked, holding it up for Maggie to see.

"It's a toothpick," Maggie teased.

"My, what big teeth you have," Thomas replied with a smile. "What is it really?"

"It's really for baking," Maggie lied. "You stick it in cakes or pies to determine if they're done. That's another thing I don't really use, since I don't have an oven." Maggie hoped Thomas didn't have an oven, either. She also hoped the questions were going to get easier.

Thomas reached back into the bag. "Since you can't cook much, you must spend a good bit of time reading. We found this book in your apartment. Is it yours?" he asked, holding up *Lady Chatterley's Lover*.

Maggie felt the tips of her ears redden and a blush come to her cheeks. "Yes, but it was a gift."

"Still, you must have enjoyed it." Thomas appeared to be beginning to enjoy the interrogation. "See how the pages are dog-eared? You must have read it several times."

"Oh no," Maggie laughed. "I kept getting embarrassed. I never finished it."

"You said it was a gift," Thomas bored in. "From whom?"

"From our mutual friend Erich Greinke."

"Ah." Thomas nodded, pressing his lips together. "Just like Erich to present an obscene present to a pretty girl. I did the best I could with him when I had him in Spain, Maggie," Thomas apologized with a grin, "but I was never able to repair his lack of social grace."

"Of course." Maggie smiled.

Outside, the air raid sirens began their low, mournful wail. Maggie guessed that meant a sunny day, although she hadn't seen the outside for a week.

Thomas carefully placed the items back in the bag and retied the drawstring. He sat back and stared at Maggie for a moment. "I want to help you, Maggie. I hope you'll help me. We'll talk again in a few days." Thomas nodded to Weiss, who opened the door. Two gray-uniformed guards came in to escort Maggie back to the cellar. Thomas shuffled the file back into order and stood. "Keep your head down, Maggie."

Maggie heard more menace in Thomas's warning than in the cry of the sirens.

◆　◆　◆

Even in the dungeon, as Maggie had begun calling her cell, she could hear the rhythmic firing of the capital's antiaircraft batteries. Without her watch, she was never sure what time it was. Her body suggested that it was nighttime, so Maggie assumed the guns were shooting at the British. It seemed like either the British or the Americans, or both, were now bombing Berlin every day. Maggie was sure the actual frequency was less, but the pounding the city was absorbing was fearsome nonetheless.

Despite her anxiety, air raids were the only time when Maggie felt some appreciation for her present situation. If she had been free, she would have had to cram into a cellar or shelter somewhere with hundreds or even thousands of strangers and likely stay the whole night. Rest was nearly impossible in such crowded circumstances. She had been caught once in the city's center and flowed into the shelter at the Zoo train station. More than twenty thousand Berliners had jammed their way in, creating a sweltering, suffocating mass. At one point, Maggie longed to bolt for the door, for the fresh air of the outside—but the sea of humanity held her wedged in place. Now Maggie sat out the raids in relative luxury, with nearly fifty square feet of space all to herself.

Of course, the intervals between raids were difficult. Maggie was fed twice a day and always the same fare: a thin, potato-flavored broth. She was allowed to exercise once a week, after which she could wash. Her pail was emptied daily, but between emptying, Maggie was forced to endure its stench. And then there was the cold: unrelenting, ever present. Maggie wore her overcoat constantly and usually wrapped her threadbare blanket over her head and shoulders like a shawl. Even so, the cold was her most reliable companion. She wasn't allowed to speak to other prisoners, which was a moot point since she was never in the presence of other prisoners to begin with.

To pass the time, Maggie would work on her story, anticipating the questions Thomas would ask and practicing the answers she would give. Even with the stakes at hand, practice got old in a hurry. Maggie felt she had acquitted herself successfully during the first session with Thomas. She wasn't sure he had completely accepted her explanation of the items from her apartment, but she also didn't think he had been able to incriminate her. Maggie wondered what Thomas would have in store for her next.

It was a week later before she found out.

◆ ◆ ◆

"Hello, Maggie," Thomas greeted her informally as the guards returned her to the same interrogation room. Everything seemed as it had been when she was last here, including the thick file folder under Thomas's arm.

"Hello, Thomas," Maggie replied. "Hello, Oberscharführer Weiss." Weiss nodded and took up his position beside the door, pushing it shut.

"How are you holding up?" Thomas asked, motioning for her to sit. Maggie took off her overcoat and hung it on the back of her chair.

"I've stayed in nicer places," she said. "I think I'll go ahead and check out, if it's all right with you and Oberscharführer Weiss there." Maggie tilted her head toward Weiss and sat down.

"Actually, I was thinking you might still be here for a while." Thomas smiled gently. "At least until you answer some more questions for us."

Great, Maggie thought. "OK," she said, "fire away." She was weary already; not the best condition in which to begin an interrogation, but what choice did she have? Maggie noticed that the cloth bag was not in the room. A good thing, she hoped.

"Maggie," Thomas began, "tell us about your lunches at Adolf Hitler Platz."

The fine hair on the back of Maggie's neck bristled. *What does he know?* she asked herself. "I usually eat a sandwich or a wurst and have a beer."

"And where do you usually eat?"

"At my desk most days. In the park if the weather is nice."

"Let's stick just to lunches in the park," Thomas directed. He opened the folder on his lap and flipped through its loose pages. "What do you do there?"

"I eat?" Maggie replied, as though trying to guess the right response.

Thomas looked up. "I know you eat. What else do you do there?"

"I read the paper, I eat, I go back to work," Maggie said, letting her impatience show.

"And . . . ?" Thomas fixed her with his stare. *He has deep-blue eyes,* Maggie thought, *and he's looking right through my soul.*

"And what, Thomas? What is it you want to know?"

"I want to know about the notes, Maggie. Don't play stupid with me, because we both know you are not."

"What notes?" Maggie shook her head, feigning annoyance to cover up her shock.

"Don't play stupid with me, Maggie," Thomas repeated, with a stern edge to his voice. "Tell me about the notes."

Maggie looked down at her hands in her lap. *Careful, now,* she told herself. "The notes were private, none of your business. They were intended for a friend."

"Who?"

"A friend."

"Come on, Maggie," Thomas said, irritation in his voice. "You have to do better than that. Much better, in fact. Who is your friend?"

Maggie's eyes filled with tears. "Oh, Thomas, must we go through this? It's—it's just very personal. It's nobody's business, certainly not the Gestapo's."

"Really?" Thomas was annoyed. He nodded to his colleague. "Oberscharführer Weiss, if you please."

Weiss disappeared into the hallway. Thomas sat quietly, his gaze never leaving Maggie as he tapped a pencil on the folder in his lap. After a few minutes, she couldn't tell exactly how long, Weiss reappeared, shoving before him an emaciated prisoner in a tattered coverall.

"Proceed, Oberscharführer," Thomas commanded.

Weiss pulled on a pair of leather gloves and advanced on the prisoner, who retreated to the corner of the interrogation room. Weiss landed a heavy blow to the man's head, causing Maggie to flinch. The prisoner fell to his knees and Weiss's jackbooted foot caught him in the ribs, sending him the rest of the way to the floor.

"Stop! Stop it!" Maggie cried, half rising from her chair.

Weiss kicked the prisoner again, catching the man in the back.

"Oh, you can stop it anytime, Maggie," Thomas replied, continuing to stare at her. "All you have to do is start answering my questions."

Maggie hesitated, then blurted, "The notes were intended for Gino, my lover. There. I've confessed. Stop this." She gestured toward the contorted figure on the floor. Tears welled in her eyes. "Can we move on now? You have the notes." Maggie looked up, hoping to see in Thomas's reaction whether any notes were in his possession.

Thomas kept a stone face. "Enough, Oberscharführer." Weiss stepped away from the prisoner, now curled into the fetal position and moaning pitifully. "Who is Gino? Why were you passing notes to him in secret, using a courier?"

Maggie felt a chill. Thomas knew about the courier. Did he have the notes, too?

"Gino was married." Maggie began to cry. "I was involved with Dieter. We couldn't be together very often and certainly not in public. We used the notes to arrange our . . . our visits."

"How did you meet this Gino?"

"We met at an embassy function back before America got into the war."

"Is Gino an American?"

"Oh no," Maggie chuckled beneath her tears, "he's all Italian."

"What was he doing at your embassy?"

"Gino worked for the Italian embassy. He was the ambassador's driver. I think he was there to deliver something or maybe pick something up. I—we—well, you know how these things work, it just sparked," Maggie reminisced, a smile on her face.

"What's his last name?"

"Lombardi. Gino Lombardi. Oh, Thomas," Maggie pleaded, "please don't drag him into this. He's married. This would ruin him. He'd probably lose his job, too."

Thomas made a note in the file. "Describe Gino Lombardi," he said without looking up.

Maggie calmed down. She stared off to the side, a dreamlike smile on her face. "Oh, he's very handsome . . ." Maggie spent the next few minutes giving a detailed description of her Italian lover. Thomas made notes, interrupting only occasionally for clarification.

"What was in the notes?" Thomas asked.

"Oh, you know," Maggie answered. "Silly stuff people say to each other when they're in love. Sometimes we'd talk about books or places we'd been or people we'd seen. Gino would tell me who had been to the embassy parties and which soirees he'd taken the ambassador to." Maggie paused. "And we would arrange to rendezvous."

"Where?"

"Where?"

"Yes, where would you meet Gino?" Thomas persisted.

"We usually met at a flat on Herbststraße. It belonged to a friend of Gino's."

"What is the friend's name?"

"I never knew," Maggie answered, looking directly at Thomas.

"Weren't there any personal items in the apartment, a name on the mailbox, something like that to give away the name of the owner?"

"Thomas, it was, um, sort of a love nest, for lack of a better term. I don't think anyone lived there full time. I think these were rooms of convenience."

"When was your last rendezvous with Gino?"

"Just before Christmas." Maggie grinned wistfully. "I've lost track of time. I don't even know what day it is."

Thomas nodded. "It's Tuesday, the thirtieth. Who else was around when you met with Gino?"

"No one. We worked hard to keep it that way."

"So, no one can corroborate this story?"

"No, of course not."

"And you expect me to believe that you did all this behind Dieter Schmidt's back, even as you worked side by side with him every day?" A judgmental tone had crept into his question.

"Actually," Maggie said, weeping quietly, "I'd prefer that you didn't."

CHAPTER 31

Berlin, Germany
February 1945

The session had been very emotional for Maggie, and she had been relieved when it came to an end. The beating of her fellow prisoner had unnerved her. She felt guilt for causing his suffering and fear that Weiss's style of persuasion might soon be directed at her. Still, she'd been able to hold on. Despite the brutality, she had stretched herself as never before, displaying guilt, shame, and wistfulness, all according to the script she had worked out in her mind. She hoped Thomas had been taken in. She wondered what had happened to the other prisoner.

On the way back to the cellar, she kept waiting for the guards to turn her around, to take her back to the interrogation room, where Thomas would dismantle her alibi point by point. When they had finally locked her in her cold cell, she had trembled for what seemed like hours as the tension seeped from her body. Late that night, when the sounds of the prison had faded away to the relative silence of the dripping and scurrying and moaning, she had allowed herself a moment of pride in her ability to turn the interrogation away from reality. How long, she had wondered, would she have to keep it up? The answer came a few days later.

◆ ◆ ◆

"So, here we are again," Thomas said, smiling, after they had taken their accustomed seats across from each other.

Maggie was bone tired. It was nearly impossible to sleep in the icebox of the dungeon. The best she could do was doze fitfully, then pace for a while to warm up, then doze some more. Still, she decided to put her best face on the interview. "Yes," she replied with a weary grin. "We've really got to stop meeting like this."

Thomas looked back at Maggie's sunken eyes, underlined with dark half-moons of flesh. Her auburn hair was matted and tangled. She smelled like livestock; her hands, face, and clothes were dirty. He judged that she was mentally and physically vulnerable for what he intended to be her last interrogation.

"What day is it?" Maggie asked. Thomas made a mental note that for the first time Maggie had kept her overcoat on.

"It's Saturday, the third," Thomas answered, staring into her listless green eyes.

"How goes the war?" Maggie asked, the fatigue evident in her voice.

"About the same," Thomas answered, his eyes never wavering. "How goes it with you?"

"About the same." Maggie attempted to smile. Her teeth felt grimy.

"I'd like to ask you a few more questions about Gino," Thomas began. "And don't make me bring that filthy punching bag back in here this time. When I ask you a question, tell me the truth. Agreed?"

"Shoot," Maggie said, trying to sound chipper.

"When was the last time you saw Gino?"

"Right before Christmas. At the apartment on Herbststraße. We were alone."

"I see. And you said his name is Gino Lombardi, a driver for the Italian embassy." Thomas was looking at his notes from their previous conversation. "Is that correct?"

Maggie nodded. "Yes." They'd been over this before. *No new news here,* she thought.

Thomas glanced over his shoulder toward the door where Weiss stood silently. Thomas pursed his lips. "I'm sorry to tell you that Gino Lombardi returned to Italy last spring, Maggie. It seems you've been less than candid with some of your answers. Your secret love nest seems not to exist, either. Oberscharführer Weiss and I spent a very tiring day and a half inspecting every apartment in the area. You can't imagine the terror we caused, knocking on the doors of unsuspecting citizens and telling them we were from the Gestapo and we just needed to look around."

Oh, can't I?

"I'm your friend, Maggie, but you've been lying to me," Thomas said, leaning forward, his eyes as cold as ice.

Maggie stared back, her mind on full alert. Her story was beginning to unravel. Her mind raced back over their previous conversation. She'd been caught in one lie, but how important was it? As long as Thomas didn't have the actual notes that she'd left in the park, he'd have a hard time making any charge stick. But did he have them? Maggie guessed he did not. If he did, he would have used them from the beginning.

Thomas cleared his throat. He was still staring at her. "Who's John Reilly?"

Maggie's mind was jerked back to the present. "An old friend of my father's. Before the United States entered the war, he went to Switzerland. He's still there. He works for Nestlé."

"Another of your imaginary lovers?" Thomas sneered.

"Oh no," Maggie laughed. "He's closer to my father's age. Too old for me."

"What kind of work does he do at Nestlé?"

"I don't know. He was a dairy farmer. That's how we got to know him. He borrowed money from my father's building and loan. It's like a bank," Maggie explained.

"I see. You write to him now, don't you, Maggie?"

"Yes. I've sent him a few letters over the past few years. Just to ask how are you?"

"What else do you put in your letters?"

"Oh, the usual stuff. Life in Berlin. I write about how the war is affecting us. Things like that."

"And where is it that he lives? I have it here somewhere." Thomas made a point of looking through some notes.

"Bern. He lives in Bern," Maggie said. "He works for Nestlé and lives in Bern." *Stop, Maggie!* she told herself. *You're talking too much.* "May I have a drink of water, please?" she asked.

Thomas nodded toward Weiss, who ducked out of the room.

"Yes, Bern," Thomas echoed. "Can you tell me what Mr. Reilly looks like? I don't seem to have a picture."

"He's about fifty-five, I guess, stocky with dark-gray hair, but bald on top. I haven't seen him in many years, you understand, not since before I left to come here."

"I see. And does Mr. Reilly write letters back to you?"

"Yes, from time to time. And I must tell you, Thomas, that life in Bern seems a little better than life in Berlin right now," Maggie needled. Maybe that would distract him.

Thomas's face smiled, but his eyes remained cold. Weiss returned and sat the cup on the table next to Maggie. "Thank you," she said.

"We have friends in Bern, too, Maggie. Our friends tell us that your Mr. Reilly looks a great deal younger than fifty-five. They say he is athletic and has a full head of hair. In fact, the man who retrieves the letters from Mr. Reilly's mailbox looks just like Erich Greinke." Thomas held his hand out to his right with the palm up. Weiss approached and laid a letter across it. Thomas held the letter up for Maggie to read the address. "This is one of yours, is it not?"

"Yes." *Uh oh,* she thought. *This is really starting to go downhill fast.*

"Well, let's see what you've been writing to Mr. Reilly. Or should I say Mr. Greinke?" Thomas removed the letter from the already open envelope and carefully unfolded it. "'Dear John.' Oh, I like how you start it off," Thomas teased menacingly. "Berlin in winter . . . lots of snow . . . Christmas coming up . . . how's Switzerland . . . how's the milk business. Hardly seems worth writing, Maggie." Thomas folded the letter and placed it back in the envelope. He held the envelope by the short edge and slapped it against his thigh, his eyes still fixed on Maggie. "I wonder," he said. "Oberscharführer, if you please."

Weiss opened the door and stepped through it. Off in the distance, air raid sirens began their slow howl. Thomas continued to tap the letter against his wooden leg. "What are we going to do, Maggie?" Within a few moments, Weiss was back. He carried a kettle and a hot plate, which he plugged into the wall behind Thomas. Sheer terror tore through Maggie's mind. *He knows!* "I wonder," Thomas repeated. Outside, the sirens grew louder.

Thomas held the envelope up and Weiss took it over to the kettle. Weiss removed the letter and unfolded it. The kettle began to whistle. The sirens wailed. Weiss held the letter to the steam. *Shit!* Maggie thought. Thomas continued to stare at her.

Weiss gently moved the paper back and forth. Maggie's eyes were fixed on the horrible sight of rows of brown numbers appearing on the page. *Shit!* her mind repeated. Her hands began to tremble. She clasped them in her lap, hoping Thomas hadn't noticed—not that it would matter at this point.

"Herr Sturmbannführer." Weiss handed the now exposed letter back to Thomas. The kettle continued its shrill whistle.

"I think you can turn off the water now," Thomas said without taking his eyes off the letter.

Weiss unplugged the hot plate and the kettle fell silent. In place of its high note was a low, throbbing drone. In the distance, an antiaircraft battery opened up, spitting shells twenty thousand feet into the sky.

"My, my, my, Maggie. What have we here?" Thomas asked with false surprise. "Why, it looks like some kind of code." He raised his eyebrows theatrically. The muffled whump of exploding bombs penetrated the interrogation room. Maggie prayed one would fall on her head. "Time's up, Maggie. Tell me what you've been up to."

"Nothing. I haven't done anything wrong. It's not what it looks like," Maggie stammered.

"Well, that's good," Thomas said, leaning forward, his voice increasing in volume. "Because it looks very bad." The explosions were getting closer, as though an angry giant were stomping across the city, squashing everything underfoot. "What kind of code is this, Maggie? What information were you sending to Erich?" Thomas had to shout to be heard over the bombs, which sounded and felt ever closer.

"I don't know," Maggie cried. She covered her ears as a bomb exploded nearby, the concussion radiating shock waves that rattled the building and sent plaster dust drifting down from the ceiling. She was weeping now. There was no way out. Hell was breaking loose and she was caught in the middle of it. She wouldn't catch up with Clive. She wouldn't see Dieter again. Her father would wonder what happened to his daughter. A tremendous blast rocked the building; then another; then three more in rapid succession. The lights went out. Maggie was tossed sideways like a discarded doll. Black smoke filled the room. Maggie couldn't see. She couldn't hear. Everything went black.

◆ ◆ ◆

Maggie's head throbbed. She was lying on her side. She blinked her eyes open. It was dark, and what she could see was fuzzy. Her ears were fuzzy, too. She could feel the shock of the bombs as they continued to fall nearby, continued to shake the building. She struggled to her knees and looked around. There was a fire burning over to her left. More explosions. *Move! Go!* Maggie got to her feet and stumbled. She had tripped over her chair. A large explosion caused her to duck. An oblong chunk of plaster smacked into the floor next to her, missing her by a hand's width. She tried to move toward the door—or at least where the door had been. A jagged hole had been ripped through the wall. The door was gone. Maggie moved toward the opening. She was dizzy, unsteady on her feet. Thomas was lying on his face, dust and ash covering his body, his leg twisted off to one side, blood trickling out of his ear. Maggie stepped over him. Weiss was partially buried under the collapsed wall. Maggie picked her way through the rubble as a bomb shattered the north side of the lobby, shrapnel ricocheting along the hallway. She coughed her way down the dark, smoke-filled corridor. She headed toward a hazy glow, the only light she could see except for the white-orange flash of the bombs. She felt the bombs more than she heard them. Her ears hurt and she covered them with her hands, only to find them both bleeding.

Maggie stepped through the opening where double doors had once stood like sentinels. The air was cold and filled with dust, ash, and smoke. Another explosion behind her punched her on the back of her shoulder and sent her sprawling into the snow. She pushed herself to her knees, gasping at the pain in her shoulder, and then stood. Maggie began to shuffle away from the building, away from the bombs that continued to rain down on the government quarter of the capital. A piece of something whooshed past her head. She kept moving.

Maggie began to run. *You've got to get away from here,* she thought. She instinctively headed west, toward Broadcasting House and her apartment. While the bombs were still falling, there would be no one aboveground. Now was her best chance to put some distance between herself and her captors. Berlin was getting a heavy pasting from the Americans. Sticks of bombs continued to fall in the vicinity, erupting into fireballs of flame, ripping the air apart and knocking Maggie to the ground. But she would not stop. She continued to hurry westward.

The bombs continued to fall for another hour, but once the enemy planes had departed, the city slowly came back to life. Berliners shuffled from their underground shelters into a garden of death. Blackened tree trunks, shattered buildings, heaps of rubble gave silent testimony to the heaviest raid yet. The authorities concentrated their efforts on firefighting and search and rescue. Maggie calculated that it would be some time before she was missed, and even longer until a search for her was mounted.

Maggie had hoped to get out of town before nightfall, but Berlin was a sprawling city. In the end, she didn't have the stamina for it. Deprived of sufficient food for six weeks, her body gave out. She found a makeshift soup line set up near the ruins of Saint Canisius Church, where she had worshipped in happier days. The church had been destroyed during a bomber raid over a year earlier. Maggie had not been there since, and, in her current state, she doubted anyone would recognize her even if they had seen her before. The soup was not much thicker than the broth she'd received in the dungeon, but it came with a thumb-size piece of bread that Maggie found heavenly. As she ate, she continued to look around her, studying her surroundings for anyone who looked out of place or who looked like they had authority.

Sounds were still muffled; both her head and her shoulder throbbed. Maggie had to be careful not to lean over too far. If she did, she quickly lost her equilibrium and found her vision blurring. Maggie set down her bowl on the knee wall that had once formed the perimeter of Saint Canisius and drifted away into the late-afternoon darkness, keeping the glow of the fires from the city center behind her.

She walked three more blocks and could go no farther. Maggie wandered into the Grunewald cemetery. She moved slowly in the dark, down a row of marble mausoleums. She found one with an unsecured gate and opened it. *It's not the Adlon,* she thought as she lay down to rest, *but I've stayed in worse places.*

◆　◆　◆

The cold woke her. She didn't know how long she had slept, only that she was freezing. Thank God she still had her overcoat. Maggie sat up and waited a moment for her head to stop spinning, then pulled herself up and looked around. *Sleep like the dead? My ass,* she thought. If this was how the dead slept, she'd stay with the living. She was colder even than she'd been in her basement cell.

A misty rain was falling, intermingled with the occasional snow-flake. It was still completely dark, and it took Maggie a moment to reorient herself. She turned up the collar of her overcoat and stepped out of the mausoleum. She needed rest, but she also needed to put more distance between herself and Thomas. And she needed food. She couldn't risk going to her friends; most of them worked for the government. Besides, she didn't want to hang around in the city any longer.

Maggie began walking in what she hoped was a westerly direction. Her eyes slowly adjusted to the darkness, but she still couldn't hear well; everything sounded muffled, as though she were holding a pillow over her ears. She walked on the empty streets, keeping watch for any light or movement that would indicate the presence of another person. She approached intersections cautiously, on the lookout for the *Polizei.*

Maggie wandered down the road, coming to the suburb of Zehlendorf. She realized she had been walking more south than west. As the sky to her left was showing the first streaks of a gray dawn,

Maggie knew she would soon have to leave the road anyway. But first: food. She was famished. She cut to her left, down an alley between two storefronts. She hoped to find a restaurant or Gasthaus and its garbage. She could hear things now, could see outlines of light coming from some of the windows in the buildings she was passing. She sniffed the air for the scent of food. The sky continued to brighten, although it looked like a cloudy morning. Within a few minutes she would need to find a new hiding place.

Maggie continued to follow the road as it headed south toward the river. It remained a dull gray morning, the mist continuing to fall, but it was daylight nonetheless and she had to get off the streets. She left the road and turned east, walking through a small stand of trees until she came upon a small stream and had an idea. She followed the stream until it came to a dirt road cutting across a field. The stream flowed beneath a small bridge, which Maggie imagined was used by the farmer. She didn't expect the bridge would get much traffic on a February Sunday, so she crawled under it, being careful to avoid the water. The last thing she needed was to get wet. It was dirty under the bridge but dry; most important, it was concealed.

◆ ◆ ◆

Hunger gnawing at her stomach woke her. She had experienced her best sleep in weeks. The daytime temperature had climbed higher while she slept, providing unaccustomed warmth. The rippling sound of the creek below her had masked other noises, helping her sleep and helping her body rest. Maggie stretched and felt pain in her shoulder. It was almost dark. She guessed it was late afternoon. She eased herself down to the water's edge and washed her face and hands. The cold water refreshed her. She waited another half hour for full darkness and then began to head south again. She had to find some food.

Heading back toward the town, she watched and listened, intent on avoiding contact with people. The early winter darkness worked in her favor, but it meant that there were probably still several hours before restaurants would put out their after-dinner garbage.

◆ ◆ ◆

Her stomach was growling so loudly that Maggie was afraid someone would hear it. She had reached the outskirts of Potsdam, sitting just across the Havel River. She was sure she could find a restaurant or two there. The only problem was that to get into the town, she had to cross the river. To cross the river, she had to use one of the bridges. And the bridges were guarded.

Too risky, old girl, she told herself. Instead, she decided to head south again, avoiding the Havel. She would take her chances in Babelsberg, a smaller village just east of Potsdam. She didn't expect to find a restaurant, but maybe there would be a Gasthaus or even a farmhouse. Maggie moved quietly along the edge of the village. There were no vehicles on the roads, and she could make out the silhouettes of buildings against the dark sky. She heard a dog barking in the distance.

You've got to eat now, her brain said to her legs, and she began to walk toward the back of a house. She crept up slowly, watching for an opening door or window, ready to fade back into the darkness at the first sign of detection. Smoke curled out of the chimney, rising a few feet and then flattening out like a low cloud. *Great,* thought Maggie, *rain on the way.*

Careful, now, she coached herself, her senses on alert. *There must be someone home.* A sliver of light outlined a window of the one-story house.

Maggie could smell food. She kept her eyes focused on the back of the house—and ran into the refuse can, knocking the top off with a thud. Maggie ducked behind the barrel and froze. She heard the door open, and a shaft of yellow light reached out into the darkness. *"Ist da jemand?"* came a woman's voice.

Maggie held her breath. The shaft of light receded as the door closed. Maggie began counting. She counted to three hundred—about five minutes, she figured. She peeked around the barrel. She saw no one. The smoke continued to rise out of the chimney; the sliver of light peered from beneath the window.

Standing and leaning over the barrel, she began to feel around inside, her fingers touching slimy pieces of something. She pulled it out, sniffed it, and then quickly popped it into her mouth. She was glad it was cold: no bugs. She was glad it was dark, too, so she couldn't see what she was eating. But oh, how delicious the potato peeling tasted. Maggie quickly plunged her hands back into the barrel, mindful not to make noise. An apple core went into her pocket. She lifted a small opened tin out, but it was empty. She stuck it in another pocket. It would do for a cup. Apart from a handful of potato peeling and the tops of a couple of carrots, she didn't get a lot, but it was a start. She gingerly lifted the lid from the ground and put it back on top.

She had similar luck at the next house: a few pieces of vegetables, but no bread, and of course, no meat. Still, she had managed to take the sharp edge off her hunger.

Somewhat fortified, Maggie decided it was time to move again. She followed the river to the south, remembering that at some point it turned northwest. Then she would be able to resume her westward trek. Taking advantage of the forest that paralleled the river, she worked her way south through the trees.

She walked for the rest of the night.

As the sky began to brighten, Maggie headed deeper into the woods, putting distance between herself and the river. Once the sun was up, she gathered some fir boughs and fashioned a crude bed beside a log. After a long night, she settled down in the sun to sleep.

◆ ◆ ◆

After six days, Maggie had reached the vicinity of Möckern. Her foraging skills had improved. She had learned that in the countryside, farmers followed the schedule of the sun and the seasons more so than the time of the clock. Meals were eaten earlier than in the city, even those eaten out. By ten at night, Maggie could approach restaurants confident that the waste had been put out. She was eating better, if not well. In addition to food, she'd also managed to pick up a stray knife, a fork, and a dish towel, which doubled as a scarf when dry. Her shoulder no longer ached unless touched. Her headaches and dizziness were gone. But still, she had challenges. One of them was just a few miles ahead.

◆　◆　◆

Maggie stared at the fast-flowing, gray water of the Elbe. It was dusk. A thin streak of light was left in the western sky, coaxing Maggie forward.

The Elbe was the last great river she would have to cross until she reached the Rhine. Maggie had spent the day trying to sleep. Morning sun had given way to a cloudy afternoon, dropping the temperature and making sleep more difficult. Now, as darkness fell, she was glad to be moving again. Walking helped her stay warm. It also enabled her to find food.

The few bridges over the Elbe in and around the city of Magdeburg were all guarded. Maggie had spent the late afternoon nestled among trees, watching the guards and observing as they waved traffic past or stopped travelers to check identification. She had toyed with the idea of simply walking across on the bridge's sidewalk, but had finally rejected that plan. If she was stopped, she would be helpless. With no identity papers, she would never be able to bluff her way past the soldiers. She had also thought of hitching a ride on a truck or other vehicle, but the same fears had dissuaded her.

Now, in the gathering darkness, Maggie stared at the river and pondered her latest plan. The water was too cold and her body too weak to swim across. She would die of exposure or drown. Instead, she had decided to "borrow" a boat. After waiting impatiently for darkness to cover her approach to the riverfront and her search for a suitable conveyance, Maggie stepped out from behind the tree where she had been waiting and cautiously moved toward the river 150 yards ahead. She was west of the village of Randau, just south of and on the opposite bank from Magdeburg.

As she moved closer, the gurgling of the river became more pronounced. Pausing every few steps to listen, she scanned to her front and rear, looking for any light in the darkness. When she reached the bank of the Elbe, she began to slowly pick her way south. In the darkness, the overhanging brush along the bank took on sinister qualities. She stopped frequently to discern whether the shapes ahead were men carrying arms or simply branches silhouetted against the darkening sky.

The first boat she found was long and wooden, with its bow pointing inland and its keel pointing skyward. Maggie approached it cautiously and looked around to make sure she was alone. Satisfied, she came around to the side of the boat and bent over. She dug her hands under the gunwale and heaved. The boat rose about two inches off the ground. Maggie pulled her hands away and let the side of the craft thump back onto the ground. It was far too heavy for her to turn over, much less get to the water.

Maggie eased her way around the overturned boat and proceeded south along the riverbank. She'd have to find something smaller, something she could handle. The next vessel she came upon was again too large and too heavy. The one after that was somewhat smaller, but was holed just behind the bow. After searching for what seemed like hours, Maggie finally found a boat that she judged would work. It was constructed of rough wood and in the darkness appeared to be in need of paint, but she thought it would do to get her across.

With effort, she turned the boat over with a thud. Its two oars and a small tiller were inside. Maggie quickly placed the oars in the oarlocks. She untied the short bow rope that secured the boat to a stake in the ground and pulled it free, then set about working the nose of the boat around so that it pointed to the river. She moved around to the stern of the small boat and pushed. It was hard labor for someone on a diet of potato skins and other scraps. After several minutes of pushing and then moving to the bow rope and pulling, Maggie managed to get the boat to the water.

All right, Maggie, she told herself, *this is the moment of truth.* When the boat went into the water, she'd have to jump in before the current snatched it away from the bank. Maggie again swung the boat around by its nose, holding firmly to the rope, and with the stern facing the water, pushed on the bow, using the bank as a fulcrum. The stern met the water and Maggie moved quickly. Still holding tightly to the rope, she shoved the boat off the bank. Immediately the bow rope went taut, pulling her toward the water. She pulled on the rope, leaning back toward land as the boat attempted to free itself from her grasp. She pulled until the nose snuggled up against the bank and the boat swung parallel to the current, its nose pointing upstream. *Now or never.* She jumped.

In the darkness, Maggie managed to land in the boat, bashing her shin against its side. The boat rocked, and frigid water sloshed over its side, slicing into Maggie's ankles like an ice-cold knife. She scrambled onto the little bench seat and grabbed the tiller, dropping it into place, then took the handles of the oars. Already the boat was out in the current, moving rather rapidly north toward the city. Maggie pulled on the oars, and the little boat began to turn. She wasn't sure how far upriver she was. In the blackout, it was hard to see where the city was—and where the guarded bridges crossed the water. It was possible that, due to the moonless darkness, the boat—and Maggie—could pass beneath the bridges unseen, but it was a risk she hoped to avoid by reaching the opposite bank well before she reached the city.

Maggie had guessed the river to be about three hundred yards across. With the current pushing her steadily, she put her right hand on the tiller and pushed the handle away from her. The boat yawed to the left, toward the opposite bank. It yawed fast and began to tip over. Maggie threw her weight to the left and let go of the tiller. The little boat rocked and then settled as its nose swung back downstream. Maggie tried the tiller again, more cautiously this time, and the boat headed toward the dark western shore. Her hands were bitterly cold and chapped, her nose and lips red from the cold air on the water, but the shore was fast approaching.

Maggie continued to work the tiller, letting the current propel the boat forward. As she neared the bank, she searched for a low spot where she could beach the boat. She could make out the dark line of the bank, but no details. The riverbank crept closer in the darkness. She glanced north: still no sign of the bridges, still time to get to shore. And then it was upon her. Low branches scratched at the side of the boat, its bow glancing off a root. Maggie reached for the oars and tried to guide the boat to shore, but she was in close enough that the left oar had no room to sweep. She pulled on the right-hand oar, and the boat slid toward the shore. Maggie dropped the oar and reached up, grabbing for branches, hoping to slow her approach. The branches ripped through her grasp, causing her to lose her balance. She had to let go, but her momentum had slowed. She reached up again as the bow swung toward the bank. She grabbed a limb, and the bow bumped against the bank. It held for a moment, and the boat began to swing around. Now, with the nose stuck in the side of the bank, the boat drifted parallel to the shore for a moment. Maggie pulled with her arms and pushed with her feet, feeling the little boat give way as she swung herself up onto the bank into a tangle of brush.

She held tightly to the bushes, and satisfied that she was on land, stood up and looked back toward the black water in time to see the rowboat drifting away downstream. She'd made it across!

◆ ◆ ◆

Captain Erich Greinke walked down the ornate corridor of the Citadelle de Namur, his boots clicking on the tiled floor. He pushed open a door on the right and stepped into the OSS liaison office to General Omar Bradley's Twelfth Army Group. Erich, along with many of his colleagues, had been commissioned into the army in order to give them greater credibility and standing in their work with partisan fighters in the occupied countries. Now, with the Allies having advanced nearly to the German border, the French and Belgians were more concerned with rebuilding their countries than with carrying the fight to the German homeland. That was a job they would gladly leave to the Americans and British.

Erich tossed his cap on his desk and looked through the morning's dispatches. Nothing much seemed to be happening. The Allies had taken the worst the Germans had left during the Battle of the Bulge. Now, back on the offensive again, the Allies were battling not only the Wehrmacht but also the weather. Shattered dams in the Ruhr Valley had rivers three feet and more above flood levels. To make matters worse, a midwinter thaw, coming after the bitter cold and heavy snows of December and January, was adding snowmelt to the already swollen rivers. As a result, General Bradley had delayed the start of his offensive rather than risk disaster attempting to cross raging rivers.

Everyone, it seemed, was stuck, waiting for better weather and receding waters. Even so, the OSS still had work to do. Erich and his colleagues at Bradley's headquarters were busy studying the growing lists of refugees and displaced persons that the G-5, the civil affairs officer, was producing. Tens of thousands of desperate souls were crossing the lines each month seeking food, shelter, medical treatment, and asylum. Erich compared the G-5's list with a confidential list from OSS headquarters, hoping for a match. The OSS roster listed people the Americans wanted to talk to—suspected war criminals, collaborators, and key scientists. When a person from the OSS list was identified, Erich or one of his staff requisitioned a jeep and drove to the camp where the person was held. Once there, the OSS men would confirm the subject's identity. A positive match would result in the person being removed to special custody. So far, the G-5's list had contained few Germans; most of the displaced were from countries still occupied by the Axis, but that was soon to change as the Allies closed on the Rhine and the German frontier.

CHAPTER 32

Near Hameln, Germany
March 1945

Maggie was asleep, but the humming of the bees kept intruding on her dreams. She had walked through the previous night, first foraging for food in the town, then retreating to the safety and shelter of the forest to its south. She had grown bolder in her search for food. In addition to nightly forays to the back doors of restaurants and Gasthauses, she had also marshaled the courage to stand in soup lines. She realized that she was far from the only refugee traveling across Germany by foot. Frequently, she found villages and towns with church-sponsored food lines. Here no identity or ration card was required. On two occasions, when hunger and fatigue had overcome her, Maggie had simply knocked on the door of a home and asked for a meal. The old woman who had answered the door the first time looked as tired as Maggie felt, but had invited her into the small, warm kitchen and fed her a wonderful meal of beets, potatoes, and fowl. On the other occasion, Maggie had begged a breakfast of eggs, bacon, potatoes, toast, and jam. The coffee she had washed down the meal with had been made from barley, but was still the most flavorful beverage she'd had in two months.

Maggie lay beneath the tall pines of the forest, shafts of sunlight penetrating the green boughs overhead. It was a relatively warm morning, with a bright-blue, cloudless sky; a perfect day to be outdoors, except for the bees. Maggie blinked and shielded her eyes from the brightness. The hum of the bees was steady and loud. She sat up and looked around at the small clearing where she had fashioned a nest of pine needles. She blinked again and looked around for the bees whose buzzing had awakened her. Slowly, her head cleared of sleep, and she looked up into the morning sky. Dozens of specks filled the sky, each trailing white tails of vapor. The droning, Maggie realized, was coming from a fleet of American bombers heading east.

Maggie stood and shielded her eyes with her hand as she continued to stare at the airplanes. The formation covered as much of the sky as the tall trees of the forest allowed her to see. The stream of bombers seemed endless, and Maggie watched them float noisily overhead for several minutes. *Somebody's going to get pounded,* she thought, glad once again to be out of Berlin, even if it meant living a vagabond's life.

◆ ◆ ◆

Maggie's trek took her near Bielefeld, and she thought of Chesney Nutt and his never-written story about the Bethel asylum. She wondered what had become of the courageous pastor and his patients.

By late March, she began to find herself surrounded by more and more refugees, most of them moving from west to east to escape the advancing Allied armies. Food was becoming harder to find. Begging was becoming dangerous, too, as local residents were overwhelmed with the needs of transients. Often now, Maggie was greeted with hostility when she asked for food. She was hungry all the time, and her strength began to flag. She also began to hear things.

The sounds of war were prevalent. Silver-bodied Allied fighter planes ruled the skies, skimming the trees and firing at anything that moved. Artillery fire thundered in the west. At night, when the skies were less crowded, Maggie observed German army units on the move. Mostly they traveled by foot or cart. Few trucks or other motor vehicles moved along the roads. She was careful to avoid any Germans in uniform or anyone who looked official. Even with her linguistic skills, honed over nearly seven years, she had no desire to have to explain herself to someone in authority.

Nonetheless, hunger was a powerful motivator, and Maggie soon discovered that Wehrmacht and Waffen SS units, if not well supplied, usually enjoyed at least adequate rations. As she neared the front, she wandered more frequently into the rear areas of army units, all of which were painstakingly making their way east. She was careful to hide from soldiers, but she felt compelled to continue to the west, and in doing so inevitably found herself in close proximity to large numbers of uniformed men. The disadvantage was that her risk of detection increased exponentially with the population, military or civilian, of a given area. The advantage was that the soldiers often discarded food—and scraps, multiplied by a hundred or even a thousand troops, added up to a feast.

◆　◆　◆

It was very late, Maggie guessed well past midnight, and she was poking slowly and quietly through a mound of rubbish behind a small house near the village of Borken. At irregular intervals, Maggie heard artillery fire coming from the west, but the rounds were falling some distance away. She was alert. She had seen the glow of a cigarette earlier. She knew there were sentries posted around the house and suspected that it was being used to billet soldiers.

Digging through the trash, her fingers closed on a half-full tube of cheese that had been discarded. Lately, as she prowled in areas recently vacated by soldiers, she had found more and more of the pale yellow cheese. Apparently, the soldiers didn't like it much. Maggie understood why. It would never replace Camembert, but it was food. She squeezed some of the cheese into her upturned mouth, then almost choked when a deep voice behind her said, *"Guten Abend, meine Dame."* Maggie had been focused so intently on the cheese that she'd failed to hear the soldier's approach. "You will please come with me," he said, clamping a viselike grip on her arm.

The soldier led her through the darkness to the back steps of the house. No light was visible from outside. He knocked softly once on the wooden door, then pushed it open and shoved her inside.

"What have you got there, Hoegg?" came a low, sleepy voice from the dark interior.

"A prowler, Herr *Sturmscharführer*," the soldier answered quietly.

"Take him out and shoot him."

"It's a woman, Herr Sturmscharführer," the soldier explained, his voice still barely above a whisper. Maggie could now make out the shapes of other soldiers on the floor of the small room.

"Scheiße!" snorted the Sturmscharführer sleepily. "We get two hours for sleep before we move out again, and you interrupt it with a prowler! You should have just kicked her in the ass and sent her away," he muttered, throwing aside his bedding and pushing himself to his feet. "Bring her," he ordered as he tiptoed around the sleeping men and out of the room.

The house was small and crowded with sleeping bodies. Maggie could hear them snoring and shifting. She and the two soldiers crossed through another room before the Sturmscharführer stopped at a doorway. She could see a dim glow seeping from the bottom of the closed door. The sleepy soldier rapped his knuckles softly on the door frame.

"Kommen Sie," commanded a muffled voice from within.

The Sturmscharführer cracked open the door, allowing light to spill into the outer room. "I beg your pardon, Herr Sturmbannführer, but Hoegg has captured a prowler," the soldier reported without entering the room.

"Shoot him," said the voice from within.

"It's a civilian, sir. A woman."

Maggie craned her neck, trying to peer around her captors and into the room.

"Damn it! All right, bring her in."

The Sturmscharführer stepped aside, and Hoegg guided Maggie into the room. A small kerosene lantern cast a pale-yellow circle of light on a map spread across a table. Beside it, a Waffen SS officer was rubbing his eyes, obviously tired. Another figure lay in a corner, snoring beneath a muddy blanket. "All right, Hoegg. Good job. You may wait outside." Hoegg nodded and disappeared back into the dark. "Now, tell me, *meine Dame*, why I shouldn't have you shot," demanded the officer. He appeared to be struggling to keep his bloodshot eyes open.

"I was hungry."

"We're all hungry and tired and dirty. What are you doing sneaking around my headquarters in the middle of the night? Don't you realize that's a good way to get shot?" He sighed and picked up a smoldering cigarette that had been balanced on the edge of the table. His mud-spattered uniform had been unclasped at his neck, and he had not shaved in several days. "Where did you come from?"

"Berlin," Maggie answered, too tired to think up a lie.

He half turned and squinted at her in the dim light from the lantern. "What are you doing here?"

"I had to get away from the bombing."

He snorted, then wiped his sleeve under his nose. "I'm afraid you've gone from bad to worse. We're only a hundred or so meters from our forward positions." He glanced at the round face of his wristwatch. "Positions we will abandon in less than an hour. I would offer to take you along with my Mercedes"—he forced a laugh—"but I fear you would get tired of pushing." The officer took two slow strides and opened the door. "Hoegg!" he called softly.

"Herr Sturmbannführer!"

"Put this woman in the root cellar. Give her one ration pack." He turned back toward Maggie. "You will stay there until we're gone. If you interfere with any of my soldiers, I will shoot you myself. Understood?"

"*Jawohl*, Herr Sturmbannführer," Maggie replied.

Hoegg guided Maggie back through the darkened house, where the sleeping men were beginning to stir. They exited into the stillness of the starry morning and walked around to the side of the house. Hoegg pulled open the broad wooden door leading down to the cellar, and Maggie felt her way down the steps. In her hand was one field ration—not much, but more food than she'd possessed at any one moment in the last several months. Maggie looked up as the door closed, erasing the stars from her view.

The SS unit had been gone for several hours, and still Maggie huddled in the corner, the earthen floor of the cellar cool and damp beneath her. The whump of artillery fire and the popping of small arms had gradually increased as the night had given way to day. Now it sounded as though the war was right overhead. Gunfire echoed through the cellar along with the clatter of running boots and the occasional teeth-jarring rumble of tracked vehicles passing nearby. Judging from the intensity of the sounds and vibrations around her, the Sturmbannführer was right. She had indeed reached the front lines—or rather, they had reached her.

Maggie replayed the night in her mind: the mistake of getting caught, her good fortune in not being shot—or perhaps worse, turned over to the authorities. She laughed at the thought: there were no authorities here.

A loud pop intruded on Maggie's thoughts, and she heard a pained howl. The outer door to the cellar rattled and was thrown back, daylight flooding into the underground chamber. "Geez! Geez! Ow for Chrissakes! Shit!" a voice in pain shouted.

"Easy now, Reg," said a second voice. "Easy now, I've got you. We're just going to ease down these steps here and fix you up right as rain, right as rain, you'll see. Step here. That's it."

Maggie shrank back into the shadows. The voices were speaking English.

Two soldiers were silhouetted in the dusty light from above. One was bleeding from the leg. His hand pressed against his thigh, he continued a painful moan. The other soldier held his comrade around the waist with one hand while in his other hand he clutched a rifle. "Here we go. Easy now. Just lie down and let's have a look at that leg." He helped his friend to the ground and set the rifle to his side. He pulled out a bayonet and quickly sliced through the leg of the wounded man's trousers. "Aw, what's all this howling about? It's naught but a scratch, Reg!"

Reg propped himself up on his elbows and peered at his right leg. From the corner, Maggie could see the pale-white flesh smeared with the vivid crimson.

"Here," his friend said, replacing the bayonet in its scabbard, "and I thought you was going to lose your bleeding leg, the way you was carryin' on."

Reg lay back on the dirt floor. His comrade reached into the pocket of Reg's jacket and pulled out a small, green package. He tore it open and pulled out an envelope of something that he sprinkled on the wound. Next, he unfolded a bandage and quickly tied it around Reg's wound. "Now, then," he said, smiling, "good as new—almost." He patted Reg on the shoulder. "I'm going to go get some help to get you back to the aid station. Now, don't go wandering off anywhere," he teased. "I don't want you to get lost after all we've been through!"

"All right, Jackie," the wounded soldier replied. "But don't dawdle. I don't want Montgomery to be worrying about me." He smiled weakly.

"I hate to leave you, lad," Jackie replied, a grim look on his face. "I'll be back as soon as I can."

Maggie spoke. "I'll look after your friend."

Jackie whirled toward her voice, his left hand reaching desperately for his rifle. "Who are you?" he shouted. "Show yourself!" he commanded, bringing the rifle to bear in Maggie's direction.

Maggie eased out of the shadows. "It's all right," she said, holding her hands up. "I'm not armed. I'll stay with your friend. You go get help."

"Who the hell are you and what are you doing here?" Jackie demanded.

"My name's Maggie, and it's a long story. I'm an American."

Jackie looked at Maggie and then at Reg. Reg nodded his head. "Go on, mate. I reckon she's as good a nurse as you'd be. The sooner you get going, the sooner you get back—and the sooner we get out of this bloody hole."

◆ ◆ ◆

"Name, please," said the sergeant from behind the folding desk. He was from the same division, the Fifty-First Highland, as Jackie and Reg.

Once Jackie had returned with litter bearers and they'd gotten Reg to the medic's station, he had taken Maggie to the headquarters section responsible for processing displaced persons.

"Margaret O'Dea, but you can call me Maggie."

The sergeant looked up to see a dirty woman of undetermined age standing before him. Her hair was a filthy, tangled mess, and she had dark circles under her eyes. Her hands and face were both darkened by layers of dirt and mud. "Very well, Miss O'Dea," he said without enthusiasm, "please take this form and fill it in completely. There are pencils on the counter over there." He pointed to his right.

Maggie took the form and moved to the counter. She was inside some kind of store—at least it had once been a store. Empty shelves lined the walls, climbing up to the pressed tin of the ceiling. Display cabinets with glass tops stood guard in front of the shelves. Maggie leaned over the display cabinet and began to work on the form. She marveled that the glass top of the cabinet was still intact.

The sergeant glanced over her completed form and dropped it into a file box on the desk, next to his tam-o'-shanter. He issued Maggie a numbered card and directed her to an exit where she could catch a truck to a camp for displaced persons. He would later file the day's list of DPs processed by the Highlanders with the civil affairs section at army group headquarters.

◆ ◆ ◆

Maggie waited in a light rain with about two dozen others. A British army truck pulled up shortly before dark, and they climbed aboard. The DPs, Maggie included, were packed in tightly. There was room only for about twelve to sit on the truck's benches, so she had to sit on the floor. The truck lumbered slowly down the road, its velocity decreasing as night fell. Crowded in on all sides by people as dirty and smelly as she,

Maggie was miserably uncomfortable. Her legs and butt ached from the bouncing ride and from her inability to stretch. Finally, after what seemed like hours, the truck pulled up to a gated fence. The tailgate was dropped, and soldiers assisted the passengers to the ground.

Army clerks directed the group through the gate, sending women to one side and men to the other. A basic meal of soup, bread, and tea was served. It was the most relaxed meal Maggie had enjoyed since before Christmas, the first one she'd eaten in relative security. After the meal came a chance to wash with warm water. Maggie stared in astonishment at the color of the water running off her face and hands. It was light brown with dirt! To be even partially clean was a luxury she had not known in three months.

CHAPTER 33

Near Bocholt, Germany
April 1945

Erich Greinke fidgeted, his fingers tapping impatiently on the steering wheel of the jeep. He was waiting behind a long string of vehicles at yet another of the endless checkpoints established by the military police. Erich supposed the checkpoints were necessary to keep traffic moving and to give priority to the endless supply convoys moving fuel, food, and ammunition to the front. Still, he was impatient to reach his destination.

The previous day, Erich had reviewed the Displaced Persons lists from both Twelfth Army Group's G-5 and his counterpart from Montgomery's Twenty-First Army Group. He was pretty bored by the daily routine, but there wasn't much else to do. He had completed the G-5 report and had moved on to his second cup of coffee and the report from Monty's headquarters. Two-thirds of the way down the page, Erich's eyes had locked on a name. Next to the name had been a place. Erich had grabbed the *Michelin Guide* from the map table and had quickly located Bocholt, Germany, site of one of the many DP camps dotting the Twenty-First Army Group's rear area.

Now, Erich was just two vehicles back from what he hoped would be the last checkpoint between him and the camp, between him and Maggie O'Dea. His travel orders were personally signed by General Bradley. He would have no problem passing the checkpoint, if he could only get up to it. Finally, the last truck pulled away. Erich presented his orders to the British MP sergeant, who gave him quick directions to the camp and a salute. He gunned the jeep and sped off.

◆ ◆ ◆

"O'Dea, Margaret O'Dea!" shouted the corporal as he strolled through the yard of the camp. The DPs were all outside of the tents today as it was a warm and sunny afternoon. Maggie heard her name called and waved at the corporal. "I'm Margaret O'Dea," she said. She still wore her battered and torn overcoat, although she had unfastened the buttons due to the pleasant weather.

"Please come with me," the young soldier replied.

Maggie followed him to the camp administration building, uncertain whether her summons meant trouble. She was in a British camp, and if her hosts had discovered that she was actually Betty from Berlin, she suspected she might be in for far worse than a dry tent and two meals a day. In her several days in the camp, she had seen people come and go. According to camp scuttlebutt, some DPs had been discovered to be Nazis in hiding. Once discovered, they had been turned over for special handling. Maggie wasn't sure what "special handling" meant, but imagined it wasn't very special to the person on the receiving end.

Maggie trailed the corporal as he opened the outer door to a long corridor off which, on each side, were several small offices. Maggie's eyes were still adjusting to the dim light inside the building when the corporal stopped and motioned her into an office on the left.

Maggie stepped into the room. A sergeant was standing behind the desk, looking as though he'd been interrupted by the presence of a British captain—his boss? Maggie wondered—and another officer, an American. Maggie glanced at the American, a captain, with a familiar face.

"Hello, Maggie." Erich Greinke smiled. "I'm so glad to see you again."

Maggie tried to smile, but instead began to weep. At last a friendly face, but she wondered how much of the fear, hunger, and plain misery of the last three months had been due to this man who now stood before her. Maggie found herself in Erich's embrace, felt his strong arms encircling her shoulders and her head resting on his. The British soldiers looked on stoically.

"It's OK now, Maggie," Erich said softly as she continued to sob. "Everything's going to be OK."

◆ ◆ ◆

Luxury. That was the only thought that entered Maggie's mind as she rolled over. The morning sun streamed through the window of her room in the small hotel in Reeves Mews, just off Hyde Park. She breathed deeply, inhaling the scent of the clean sheets. The bed was clean, the floor was clean, the bathroom was clean, and, most wonderful of all, Maggie was clean!

She had arrived in London the previous evening after a dizzying trip with Erich from the camp at Bocholt. His travel orders signed by General Bradley had proven more valuable than gold. After a long, cold jeep ride, Erich had bundled her onto a C-47 transport plane at the army's airfield near Namur. He had used Bradley's authority to bump a major and a lieutenant colonel off the flight to London. The flight, like the ride in the jeep, had been cold and bumpy, and Maggie was afraid she would get sick; but she'd managed to outlast the turbulence and had quite enjoyed the dusky descent into London.

A driver and staff car had greeted them at the airstrip and carried them to the Ambassador Arms Hotel. Erich had checked her in and asked her sizes. He had arranged with the desk clerk to send up a tray of sandwiches and a pint of Guinness. "I'll pick you up here in the morning at eight o'clock. I want you to tell me everything that's happened since I left Berlin. Get a good night's rest, and I'll see you in the morning."

Maggie had been so tired and so eager for a proper bath that she hadn't asked Erich any questions, simply wished him a good night. She had gobbled three sandwiches and washed them down with her pint as she soaked in the warm bath. Then she had slept.

The morning sun brightened not only the room but also Maggie's mood. Maggie heard a knock on her door and glanced at the metal alarm clock beside her bed. It was seven o'clock. She pushed back her covers and put on the robe that the hotel had supplied. She opened the door to a chambermaid carrying a stack of olive-colored clothing. "Special delivery, love," the maid sang.

Maggie took the clothing and laid it out on the bed. It included a khaki blouse and necktie with a dark olive skirt and jacket, a pair of shoes, undergarments, and, wonder of wonders, a pair of nylons. She smiled and shook her head; only Erich would think of that.

At quarter to eight, Maggie was downstairs in the tiny lobby. Two minutes later, Erich strolled in wearing his army uniform, the twin silver bars of a captain adorning his shoulders. "Good morning, Maggie," Erich said, extending his hand. "You look terrific! I see we did all right on the sizes," he said, looking her up and down.

"Yes," she answered, smiling, "you did quite well. Tell me how you were able to gather all of these things so quickly."

"Let's just say I have access to resources." Erich smiled. "C'mon"—he nodded his head toward the door—"we've got plenty of work to do."

◆ ◆ ◆

From Reeves Mews, the trip to Whitehall took fifteen minutes. Erich and Maggie sat in the backseat while their driver negotiated London's streets. Maggie's attention was fixed on the people and the buildings of London. While occasionally they passed a bombed-out shell, most of the structures seemed sound and in good repair. Nowhere did they encounter a blockaded street or blocks of rubble as they would in Berlin. It was as if the mighty Blitz had never occurred. The car eased onto Whitehall, and Maggie noticed the throngs of people on the streets going about their daily business. Other than mounds of sandbags and uniformed sentries around building entrances, the area looked remarkably normal.

"Here we are," Erich announced as the staff car turned into a small courtyard. The car came to a stop, and the driver hopped out and held the door for Maggie. She followed Erich through a sandbagged, arched doorway and then up a flight of stairs to the building's second floor. "Right in here," Erich said, opening a door on the right of a long hallway and standing aside to let her enter. The room was small, with one window set into the wall behind a wooden desk. In front of the desk sat a single upholstered chair.

"Please, Maggie, have a seat," said Erich, pointing to the chair as he moved behind the desk. She sat as he pulled a writing tablet from a desk drawer, removed his uniform jacket, and took his own seat behind the desk. "I'd like to hear your story," he began. "Everything from our last meeting at Alois's to when I found you at Bocholt." He peered across the desk at Maggie as he unscrewed the cap to a fountain pen.

"I hardly know where to begin," Maggie laughed. The last few days had been so emotional, so searing, and now here was Erich asking her to think back nearly four years. Maggie started by describing her first trips to Adolf Hitler Platz and what she had seen and observed at the ministry. She recalled her visits to Goebbels's country estate and the broadcast that had led to Clive's arrest and Dieter's exile. She told of her surprise and concern when she'd received her first letter from the front only to learn that Dieter had landed in Kurt Engel's battalion. Erich looked up with arched eyebrows.

"Really?" he asked, a thin smile on his face. "What were the odds of that? Did you continue to get regular letters from Dieter?"

"I continued to get letters, but not on a regular basis. Apparently, at the front his schedule wasn't quite as fixed as at Broadcasting House." Maggie smiled wistfully.

"Did Dieter tell you where he was or the name of his unit?"

"Oh, he could never say where they were—military secrets, you know," Maggie recalled. "I assumed his unit was the same one Kurt had been in all along, the Leibstandarte SS Adolf Hitler."

"Go on," Erich said, scratching a note on his tablet.

Maggie shared her acquisition of tidbits about the Germans' special weapons. She recounted some of English Section's programming decisions and the discussions behind them, including the radio drama that had aired shortly before the invasion.

"Let me stop you there, Maggie," Erich interrupted. "Did anyone in the ministry ever imply to you that the Allied invasion was imminent? Did anyone ever say, 'Oh, they're going to invade on this date'?"

"No, nothing specific was ever mentioned in my presence. But they—Goebbels and Bauer—they seemed to be on edge last spring, as though they expected the invasion at any time."

"I understand. Maggie, you were wise never to use your real name on the air," Erich said. "That drama of yours really angered a lot of our people; they felt it was treasonous. Of course, we—the government, that is—know who you are, but the general public doesn't. Let's keep it that way. Some of your less discreet American colleagues from Broadcasting House are going to have a lot of explaining to do once things settle down again."

Maggie told Erich about the gradual changing of the mood of the propaganda ministry's leaders following the invasion and the resumption of the heavy bombing of Berlin. "They became less sure of themselves, and some of our programming began to reflect that. Some of the commentaries veered so far off course that they couldn't have been taken seriously by many listeners."

"Tell me what happened in December," Erich probed gently. "We began to get worried when we quit hearing from you."

Maggie told about Thomas Müller's Christmas Day visit to her apartment and her incarceration at 8 Prinz-Albrecht-Straße. She described her interrogations and her escape. Erich continued to make notes as she talked, occasionally interrupting to ask for a clarification.

"And then," Maggie recalled, "I was foraging for food and I got a little careless. The best way to forage is to find stuff you can eat or use and shove it in a pocket. You have to stay alert, always looking around for the police—or really anyone else. Well, I found a pile of discarded army rations, and I made the mistake of eating when I should have been watching—and I got nabbed." Erich nodded. "So, this young soldier takes me into this house and turns me over to his commander. The commander—he never gave his name—had me shut up in a cellar. A couple of Tommies came along the next morning. One of them was wounded. I looked after him while his friend went for help. They turned me over to the British army. Then you found me." Her eyes began to tear up and she wiped them quickly.

Erich shook his head. "So, after walking across half of Germany, you stumbled right through the front lines? Amazing! Maggie, if I show you a map, do you think you could point out your route?"

"I think I could get pretty close." Erich rummaged through one of the desk drawers and pulled out a large-scale map of Germany. He spread it across the top of the desk, setting his pen and tablet to the side. Maggie stood and leaned over the desk. She pointed out the towns she passed through on her long trek. Just east of the Rhine River, her fingertip paused on the map. "Here. This is where I was captured, near this little town, Borken."

"Could you tell how many men were there, what size unit it was?"

"Well, it was the middle of the night and most of them were asleep. I'd guess maybe forty to fifty men total."

"What type of vehicles did they have?"

"I didn't see any. But remember that I wasn't there on a reconnaissance mission—I was just hungry." Maggie smiled.

"Of course, of course." Erich smiled in return. "Given your situation and the darkness and all of that, did you happen to see what kind of weapons they carried? No?" Erich asked as she shook her head. "These aren't normally questions I'd ask, Maggie," Erich explained. "It's just that we're watching the Germans collapse, and any information we can pick up helps us better understand their true condition." Erich paused for a moment to review his notes.

"I'm sorry I didn't do a better job of seeing what was around me, but, well, I had survival on my mind." Maggie smiled again.

"Sure you did," Erich said, glancing at his watch. "I understand. I'm just glad you're here now and safe."

Maggie ventured a question of her own. "Tell me, Erich, how much longer can the Germans hold out?"

"Not long, from what we hear. Weeks, maybe a month. The fact that you didn't see any vehicles fits with the general picture we have, which is that they are out of fuel stocks. In the west, at least, the Germans are falling back and conducting a delaying action." Erich saw a quizzical look on Maggie's face. "All that means is that they are retreating, but trying to do so as slowly as possible. The Russians seem to be closing in from the east, too. This thing should be over soon. Tell me, Maggie," Erich said, screwing the cap back on his pen, "when did you last hear from Dieter?"

"I got a letter from him in early December, just before that big battle."

"Did he refer to the offensive in his letter?"

"On no. I don't even know if he was in it."

Erich nodded. "We think he probably was. We think the Leibstandarte was up to some of its old tricks."

"What do you mean?"

"Just that we have some questions about the tactics they employed. We'd like to talk to members of the unit—if we get a chance, that is."

Maggie appeared to miss his meaning, for she smiled, then as tears again welled in her eyes she said, "Well, that should be easy enough to arrange. Dieter proposed we meet at the Brandenburg Gate on the first day of summer. I intend to keep our date."

"I hope you can, Maggie. I hope you can. Well, thanks for going over all that for me. I know it must have been quite an ordeal—all of it—from passing us information to your experiences with Thomas and your miraculous escape." Erich looked down at the map on the desktop and slowly shook his head. "There's nothing I can ever say or do to repay what you've done, Maggie. So I'll just say thanks." He stood and extended his hand. Maggie stood and shook it, a lump in her throat.

"Now, I've got someone I want you to meet," Erich said, pulling his uniform jacket on.

◆　◆　◆

The staff car turned north on Whitehall and skirted Piccadilly. There was more traffic on the sidewalks and streets now. The contrast between Berlin's shattered, car-less streets and London could not have been more pronounced. Maggie noticed that Londoners were walking purpose-fully, that stores were stocked, and that life looked nearly normal com-pared with the last capital she'd lived in.

"Where, exactly, are we headed, Erich?" she asked as the car turned onto Grosvenor Street.

"Claridge's."

Maggie groaned. One of London's grand hotels, Claridge's was famous (infamous, in Maggie's view) for the number of the empire's aristocrats who maintained suites there. "You may recall that I am not, like most Americans, enamored of all things British. Why would you take me to a place like Claridge's, which represents so much of what I dislike about the English?"

"Easy, Maggie," Erich said, a worried expression on his face. "I'm not taking you there to pay tribute to the empire. I'm taking you there to meet someone."

"Who?"

"You'll see."

After only a couple of minutes of riding in silence, the car pulled up to Claridge's Hotel. A liveried doorman stepped forward, opened the car door, and extended his hand to Maggie. "Good morning, ma'am," he said with a friendly smile. "Welcome to Claridge's." Maggie smirked in return until Erich grabbed her by the elbow and pulled her through the revolving door and into the grand lobby.

"Why are we here? Who are we meeting?" Maggie asked as she tried to match Erich's brisk pace. Maggie looked around at the luxurious lobby, dotted with military men in uniforms of olive, navy, khaki, and other colors.

"Yours not to reason why, Maggie," Erich muttered, smiling. He guided her onto the lift and said, "Fourth floor, please," to the operator. The cage was pulled across the opening, and the elevator's glass doors closed. Maggie felt the slight lurch as the elevator began to ascend. Exasperated at the lack of information she'd been able to extract from Erich, she kept her smirk in place and her eyes on the lighted numbers above the door.

The elevator came to rest smoothly, and the operator pulled the cage open again. Erich pushed on the glass doors, and they exited into a richly carpeted corridor. "This way," Erich said as he headed to the left, Maggie trailing two steps behind.

He stopped in front of suite 408 and rapped sharply on the door. She heard no reply but watched as he pushed down on the handle and opened the door. "This way," he said again over his shoulder. He ushered Maggie into a large living room with twin sofas, their corners set perpendicular to each other. A heavy leather-upholstered chair sat directly opposite the corner formed by the two sofas. A tea service cart sat to the side of the chair. Large windows on the Brook Street side of the building were open, letting in sunlight and fresh air. A handsome, dark wooden desk and chair sat in a corner of the room. A lamp on the desk was on, illuminating several neatly stacked folders and writing tablets.

"Have a seat, Maggie," Erich said. "I'll let our host know you're here." Without waiting for a reply, he turned and walked across the room to a door that appeared to lead to a bedroom. He knocked softly on it and said, "Sir, it's Erich, here with our guest." Maggie heard a muffled reply as she sat down on one of the sofas.

Within a moment, the door opened and a silver-haired man wearing a khaki uniform shirt and tie stepped out. He nodded a greeting to Erich and strode across the carpeted floor straight toward Maggie, his large, blue eyes accentuating a friendly smile. "So, this is Miss O'Dea, about whom I have heard so much!" He extended his hand as Maggie stood. It was strong, solid, all muscle, but he didn't squeeze her hand like some men did. Instead, he held it as though he was protecting it. "I'm Bill Donovan," he said, still smiling, "and I'm very proud to finally meet you."

"How do you do?" Maggie replied, trying to remember why Donovan's name sounded familiar.

"General Donovan is head of the OSS, Maggie," Erich interjected, moving to stand beside her. "He's my boss."

"Please sit," Donovan said, motioning toward the sofa. "I know it's a little early for *elevenses*, as our cousins like to say, but I think we can take tea without causing any offense to our hosts. Erich, would you assist?"

"Yes sir." Erich moved to the cart as Maggie resumed her seat.

"You do like tea, don't you, Miss O'Dea?" Donovan asked, still smiling.

"Please, call me Maggie. And I'm Irish. I'm not much of a tea drinker."

Donovan chuckled. "I'm Irish, too. Erich's told me about your sentiments toward our hosts." Donovan's smile faded away and his clear, blue eyes took on a more serious look. "I wanted to tell you how much your country appreciates all you've done during this war. I know you were in mortal danger at times, and that your work for us caused you quite a bit of misery. Anxiety, too, I'm sure. The information you sent to us helped us better understand what Hitler and the Nazis were up to and how they intended to go about achieving their objectives." Erich brought over a cup and saucer for Maggie, winking at her while his back was to the general.

"Thank you, General Donovan," Maggie replied. "The last four months were really quite miserable." She took a sip and, realizing that it wasn't tea, understood the message behind Erich's wink.

"Your information linking Peenemünde to the Nazi special weapons program helped us connect some of the dots." Erich carried a cup of tea to Donovan, who looked up and smiled. "Thank you, Erich."

Erich took a seat next to Maggie on the sofa. "Unfortunately," Erich began, "we weren't always smart enough to figure out how your information fit into the big picture. The Ardennes offensive in December is a painful example. The German advance caught us by surprise.

Fortunately, Eisenhower and his commanders figured out what was going on pretty quickly, and they were able to blunt the attack before it achieved its objective."

Maggie took a sip from her cup. "My report on troop movements from east to west seems to have started my own journey," she remarked.

"Yes, so it would seem," Erich replied. "Tell the general what happened."

Maggie related her Christmas-morning visit from Thomas Müller and described her holiday incarceration at Prinz-Albrecht-Straße.

"Was Thomas the only interrogator?" Erich asked.

"Oh yes. Good old Thomas," Maggie said with a bitter smile.

Donovan leaned back in his armchair, holding his teacup above his lap. Erich asked another question. "What did you tell him?"

"Nothing. I didn't tell him anything, though I think he had it pretty well figured out. I don't think they ever intercepted any of the notes from the dead drop, but he showed me one of the John Reilly letters that they had opened. He even mentioned that someone who looked a lot like you, Erich, had been retrieving the letters in Bern. That's when I got really nervous. But the rest of the time I just stuck to the story about Gino."

"Did Thomas believe it?" Erich asked.

"No. He said Gino had left Berlin months before our last meeting was alleged to have taken place."

"Maggie, if I may interject a question?" It was Donovan. Maggie turned toward the general. "Did the Gestapo use any physical coercion, any violence on you?"

"No," Maggie answered, glancing down at her feet. She looked back up, meeting Donovan's eyes. "But they did brutally beat another prisoner as my surrogate. The closest they came to physically abusing me was the cold in my cell and the lack of exercise and diet. But I was never hit or beaten or anything like that."

"Most of their other prisoners weren't so fortunate," Erich interjected.

Maggie felt a flare of annoyance toward Erich. He was the indirect cause of the misery of the past few months. "I'll have you know that I was held in an unheated cell for six weeks in the middle of the coldest winter this century. I was repeatedly interrogated and expected to be shot. I was nearly killed by our own bombers. I spent two months as a fugitive traveling across northern Germany in the dead of winter with no money and no papers. I lived by my wits and half-starved to death. I'm grateful I wasn't beaten or—or worse, but don't think that I didn't suffer."

"Of course not," Donovan reassured with a smile.

"Thomas always liked you, Maggie," Erich said. "That's probably why you were never beaten. Usually the Gestapo is pretty, shall we say, relaxed when it comes to protecting the health and welfare of its prisoners. I don't know if you remember it or not, but Thomas and I fought together in Spain. After he came back from Poland, he was disillusioned with the brutality he witnessed by the SS. Then, when he came back from France, despite the stunning victory, he couldn't stomach the treatment of civilians and prisoners of war he'd seen. He couldn't abide cruelty. He saved my life once, and he probably saved your life—or at least kept you alive long enough for you to escape."

Maggie stared into her cup and thought about Thomas's round face and dimpled smile. "He kept saying he was my friend and he wanted to help me," she recalled. "I couldn't figure out how, though."

"I guess we'll never know," Erich said. "You said he was killed during the bombing, the one when you escaped?"

"I didn't stop to check his pulse, but he looked in a pretty bad way."

The trio sat in silence for a moment.

"Maggie," Donovan began, "we'd like to help you get on with your life. Erich will assist you with a new passport and an official letter of commendation for wartime service. We want to equip you with official documentation that proves you were working on behalf of your country even before we formally entered the war. We'll also help out should any legal questions come up concerning your work for the Nazis."

"Thank you, General."

"Erich, you can see to that, can't you?" Donovan looked to his younger colleague.

"Yes sir."

"And some travel funds, too. Back pay for Maggie's years under cover." Donovan looked back to Maggie. "Is there anything else we can do for you, Maggie?"

She hesitated. *What the hell,* she thought. "Yes sir, there is. I'd like to find Dieter Schmidt. He was a colleague of mine at the propaganda ministry. He was conscripted and sent to France. I'd like to go back and find him."

Donovan chuckled and shook his head. "Maggie, I never doubted it, but now I know you're Irish! I'm afraid you can't go back. Even though the Germans are on their last legs, the fighting still isn't over. Frankly, I don't think your going back to Europe is a good idea right now. But," he said, setting the teacup on the carpeted floor and pushing himself up, "I'll make some inquiries and see what we can find out. I am proud to have met you, Maggie," he said again, taking her hand in his, his blue eyes beaming above a genuine smile. "You've done a great service for your country and for the cause of freedom. If there is anything else we can do to help you, let Erich know. I wish we could visit longer and I could hear more of your exploits, but that will have to wait for another day, I'm afraid. I must excuse myself now to prepare for a conference. Thank you, Maggie." With that, Donovan released her hand, turned, and walked back through the bedroom door, closing it behind him.

◆ ◆ ◆

Maggie strolled alone through Hyde Park, enjoying the warm sunshine, the stares of free men, and the rose blossoms. Maybe Thomas had really been her friend, had kept her alive until she could escape. She wondered what his plan had been, if he'd really had one. She guessed she'd never know. With her hands behind her back and her head down, Maggie sauntered along the paths of the great park, wondering if Dieter was still alive—where he was, what he was doing, and whether the bedlam of war had altered his gentle nature. *I will go back,* she promised herself. *Some way, somehow, I will go back and I will find Dieter Schmidt.* The warm spring afternoon began to yield, the sun sinking slowly. "Hurry, sun!" Maggie whispered as she looked ahead to the first day of summer.

Author's Note

For me, writing begins with reading. I love to read, especially history and historical fiction. One day I came across the story of Mildred Gillars, an American who broadcast Nazi propaganda during the war. What an intriguing story, I thought. What would motivate someone to undertake such a mission? There are any number of answers, of course, and in the case of the fictitious Maggie O'Dea, romance started her down the long and twisting path.

I've had the opportunity to visit Berlin on three occasions. My first visit was in the spring of 1984. My parents, Harry and Ina, to whom this book is dedicated, came to Germany, where I was stationed with the US Army. We spent a fascinating weekend in the divided city, including an afternoon in the Soviet sector. A few months later, I was back in Berlin with my colleagues Rich Gamble and Bobby Joe Harris on assignment to photograph Warsaw Pact military hardware during the East Germans' annual October 7 parade. My most recent visit was with our extended family in 2004, when we were finally free to stroll through the Brandenburg Gate.

Several historical figures appear in the pages of *Berlin Calling*. While they have been plucked from reality and inserted into a work of fiction, they are true to character as I understand their characters to have been.

Although I bear the responsibility for errors both great and small, *Berlin Calling* is assuredly better for the generosity of friends who have taken their time to read it and offer their criticism and advice. Chuck Driskell, author of several thrillers, provided thoughtful suggestions concerning content and marketing. John Harden applied his distinctive perspective and offered great advice on the portrayal of Maggie's incarceration. Don McKale, emeritus professor of history at Clemson University, encouraged my writing even as he admonished me for not being hard enough on the Nazis. Troy Terry helped me strengthen the beginning of the book and offered guidance on making it a more enjoyable read.

My business partner, Joe Turner, tolerated my writing addiction with patience and encouragement. These are marks of his generous character, for which I am grateful.

I was intrigued when one spring afternoon I received an e-mail from Miriam Juskowicz at Lake Union Publishing expressing an interest in publishing this book. It has benefited greatly from the attention of developmental editor David Downing and copy editor Sarah Engel. David and Sarah identified numerous errors ranging from plot and character development issues to historical facts and grammar. Any errors that remain—despite their diligent scrutiny—belong to me. The mysterious and enticing cover was designed by Rachel Adam Rogers. My thanks to Miriam for assembling such talented collaborators and for showing me that the work I do as part of a team is invariably better than that which I do by myself.

Thanks are always in order for my wife, Yvonne, and our children, Mary Kate, Addison, and Callie. They allow me to slip away into the back of the house and write for long stretches. This book is proof that I was not merely sneaking naps! My family is my favorite place to be and my favorite thing to do.

Kelly Durham
Clemson, SC
September 2016

ABOUT THE AUTHOR

Kelly Durham lives in Clemson, South Carolina, with his wife, Yvonne; their daughters, Mary Kate, Addison, and Callie; and their dog, George Marshall. He is the author of four previous novels, including *Wade's War, The Reluctant Copilot, The War Widow,* and *The Movie Star and Me.* A graduate of Clemson University, Kelly served four years in the US Army with assignments in Arizona and Germany before returning to Clemson and entering private business. He was an award-winning Wendy's franchise owner for more than twenty-five years, as well as a private pilot, and he was named a distinguished alumnus of Clemson University in 2012. For more information about the author and his work, visit www.kellydurham.com.